Buffy the Vampire Slayer™

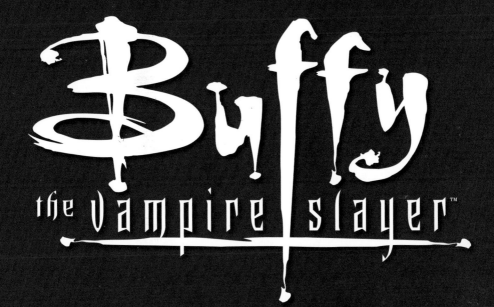

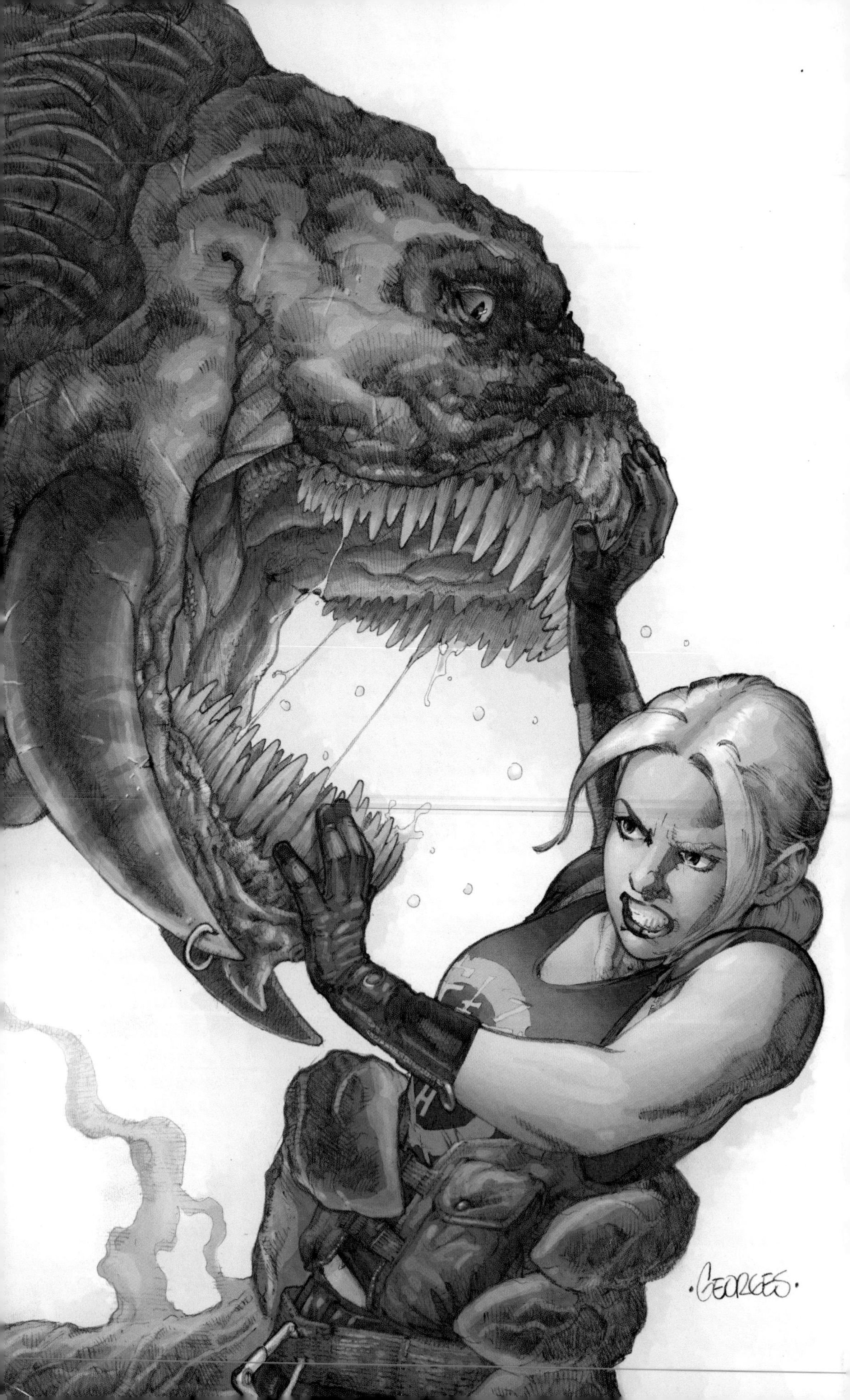
·GEORGES·

Buffy the Vampire Slayer™

SEASON EIGHT VOLUME I

THE LONG WAY HOME

Script JOSS WHEDON

Pencils GEORGES JEANTY

Inks ANDY OWENS

Colors DAVE STEWART

Letters RICHARD STARKINGS
& COMICRAFT'S JIMMY

Cover Art JO CHEN

Guest Pencils for "The Chain" PAUL LEE

Executive Producer JOSS WHEDON

Dark Horse Books®

Publisher MIKE RICHARDSON

Editor SCOTT ALLIE

Assistant Editors KATIE MOODY & SIERRA HAHN

Collection Designer HEIDI FAINZA

This story takes place after the end of the
television series *Buffy the Vampire Slayer*
created by Joss Whedon.

Special thanks to Debbie Olshan at Twentieth Century Fox, Crystal Shand, and Michael Boretz.

This volume reprints the comic book series *Buffy the
Vampire Slayer* Season Eight #1–5 from Dark Horse Comics.

Published by
Dark Horse Books
A division of
Dark Horse Comics, Inc.
10956 SE Main Street
Milwaukie, OR 97222

darkhorse.com

To find a comics shop in your area,
call the Comic Shop Locator Service toll-free at (888) 266-4226.

First edition: November 2007
ISBN-10: 1-59307-822-6
ISBN-13: 978-1-59307-822-5

3 5 7 9 10 8 6 4

Printed in Canada

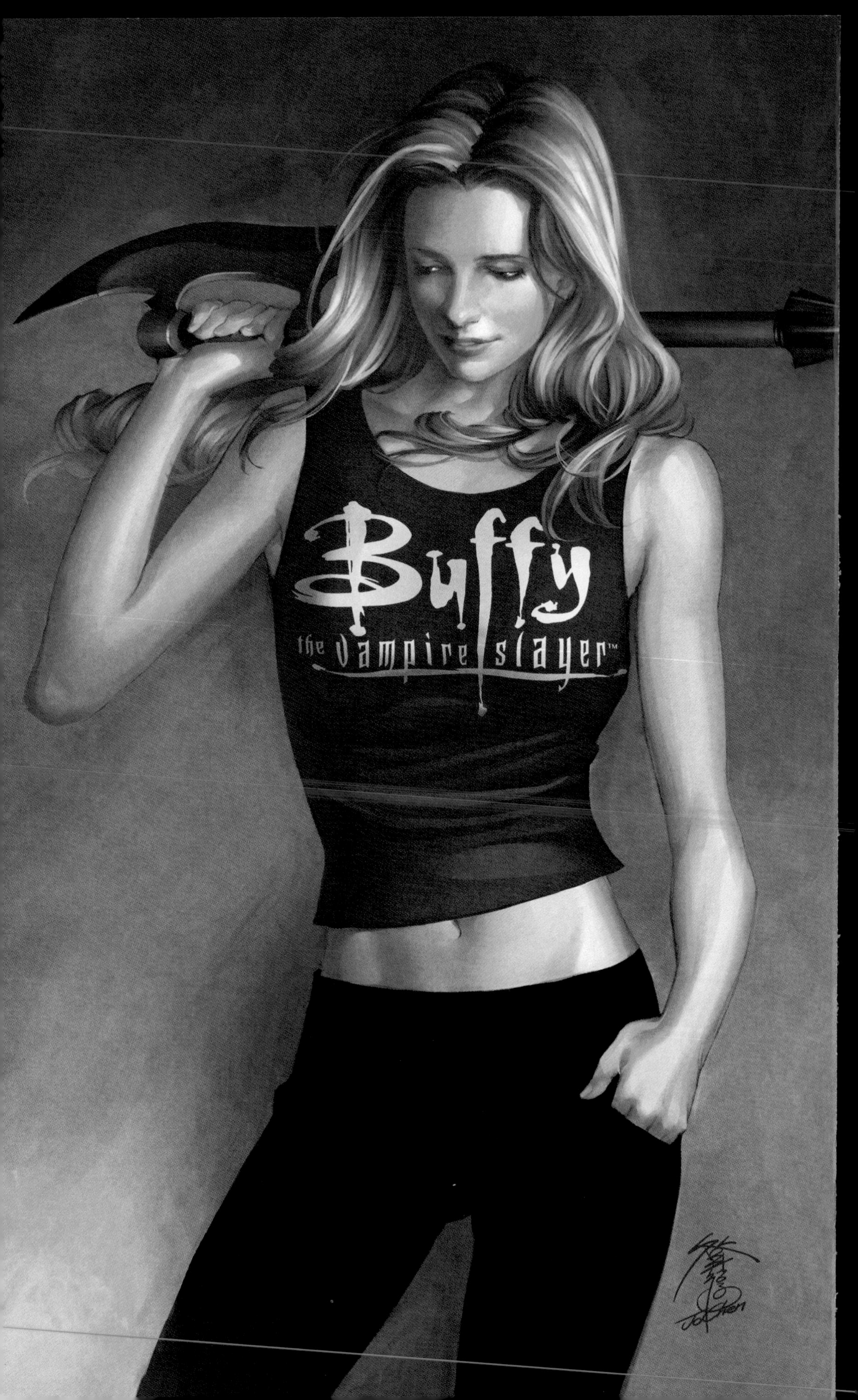
Buffy
the vampire slayer™

The LONG WAY HOME

THE THING ABOUT CHANGING THE WORLD...

ONCE YOU DO IT, THE WORLD'S ALL DIFFERENT.

Part One

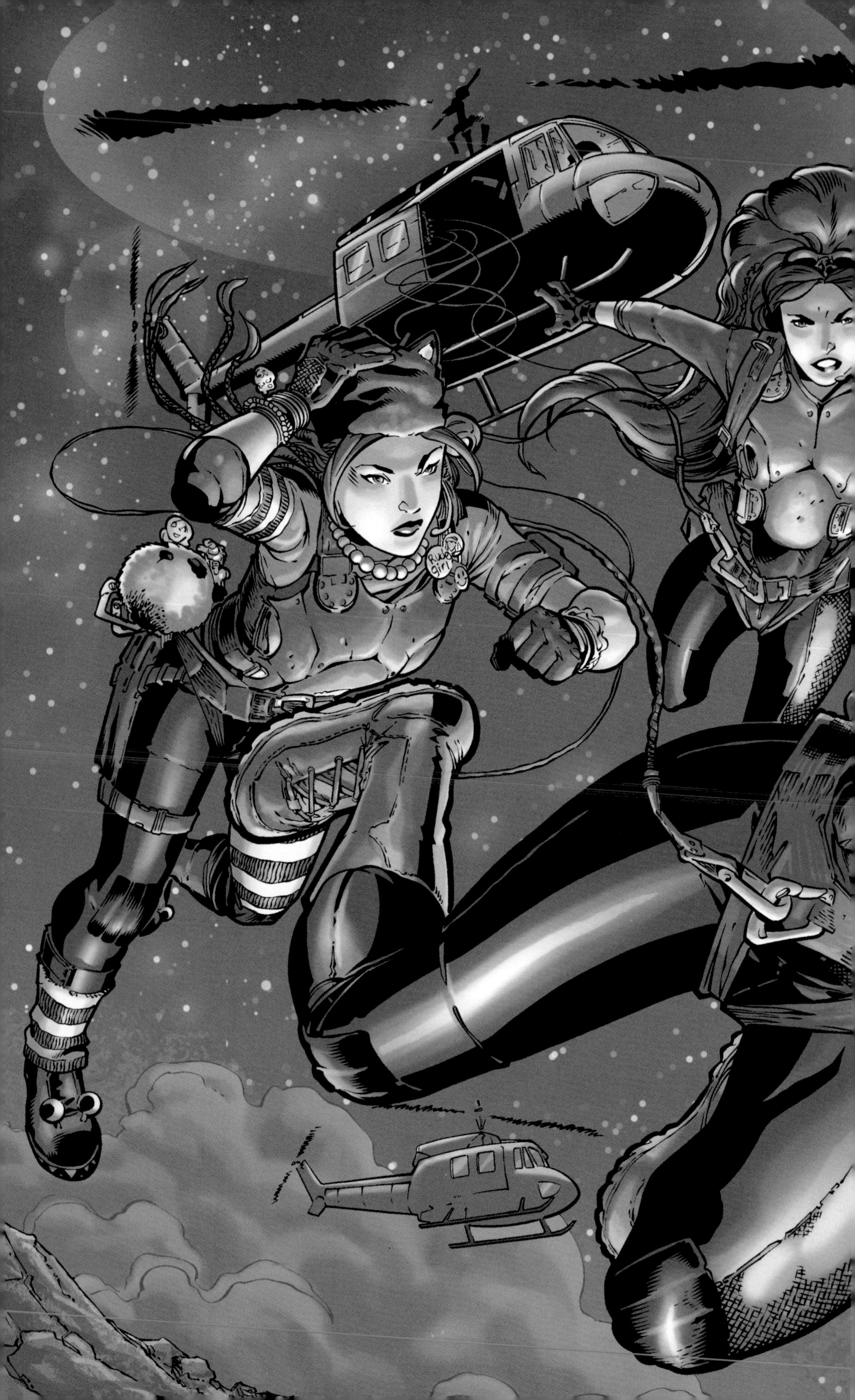
Rude girl

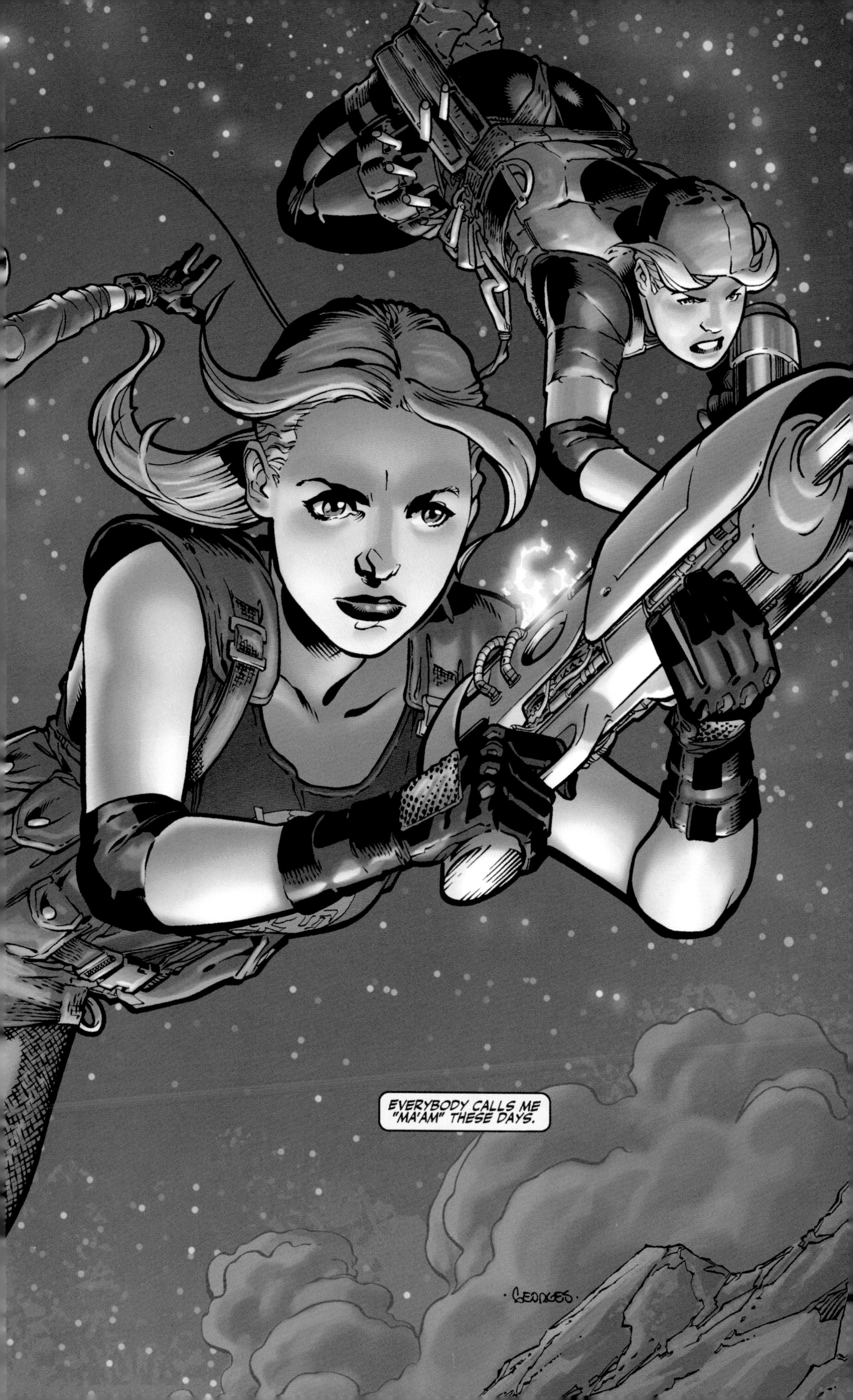
EVERYBODY CALLS ME "MA'AM" THESE DAYS.
·GEORGES·

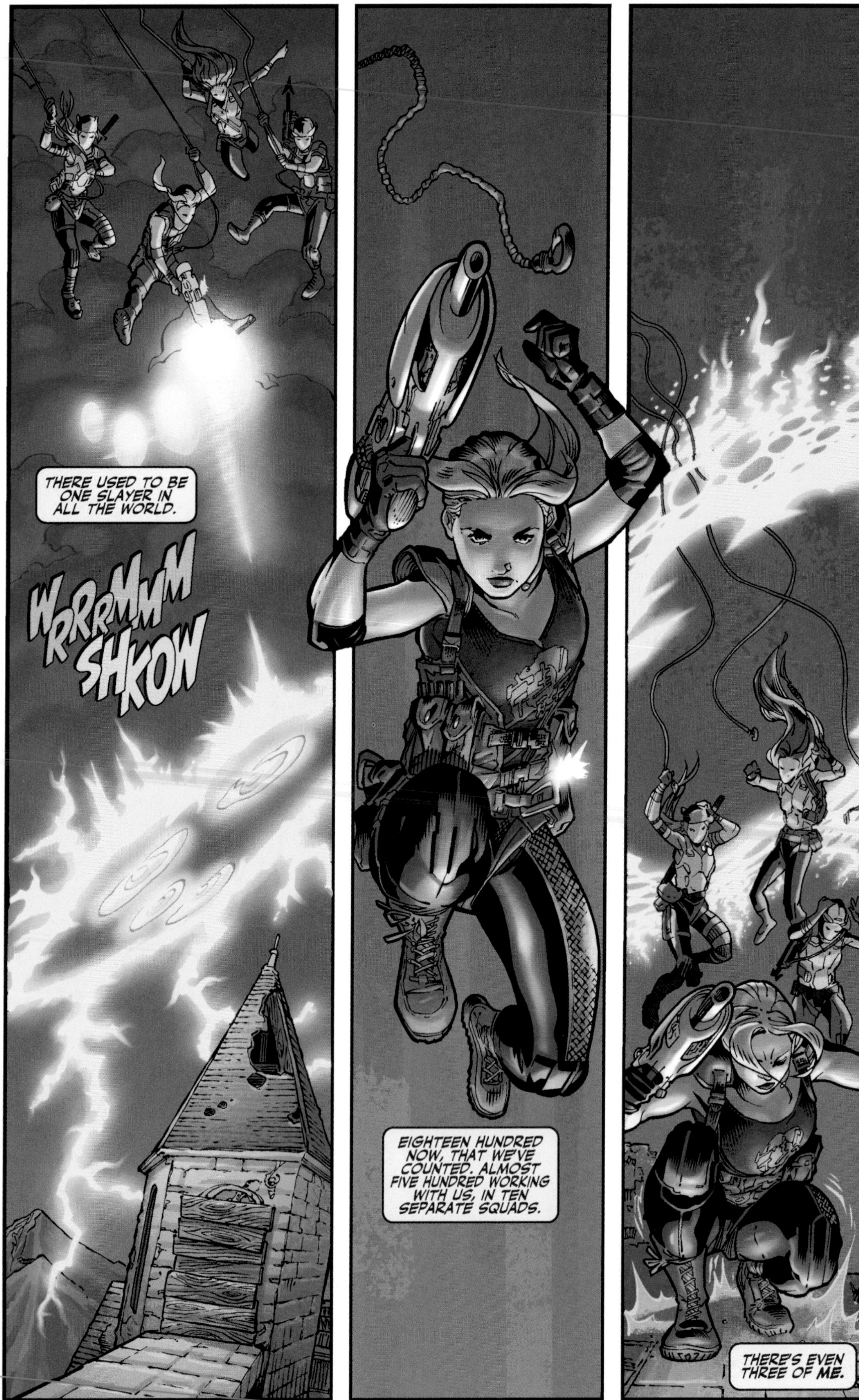
THERE USED TO BE ONE SLAYER IN ALL THE WORLD.
WRRRMMM
SHKOW
EIGHTEEN HUNDRED NOW, THAT WE'VE COUNTED. ALMOST FIVE HUNDRED WORKING WITH US, IN TEN SEPARATE SQUADS.
THERE'S EVEN THREE OF ME.

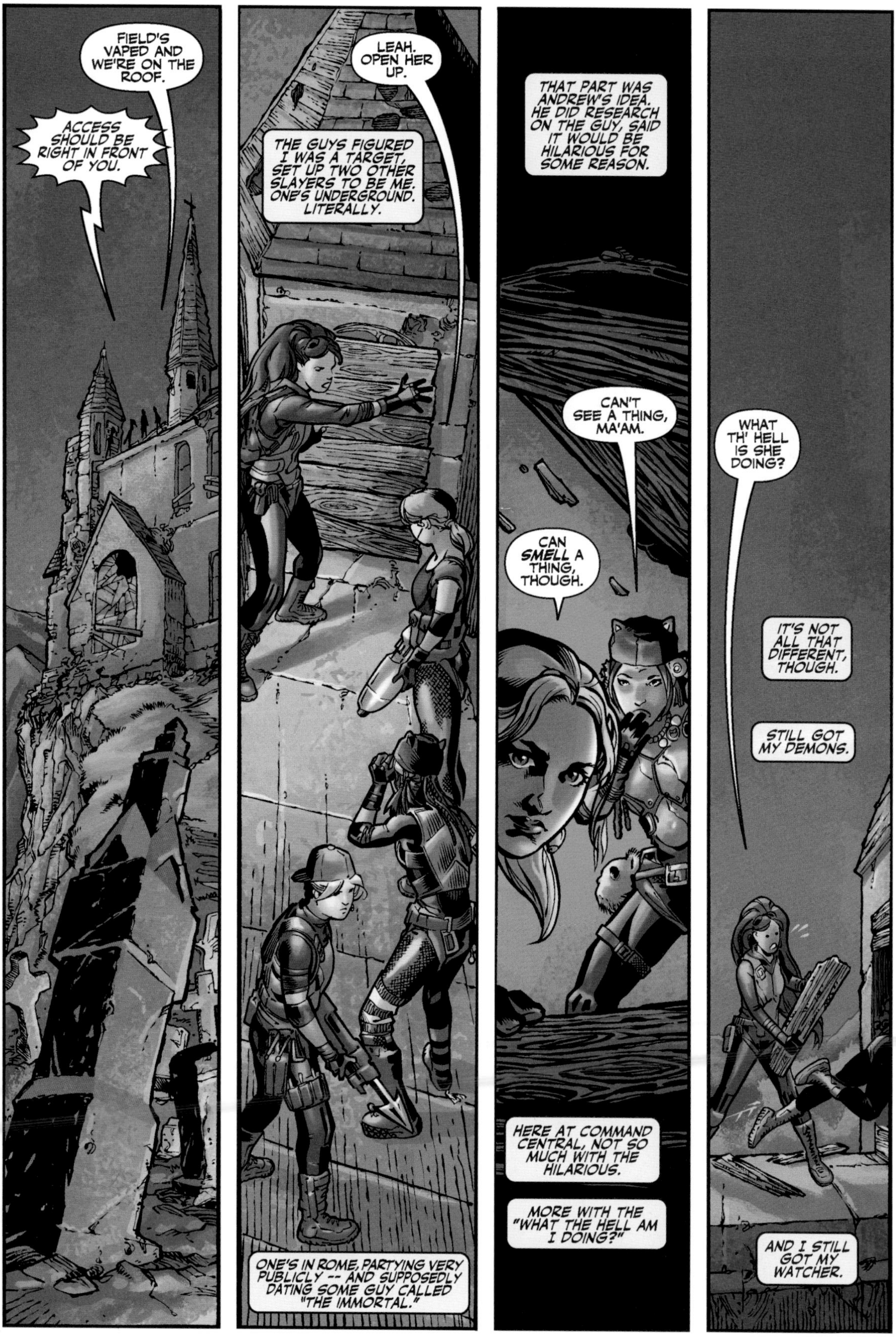
FIELD'S VAPED AND WE'RE ON THE ROOF.
ACCESS SHOULD BE RIGHT IN FRONT OF YOU.
LEAH. OPEN HER UP.
THE GUYS FIGURED I WAS A TARGET, SET UP TWO OTHER SLAYERS TO BE ME. ONE'S UNDERGROUND. LITERALLY.
ONE'S IN ROME, PARTYING VERY PUBLICLY -- AND SUPPOSEDLY DATING SOME GUY CALLED "THE IMMORTAL."
THAT PART WAS ANDREW'S IDEA. HE DID RESEARCH ON THE GUY, SAID IT WOULD BE HILARIOUS FOR SOME REASON.
CAN'T SEE A THING, MA'AM.
CAN SMELL A THING, THOUGH.
HERE AT COMMAND CENTRAL, NOT SO MUCH WITH THE HILARIOUS.
MORE WITH THE "WHAT THE HELL AM I DOING?"
WHAT TH' HELL IS SHE DOING?
IT'S NOT ALL THAT DIFFERENT, THOUGH.
STILL GOT MY DEMONS.
AND I STILL GOT MY WATCHER.

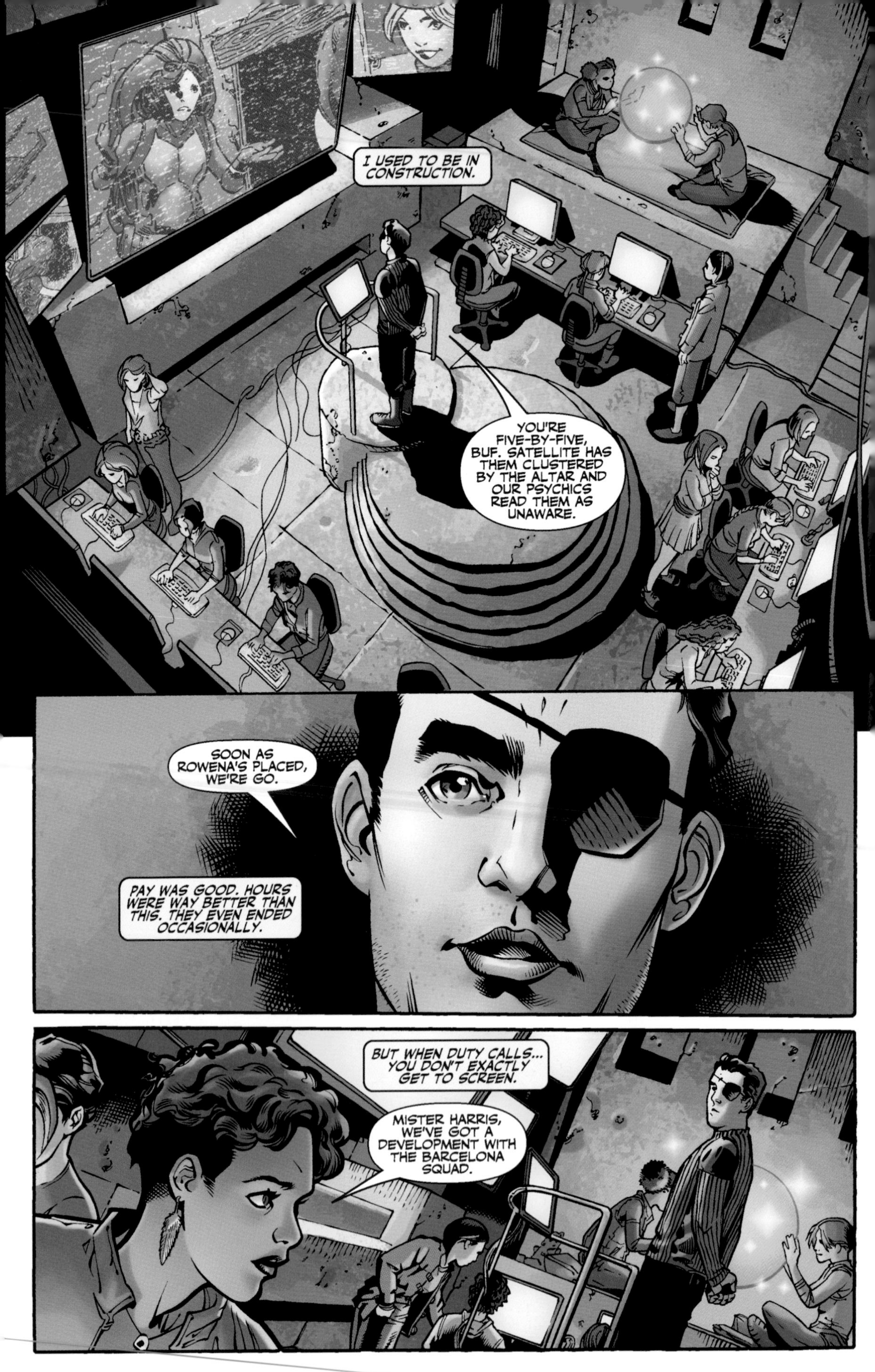
I USED TO BE IN CONSTRUCTION.
YOU'RE FIVE-BY-FIVE, BUF. SATELLITE HAS THEM CLUSTERED BY THE ALTAR AND OUR PSYCHICS READ THEM AS UNAWARE.
SOON AS ROWENA'S PLACED, WE'RE GO.
PAY WAS GOOD. HOURS WERE WAY BETTER THAN THIS. THEY EVEN ENDED OCCASIONALLY.
BUT WHEN DUTY CALLS... YOU DON'T EXACTLY GET TO SCREEN.
MISTER HARRIS, WE'VE GOT A DEVELOPMENT WITH THE BARCELONA SQUAD.

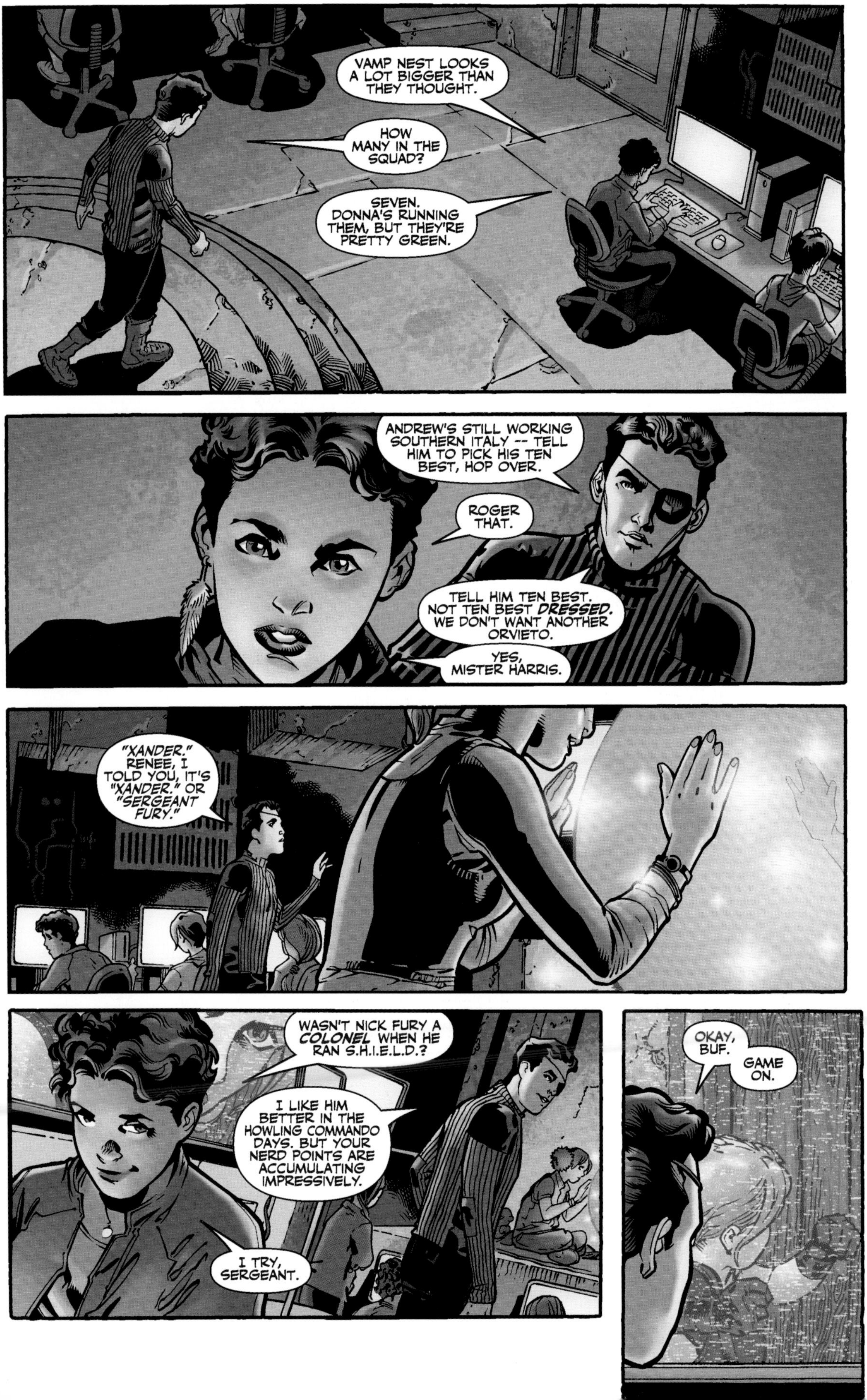
VAMP NEST LOOKS A LOT BIGGER THAN THEY THOUGHT.
HOW MANY IN THE SQUAD?
SEVEN. DONNA'S RUNNING THEM, BUT THEY'RE PRETTY GREEN.
ANDREW'S STILL WORKING SOUTHERN ITALY -- TELL HIM TO PICK HIS TEN BEST, HOP OVER.
ROGER THAT.
TELL HIM TEN BEST. NOT TEN BEST DRESSED. WE DON'T WANT ANOTHER ORVIETO.
YES, MISTER HARRIS.
"XANDER." RENEE, I TOLD YOU, IT'S "XANDER." OR "SERGEANT FURY."
WASN'T NICK FURY A COLONEL WHEN HE RAN S.H.I.E.L.D.?
I LIKE HIM BETTER IN THE HOWLING COMMANDO DAYS. BUT YOUR NERD POINTS ARE ACCUMULATING IMPRESSIVELY.
I TRY, SERGEANT.
OKAY, BUF.
GAME ON.

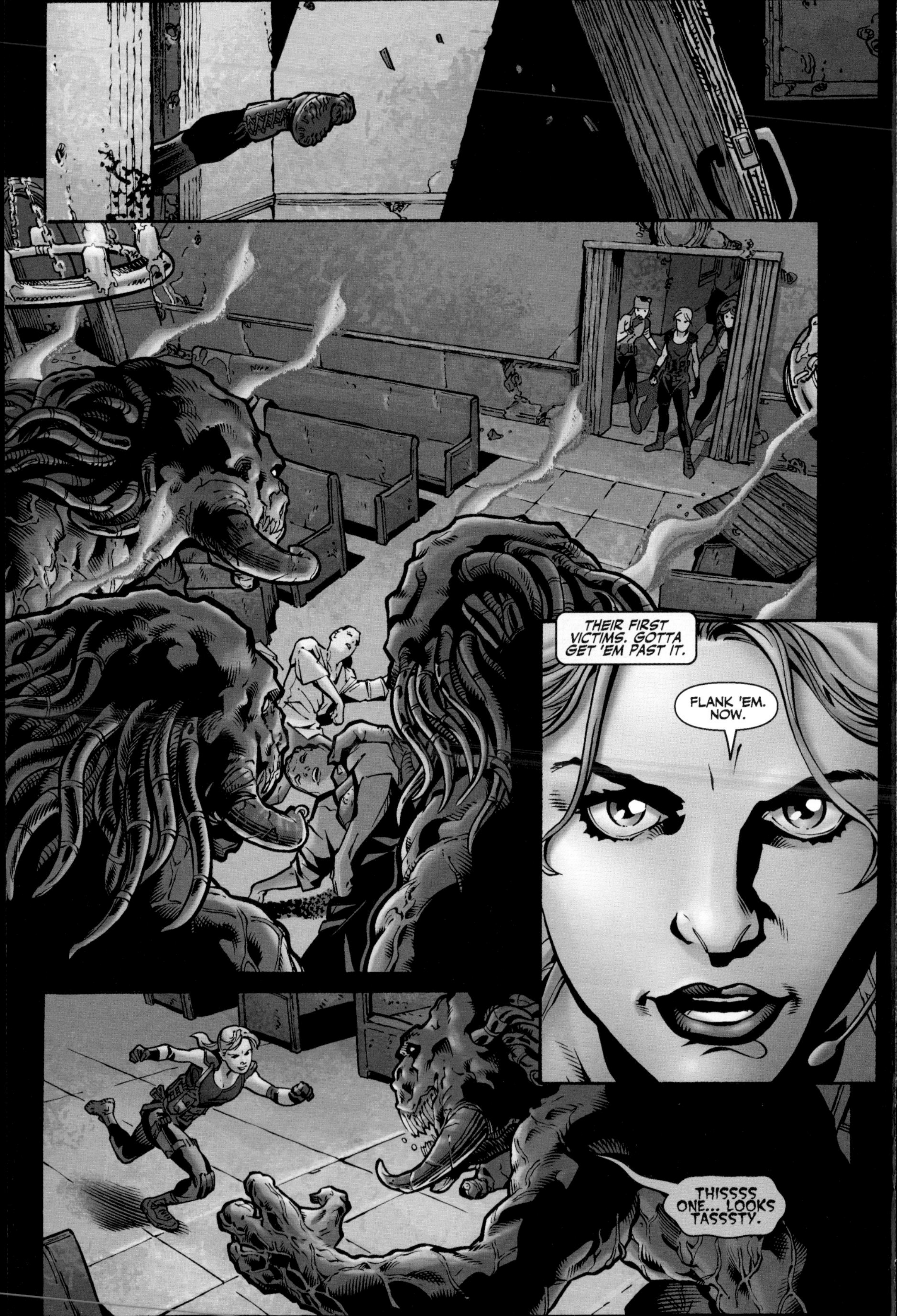
THEIR FIRST VICTIMS. GOTTA GET 'EM PAST IT.
FLANK 'EM. NOW.
THISSSS ONE... LOOKS TASSSTY.

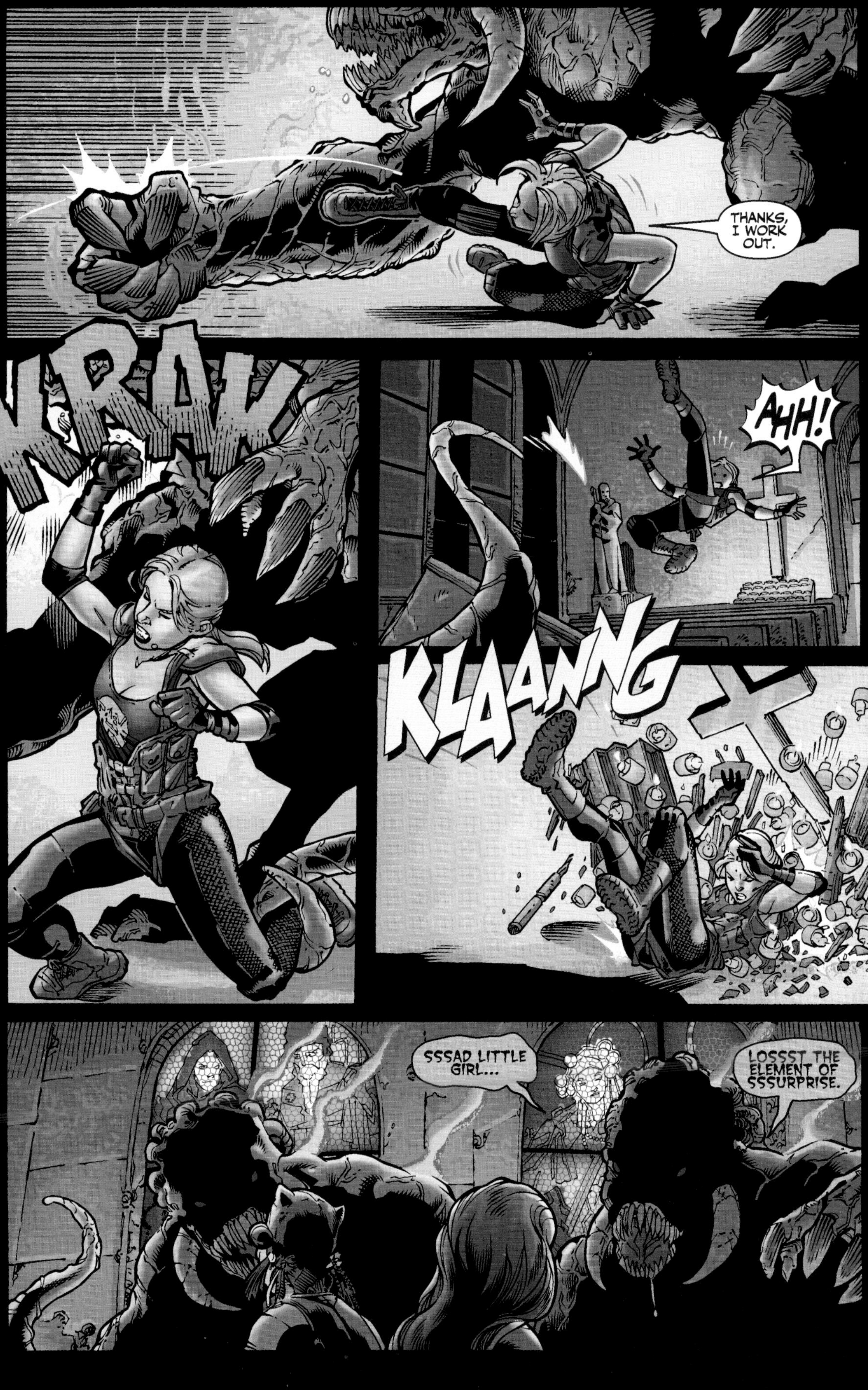
THANKS, I WORK OUT.
KRAK
AHH!
KLAANNG
SSSAD LITTLE GIRL...
LOSSST THE ELEMENT OF SSSURPRISE.

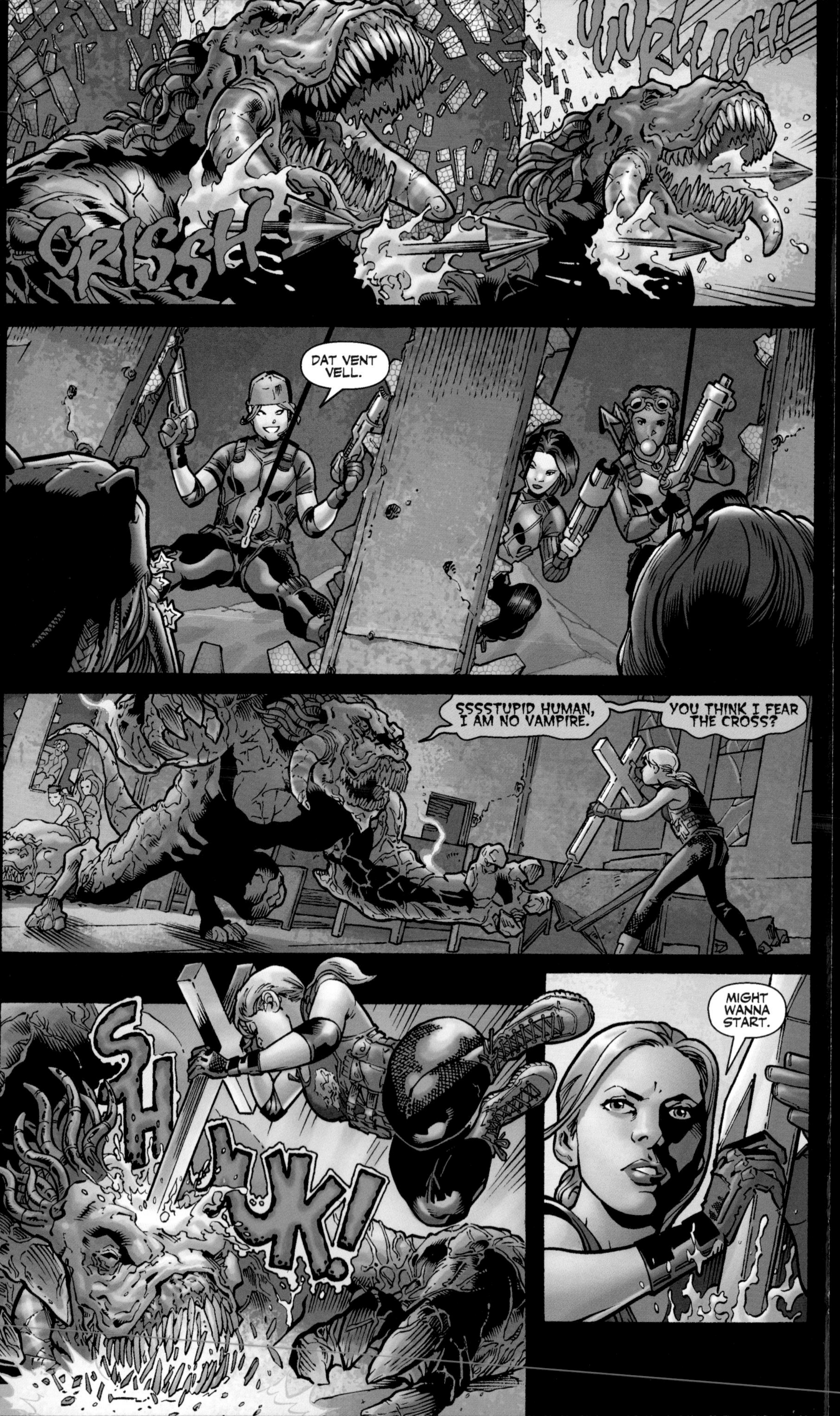
YUURLLGH!
CRISSH
DAT VENT VELL.
SSSSTUPID HUMAN, I AM NO VAMPIRE.
YOU THINK I FEAR THE CROSS?
SHUNK!
MIGHT WANNA START.

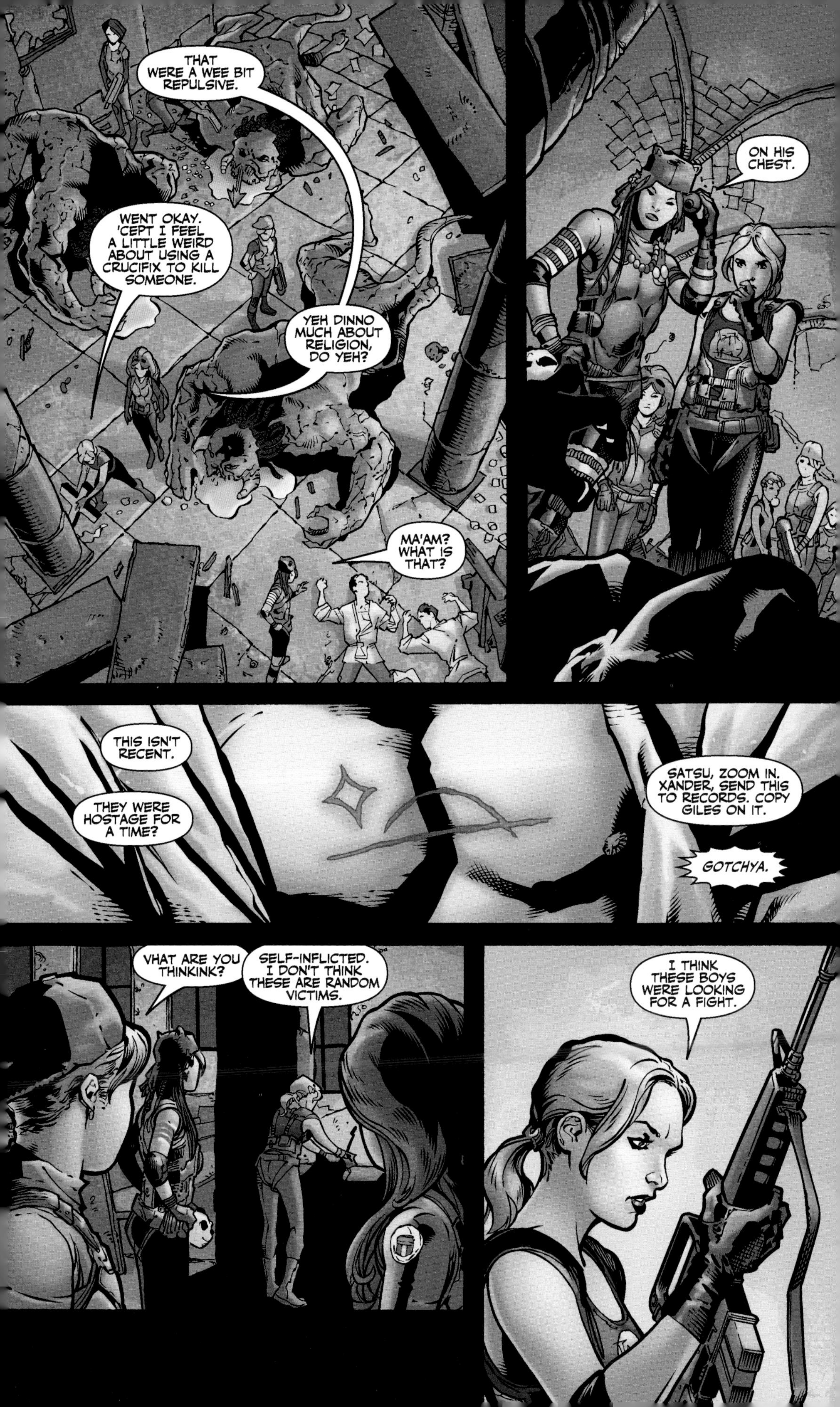
WENT OKAY. 'CEPT I FEEL A LITTLE WEIRD ABOUT USING A CRUCIFIX TO KILL SOMEONE.
THAT WERE A WEE BIT REPULSIVE.
YEH DINNO MUCH ABOUT RELIGION, DO YEH?
MA'AM? WHAT IS THAT?
ON HIS CHEST.
THIS ISN'T RECENT.
THEY WERE HOSTAGE FOR A TIME?
SATSU, ZOOM IN. XANDER, SEND THIS TO RECORDS. COPY GILES ON IT.
GOTCHYA.
VHAT ARE YOU THINKINK?
SELF-INFLICTED. I DON'T THINK THESE ARE RANDOM VICTIMS.
I THINK THESE BOYS WERE LOOKING FOR A FIGHT.

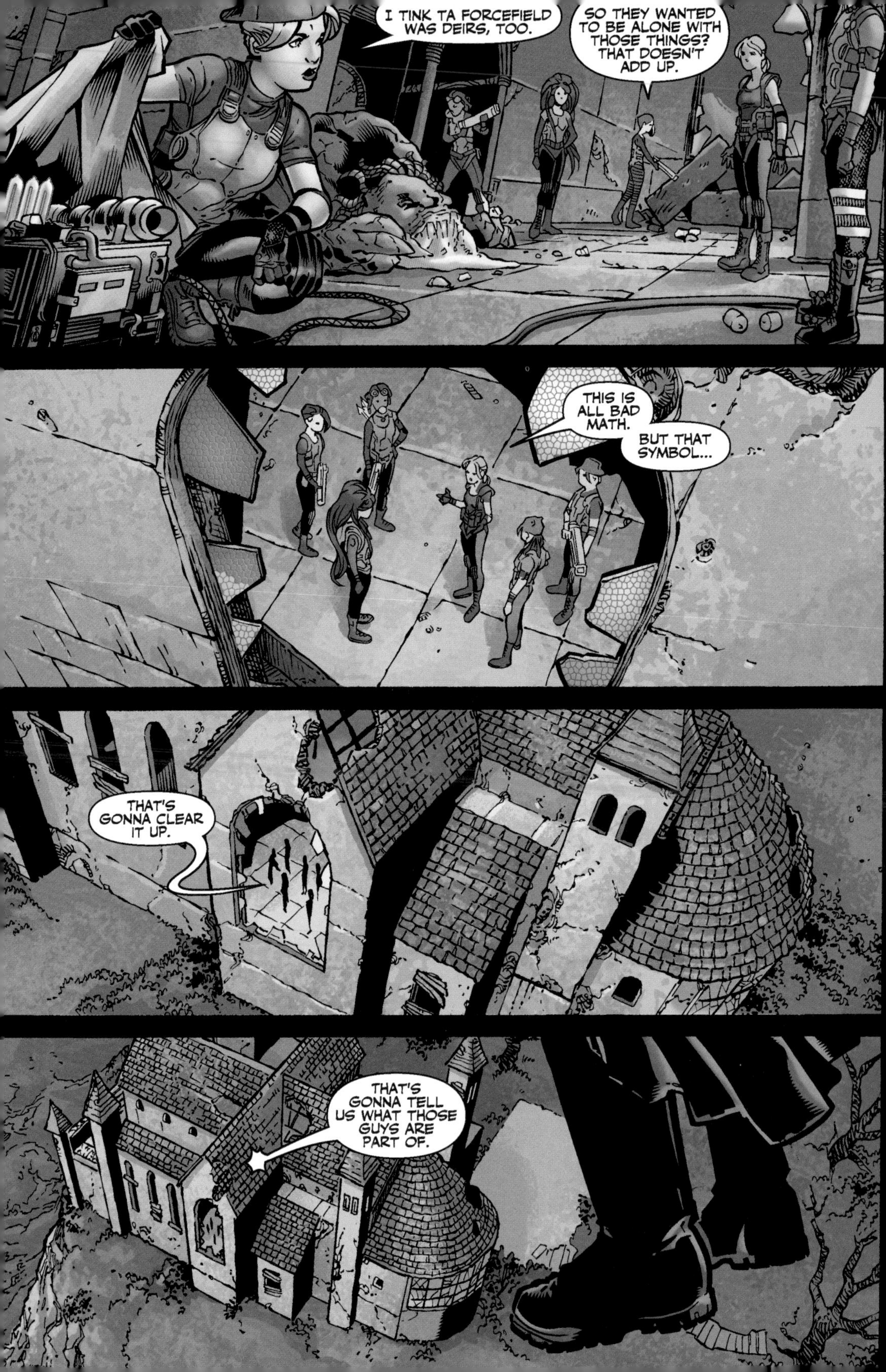
I TINK TA FORCEFIELD WAS DEIRS, TOO.
SO THEY WANTED TO BE ALONE WITH THOSE THINGS? THAT DOESN'T ADD UP.
THIS IS ALL BAD MATH.
BUT THAT SYMBOL...
THAT'S GONNA CLEAR IT UP.
THAT'S GONNA TELL US WHAT THOSE GUYS ARE PART OF.

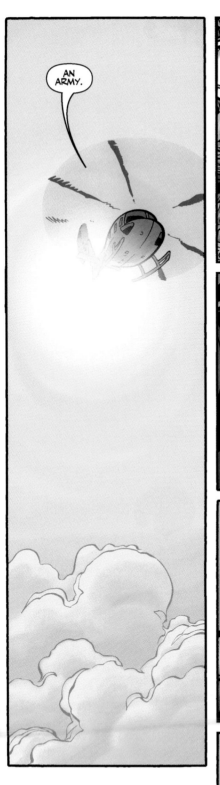

AN ARMY.

YOU DON'T THINK THAT'S OVERSTATING IT, GENERAL VOLL?

OUR INTEL SAYS THEY'RE TOO LOOSELY AFFILIATED TO... I MEAN, THEY'RE SCATTERED IN THOSE --

"SQUADS," RIGHT. TERRORISTS CALL 'EM "CELLS."

WE GO AHEAD WITH THIS, WE GOTTA BE TOGETHER ON EXACTLY WHAT WE'RE FACING. AND THAT'S AN ARMY.

THEY GOT POWER, THEY GOT RESOURCES, AND THEY GOT A HARD-LINE IDEOLOGY THAT DOES NOT JIBE WITH AMERICAN INTERESTS.

WORST OF ALL, THEY GOT A LEADER.

CHARISMATIC, UNCOMPROMISING, AND COMPLETELY DESTRUCTIVE.

I MEAN, FOR THE LOVE OF GOD...

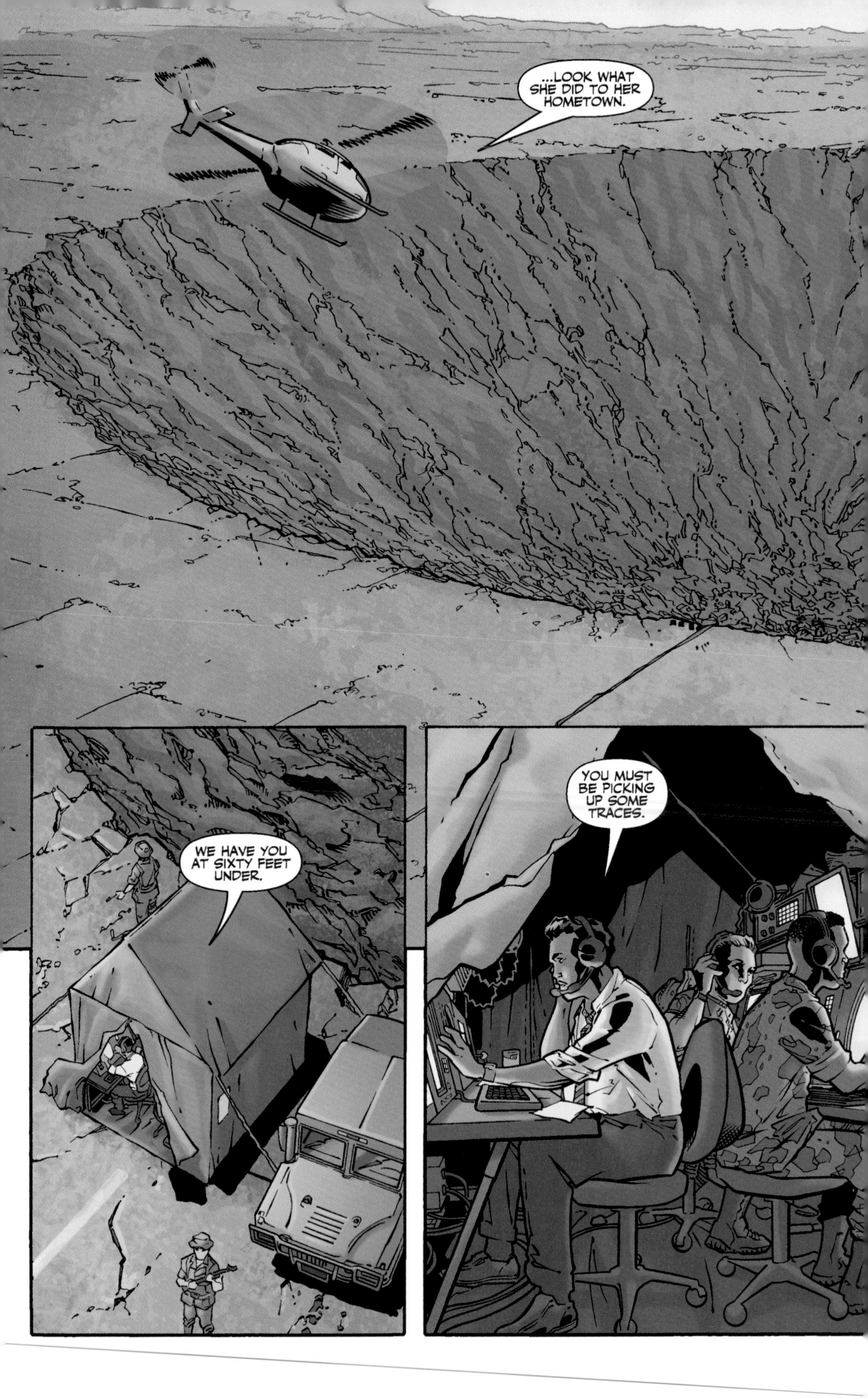
...LOOK WHAT SHE DID TO HER HOMETOWN.
WE HAVE YOU AT SIXTY FEET UNDER.
YOU MUST BE PICKING UP SOME TRACES.

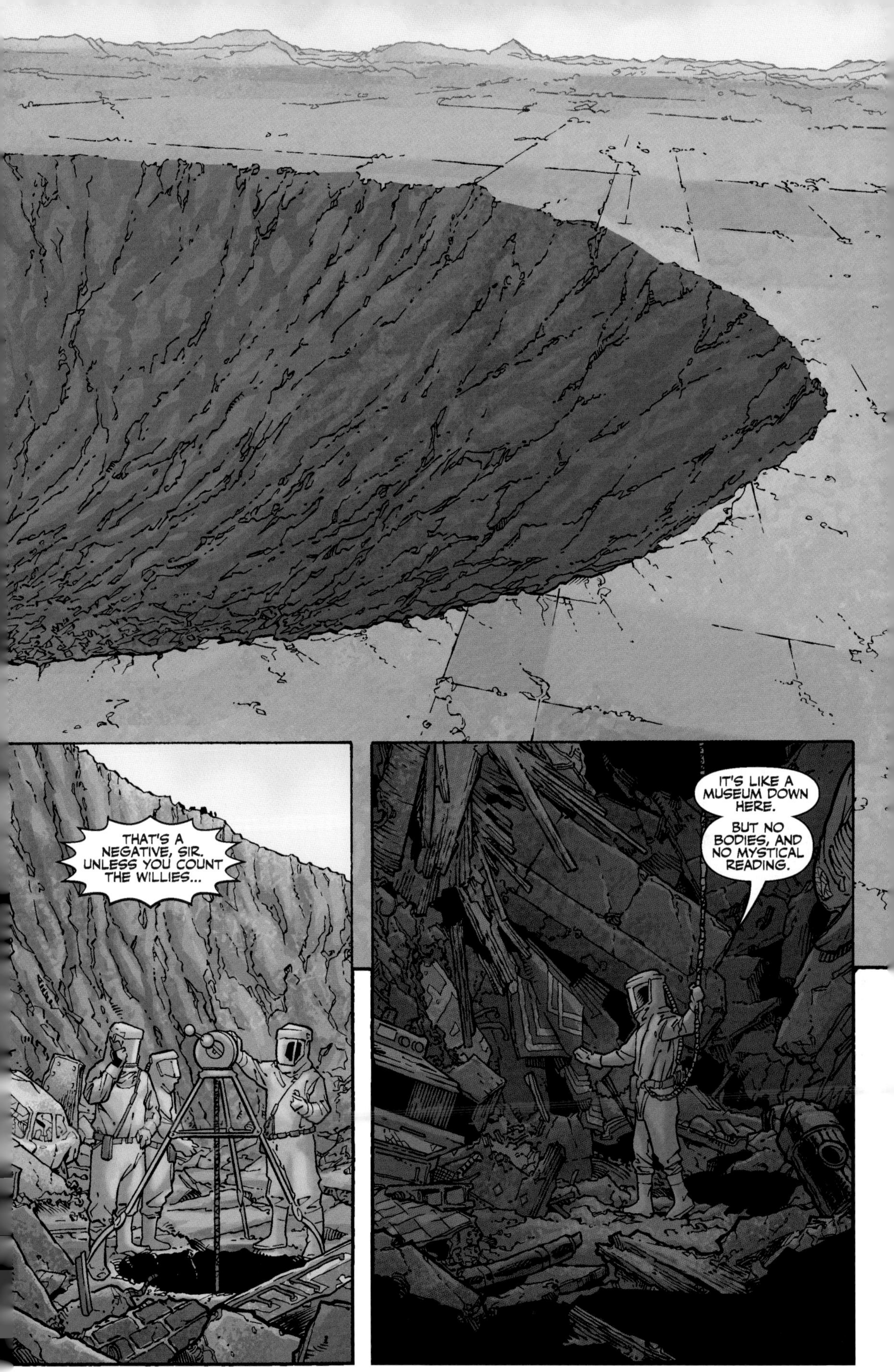
THAT'S A NEGATIVE, SIR. UNLESS YOU COUNT THE WILLIES...
IT'S LIKE A MUSEUM DOWN HERE.
BUT NO BODIES, AND NO MYSTICAL READING.

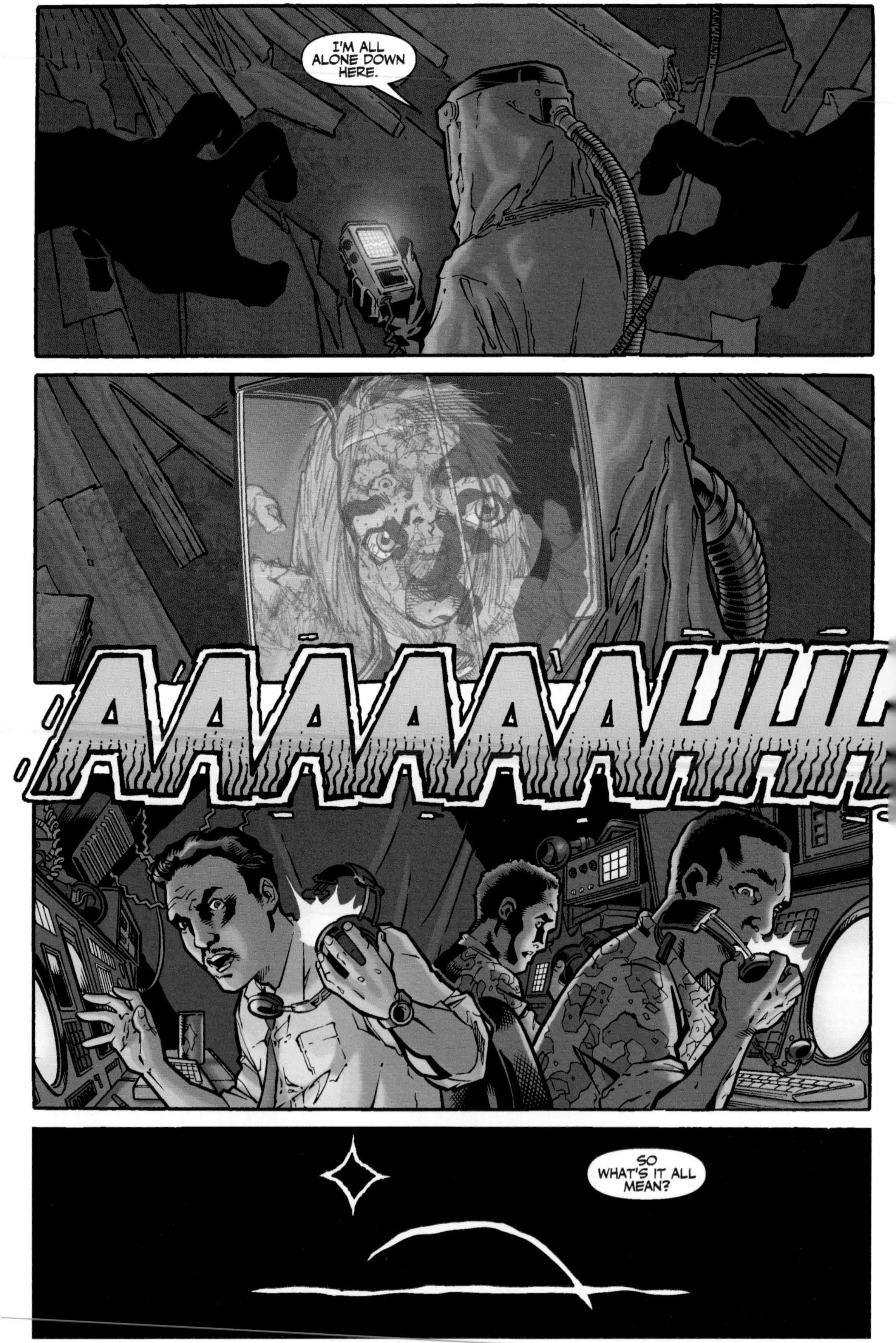
I'M ALL ALONE DOWN HERE.
AAAAAAHHH
SO WHAT'S IT ALL MEAN?

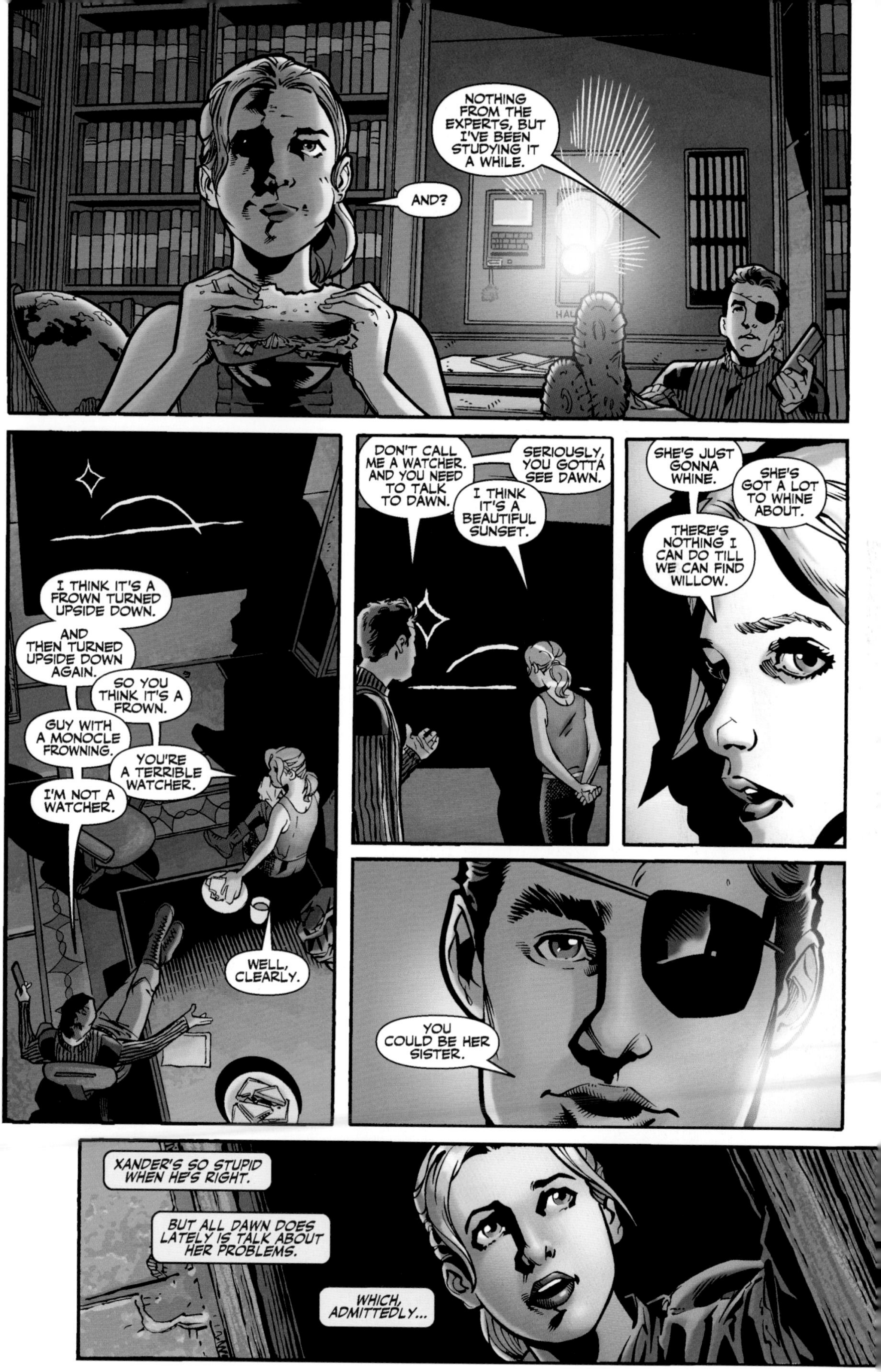
NOTHING FROM THE EXPERTS, BUT I'VE BEEN STUDYING IT A WHILE.
AND?
I THINK IT'S A FROWN TURNED UPSIDE DOWN.
AND THEN TURNED UPSIDE DOWN AGAIN.
SO YOU THINK IT'S A FROWN.
GUY WITH A MONOCLE FROWNING.
YOU'RE A TERRIBLE WATCHER.
I'M NOT A WATCHER.
WELL, CLEARLY.
DON'T CALL ME A WATCHER. AND YOU NEED TO TALK TO DAWN.
SERIOUSLY, YOU GOTTA SEE DAWN.
I THINK IT'S A BEAUTIFUL SUNSET.
SHE'S JUST GONNA WHINE.
SHE'S GOT A LOT TO WHINE ABOUT.
THERE'S NOTHING I CAN DO TILL WE CAN FIND WILLOW.
YOU COULD BE HER SISTER.
XANDER'S SO STUPID WHEN HE'S RIGHT.
BUT ALL DAWN DOES LATELY IS TALK ABOUT HER PROBLEMS.
WHICH, ADMITTEDLY...

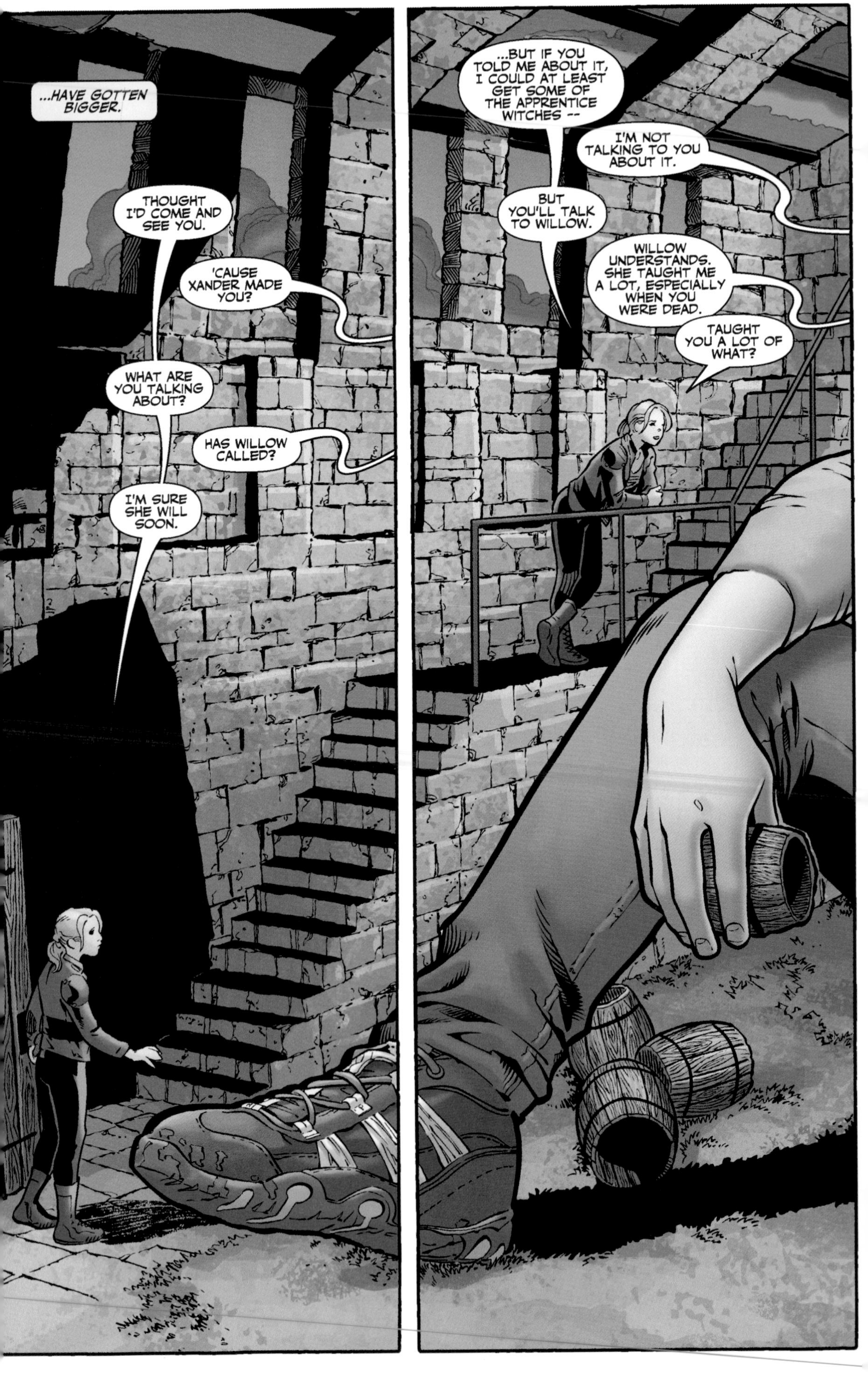
...HAVE GOTTEN BIGGER.
THOUGHT I'D COME AND SEE YOU.
'CAUSE XANDER MADE YOU?
WHAT ARE YOU TALKING ABOUT?
HAS WILLOW CALLED?
I'M SURE SHE WILL SOON.
...BUT IF YOU TOLD ME ABOUT IT, I COULD AT LEAST GET SOME OF THE APPRENTICE WITCHES --
I'M NOT TALKING TO YOU ABOUT IT.
BUT YOU'LL TALK TO WILLOW.
WILLOW UNDERSTANDS. SHE TAUGHT ME A LOT, ESPECIALLY WHEN YOU WERE DEAD.
TAUGHT YOU A LOT OF WHAT?

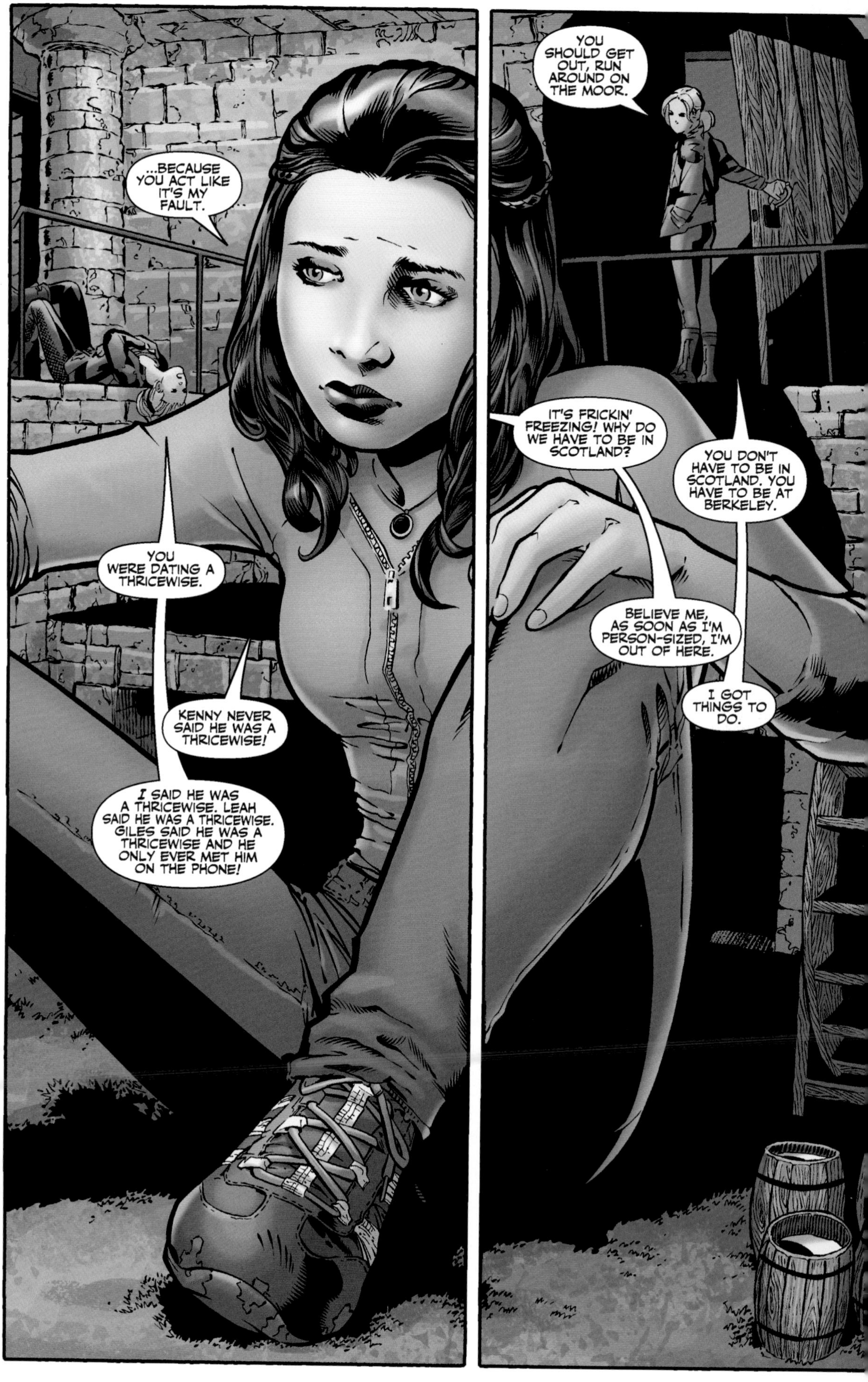
...BECAUSE YOU ACT LIKE IT'S MY FAULT.
YOU WERE DATING A THRICEWISE.
KENNY NEVER SAID HE WAS A THRICEWISE!
I SAID HE WAS A THRICEWISE. LEAH SAID HE WAS A THRICEWISE. GILES SAID HE WAS A THRICEWISE AND HE ONLY EVER MET HIM ON THE PHONE!
YOU SHOULD GET OUT, RUN AROUND ON THE MOOR.
IT'S FRICKIN' FREEZING! WHY DO WE HAVE TO BE IN SCOTLAND?
YOU DON'T HAVE TO BE IN SCOTLAND. YOU HAVE TO BE AT BERKELEY.
BELIEVE ME, AS SOON AS I'M PERSON-SIZED, I'M OUT OF HERE.
I GOT THINGS TO DO.

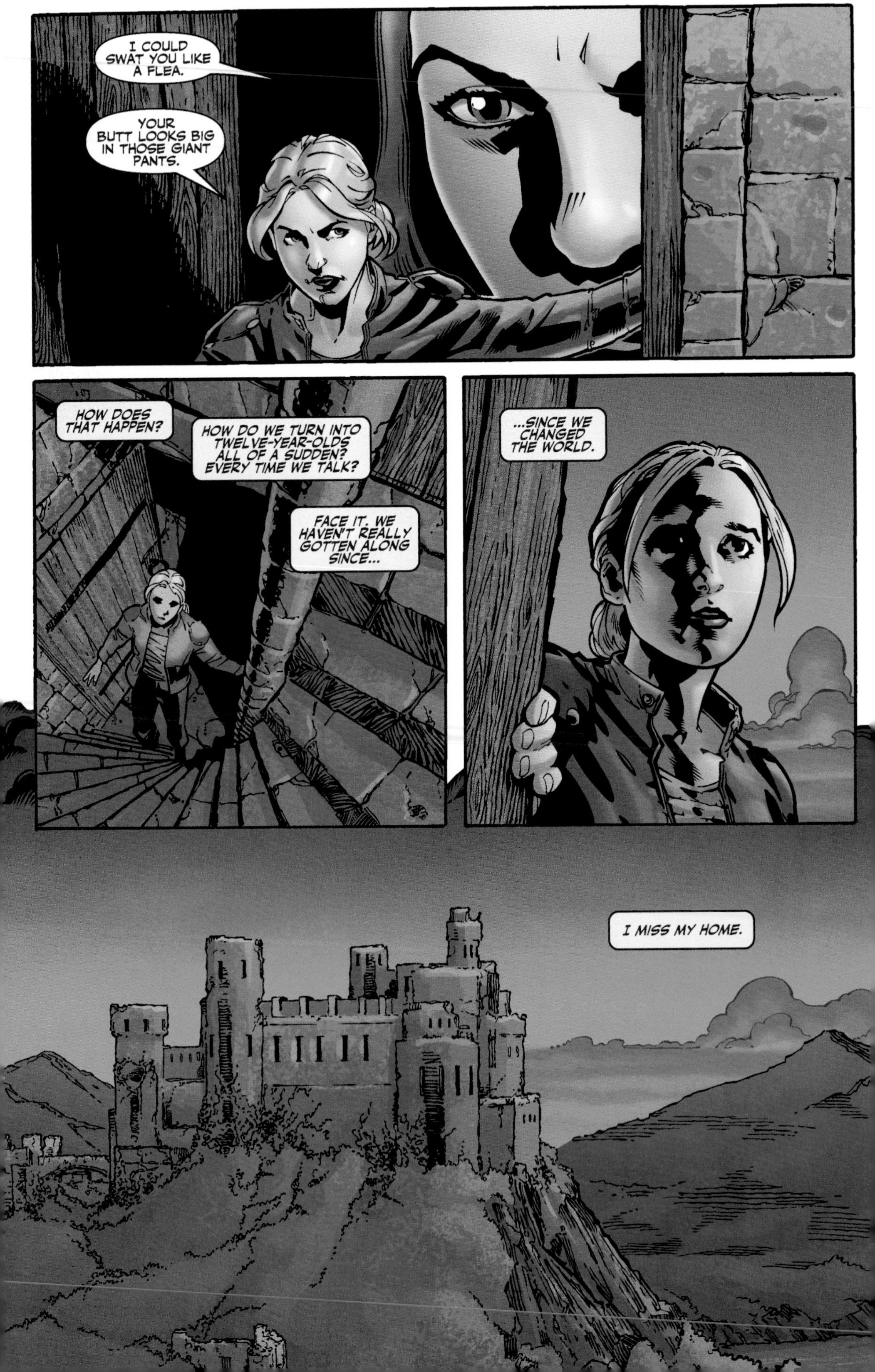
I COULD SWAT YOU LIKE A FLEA.
YOUR BUTT LOOKS BIG IN THOSE GIANT PANTS.
HOW DOES THAT HAPPEN?
HOW DO WE TURN INTO TWELVE-YEAR-OLDS ALL OF A SUDDEN? EVERY TIME WE TALK?
FACE IT. WE HAVEN'T REALLY GOTTEN ALONG SINCE...
...SINCE WE CHANGED THE WORLD.
I MISS MY HOME.

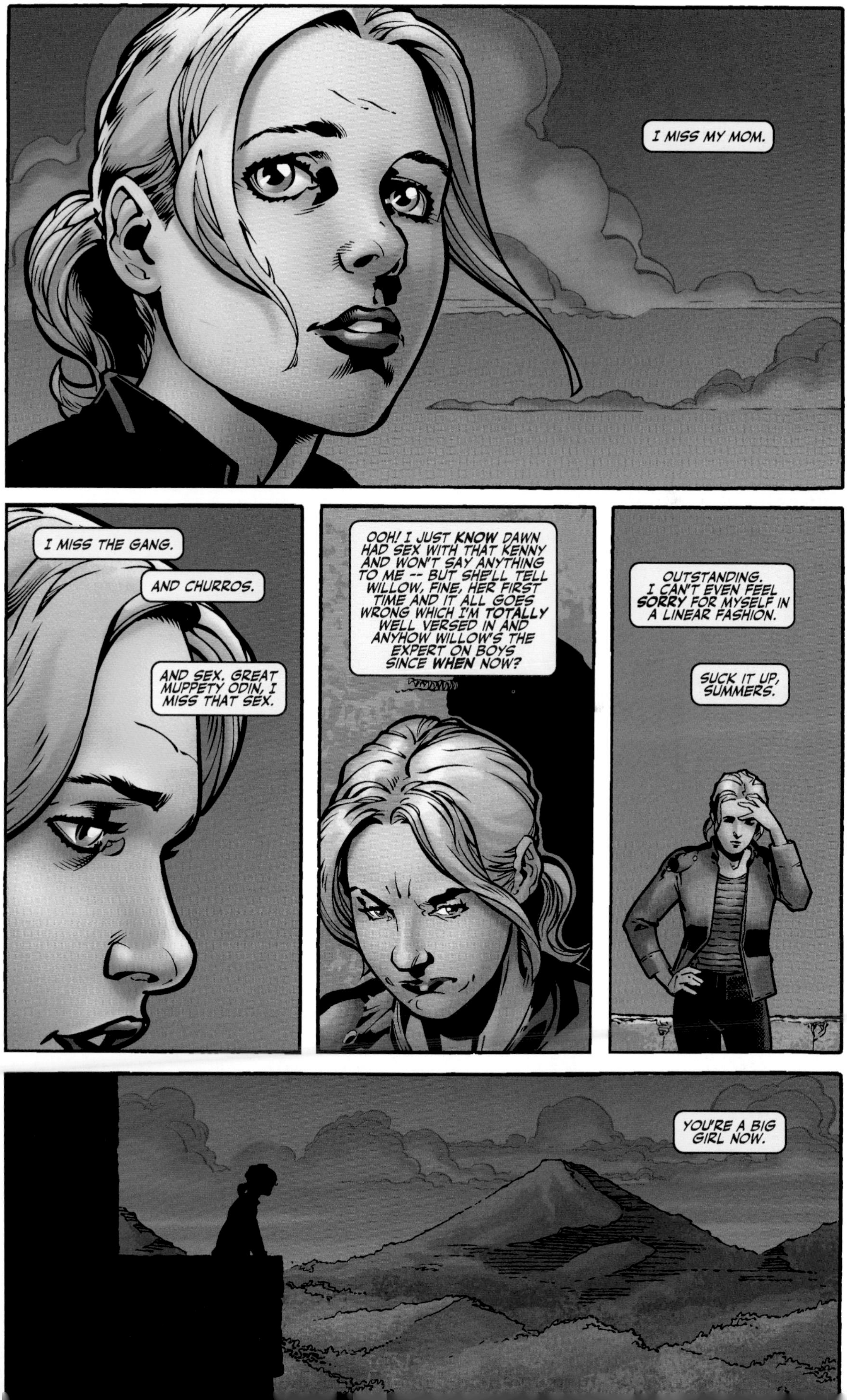
I MISS MY MOM.
I MISS THE GANG.
AND CHURROS.
AND SEX. GREAT MUPPETY ODIN, I MISS THAT SEX.
OOH! I JUST KNOW DAWN HAD SEX WITH THAT KENNY AND WON'T SAY ANYTHING TO ME -- BUT SHE'LL TELL WILLOW, FINE, HER FIRST TIME AND IT ALL GOES WRONG WHICH I'M TOTALLY WELL VERSED IN AND ANYHOW WILLOW'S THE EXPERT ON BOYS SINCE WHEN NOW?
OUTSTANDING. I CAN'T EVEN FEEL SORRY FOR MYSELF IN A LINEAR FASHION.
SUCK IT UP, SUMMERS.
YOU'RE A BIG GIRL NOW.

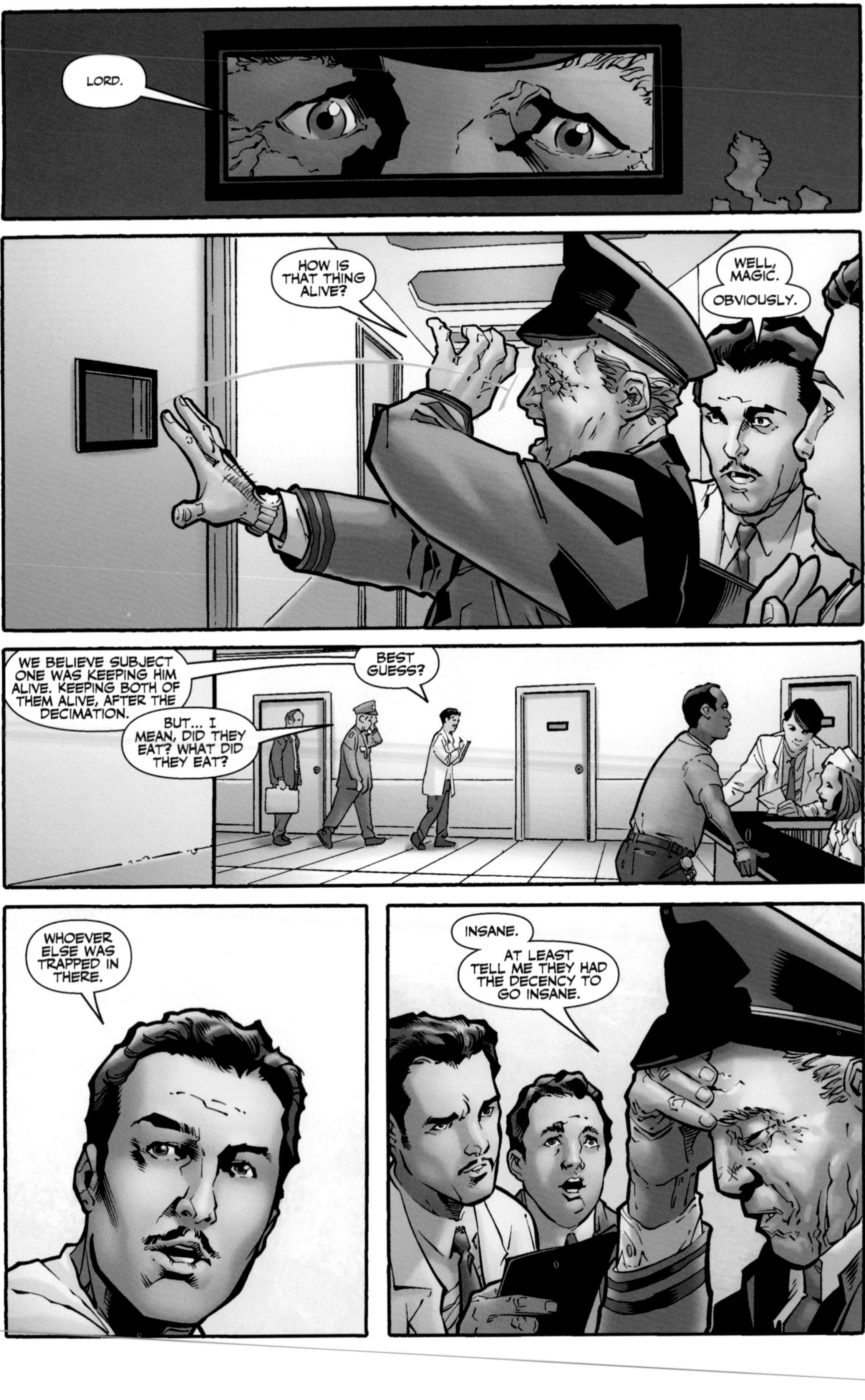
LORD.
HOW IS THAT THING ALIVE?
WELL, MAGIC.
OBVIOUSLY.
WE BELIEVE SUBJECT ONE WAS KEEPING HIM ALIVE. KEEPING BOTH OF THEM ALIVE, AFTER THE DECIMATION.
BEST GUESS?
BUT... I MEAN, DID THEY EAT? WHAT DID THEY EAT?
WHOEVER ELSE WAS TRAPPED IN THERE.
INSANE.
AT LEAST TELL ME THEY HAD THE DECENCY TO GO INSANE.

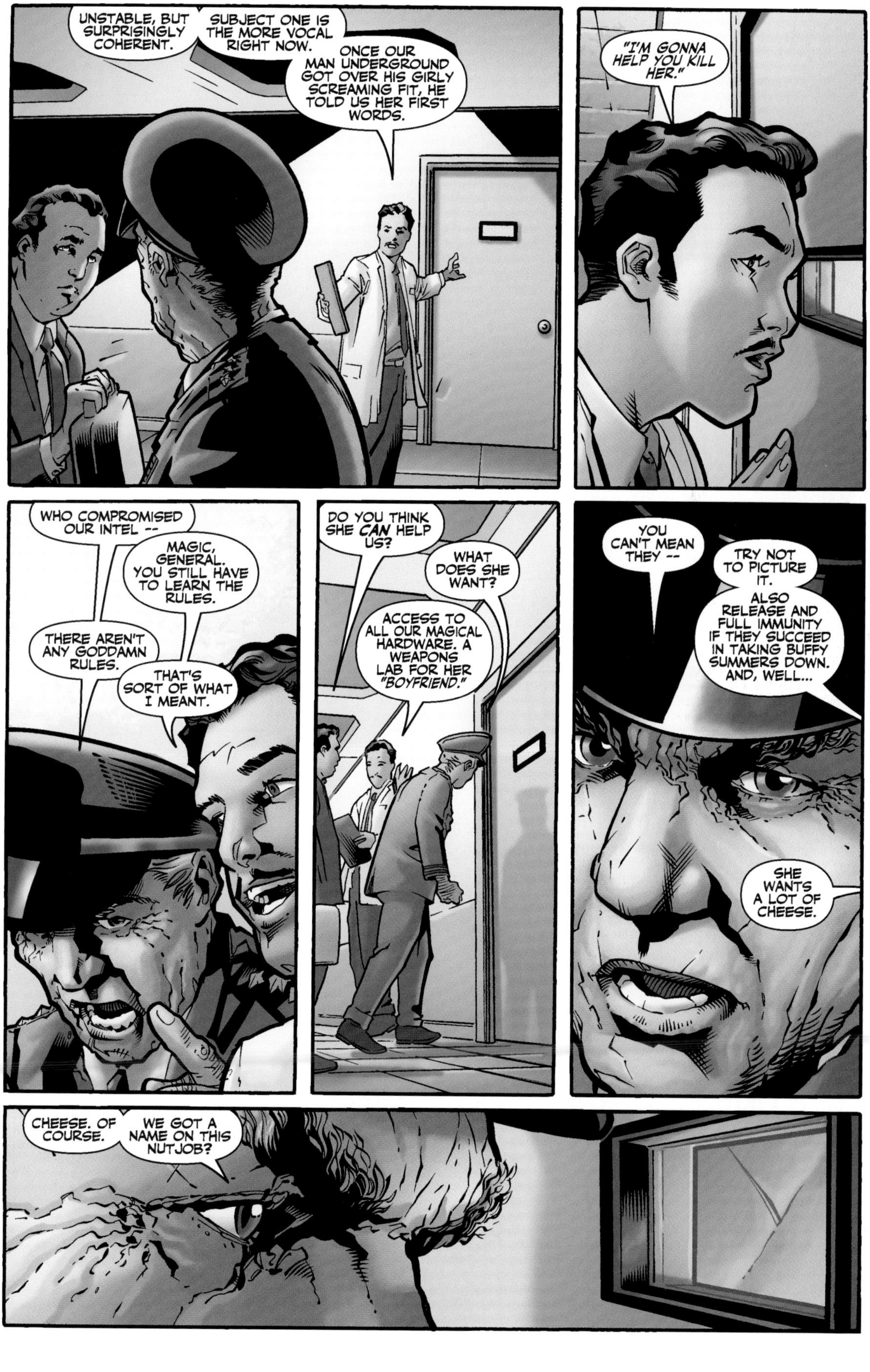
UNSTABLE, BUT SURPRISINGLY COHERENT.
SUBJECT ONE IS THE MORE VOCAL RIGHT NOW.
ONCE OUR MAN UNDERGROUND GOT OVER HIS GIRLY SCREAMING FIT, HE TOLD US HER FIRST WORDS.
"I'M GONNA HELP YOU KILL HER."
WHO COMPROMISED OUR INTEL --
MAGIC, GENERAL. YOU STILL HAVE TO LEARN THE RULES.
THERE AREN'T ANY GODDAMN RULES.
THAT'S SORT OF WHAT I MEANT.
DO YOU THINK SHE *CAN* HELP US?
WHAT DOES SHE WANT?
ACCESS TO ALL OUR MAGICAL HARDWARE. A WEAPONS LAB FOR HER *"BOYFRIEND."*
YOU CAN'T MEAN THEY --
TRY NOT TO PICTURE IT.
ALSO RELEASE AND FULL IMMUNITY IF THEY SUCCEED IN TAKING BUFFY SUMMERS DOWN. AND, WELL...
SHE WANTS A LOT OF CHEESE.
CHEESE. OF COURSE.
WE GOT A NAME ON THIS NUTJOB?

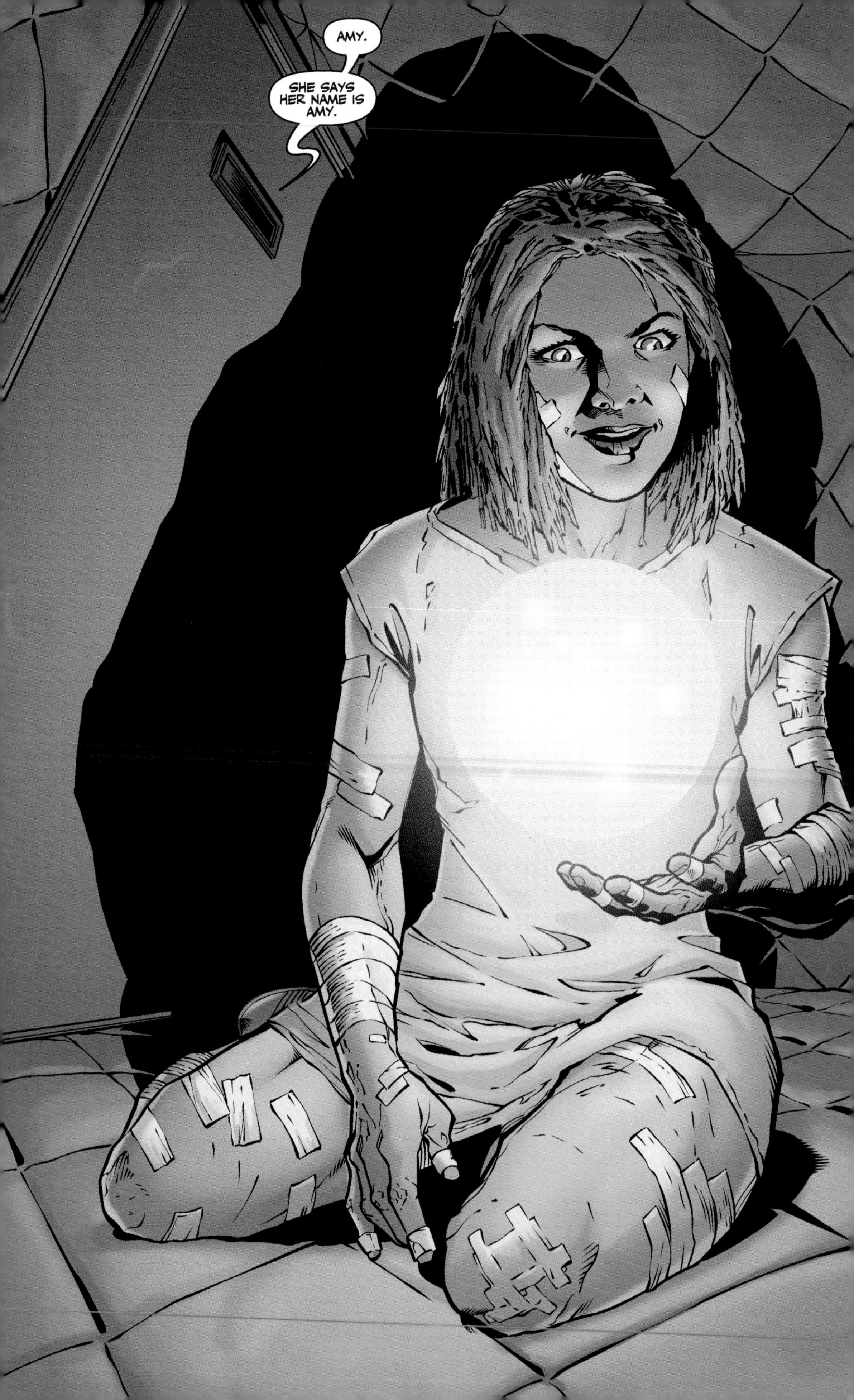
AMY.
SHE SAYS HER NAME IS AMY.

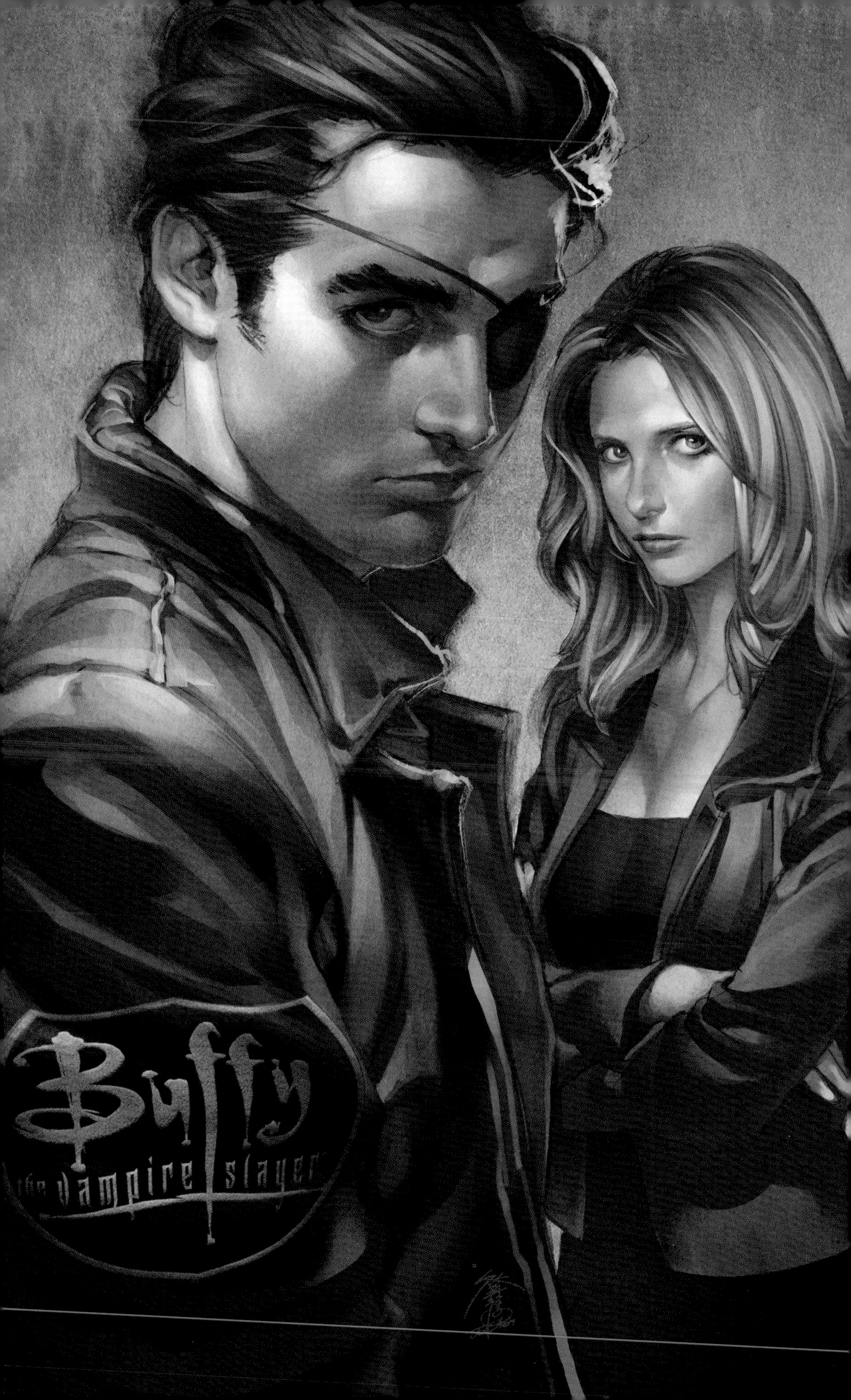
Buffy
the vampire slayer

The LONG WAY HOME

I USED TO BE A WATCHER.

Part Two

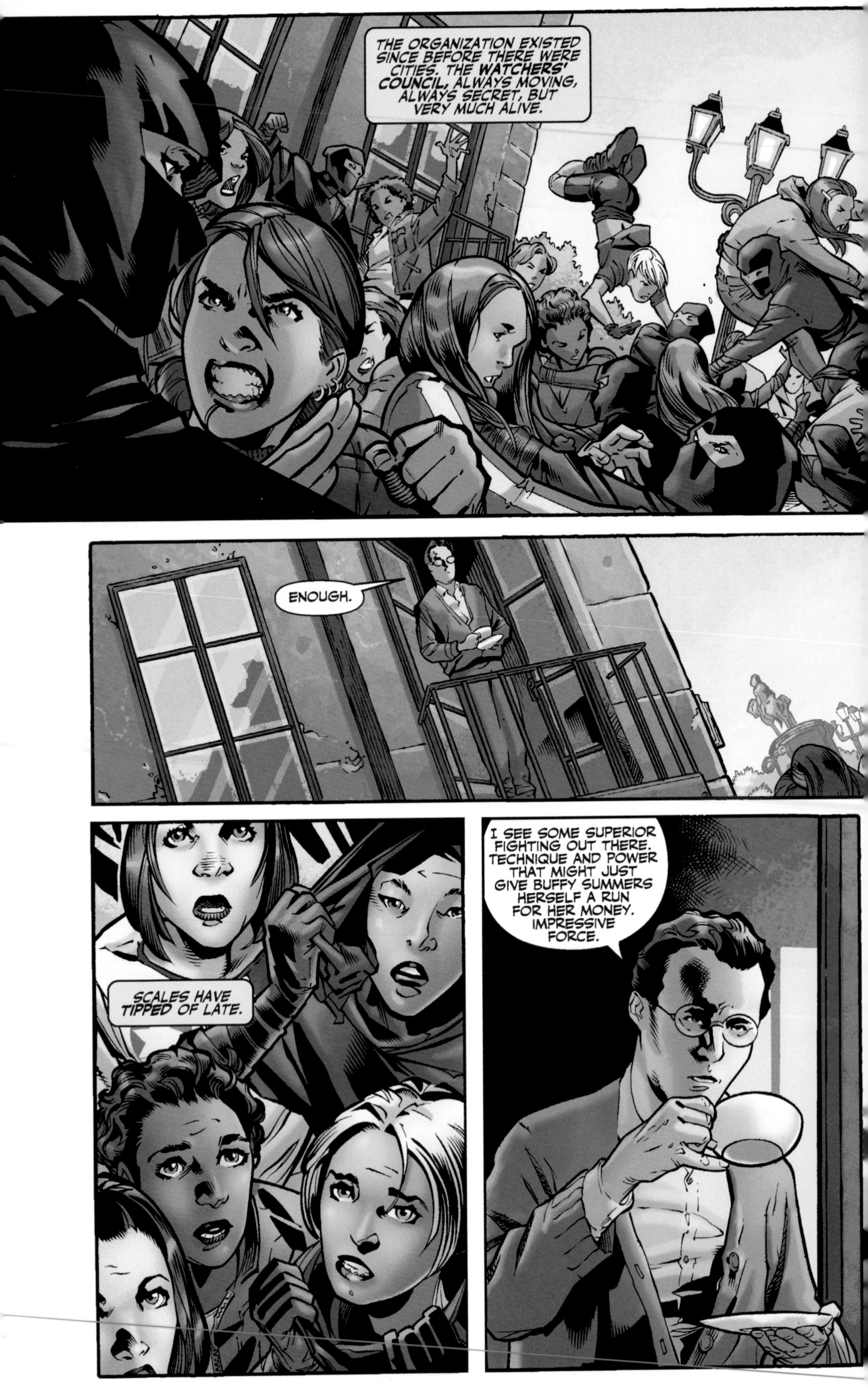
THE ORGANIZATION EXISTED SINCE BEFORE THERE WERE CITIES. THE WATCHERS' COUNCIL, ALWAYS MOVING, ALWAYS SECRET, BUT VERY MUCH ALIVE.
ENOUGH.
SCALES HAVE TIPPED OF LATE.
I SEE SOME SUPERIOR FIGHTING OUT THERE. TECHNIQUE AND POWER THAT MIGHT JUST GIVE BUFFY SUMMERS HERSELF A RUN FOR HER MONEY. IMPRESSIVE FORCE.

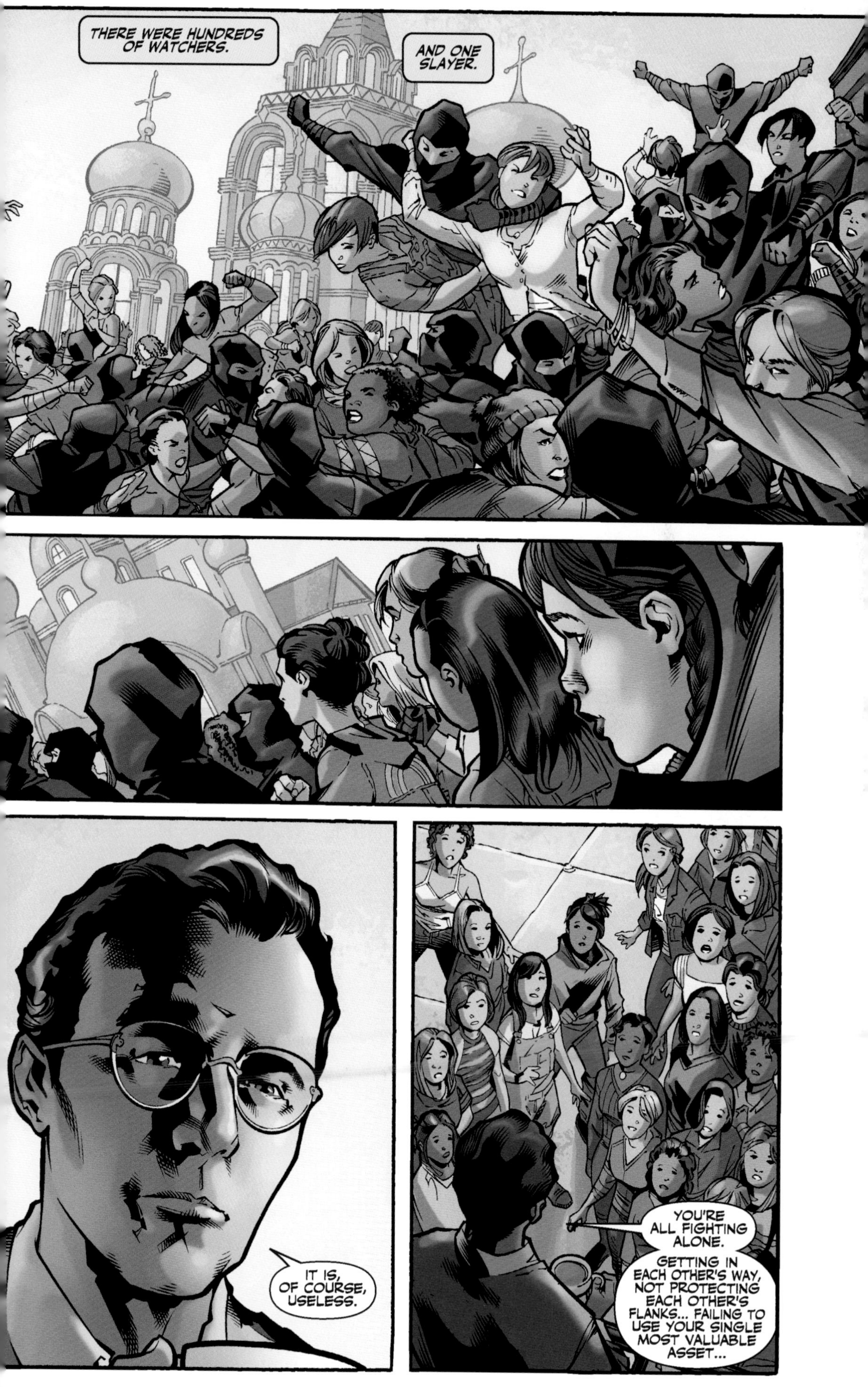
THERE WERE HUNDREDS OF WATCHERS.
AND ONE SLAYER.
IT IS, OF COURSE, USELESS.
YOU'RE ALL FIGHTING ALONE.
GETTING IN EACH OTHER'S WAY, NOT PROTECTING EACH OTHER'S FLANKS... FAILING TO USE YOUR SINGLE MOST VALUABLE ASSET...

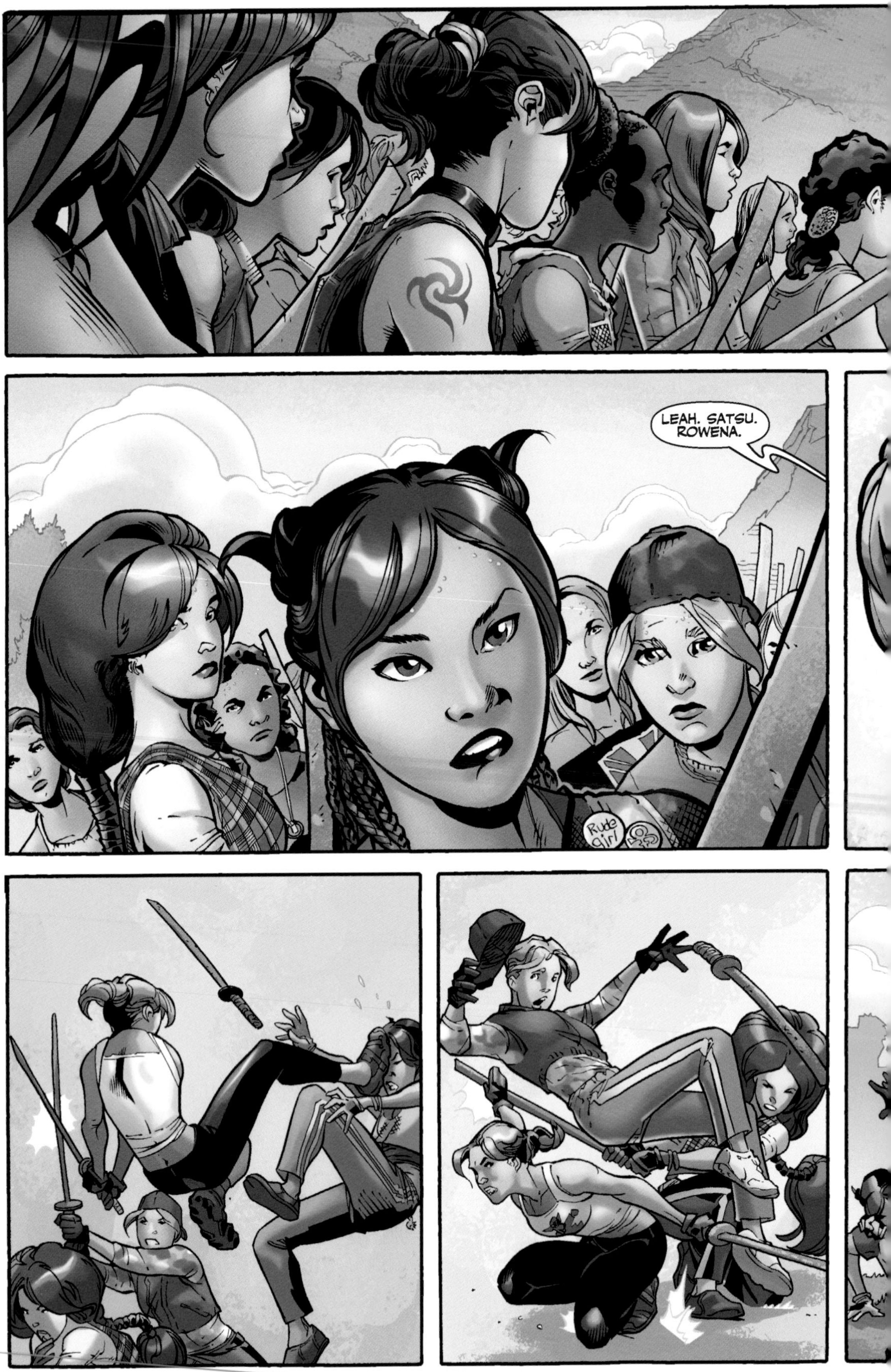
LEAH. SATSU. ROWENA.
Rude girl

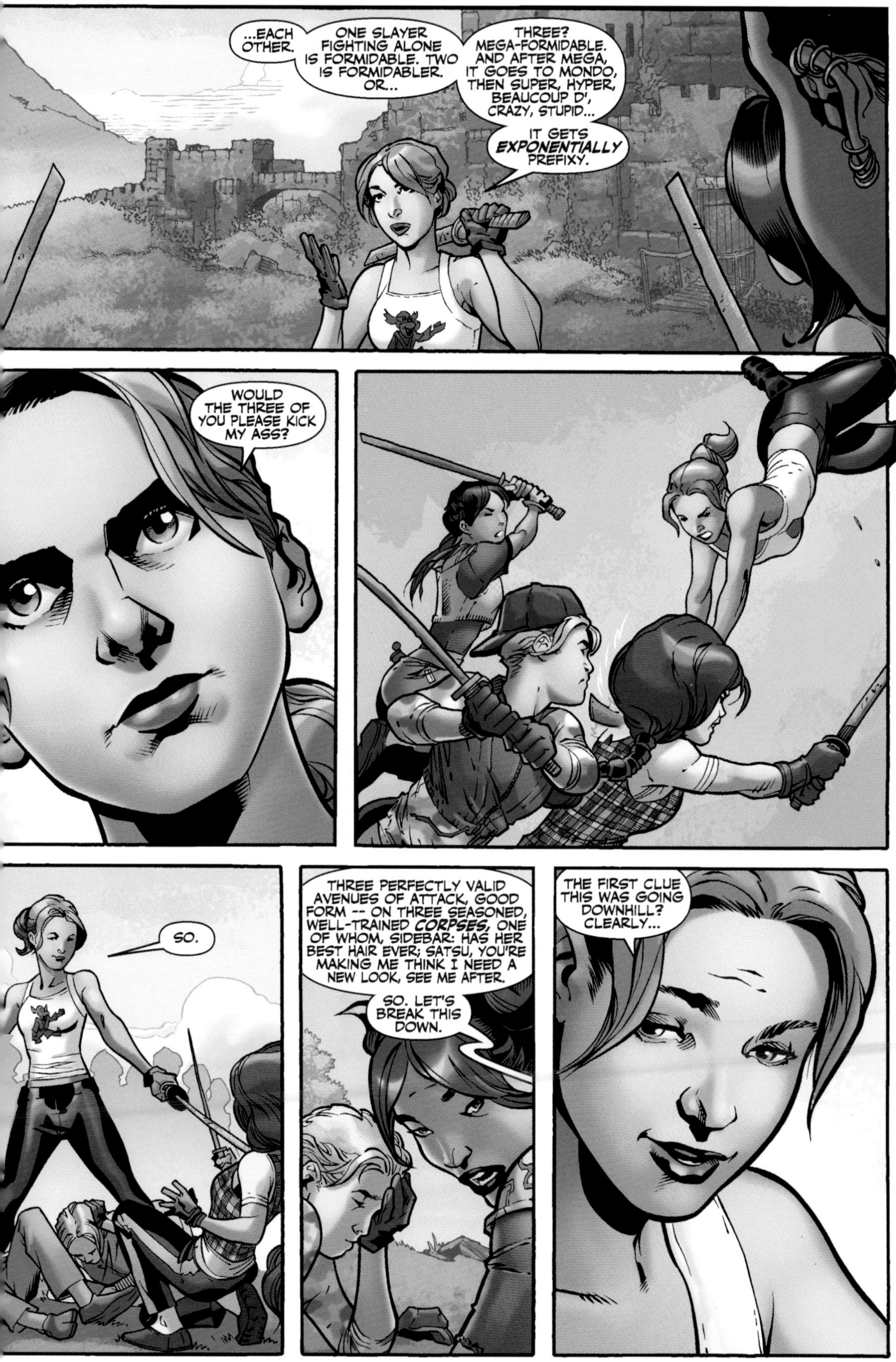
...EACH OTHER.
ONE SLAYER FIGHTING ALONE IS FORMIDABLE. TWO IS FORMIDABLER. OR...
THREE? MEGA-FORMIDABLE. AND AFTER MEGA, IT GOES TO MONDO, THEN SUPER, HYPER, BEAUCOUP D', CRAZY, STUPID...
IT GETS *EXPONENTIALLY* PREFIXY.
WOULD THE THREE OF YOU PLEASE KICK MY ASS?
SO.
THREE PERFECTLY VALID AVENUES OF ATTACK, GOOD FORM -- ON THREE SEASONED, WELL-TRAINED *CORPSES,* ONE OF WHOM, SIDEBAR: HAS HER BEST HAIR EVER; SATSU, YOU'RE MAKING ME THINK I NEED A NEW LOOK, SEE ME AFTER.
SO. LET'S BREAK THIS DOWN.
THE FIRST CLUE THIS WAS GOING DOWNHILL? CLEARLY...

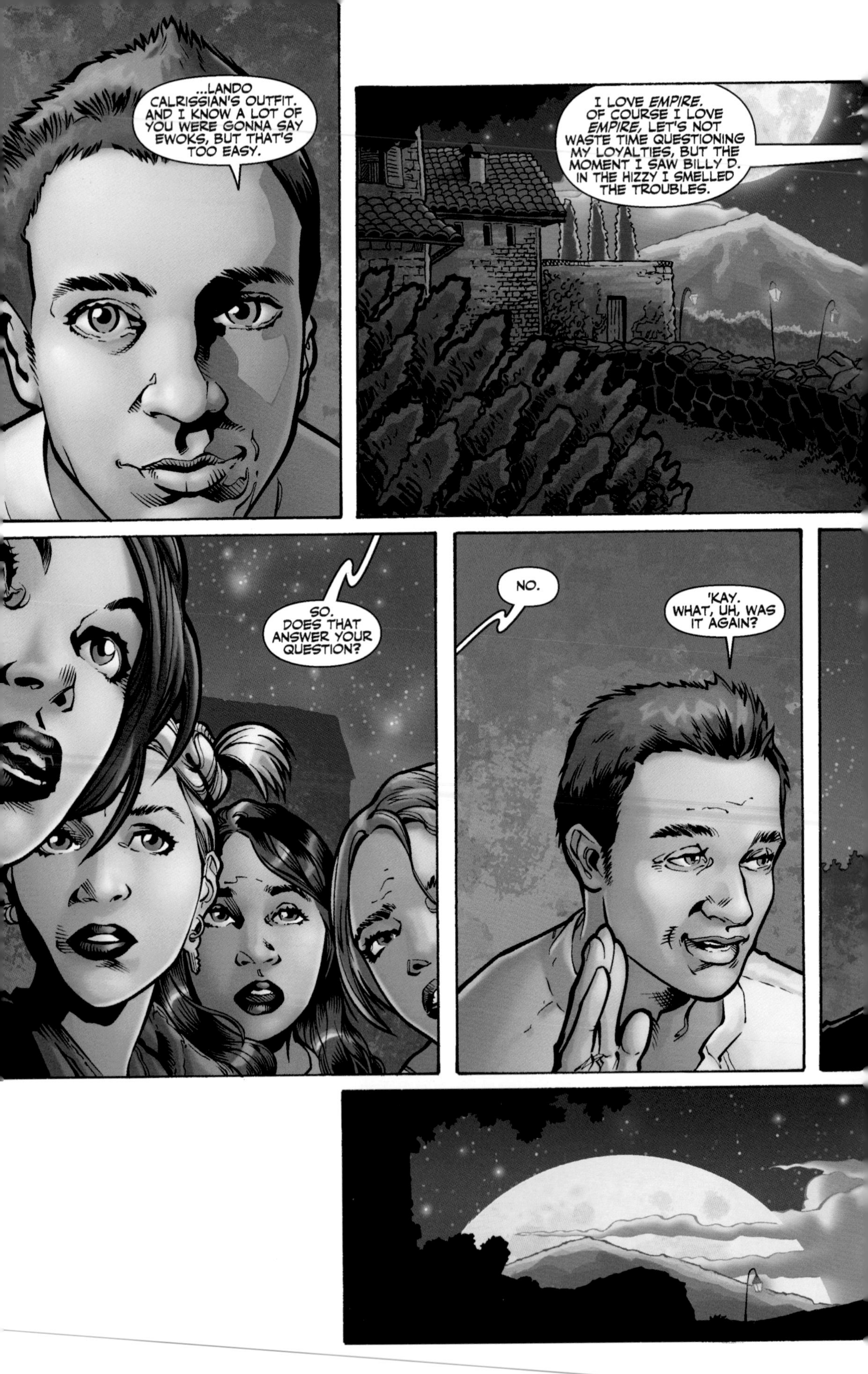
...LANDO CALRISSIAN'S OUTFIT. AND I KNOW A LOT OF YOU WERE GONNA SAY EWOKS, BUT THAT'S TOO EASY.
I LOVE *EMPIRE*. OF COURSE I LOVE *EMPIRE*, LET'S NOT WASTE TIME QUESTIONING MY LOYALTIES, BUT THE MOMENT I SAW BILLY D. IN THE HIZZY I SMELLED THE TROUBLES.
SO. DOES THAT ANSWER YOUR QUESTION?
NO.
'KAY. WHAT, UH, WAS IT AGAIN?

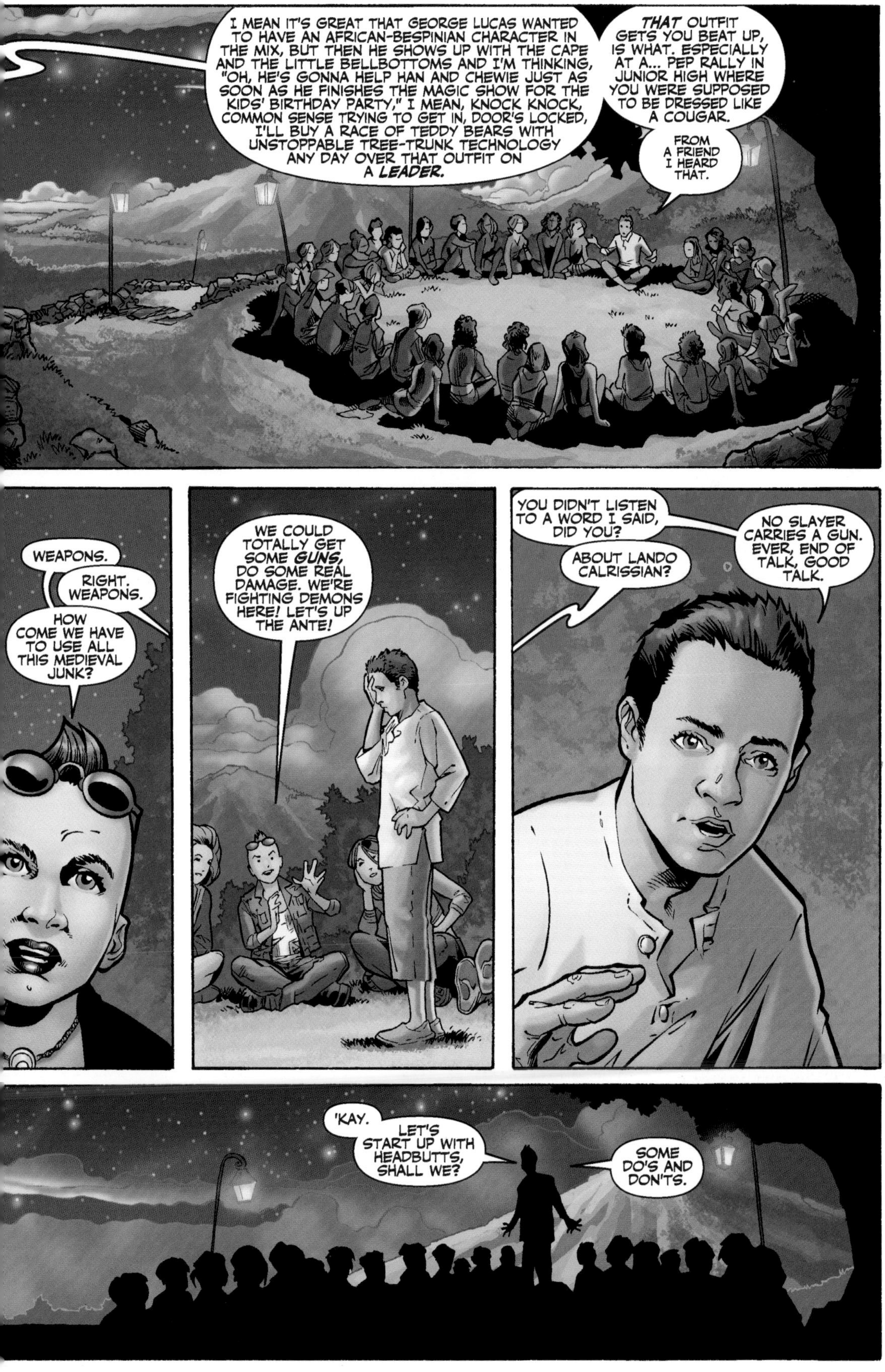
I MEAN IT'S GREAT THAT GEORGE LUCAS WANTED TO HAVE AN AFRICAN-BESPINIAN CHARACTER IN THE MIX, BUT THEN HE SHOWS UP WITH THE CAPE AND THE LITTLE BELLBOTTOMS AND I'M THINKING, "OH, HE'S GONNA HELP HAN AND CHEWIE JUST AS SOON AS HE FINISHES THE MAGIC SHOW FOR THE KIDS' BIRTHDAY PARTY," I MEAN, KNOCK KNOCK, COMMON SENSE TRYING TO GET IN, DOOR'S LOCKED, I'LL BUY A RACE OF TEDDY BEARS WITH UNSTOPPABLE TREE-TRUNK TECHNOLOGY ANY DAY OVER THAT OUTFIT ON A LEADER.
THAT OUTFIT GETS YOU BEAT UP, IS WHAT. ESPECIALLY AT A... PEP RALLY IN JUNIOR HIGH WHERE YOU WERE SUPPOSED TO BE DRESSED LIKE A COUGAR.
FROM A FRIEND I HEARD THAT.
WEAPONS.
RIGHT. WEAPONS.
HOW COME WE HAVE TO USE ALL THIS MEDIEVAL JUNK?
WE COULD TOTALLY GET SOME GUNS, DO SOME REAL DAMAGE. WE'RE FIGHTING DEMONS HERE! LET'S UP THE ANTE!
YOU DIDN'T LISTEN TO A WORD I SAID, DID YOU?
ABOUT LANDO CALRISSIAN?
NO SLAYER CARRIES A GUN. EVER, END OF TALK, GOOD TALK.
'KAY.
LET'S START UP WITH HEADBUTTS, SHALL WE?
SOME DO'S AND DON'TS.

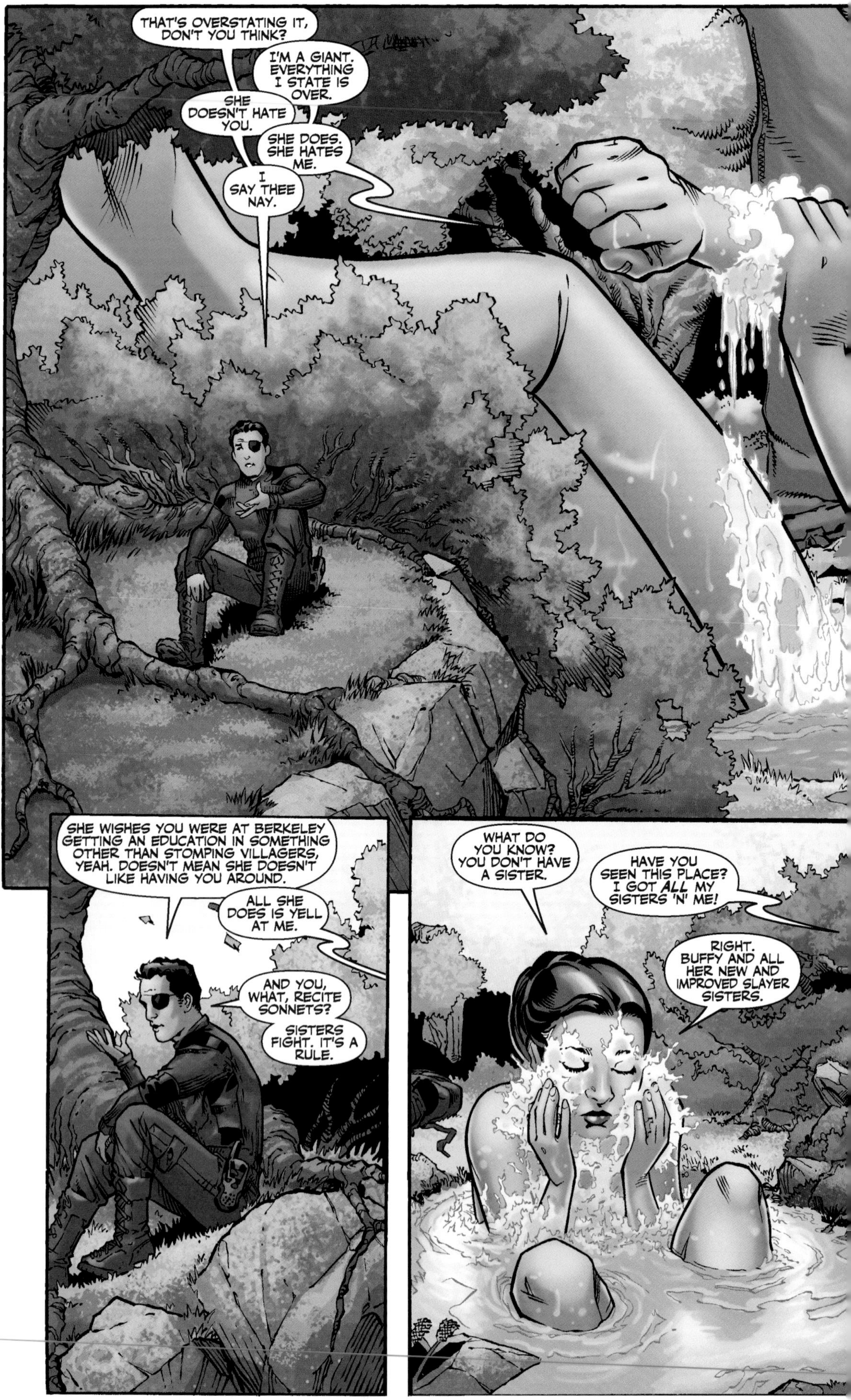
THAT'S OVERSTATING IT, DON'T YOU THINK?
I'M A GIANT. EVERYTHING I STATE IS OVER.
SHE DOESN'T HATE YOU.
SHE DOES. SHE HATES ME.
I SAY THEE NAY.
SHE WISHES YOU WERE AT BERKELEY GETTING AN EDUCATION IN SOMETHING OTHER THAN STOMPING VILLAGERS, YEAH. DOESN'T MEAN SHE DOESN'T LIKE HAVING YOU AROUND.
ALL SHE DOES IS YELL AT ME.
AND YOU, WHAT, RECITE SONNETS?
SISTERS FIGHT. IT'S A RULE.
WHAT DO YOU KNOW? YOU DON'T HAVE A SISTER.
HAVE YOU SEEN THIS PLACE? I GOT ALL MY SISTERS 'N' ME!
RIGHT. BUFFY AND ALL HER NEW AND IMPROVED SLAYER SISTERS.

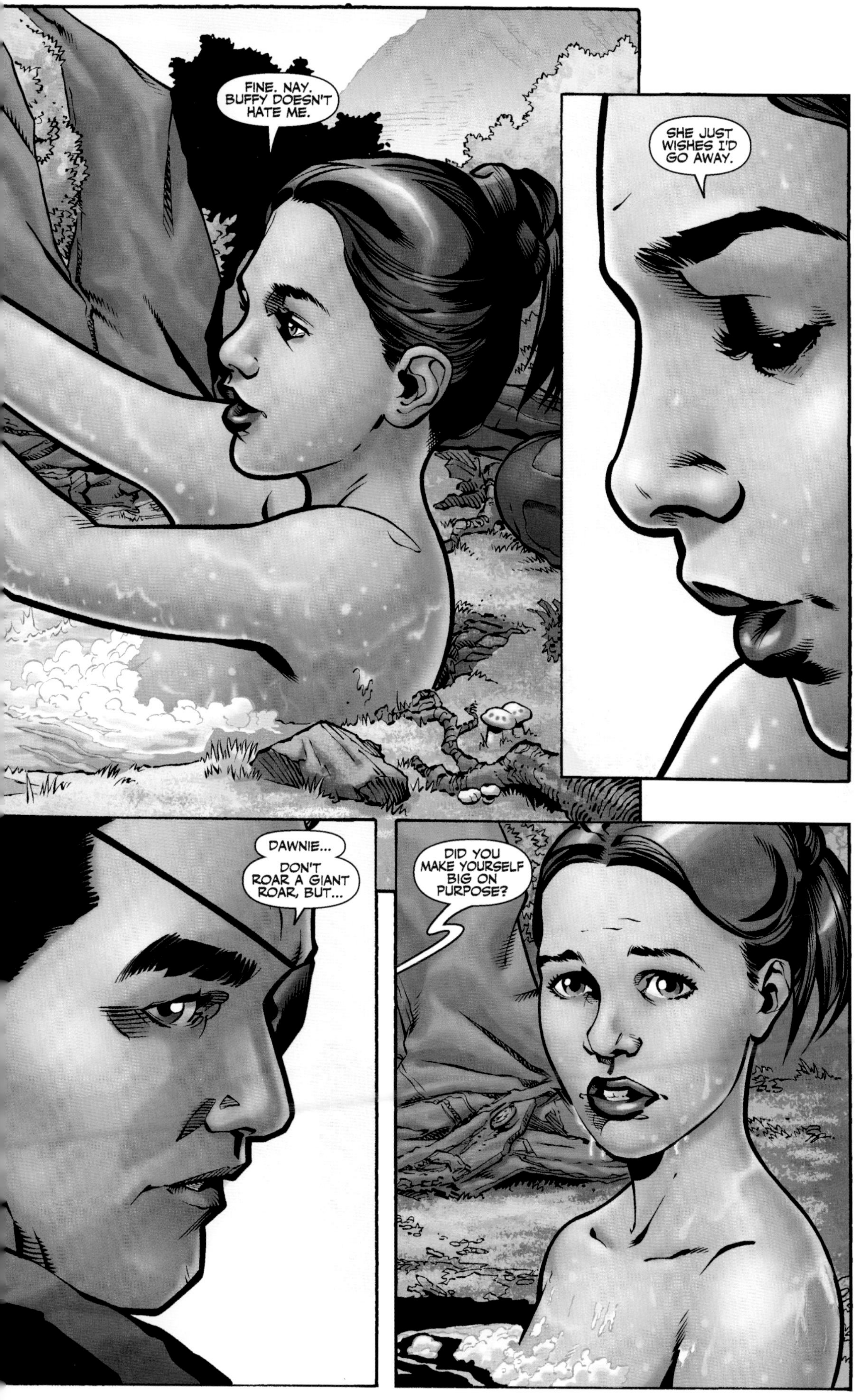
FINE. NAY. BUFFY DOESN'T HATE ME.
SHE JUST WISHES I'D GO AWAY.
DAWNIE...
DON'T ROAR A GIANT ROAR, BUT...
DID YOU MAKE YOURSELF BIG ON PURPOSE?

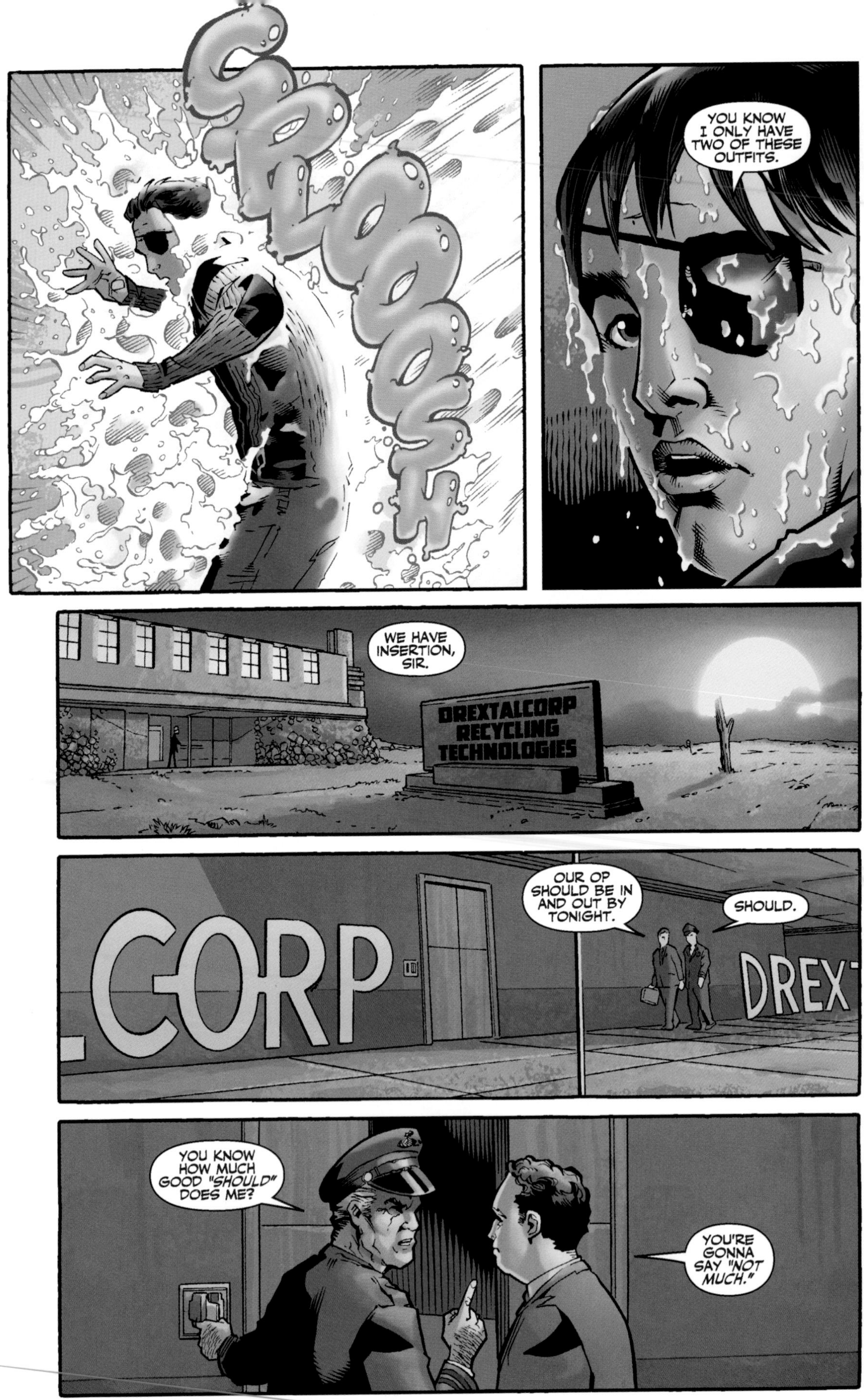
SPLOOOSH
YOU KNOW I ONLY HAVE TWO OF THESE OUTFITS.
WE HAVE INSERTION, SIR.
DREXTALCORP RECYCLING TECHNOLOGIES
OUR OP SHOULD BE IN AND OUT BY TONIGHT.
SHOULD.
CORP
DREX
YOU KNOW HOW MUCH GOOD "SHOULD" DOES ME?
YOU'RE GONNA SAY "NOT MUCH."

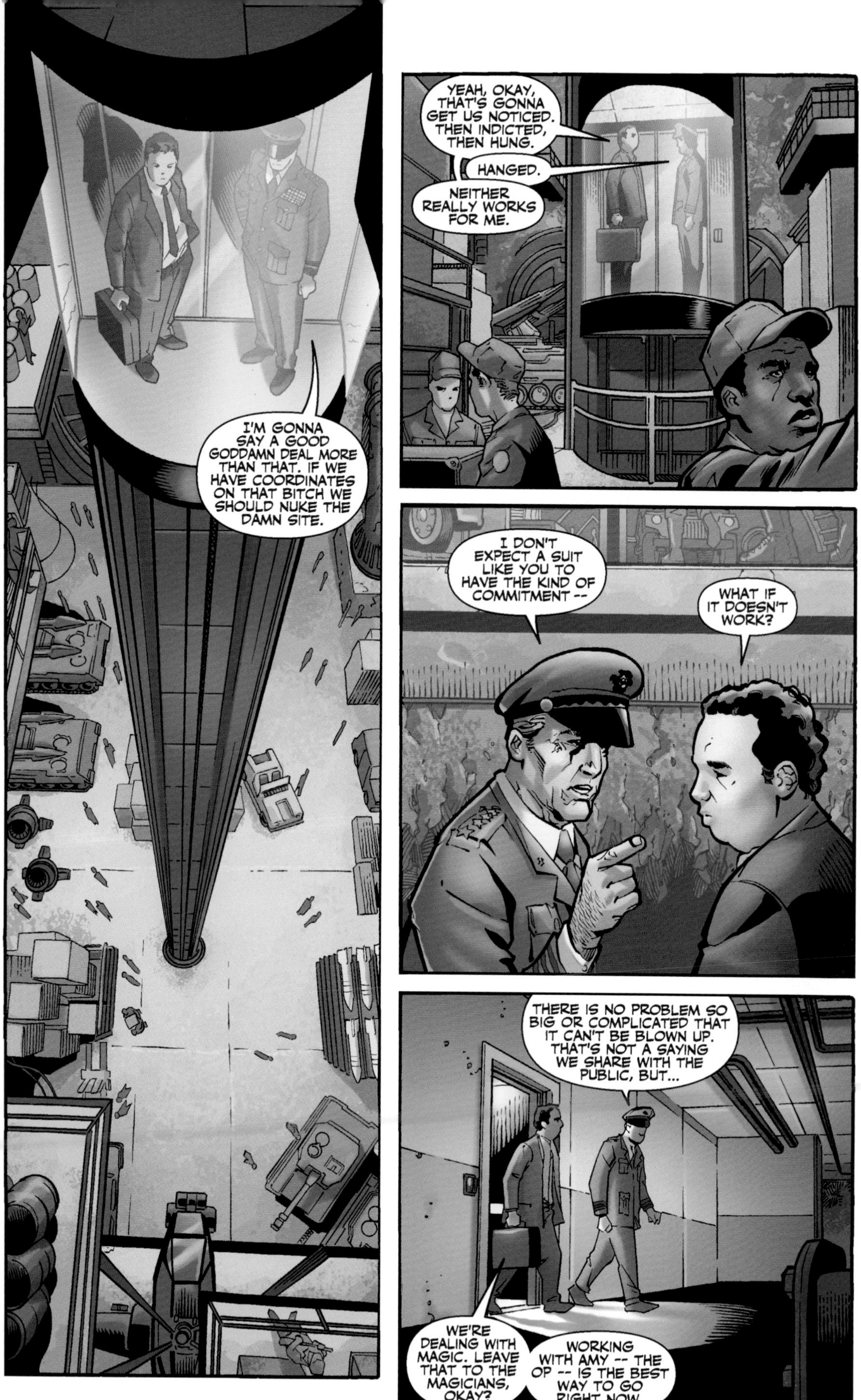
I'M GONNA SAY A GOOD GODDAMN DEAL MORE THAN THAT. IF WE HAVE COORDINATES ON THAT BITCH WE SHOULD NUKE THE DAMN SITE.
YEAH, OKAY, THAT'S GONNA GET US NOTICED. THEN INDICTED, THEN HUNG.
HANGED.
NEITHER REALLY WORKS FOR ME.
I DON'T EXPECT A SUIT LIKE YOU TO HAVE THE KIND OF COMMITMENT --
WHAT IF IT DOESN'T WORK?
THERE IS NO PROBLEM SO BIG OR COMPLICATED THAT IT CAN'T BE BLOWN UP. THAT'S NOT A SAYING WE SHARE WITH THE PUBLIC, BUT...
WE'RE DEALING WITH MAGIC. LEAVE THAT TO THE MAGICIANS, OKAY?
WORKING WITH AMY -- THE OP -- IS THE BEST WAY TO GO RIGHT NOW.

AND IF SHE BLOWS IT? WE SEND THAT MONSTROSITY SHE CALLS A BOYFRIEND IN NEXT?

THAT THING REALLY IS GROSS.

AND, YES, I THINK WE DO.

I'M GONNA GET SOME SHUT-EYE. WAKE ME WITH A REPORT.

LET'S HOPE IT'S A GOOD ONE.

SUIT.

JUST A SUIT, WALKS AND TALKS, HAS BY CHANCE A MAN IN IT.

GOT NO IDEA WHAT'S AT STAKE HERE.

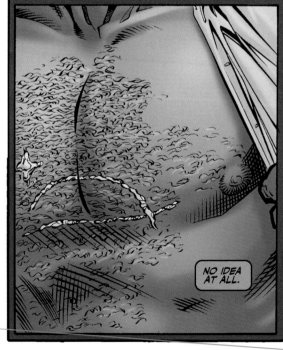

NO IDEA AT ALL.

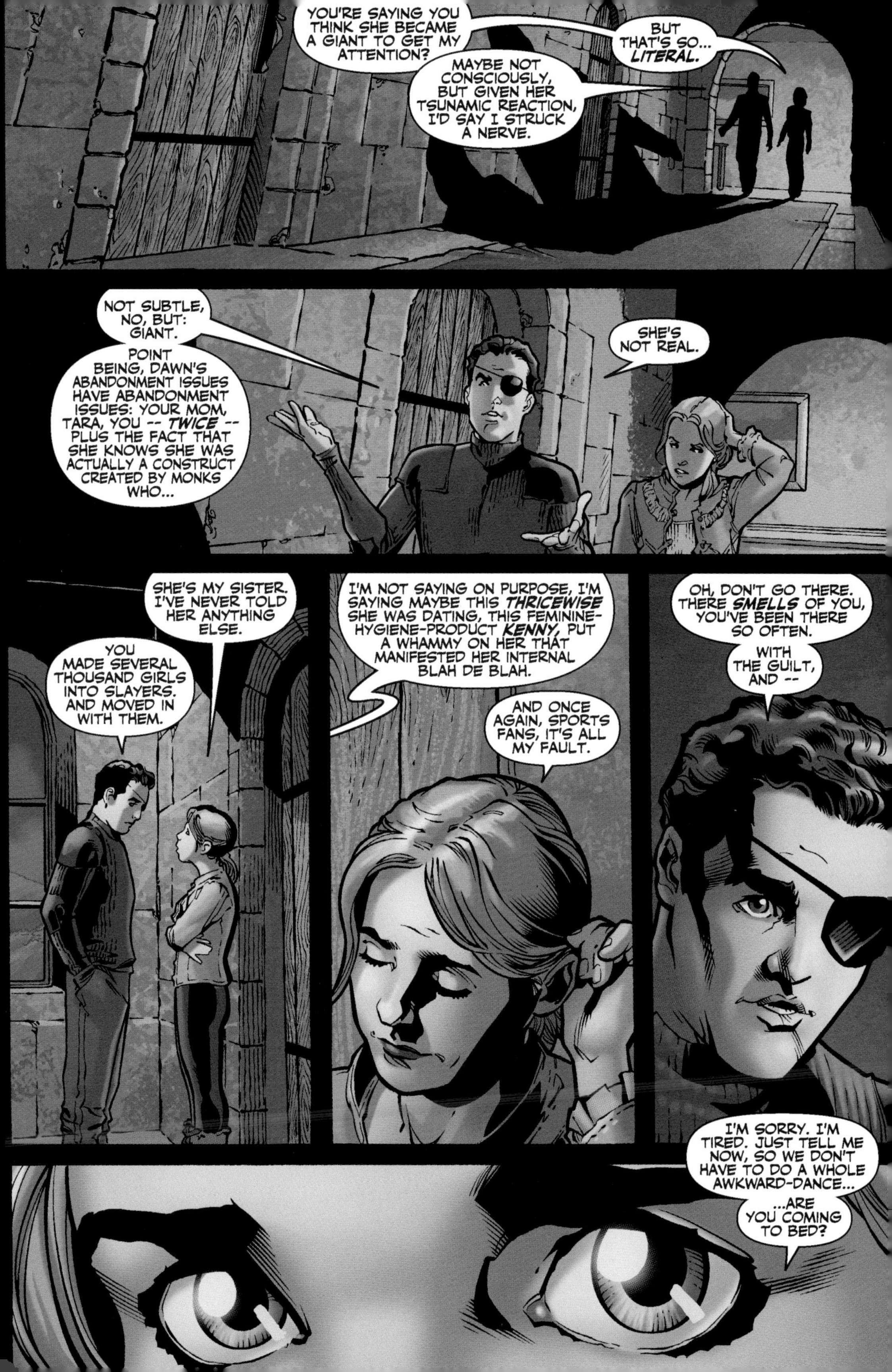
YOU'RE SAYING YOU THINK SHE BECAME A GIANT TO GET MY ATTENTION?
BUT THAT'S SO... LITERAL.
MAYBE NOT CONSCIOUSLY, BUT GIVEN HER TSUNAMIC REACTION, I'D SAY I STRUCK A NERVE.
NOT SUBTLE, NO, BUT: GIANT.
POINT BEING, DAWN'S ABANDONMENT ISSUES HAVE ABANDONMENT ISSUES: YOUR MOM, TARA, YOU -- TWICE -- PLUS THE FACT THAT SHE KNOWS SHE WAS ACTUALLY A CONSTRUCT CREATED BY MONKS WHO...
SHE'S NOT REAL.
SHE'S MY SISTER. I'VE NEVER TOLD HER ANYTHING ELSE.
YOU MADE SEVERAL THOUSAND GIRLS INTO SLAYERS. AND MOVED IN WITH THEM.
I'M NOT SAYING ON PURPOSE, I'M SAYING MAYBE THIS THRICEWISE SHE WAS DATING, THIS FEMININE-HYGIENE-PRODUCT KENNY, PUT A WHAMMY ON HER THAT MANIFESTED HER INTERNAL BLAH DE BLAH.
AND ONCE AGAIN, SPORTS FANS, IT'S ALL MY FAULT.
OH, DON'T GO THERE. THERE SMELLS OF YOU, YOU'VE BEEN THERE SO OFTEN.
WITH THE GUILT, AND --
I'M SORRY. I'M TIRED. JUST TELL ME NOW, SO WE DON'T HAVE TO DO A WHOLE AWKWARD-DANCE...
...ARE YOU COMING TO BED?

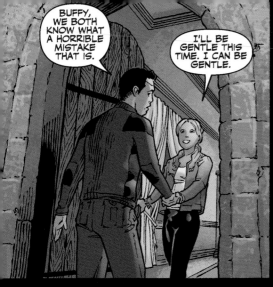

BUFFY, WE BOTH KNOW WHAT A HORRIBLE MISTAKE THAT IS.

I'LL BE GENTLE THIS TIME. I CAN BE GENTLE.

BUHMMMMMMMM!

OOH!

SO, GENTLE.

OH, BALLS.

NO, NO, I CAN'T GO OUTSIDE, I'M AFRAID OF THE DARK.

BUFFY, YOU ARE THE DARK.

THAT'S WHAT I MEANT.

THIS LINT IS SO SCOTTISH.

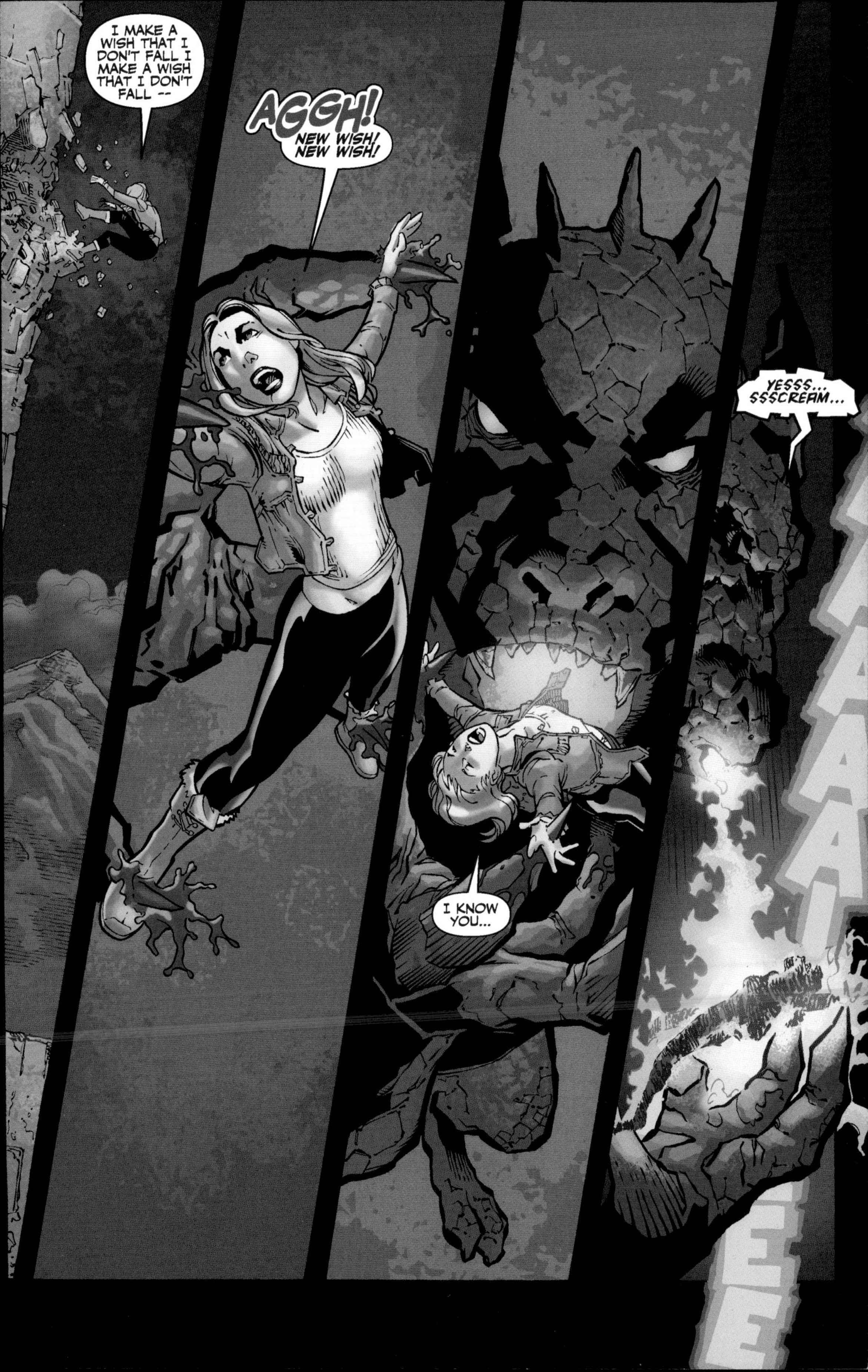
I MAKE A WISH THAT I DON'T FALL I MAKE A WISH THAT I DON'T FALL --
AGGH!
NEW WISH! NEW WISH!
YESSS... SSSCREAM...
I KNOW YOU...

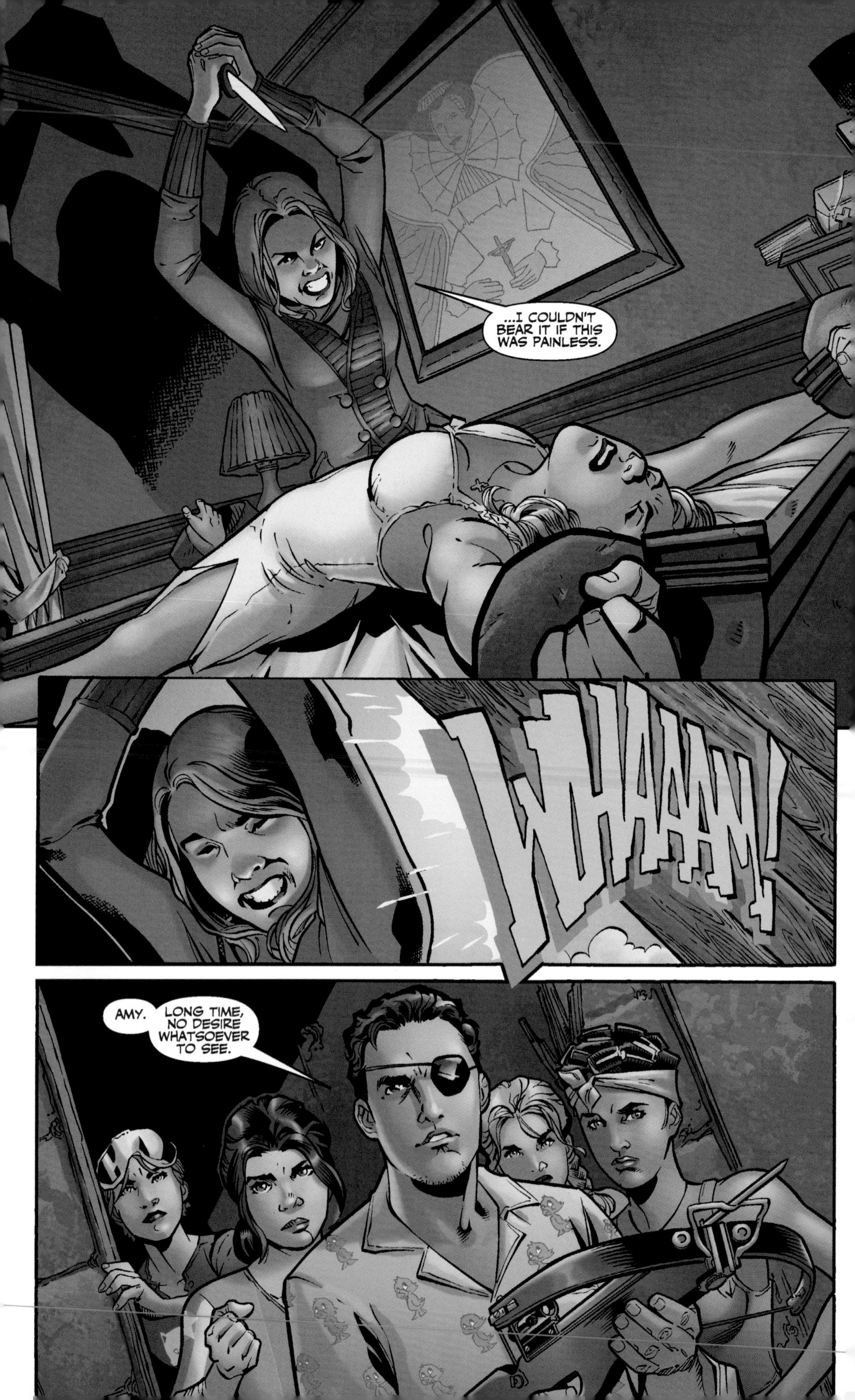
...I COULDN'T BEAR IT IF THIS WAS PAINLESS.
WHAAAM!
AMY.
LONG TIME, NO DESIRE WHATSOEVER TO SEE.

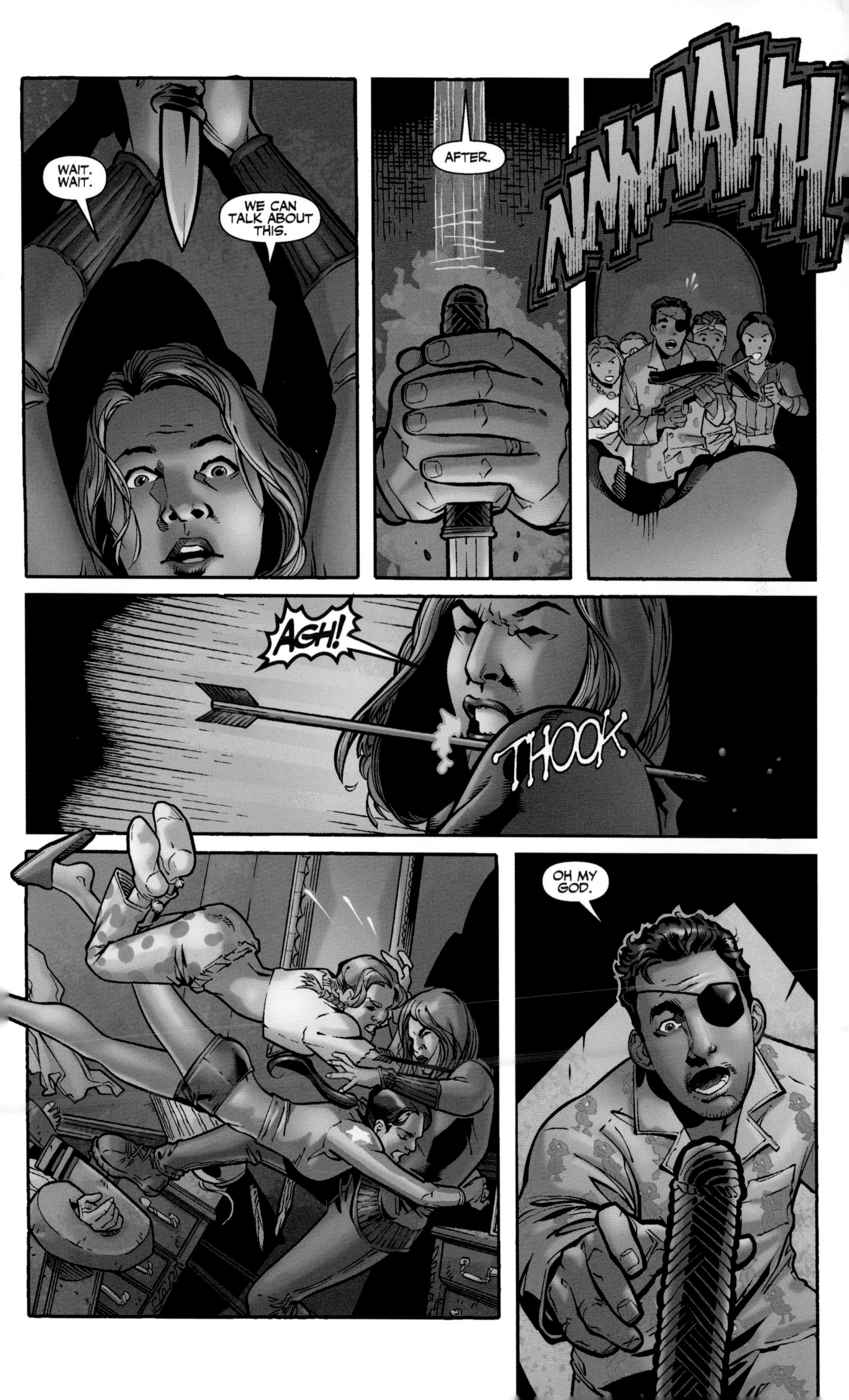
WAIT. WAIT.
WE CAN TALK ABOUT THIS.
AFTER.
AIIIAAAHH!
AGH!
THOOK
OH MY GOD.

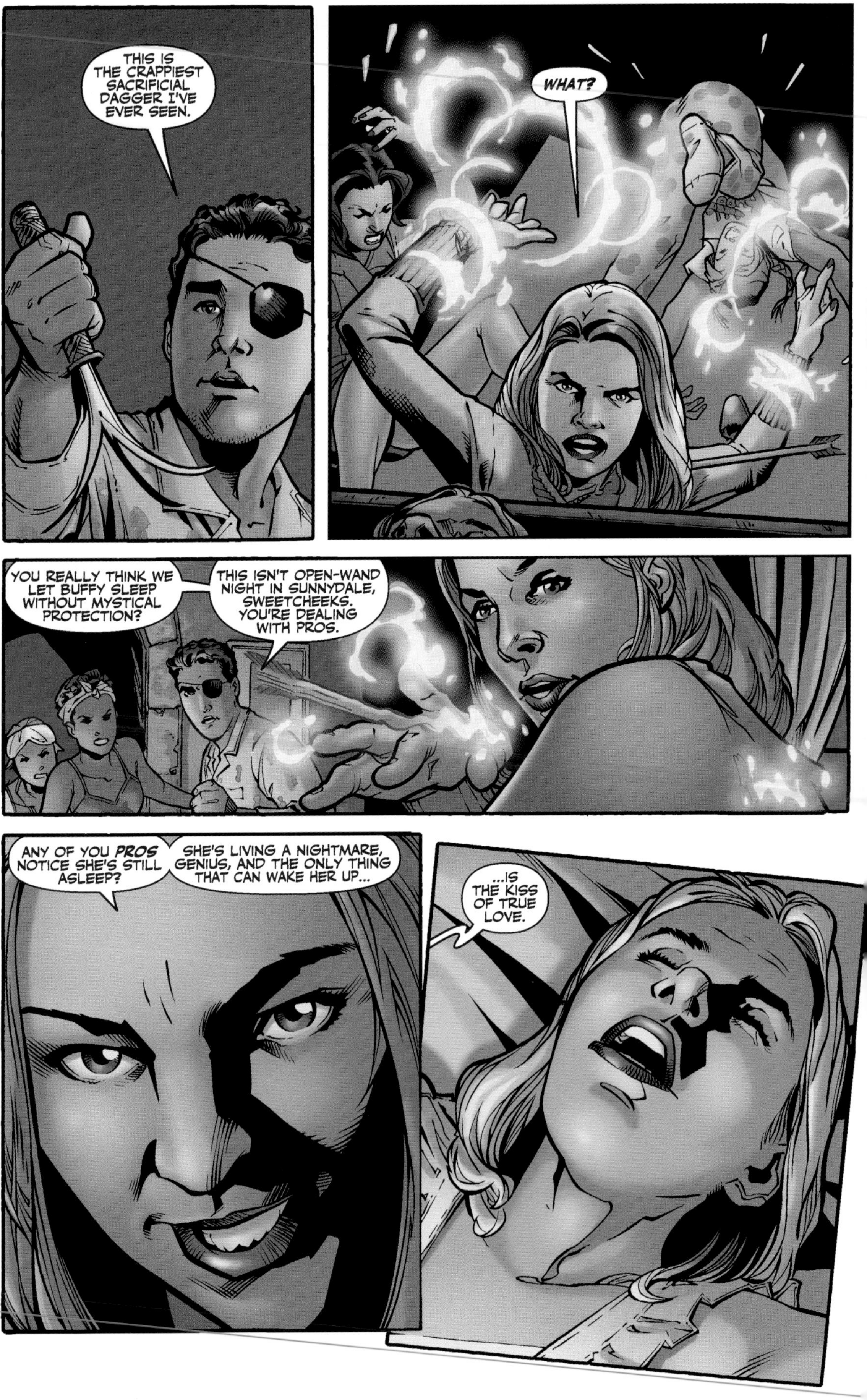
THIS IS THE CRAPPIEST SACRIFICIAL DAGGER I'VE EVER SEEN.
WHAT?
YOU REALLY THINK WE LET BUFFY SLEEP WITHOUT MYSTICAL PROTECTION?
THIS ISN'T OPEN-WAND NIGHT IN SUNNYDALE, SWEETCHEEKS. YOU'RE DEALING WITH PROS.
ANY OF YOU *PROS* NOTICE SHE'S STILL ASLEEP?
SHE'S LIVING A NIGHTMARE, GENIUS, AND THE ONLY THING THAT CAN WAKE HER UP...
...IS THE KISS OF TRUE LOVE.

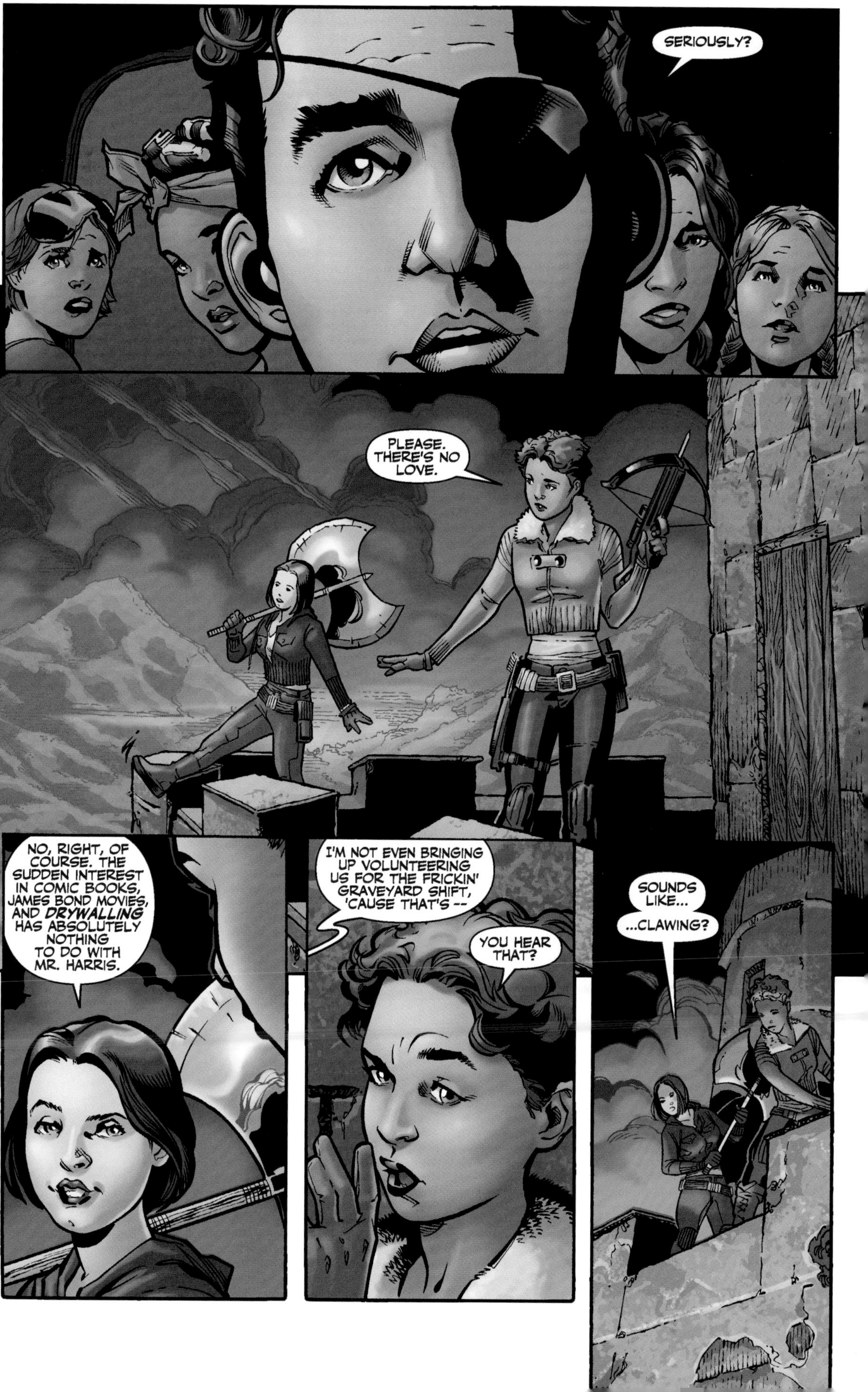
SERIOUSLY?
PLEASE. THERE'S NO LOVE.
NO, RIGHT, OF COURSE. THE SUDDEN INTEREST IN COMIC BOOKS, JAMES BOND MOVIES, AND *DRYWALLING* HAS ABSOLUTELY NOTHING TO DO WITH MR. HARRIS.
I'M NOT EVEN BRINGING UP VOLUNTEERING US FOR THE FRICKIN' GRAVEYARD SHIFT, 'CAUSE THAT'S --
YOU HEAR THAT?
SOUNDS LIKE...
...CLAWING?

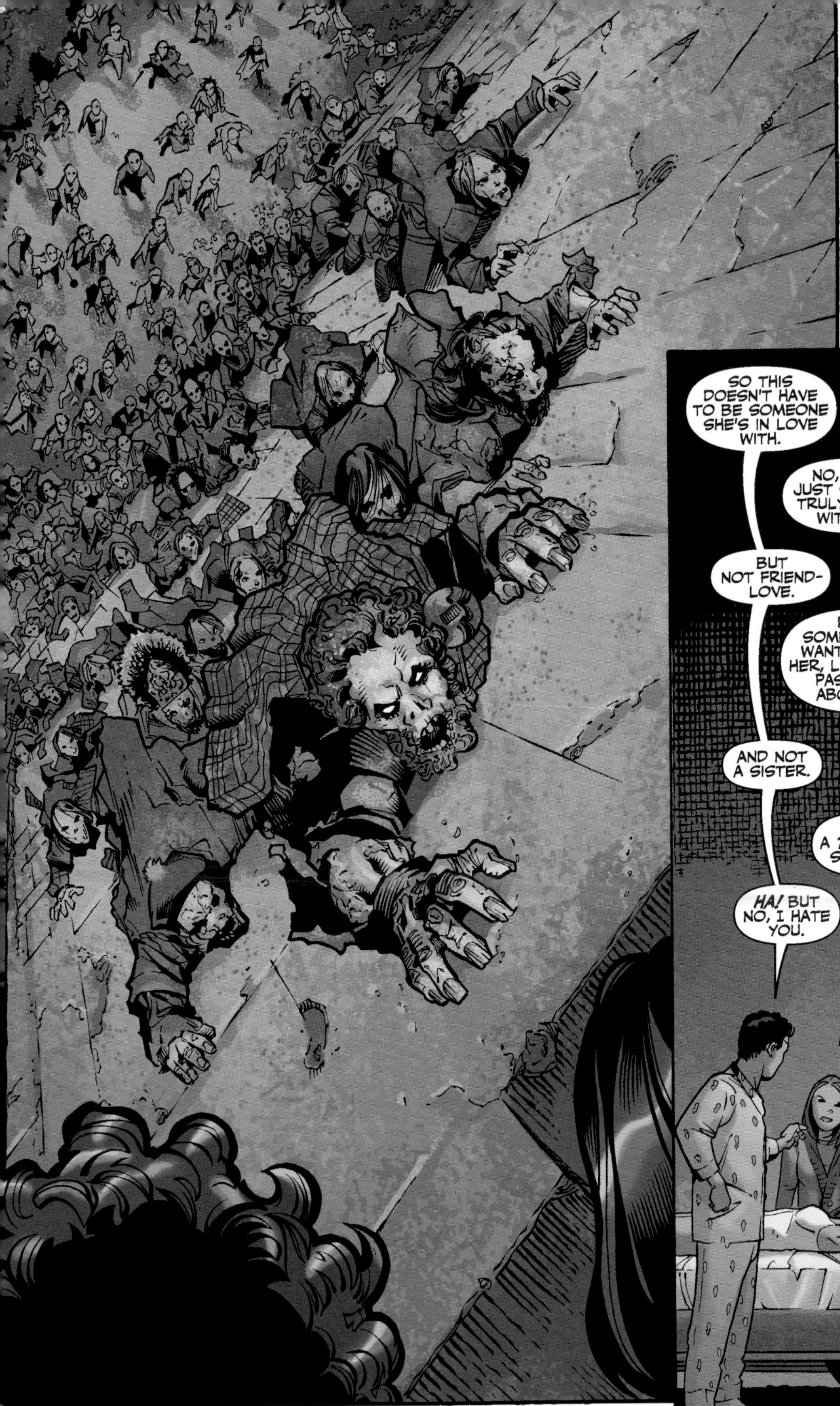

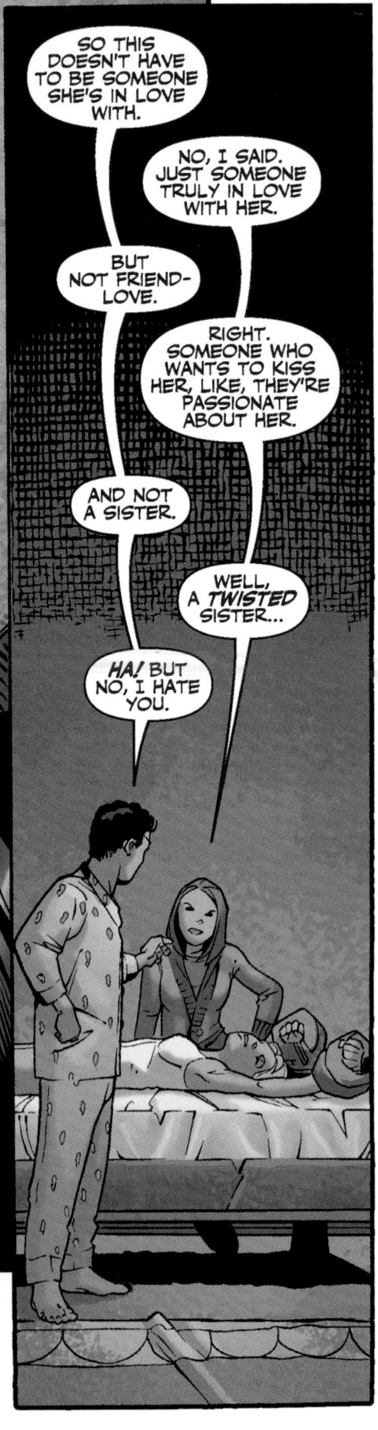
SO THIS DOESN'T HAVE TO BE SOMEONE SHE'S IN LOVE WITH.
NO, I SAID. JUST SOMEONE TRULY IN LOVE WITH HER.
BUT NOT FRIEND-LOVE.
RIGHT. SOMEONE WHO WANTS TO KISS HER, LIKE, THEY'RE PASSIONATE ABOUT HER.
AND NOT A SISTER.
WELL, A *TWISTED* SISTER...
HA! BUT NO, I HATE YOU.

WE'RE UNDER ATTACK! FULL BREACH ON THE EAST WALL!

WHO'S BREACHING?

LIVING DEAD, SIR.

MAN, AMY, YOU'RE DOING ALL THE CLASSICS TONIGHT.

I NEED YOU THREE IN THE FIELD.

WHAT ABOUT TH' BITCH A' THE WEST HERE?

SHE'S BOUND BY OUR SECURITY OR SHE'D'VE BAILED BY NOW.

KEEP A GUARD ON HER AND GET OUR WITCHES WORKING ON THIS "TRUE LOVE" CRAP.

IT'S REAL, XANDER. YOUR STAR PLAYER'S OUT UNLESS SHE RECEIVES A KISS FROM SOMEONE PASSIONATELY DEVOTED TO HER.

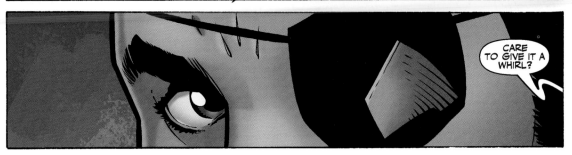

CARE TO GIVE IT A WHIRL?

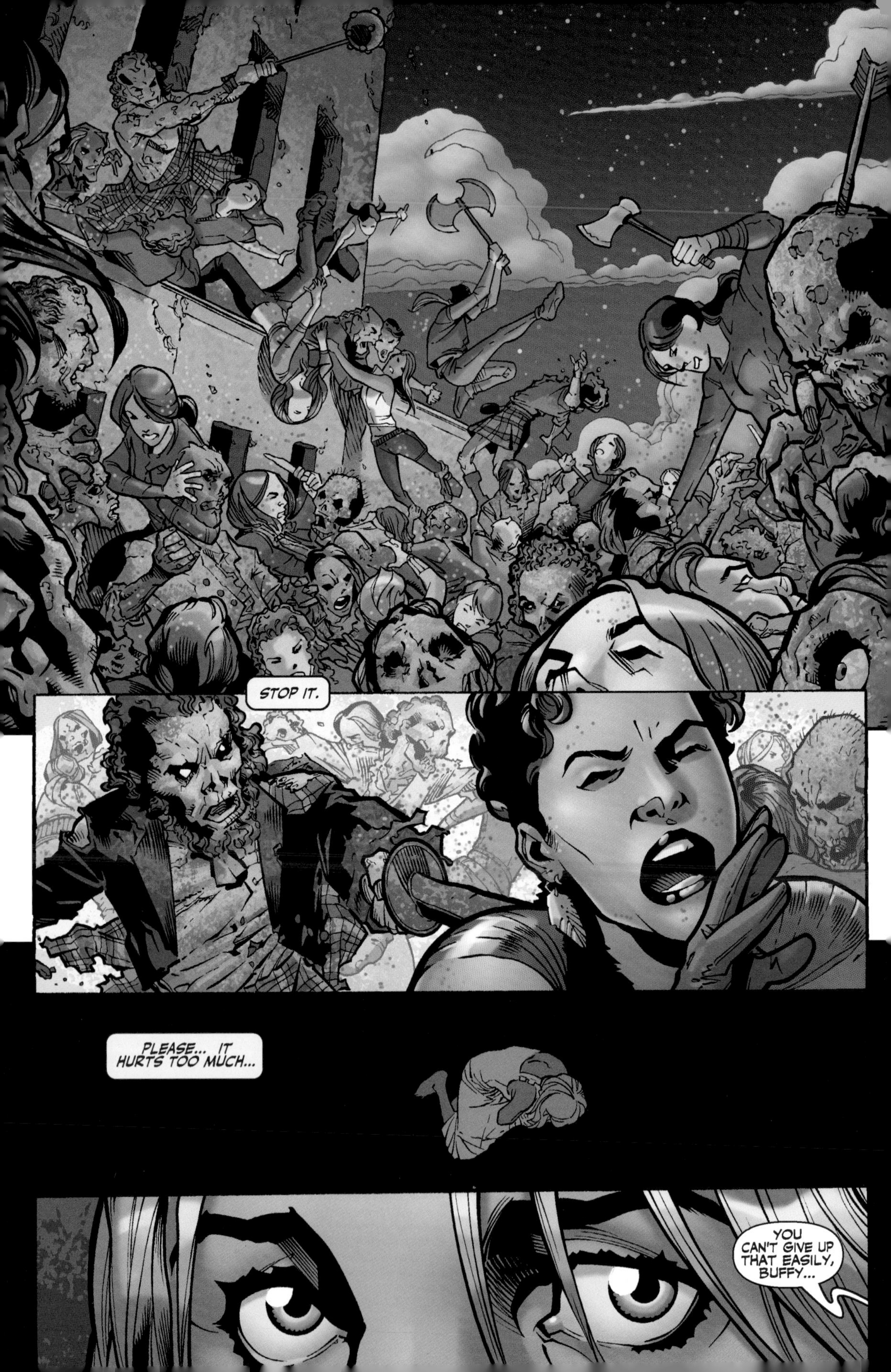
STOP IT.
PLEASE... IT HURTS TOO MUCH...
YOU CAN'T GIVE UP THAT EASILY, BUFFY...

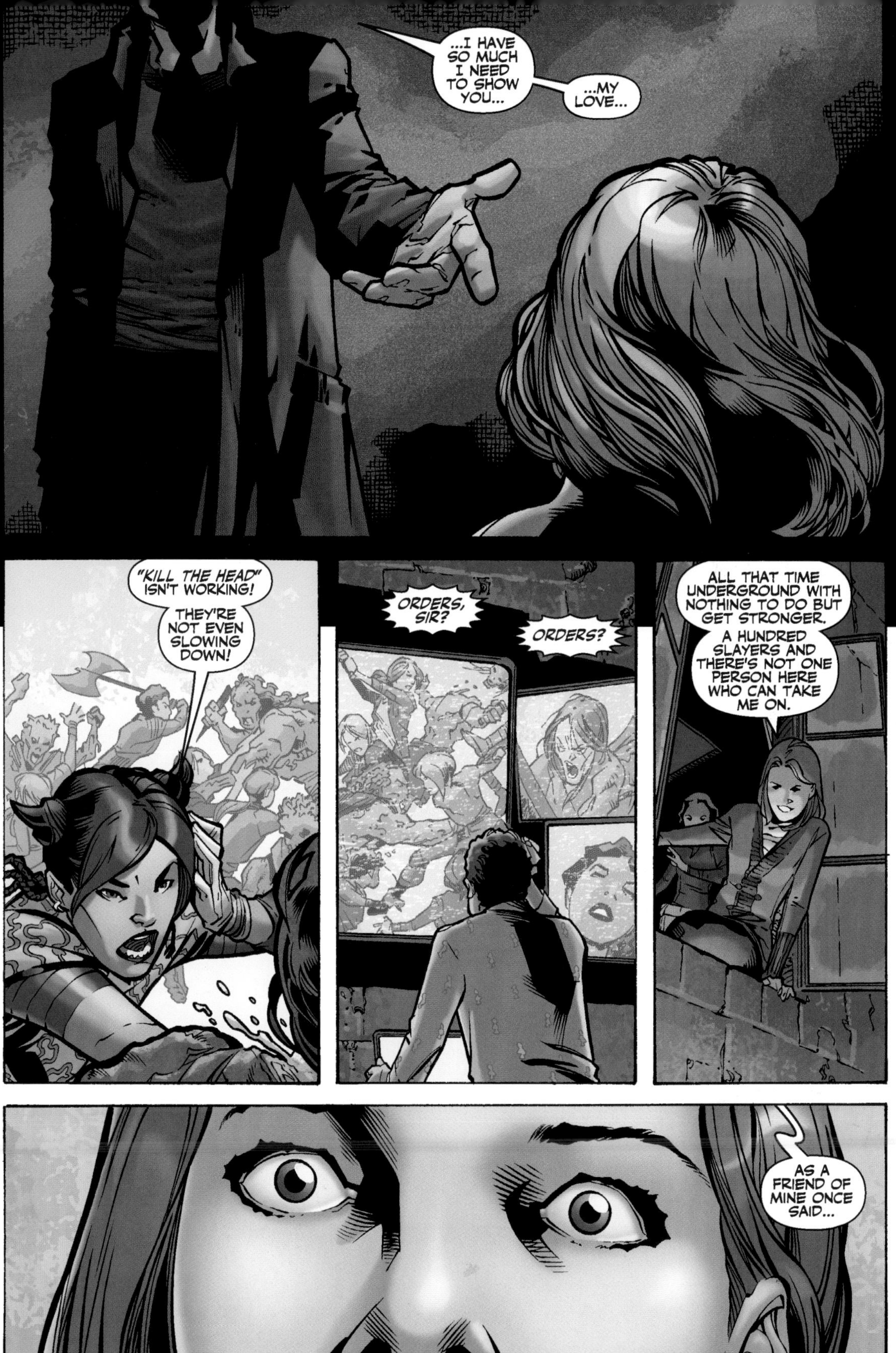
...I HAVE SO MUCH I NEED TO SHOW YOU...
...MY LOVE...
"KILL THE HEAD" ISN'T WORKING!
THEY'RE NOT EVEN SLOWING DOWN!
ORDERS, SIR?
ORDERS?
ALL THAT TIME UNDERGROUND WITH NOTHING TO DO BUT GET STRONGER.
A HUNDRED SLAYERS AND THERE'S NOT ONE PERSON HERE WHO CAN TAKE ME ON.
AS A FRIEND OF MINE ONCE SAID...

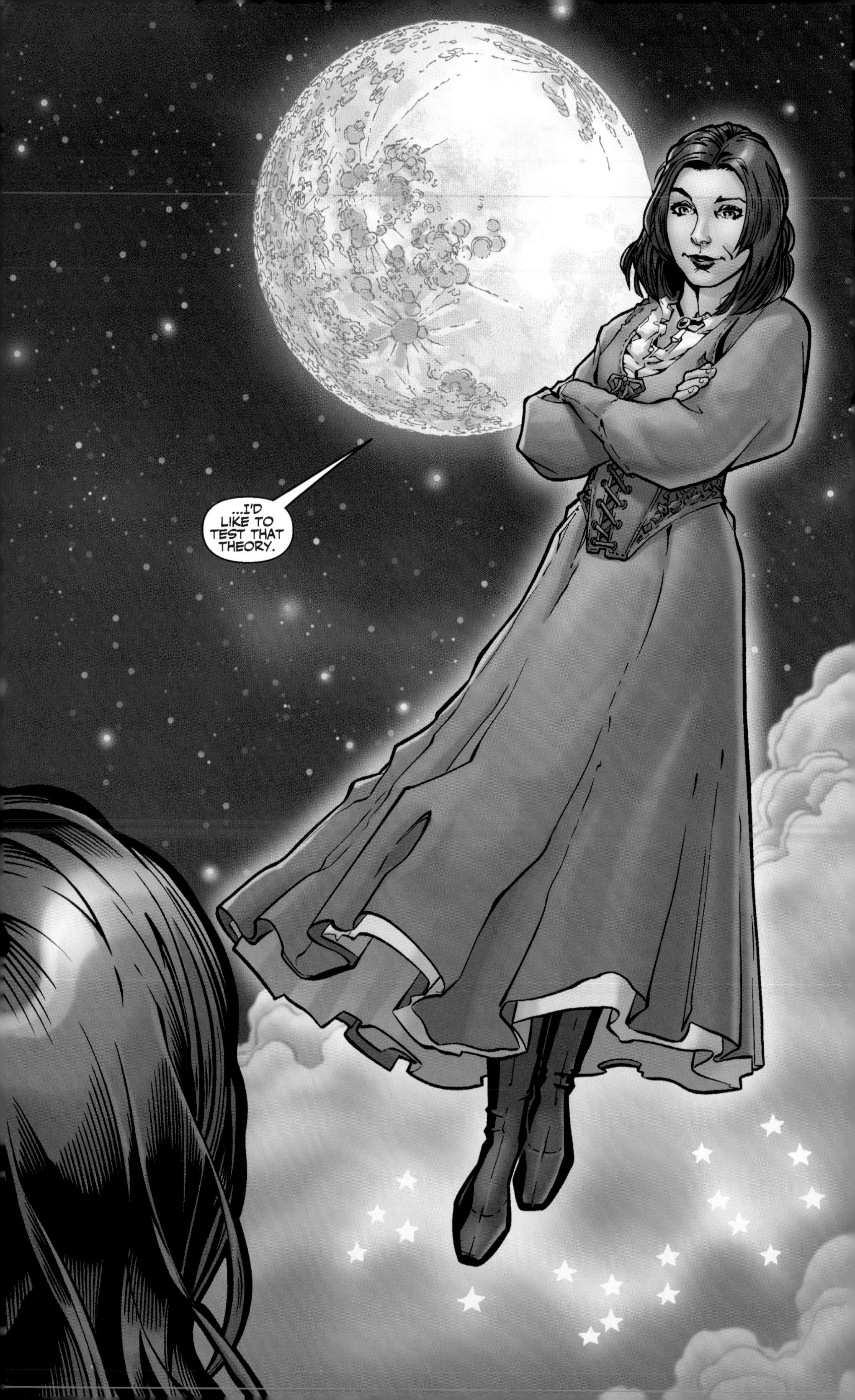
...I'D LIKE TO TEST THAT THEORY.

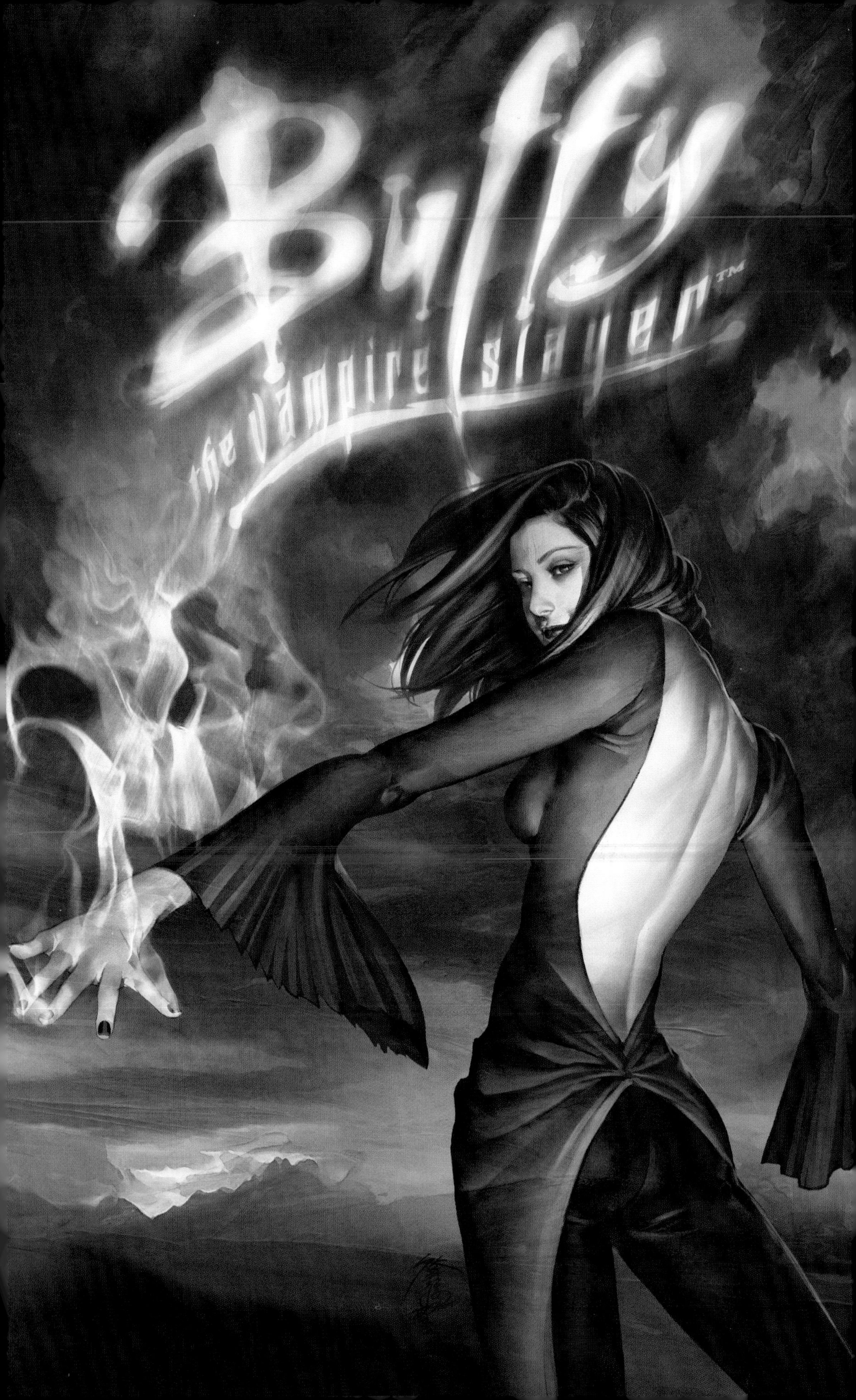
Buffy
the Vampire Slayer™

The LONG WAY HOME

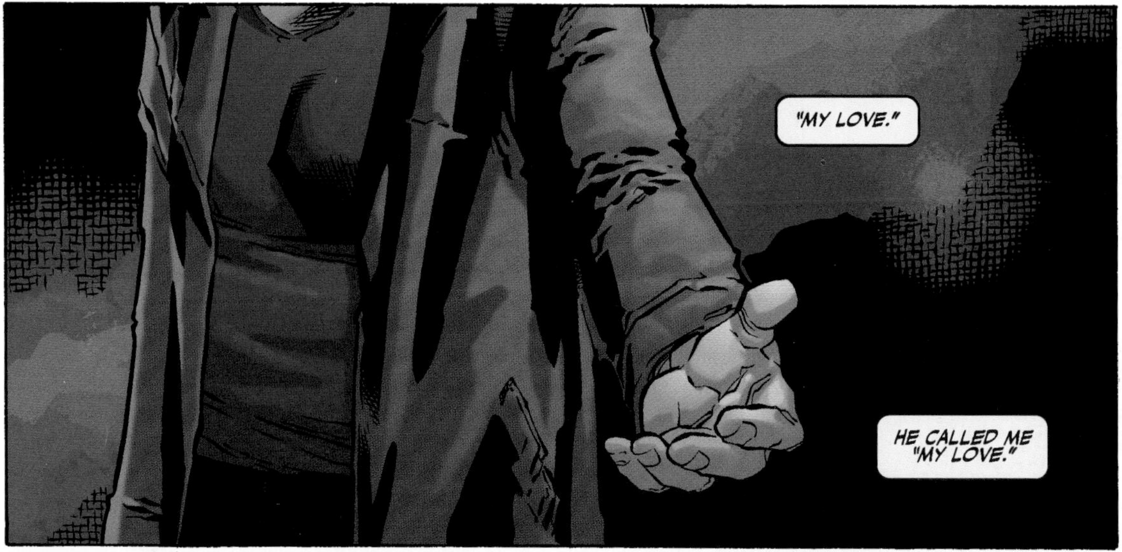
"MY LOVE."
HE CALLED ME "MY LOVE."

Part Three

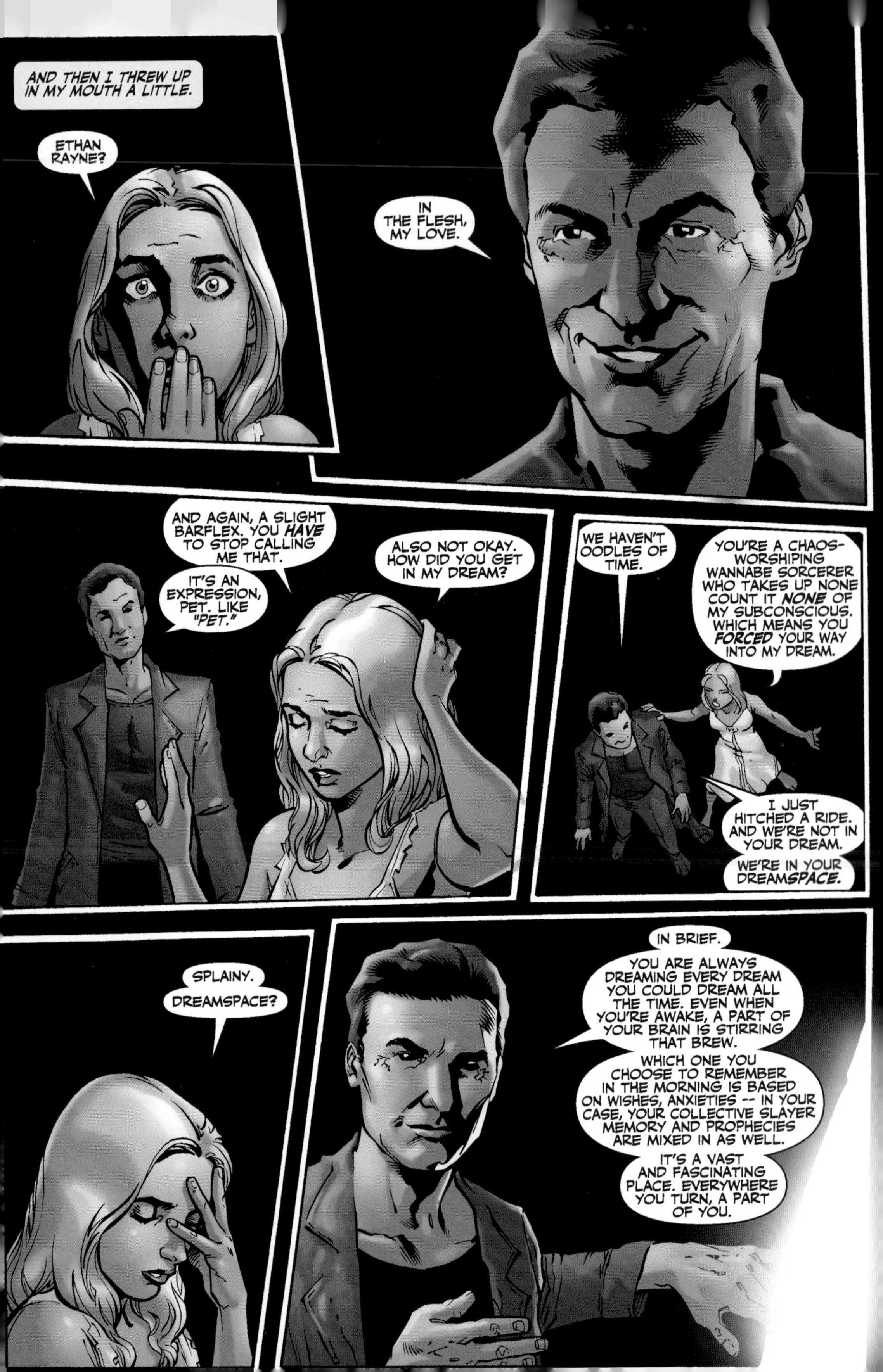
AND THEN I THREW UP IN MY MOUTH A LITTLE.
ETHAN RAYNE?
IN THE FLESH, MY LOVE.
AND AGAIN, A SLIGHT BARFLEX. YOU *HAVE* TO STOP CALLING ME THAT.
IT'S AN EXPRESSION, PET. LIKE "PET."
ALSO NOT OKAY. HOW DID YOU GET IN MY DREAM?
WE HAVEN'T OODLES OF TIME.
YOU'RE A CHAOS-WORSHIPING WANNABE SORCERER WHO TAKES UP NONE COUNT IT *NONE* OF MY SUBCONSCIOUS. WHICH MEANS YOU *FORCED* YOUR WAY INTO MY DREAM.
I JUST HITCHED A RIDE. AND WE'RE NOT IN YOUR DREAM.
WE'RE IN YOUR DREAM*SPACE.*
SPLAINY.
DREAMSPACE?
IN BRIEF.
YOU ARE ALWAYS DREAMING EVERY DREAM YOU COULD DREAM ALL THE TIME. EVEN WHEN YOU'RE AWAKE, A PART OF YOUR BRAIN IS STIRRING THAT BREW.
WHICH ONE YOU CHOOSE TO REMEMBER IN THE MORNING IS BASED ON WISHES, ANXIETIES -- IN YOUR CASE, YOUR COLLECTIVE SLAYER MEMORY AND PROPHECIES ARE MIXED IN AS WELL.
IT'S A VAST AND FASCINATING PLACE. EVERYWHERE YOU TURN, A PART OF YOU.

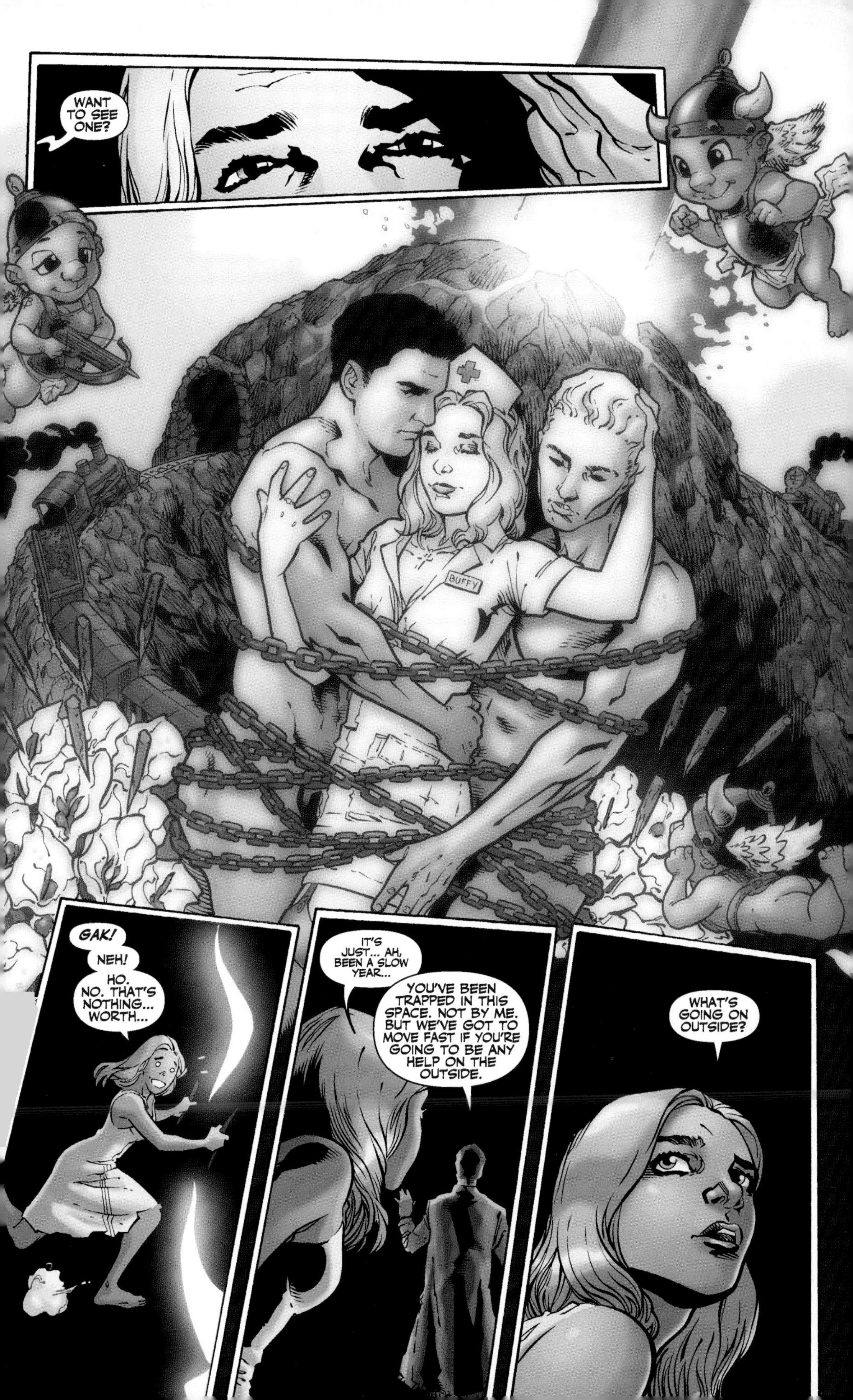
WANT TO SEE ONE?
BUFFY
GAK!
NEH!
HO. NO. THAT'S NOTHING... WORTH...
IT'S JUST... AH, BEEN A SLOW YEAR...
YOU'VE BEEN TRAPPED IN THIS SPACE. NOT BY ME. BUT WE'VE GOT TO MOVE FAST IF YOU'RE GOING TO BE ANY HELP ON THE OUTSIDE.
WHAT'S GOING ON OUTSIDE?

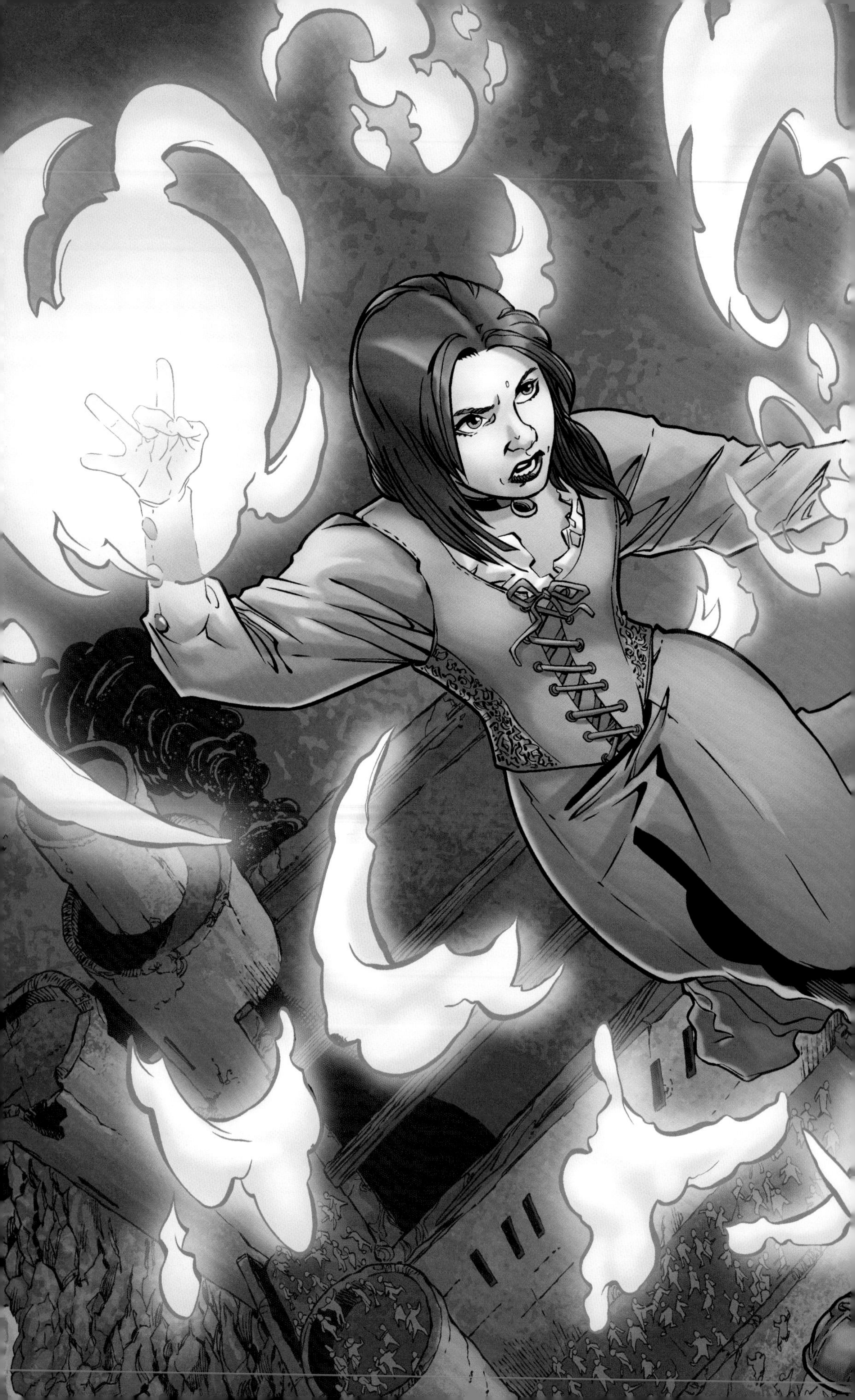

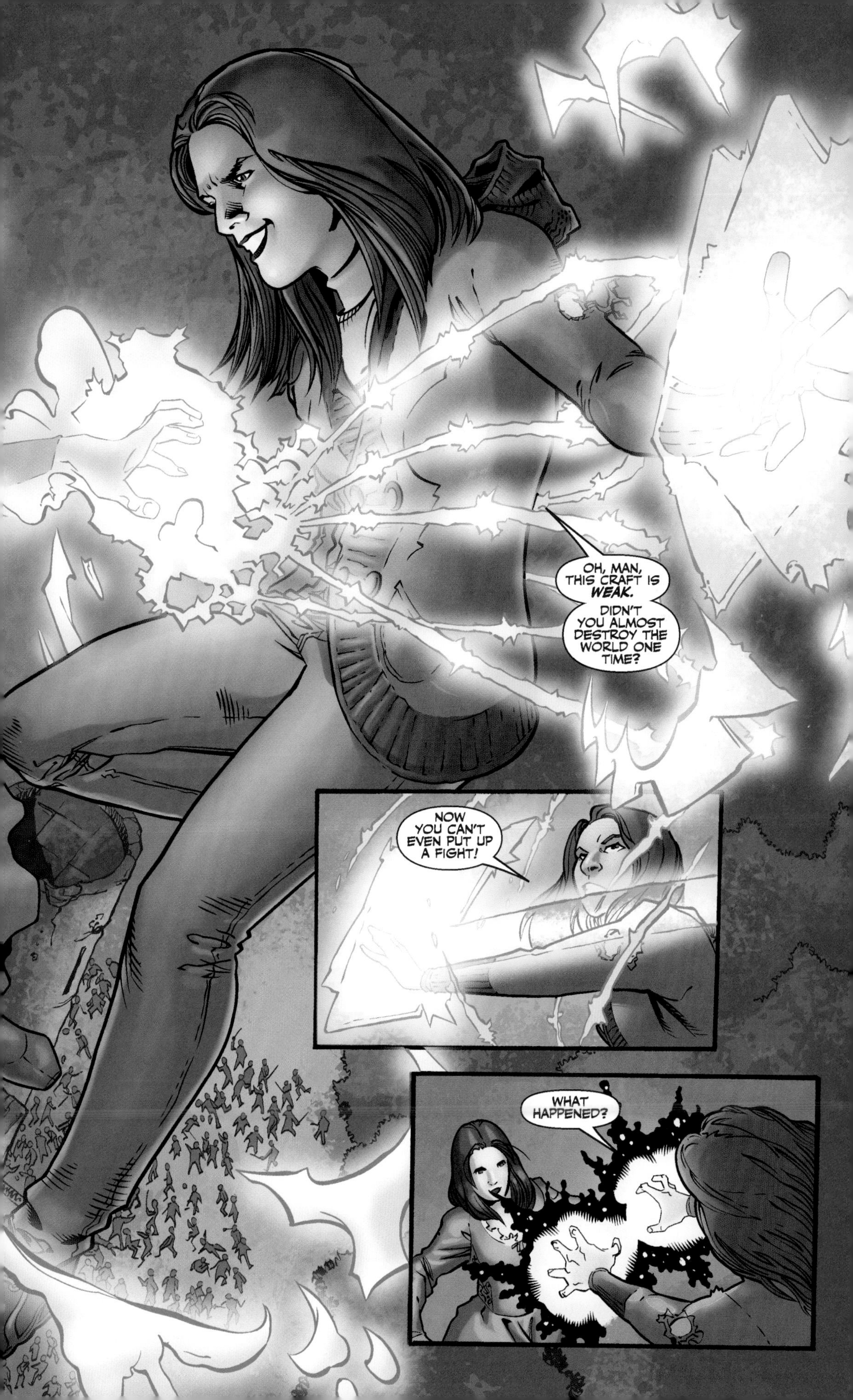
OH, MAN, THIS CRAFT IS **WEAK.**
DIDN'T YOU ALMOST DESTROY THE WORLD ONE TIME?
NOW YOU CAN'T EVEN PUT UP A FIGHT!
WHAT HAPPENED?

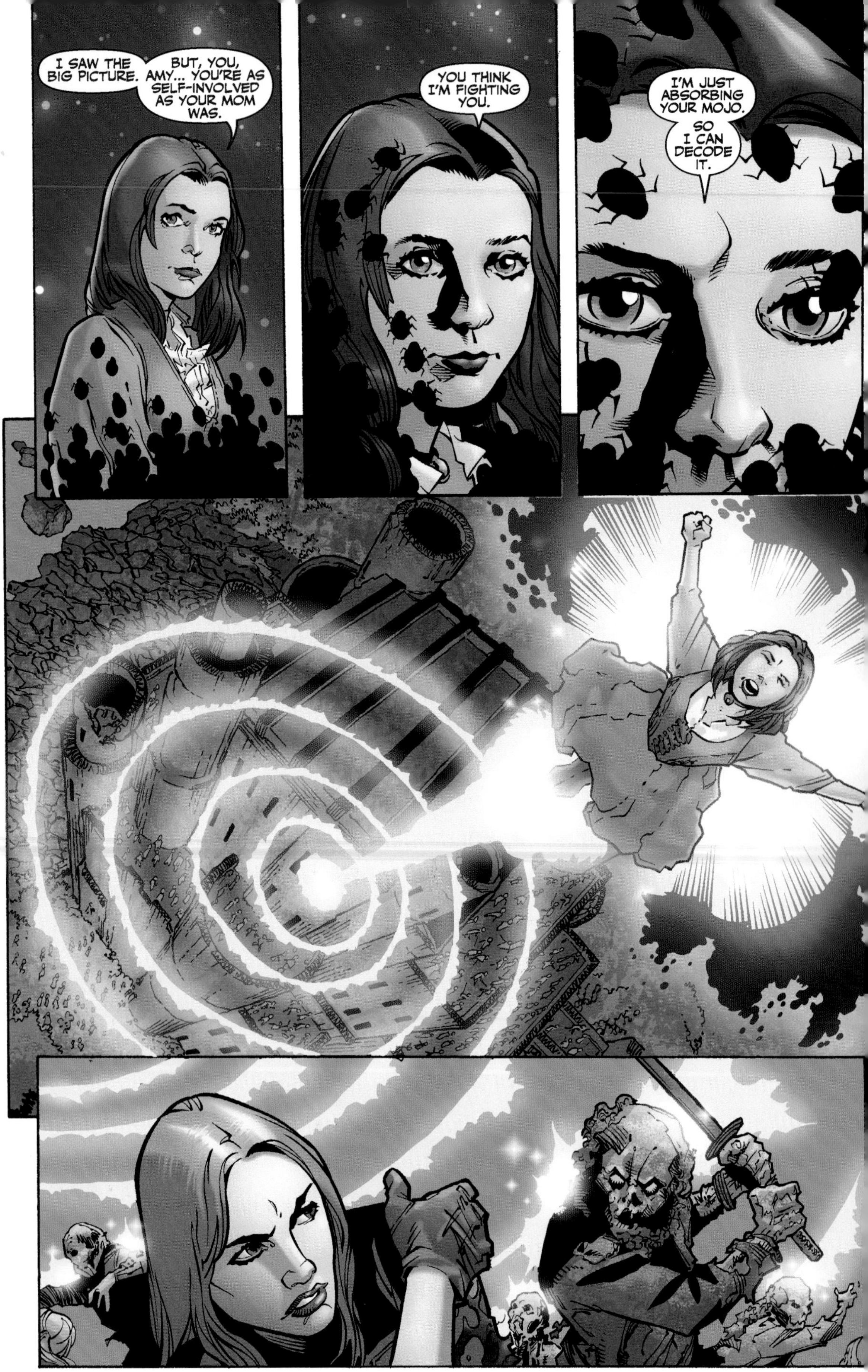
I SAW THE BIG PICTURE.
BUT, YOU, AMY... YOU'RE AS SELF-INVOLVED AS YOUR MOM WAS.
YOU THINK I'M FIGHTING YOU.
I'M JUST ABSORBING YOUR MOJO.
SO I CAN DECODE IT.

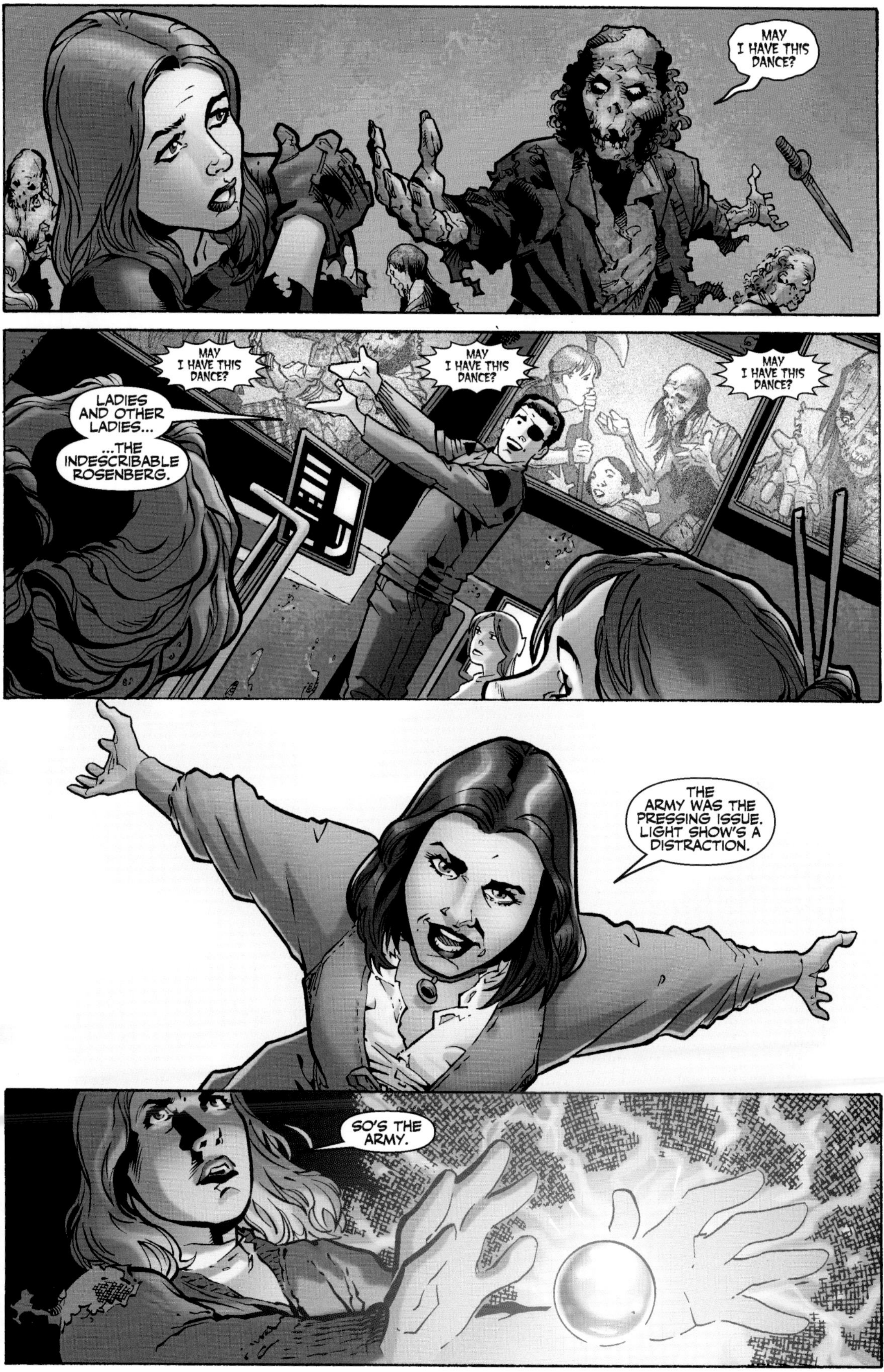
MAY I HAVE THIS DANCE?
MAY I HAVE THIS DANCE?
LADIES AND OTHER LADIES...
...THE INDESCRIBABLE ROSENBERG.
MAY I HAVE THIS DANCE?
MAY I HAVE THIS DANCE?
THE ARMY WAS THE PRESSING ISSUE. LIGHT SHOW'S A DISTRACTION.
SO'S THE ARMY.

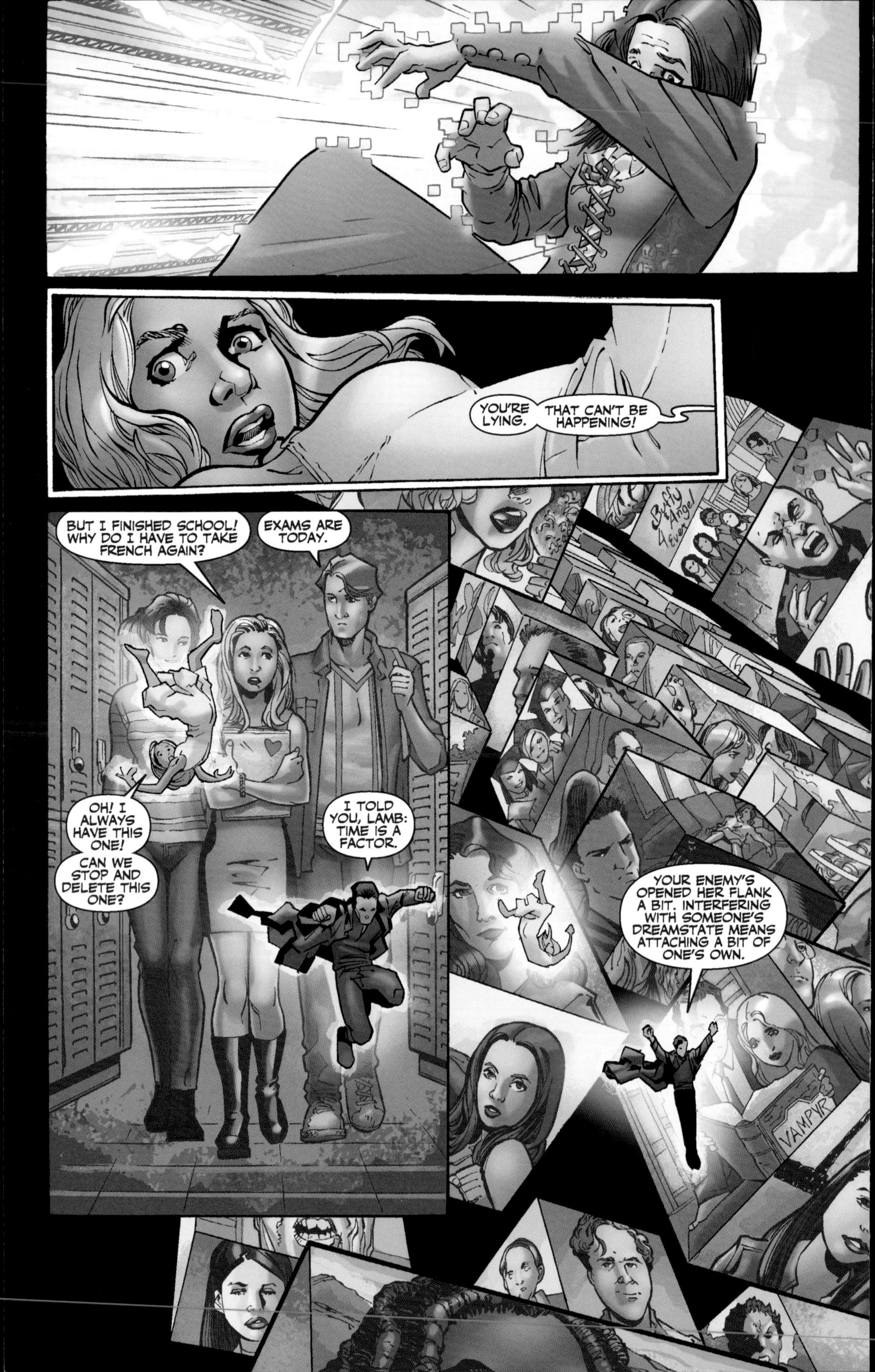

YOU'RE LYING.
THAT CAN'T BE HAPPENING!
BUT I FINISHED SCHOOL! WHY DO I HAVE TO TAKE FRENCH AGAIN?
EXAMS ARE TODAY.
OH! I ALWAYS HAVE THIS ONE!
CAN WE STOP AND DELETE THIS ONE?
I TOLD YOU, LAMB: TIME IS A FACTOR.
YOUR ENEMY'S OPENED HER FLANK A BIT. INTERFERING WITH SOMEONE'S DREAMSTATE MEANS ATTACHING A BIT OF ONE'S OWN.
Buffy 4 Angel 4 ever
VAMPYR

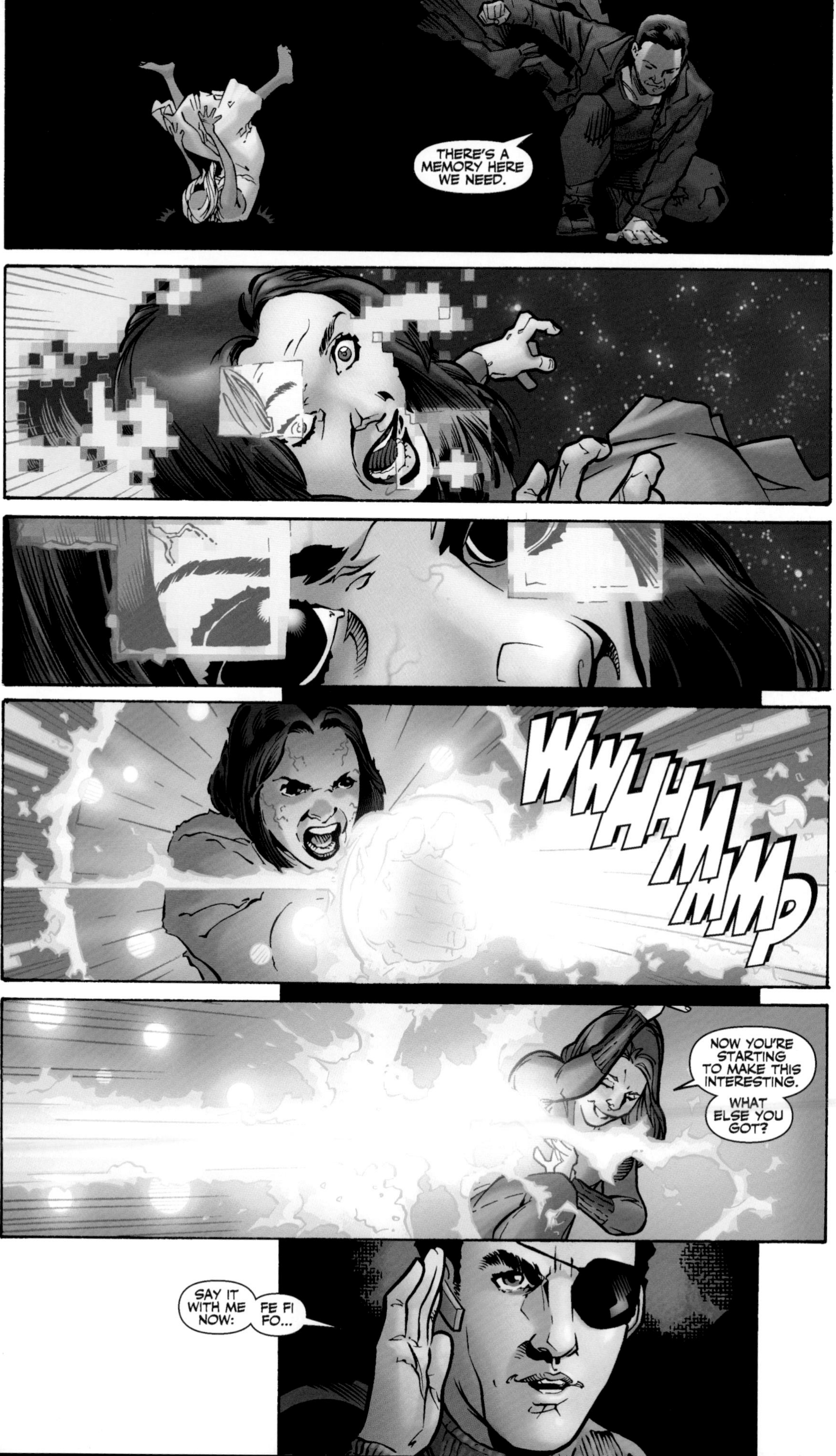
THERE'S A MEMORY HERE WE NEED.
WWHHMMMP
NOW YOU'RE STARTING TO MAKE THIS INTERESTING.
WHAT ELSE YOU GOT?
SAY IT WITH ME NOW:
FE FI FO...

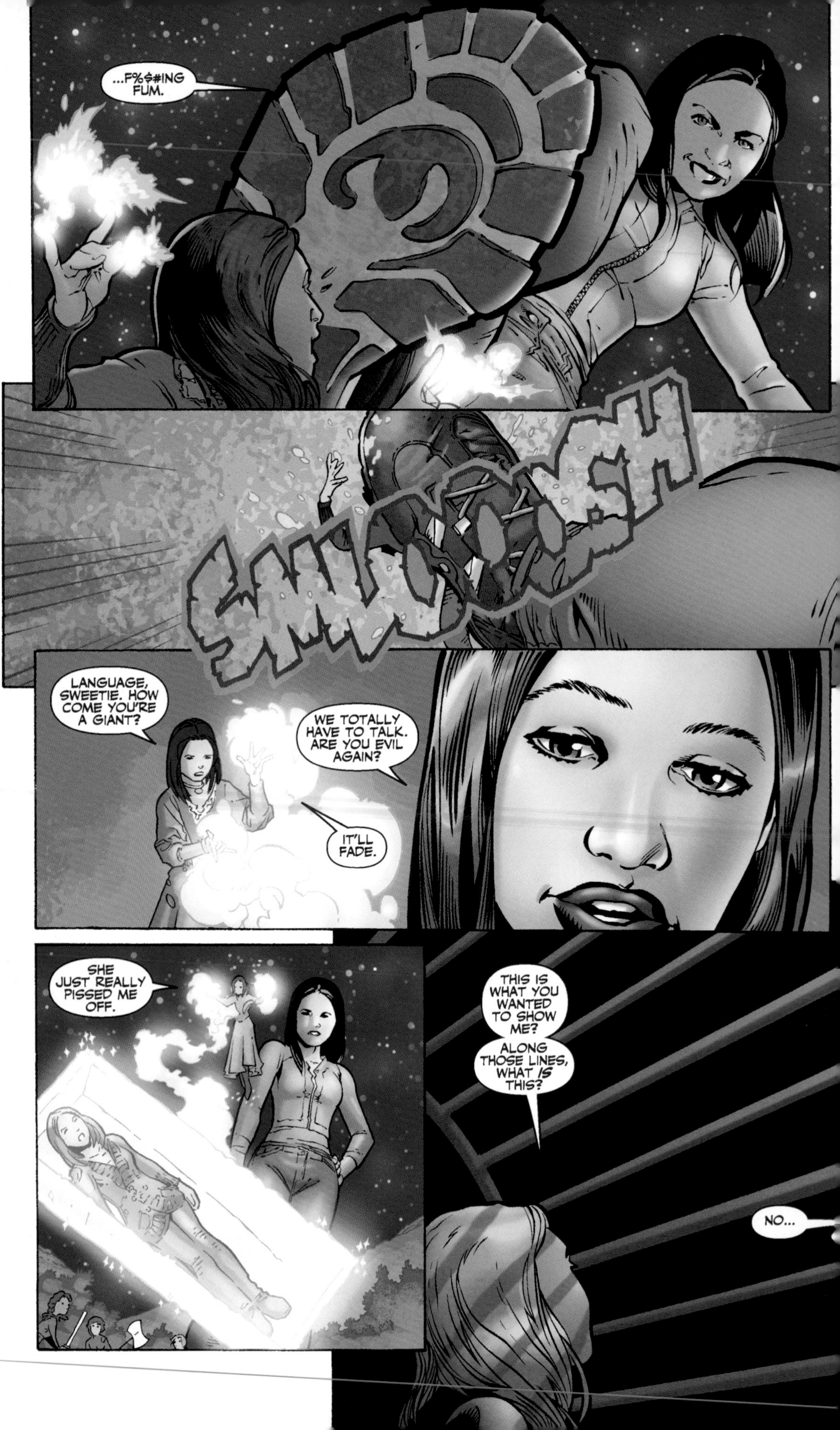
...F%$#ING FUM.
SMOOOOSH
LANGUAGE, SWEETIE. HOW COME YOU'RE A GIANT?
WE TOTALLY HAVE TO TALK. ARE YOU EVIL AGAIN?
IT'LL FADE.
SHE JUST REALLY PISSED ME OFF.
THIS IS WHAT YOU WANTED TO SHOW ME?
ALONG THOSE LINES, WHAT *IS* THIS?
NO...

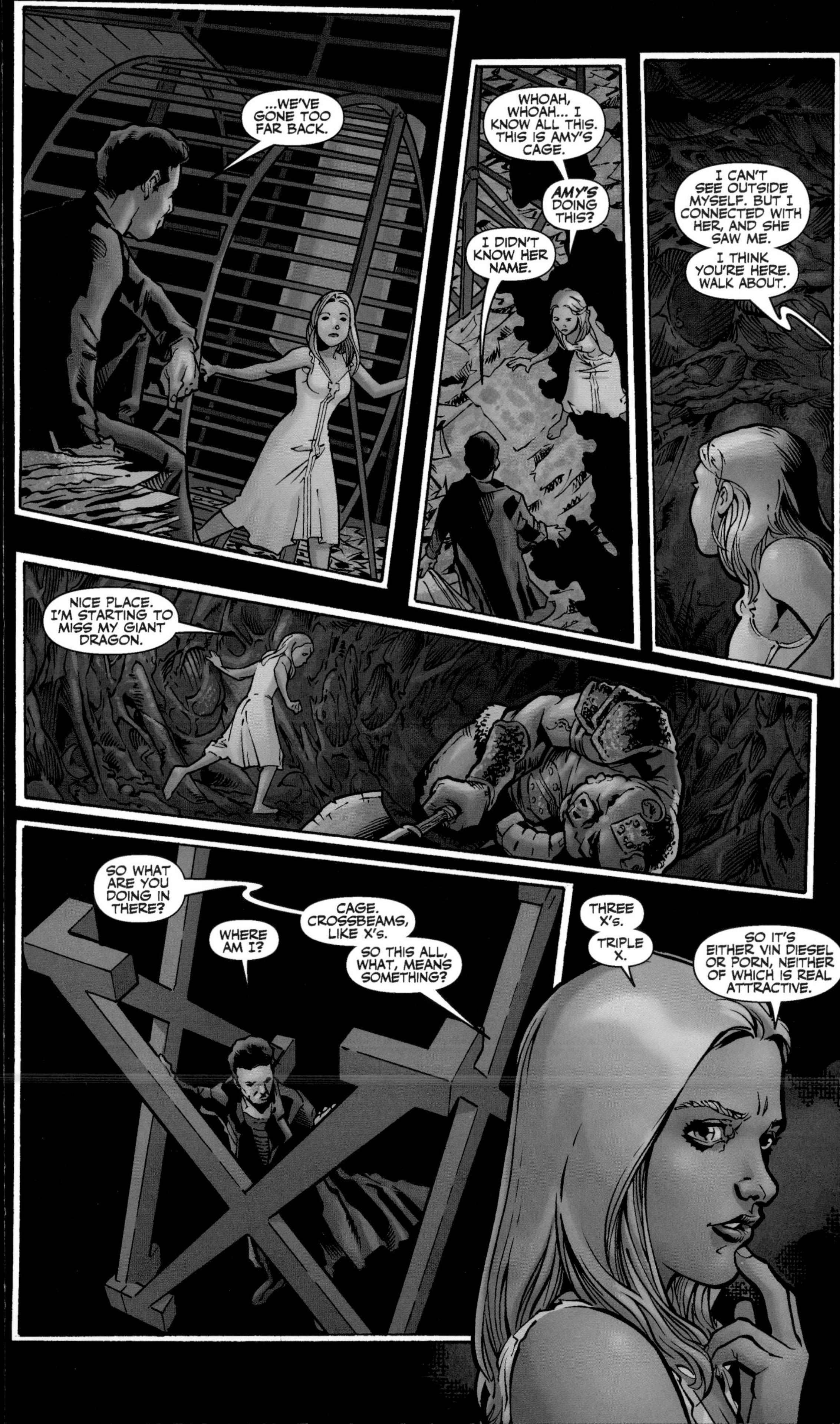
...WE'VE GONE TOO FAR BACK.
WHOAH, WHOAH... I KNOW ALL THIS. THIS IS AMY'S CAGE.
AMY'S DOING THIS?
I DIDN'T KNOW HER NAME.
I CAN'T SEE OUTSIDE MYSELF. BUT I CONNECTED WITH HER, AND SHE SAW ME.
I THINK YOU'RE HERE. WALK ABOUT.
NICE PLACE. I'M STARTING TO MISS MY GIANT DRAGON.
SO WHAT ARE YOU DOING IN THERE?
WHERE AM I?
CAGE. CROSSBEAMS, LIKE X's.
SO THIS ALL, WHAT, MEANS SOMETHING?
THREE X's.
TRIPLE X.
SO IT'S EITHER VIN DIESEL OR PORN, NEITHER OF WHICH IS REAL ATTRACTIVE.

I'M MORE AN ANTIQUE ROMAN THAN A DANE.

DID I MENTION I'M NOT CRAZY GOOD AT SYMBOLISM?

JUST REMEMBER WHAT YOU SEE HERE.

TWILIGHT IS FALLING.

YOU'RE GOING TO NEED ALL THE HELP YOU CAN GET.

PET.

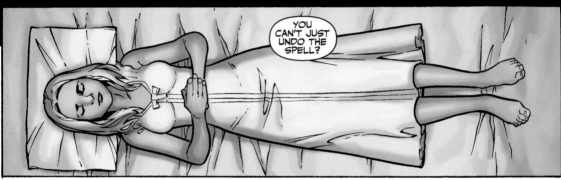

YOU CAN'T JUST UNDO THE SPELL?

SERIOUS MAGIC IS KINDA LIKE IMPROV, DAWN. YOU CAN'T JUST STOP IT COLD; YOU GOTTA ADAPT.

IS THAT WHY I'VE GOT AN ARMY OF THE UNDEAD PLAYING *PRIDE AND PREJUDICE* AROUND MY ANKLES?

DON'T WORRY; AS SOON AS THE BALL'S OVER THEY'LL LEAVE.

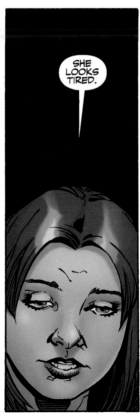

SHE LOOKS TIRED.

SHE'S ASLEEP.

YOU KNOW WHAT I MEAN.

IT'S BEEN A LONG YEAR, AND YOU'VE BEEN WHERE NOW?

WE'LL TALK. THIS IS A TRUE LOVE SPELL.

RUMOR HAS IT. HOW DO WE DEAL?

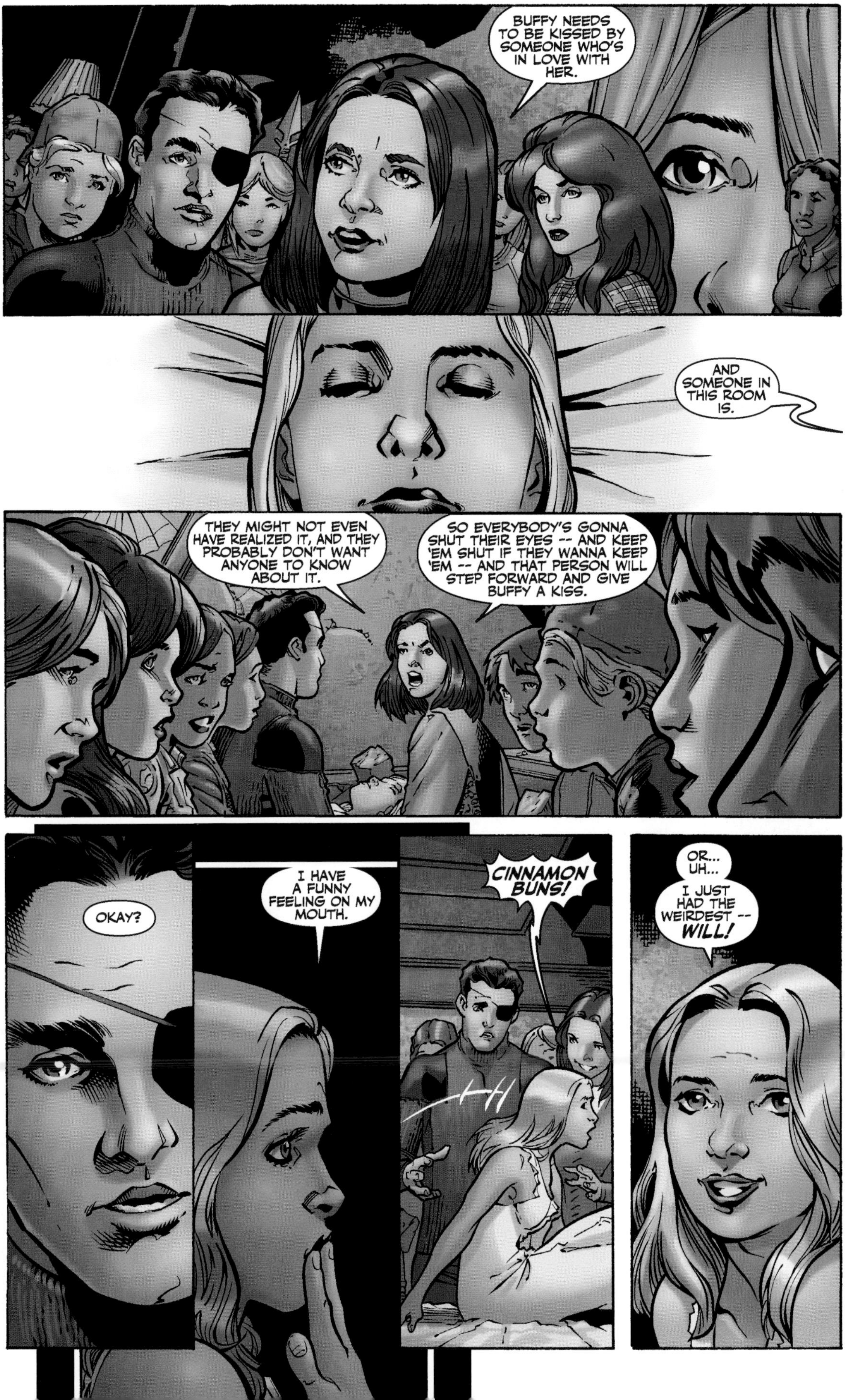
BUFFY NEEDS TO BE KISSED BY SOMEONE WHO'S IN LOVE WITH HER.
AND SOMEONE IN THIS ROOM IS.
THEY MIGHT NOT EVEN HAVE REALIZED IT, AND THEY PROBABLY DON'T WANT ANYONE TO KNOW ABOUT IT.
SO EVERYBODY'S GONNA SHUT THEIR EYES -- AND KEEP 'EM SHUT IF THEY WANNA KEEP 'EM -- AND THAT PERSON WILL STEP FORWARD AND GIVE BUFFY A KISS.
OKAY?
I HAVE A FUNNY FEELING ON MY MOUTH.
CINNAMON BUNS!
OR... UH... I JUST HAD THE WEIRDEST -- WILL!

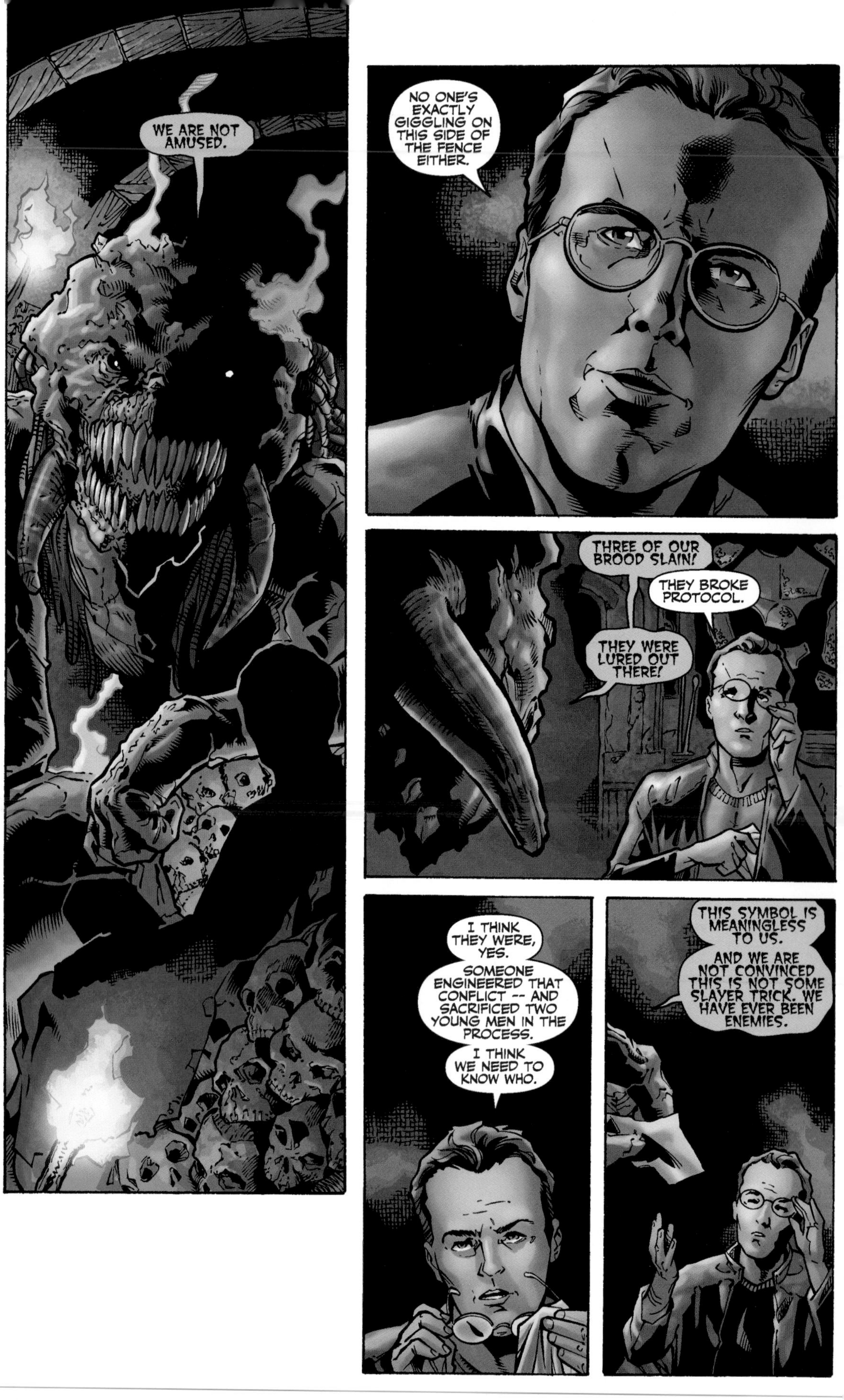
WE ARE NOT AMUSED.
NO ONE'S EXACTLY GIGGLING ON THIS SIDE OF THE FENCE EITHER.
THREE OF OUR BROOD SLAIN!
THEY BROKE PROTOCOL.
THEY WERE LURED OUT THERE!
I THINK THEY WERE, YES.
SOMEONE ENGINEERED THAT CONFLICT -- AND SACRIFICED TWO YOUNG MEN IN THE PROCESS.
I THINK WE NEED TO KNOW WHO.
THIS SYMBOL IS MEANINGLESS TO US.
AND WE ARE NOT CONVINCED THIS IS NOT SOME SLAYER TRICK. WE HAVE EVER BEEN ENEMIES.

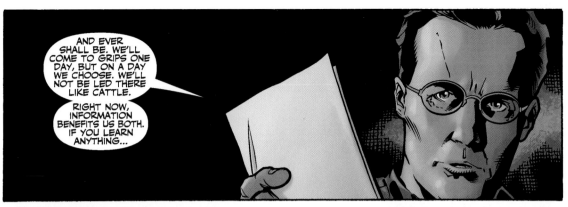

AND EVER SHALL BE. WE'LL COME TO GRIPS ONE DAY, BUT ON A DAY WE CHOOSE. WE'LL NOT BE LED THERE LIKE CATTLE.

RIGHT NOW, INFORMATION BENEFITS US BOTH. IF YOU LEARN ANYTHING...

...WE WOULD SO TELL YOU ALL ABOUT IT.

SERIOUSLY, WE GOT NOTHING GOING ON HERE. I'VE LOOKED THROUGH SO MANY BOOKS I'VE GOT PARCHMENT FINGERS. BUT MY MOM USED TO ORDER THIS SPECIAL DERMATOLOGICAL SOAP BECAUSE HOISIN SAUCE MAKES ME RASHY --

JUST KEEP AN EYE OUT.

OH, WE'RE ON ALERT. YOU THINK AMY'S ATTACK AND THE SYMBOL ARE LINKED?

JUST A WHOLE LOTTA QUESTION MARKS COMING UP AT THE SAME TIME. WANTED TO MAKE SURE YOU'RE NOT SEEING ANY ACTION.

I WISH! WE'RE JUST TRYING TO THINK OF GAMES TO STAY AWAKE. IT'S DULLSVILLE, ITALY.

SOUNDS GOOD ENOUGH TO ME.

NO, TRUST ME...

...YOU'D BE BORED STIFF.

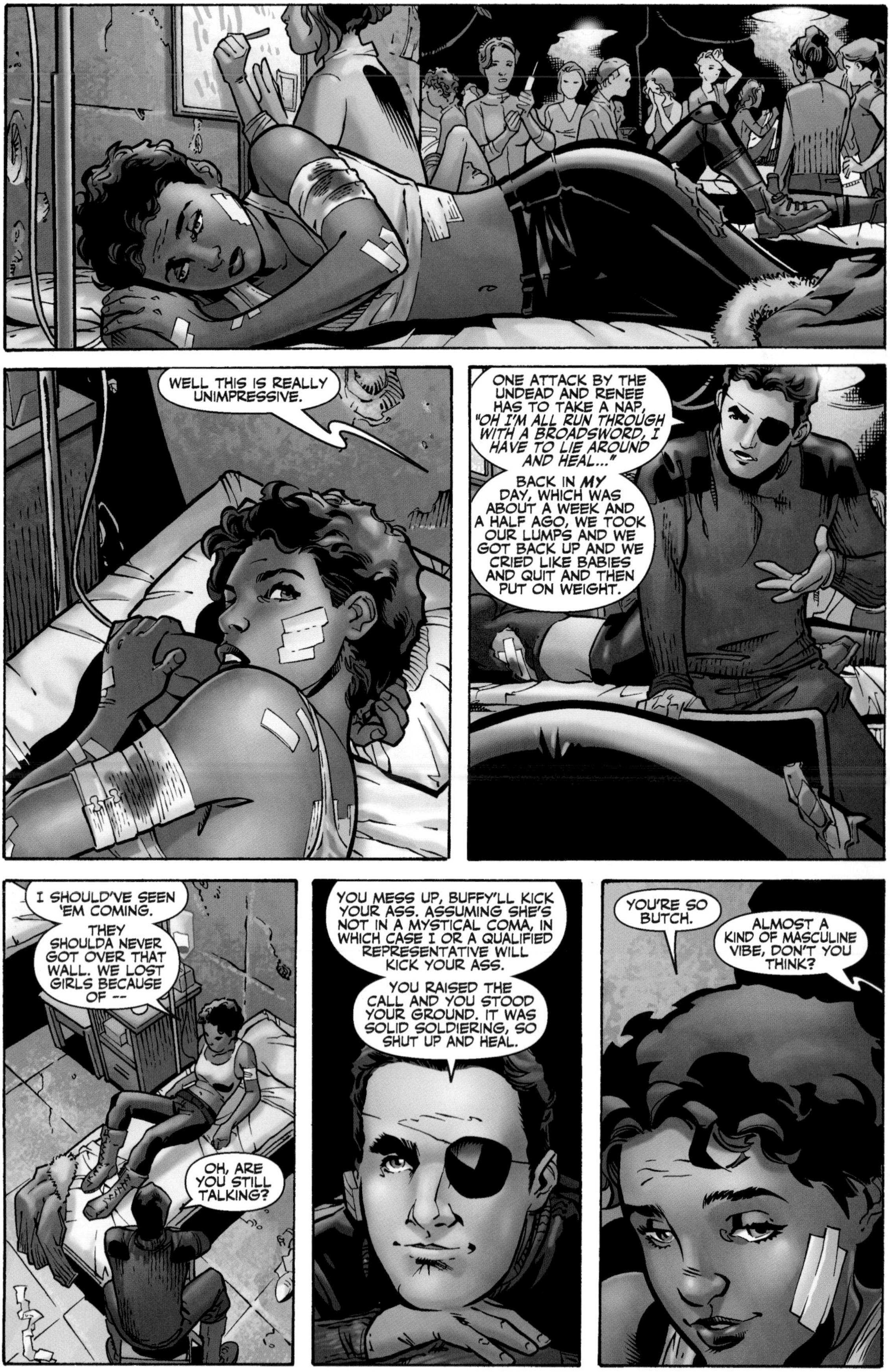
WELL THIS IS REALLY UNIMPRESSIVE.
ONE ATTACK BY THE UNDEAD AND RENEE HAS TO TAKE A NAP, *"OH I'M ALL RUN THROUGH WITH A BROADSWORD, I HAVE TO LIE AROUND AND HEAL..."*
BACK IN *MY* DAY, WHICH WAS ABOUT A WEEK AND A HALF AGO, WE TOOK OUR LUMPS AND WE GOT BACK UP AND WE CRIED LIKE BABIES AND QUIT AND THEN PUT ON WEIGHT.
I SHOULD'VE SEEN 'EM COMING.
THEY SHOULDA NEVER GOT OVER THAT WALL. WE LOST GIRLS BECAUSE OF --
OH, ARE YOU STILL TALKING?
YOU MESS UP, BUFFY'LL KICK YOUR ASS. ASSUMING SHE'S NOT IN A MYSTICAL COMA, IN WHICH CASE I OR A QUALIFIED REPRESENTATIVE WILL KICK YOUR ASS.
YOU RAISED THE CALL AND YOU STOOD YOUR GROUND. IT WAS SOLID SOLDIERING, SO SHUT UP AND HEAL.
YOU'RE SO BUTCH.
ALMOST A KIND OF MASCULINE VIBE, DON'T YOU THINK?

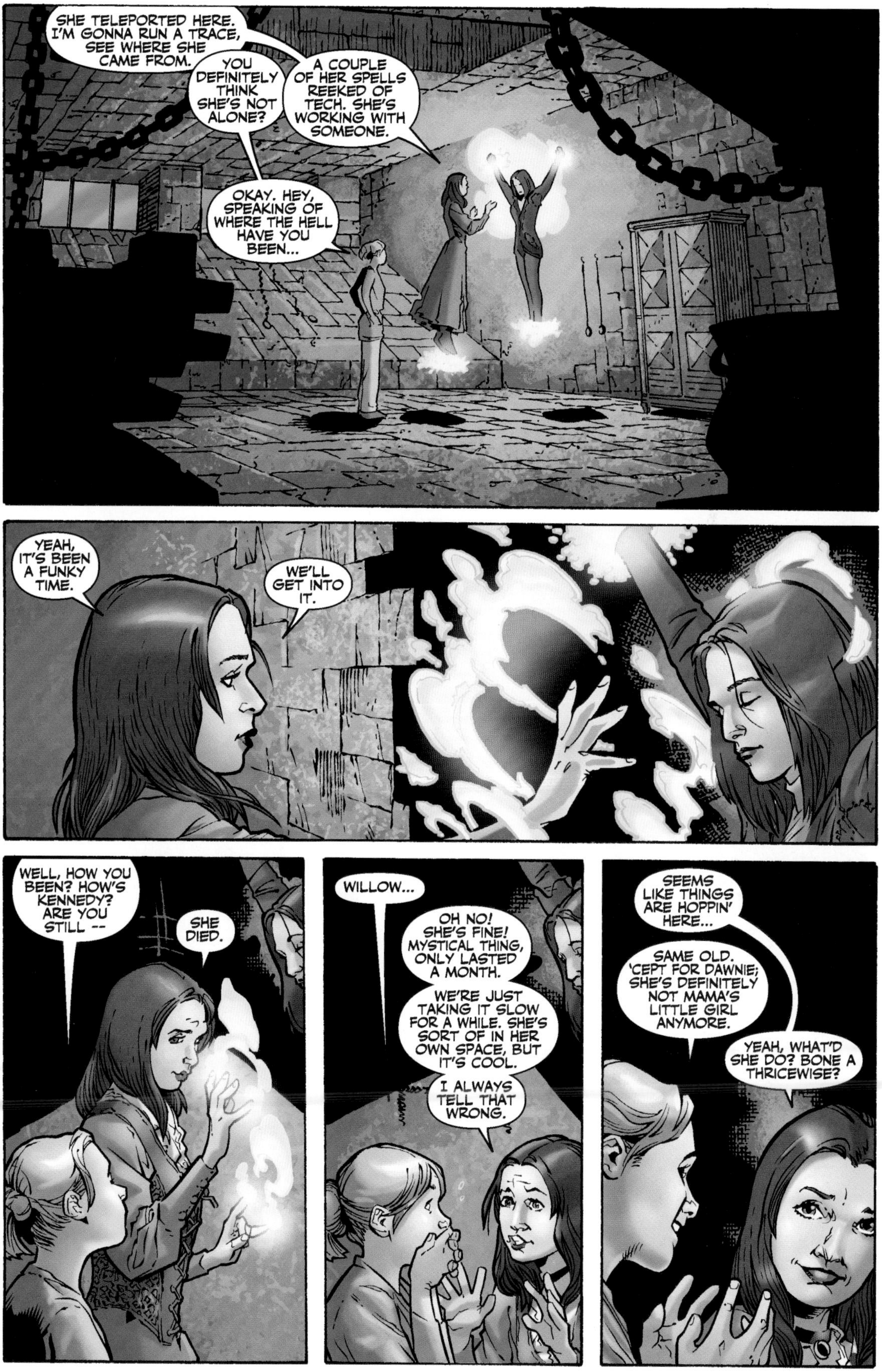
SHE TELEPORTED HERE. I'M GONNA RUN A TRACE, SEE WHERE SHE CAME FROM.
YOU DEFINITELY THINK SHE'S NOT ALONE?
A COUPLE OF HER SPELLS REEKED OF TECH. SHE'S WORKING WITH SOMEONE.
OKAY. HEY, SPEAKING OF WHERE THE HELL HAVE YOU BEEN...
YEAH, IT'S BEEN A FUNKY TIME.
WE'LL GET INTO IT.
WELL, HOW YOU BEEN? HOW'S KENNEDY? ARE YOU STILL --
SHE DIED.
WILLOW...
OH NO! SHE'S FINE! MYSTICAL THING, ONLY LASTED A MONTH.
WE'RE JUST TAKING IT SLOW FOR A WHILE. SHE'S SORT OF IN HER OWN SPACE, BUT IT'S COOL.
I ALWAYS TELL THAT WRONG.
SEEMS LIKE THINGS ARE HOPPIN' HERE...
SAME OLD. 'CEPT FOR DAWNIE; SHE'S DEFINITELY NOT MAMA'S LITTLE GIRL ANYMORE.
YEAH, WHAT'D SHE DO? BONE A THRICEWISE?

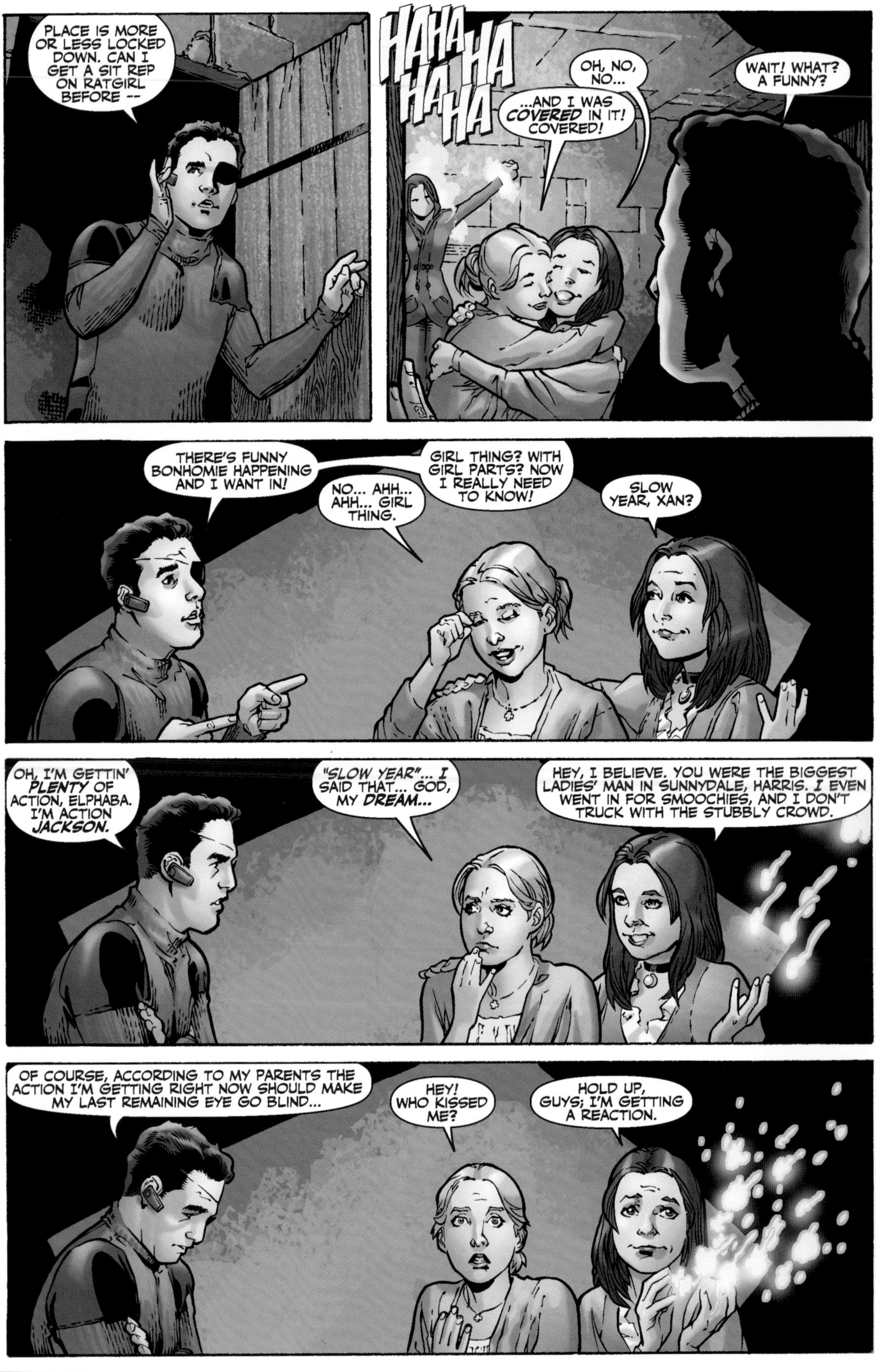
PLACE IS MORE OR LESS LOCKED DOWN. CAN I GET A SIT REP ON RATGIRL BEFORE --
HAHAHA HAHAHA
...AND I WAS *COVERED* IN IT! COVERED!
OH, NO, NO...
WAIT! WHAT? A FUNNY?
THERE'S FUNNY BONHOMIE HAPPENING AND I WANT IN!
NO... AHH... AHH... GIRL THING.
GIRL THING? WITH GIRL PARTS? NOW I REALLY NEED TO KNOW!
SLOW YEAR, XAN?
OH, I'M GETTIN' *PLENTY* OF ACTION, ELPHABA. I'M ACTION *JACKSON.*
"SLOW YEAR"... *I* SAID THAT... GOD, MY *DREAM...*
HEY, I BELIEVE. YOU WERE THE BIGGEST LADIES' MAN IN SUNNYDALE, HARRIS. *I* EVEN WENT IN FOR SMOOCHIES, AND I DON'T TRUCK WITH THE STUBBLY CROWD.
OF COURSE, ACCORDING TO MY PARENTS THE ACTION I'M GETTING RIGHT NOW SHOULD MAKE MY LAST REMAINING EYE GO BLIND...
HEY! WHO KISSED ME?
HOLD UP, GUYS; I'M GETTING A REACTION.

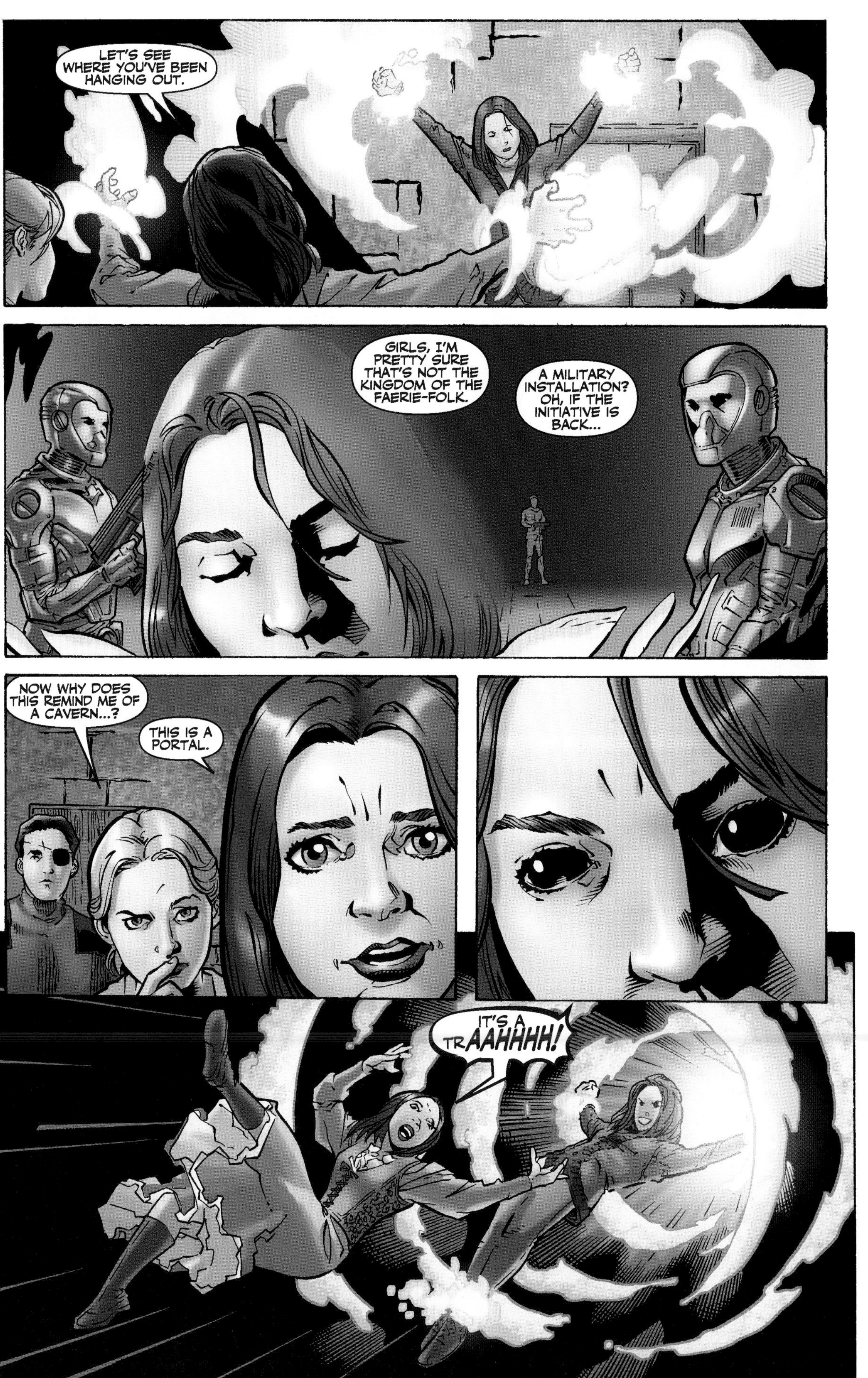
LET'S SEE WHERE YOU'VE BEEN HANGING OUT.
GIRLS, I'M PRETTY SURE THAT'S NOT THE KINGDOM OF THE FAERIE-FOLK.
A MILITARY INSTALLATION? OH, IF THE INITIATIVE IS BACK...
NOW WHY DOES THIS REMIND ME OF A CAVERN...?
THIS IS A PORTAL.
IT'S A TRAAHHHH!

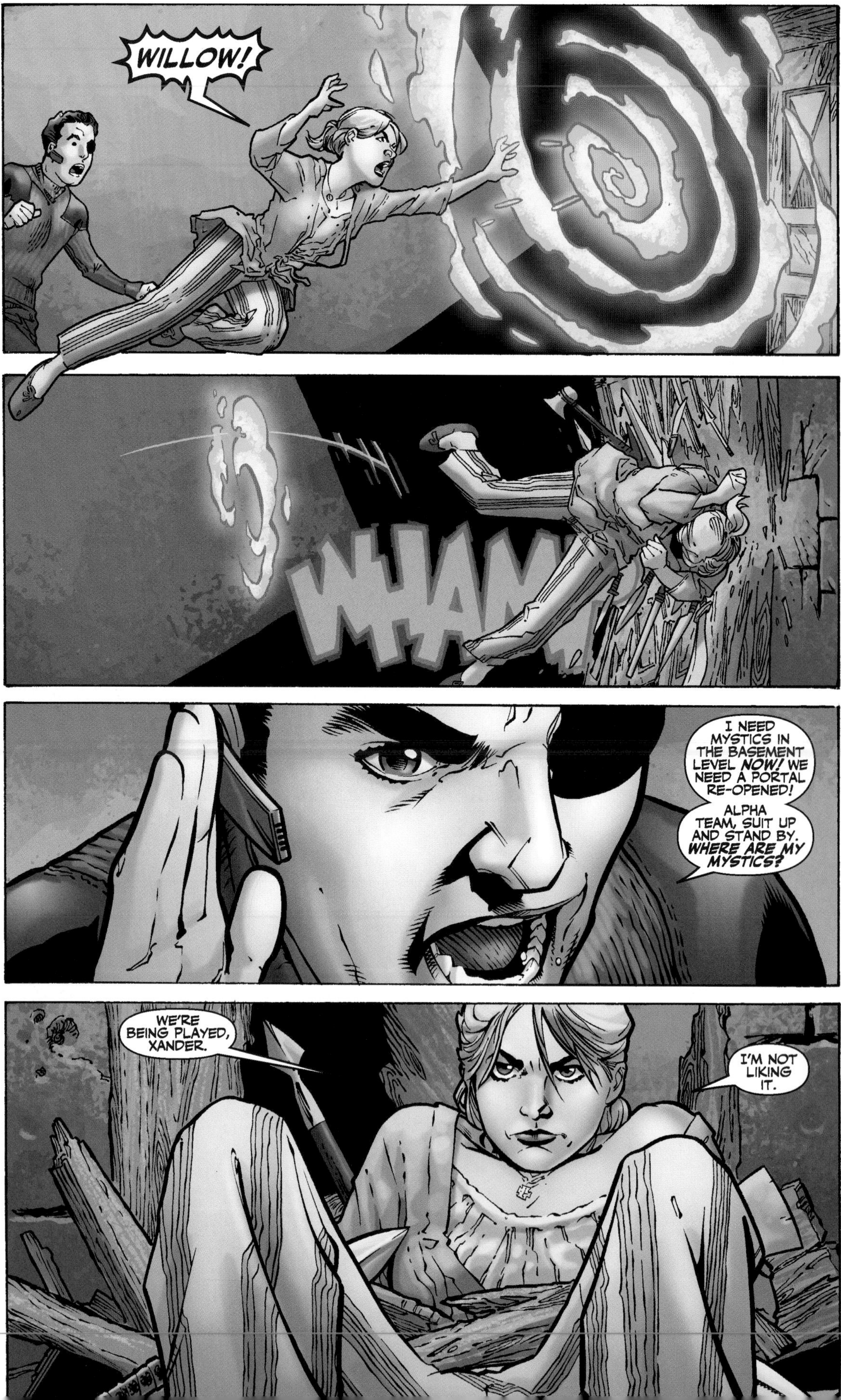
WILLOW!
WHAM
I NEED MYSTICS IN THE BASEMENT LEVEL NOW! WE NEED A PORTAL RE-OPENED!
ALPHA TEAM, SUIT UP AND STAND BY. WHERE ARE MY MYSTICS?
WE'RE BEING PLAYED, XANDER.
I'M NOT LIKING IT.

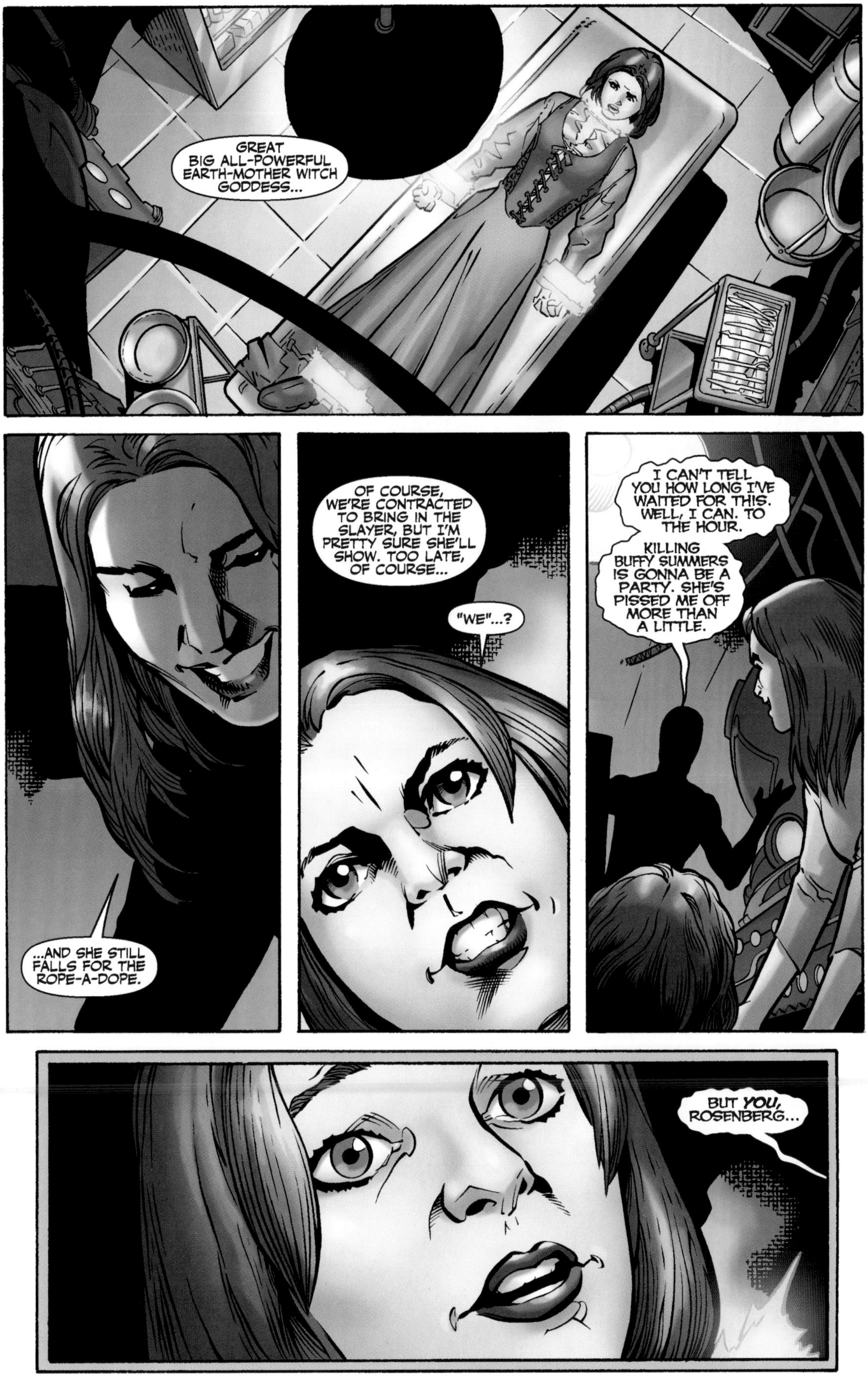
GREAT BIG ALL-POWERFUL EARTH-MOTHER WITCH GODDESS...
...AND SHE STILL FALLS FOR THE ROPE-A-DOPE.
OF COURSE, WE'RE CONTRACTED TO BRING IN THE SLAYER, BUT I'M PRETTY SURE SHE'LL SHOW. TOO LATE, OF COURSE...
"WE"...?
I CAN'T TELL YOU HOW LONG I'VE WAITED FOR THIS. WELL, I CAN. TO THE HOUR.
KILLING BUFFY SUMMERS IS GONNA BE A PARTY. SHE'S PISSED ME OFF MORE THAN A LITTLE.
BUT YOU, ROSENBERG...

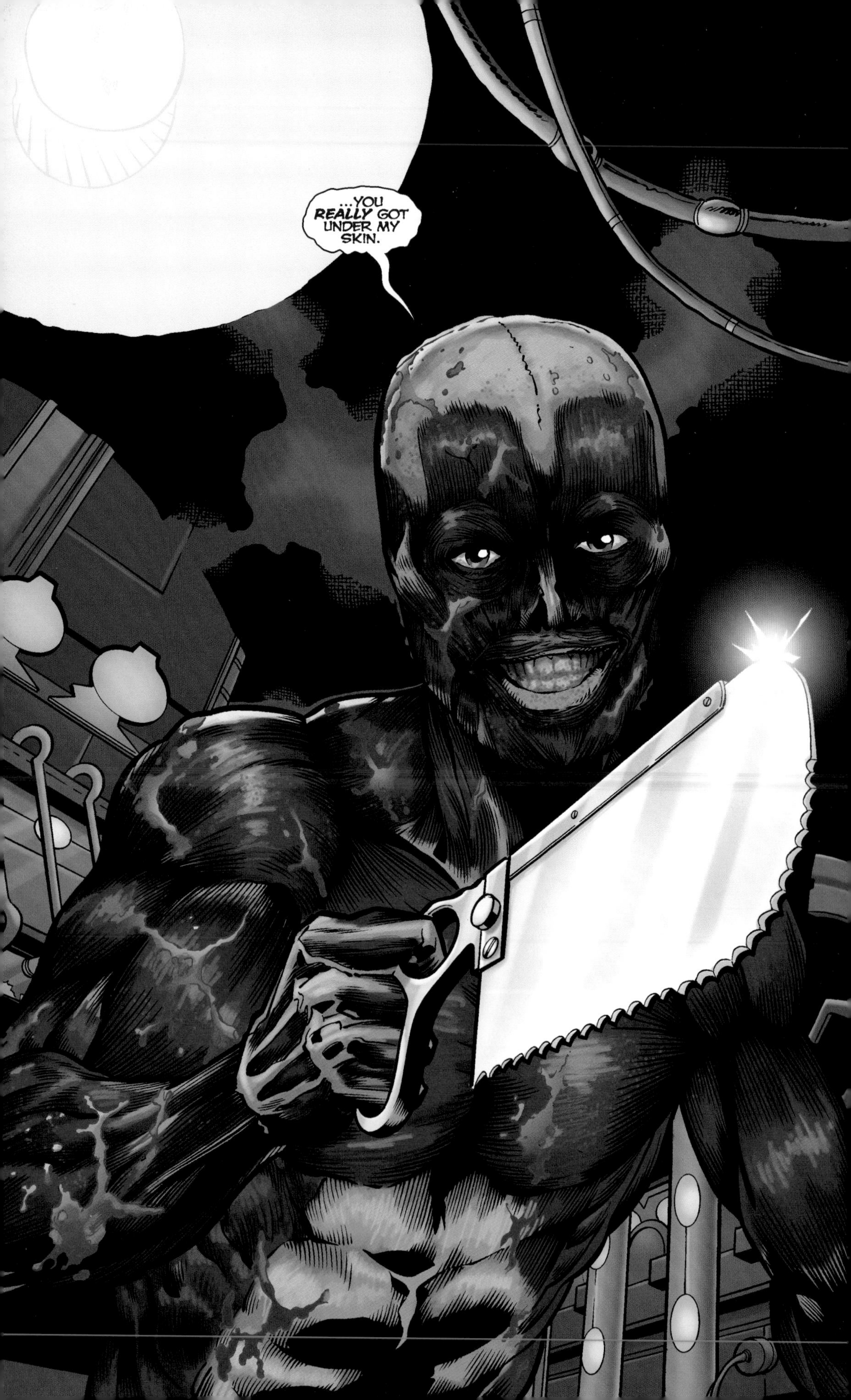
...YOU REALLY GOT UNDER MY SKIN.

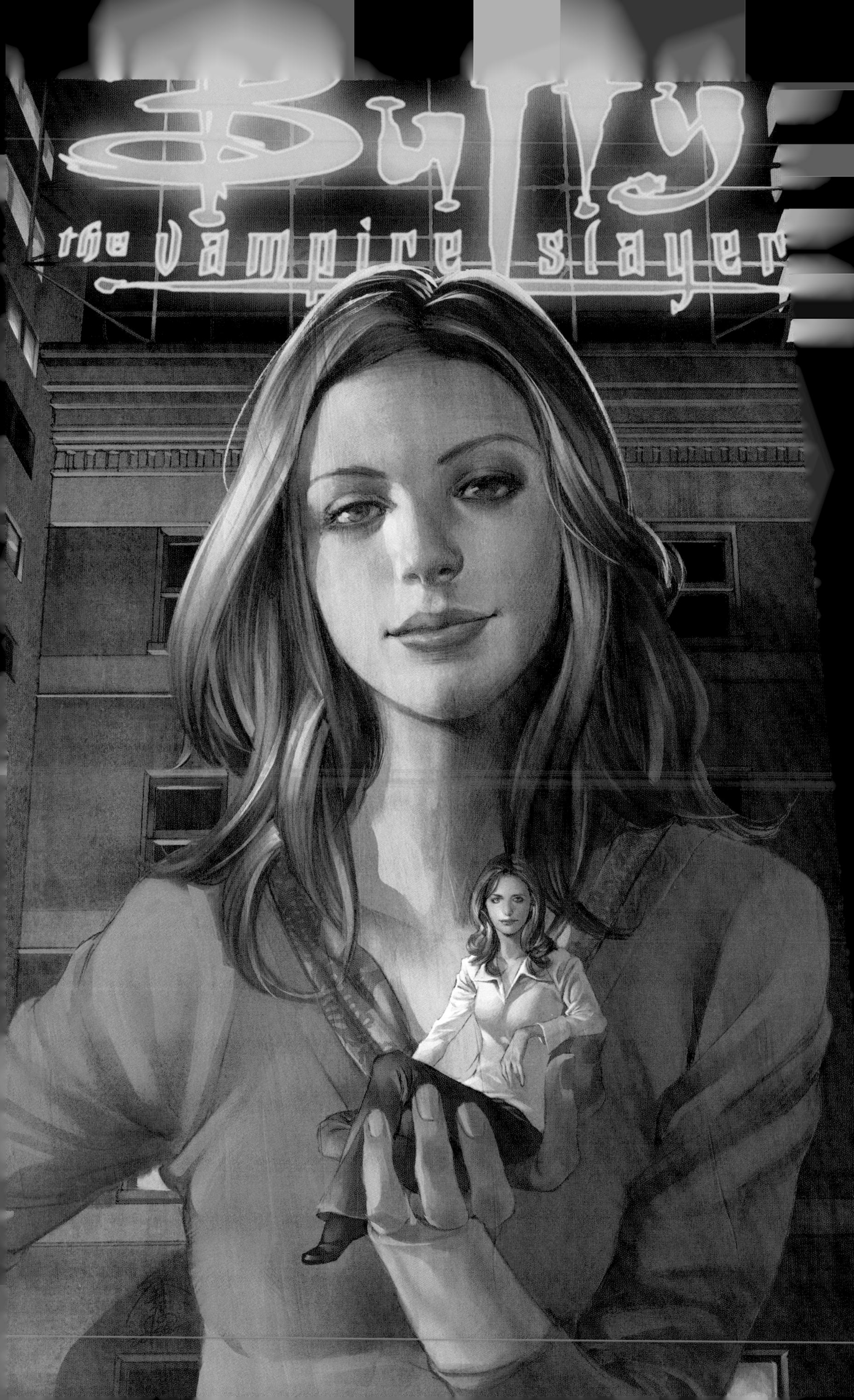

Buffy
the vampire slayer

The LONG WAY HOME

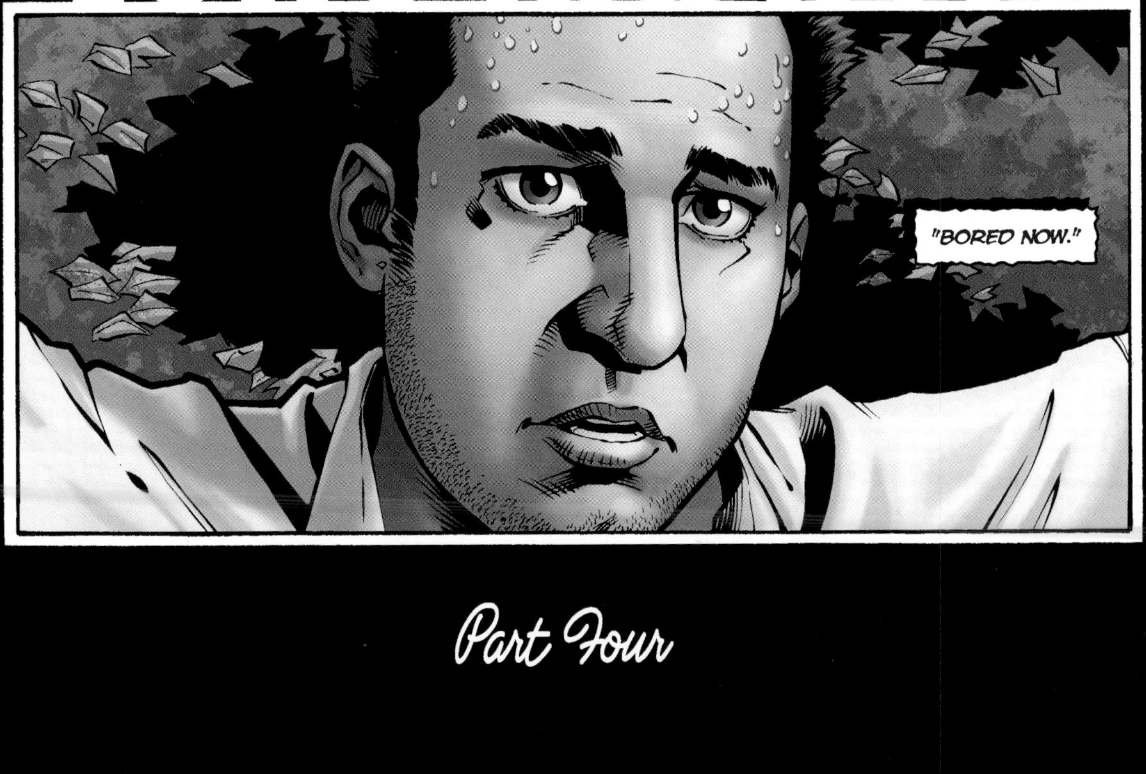
"BORED NOW."

Part Four

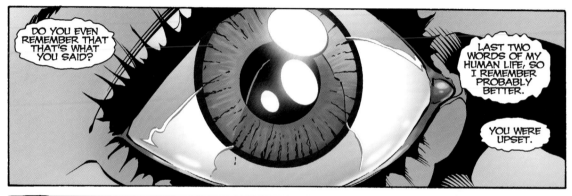

DO YOU EVEN REMEMBER THAT THAT'S WHAT YOU SAID?

LAST TWO WORDS OF MY HUMAN LIFE, SO I REMEMBER PROBABLY BETTER.

YOU WERE UPSET.

KINDA SPIRALING, IS WHAT THEY SAY.

WHICH IS, HEY--I'M NOT EXCUSING WHERE I WAS AT, SO DON'T THINK--

I MEAN YOU-- IF AMY HADN'T BEEN WATCHING YOU, SHE WOULD NEVER HAVE STARTED WATCHING ME.

WATCHING *OVER* ME.

"DO YOU KNOW SHE HAD MAYBE A FOUR-SECOND WINDOW AFTER MY SKIN CAME OFF BEFORE I DIED OF SHOCK ALONE?

"THAT FLASH-PAPER DISAPPEARING TRICK WAS PRETTY HOKEY, WE KID ABOUT THAT, BUT THINKING ON YOUR FEET? THIS IS THE GIRL.

"HER MAGIC IS MY SKIN."

THAT TIME WE CAME UP WITH THE SPELL FOR YOU AND YOUR NEW GIRLFRIEND--

--AND HEY, *THAT* WAS QUICK, I WAS STILL LEARNING TO WALK AGAIN AND YOU'RE ALREADY IN THE FRESH TRIM...

I REMEMBER THINKING AND IT COMES UP AGAIN IN THIS SITUATION, I JUST HAVE TO WONDER...

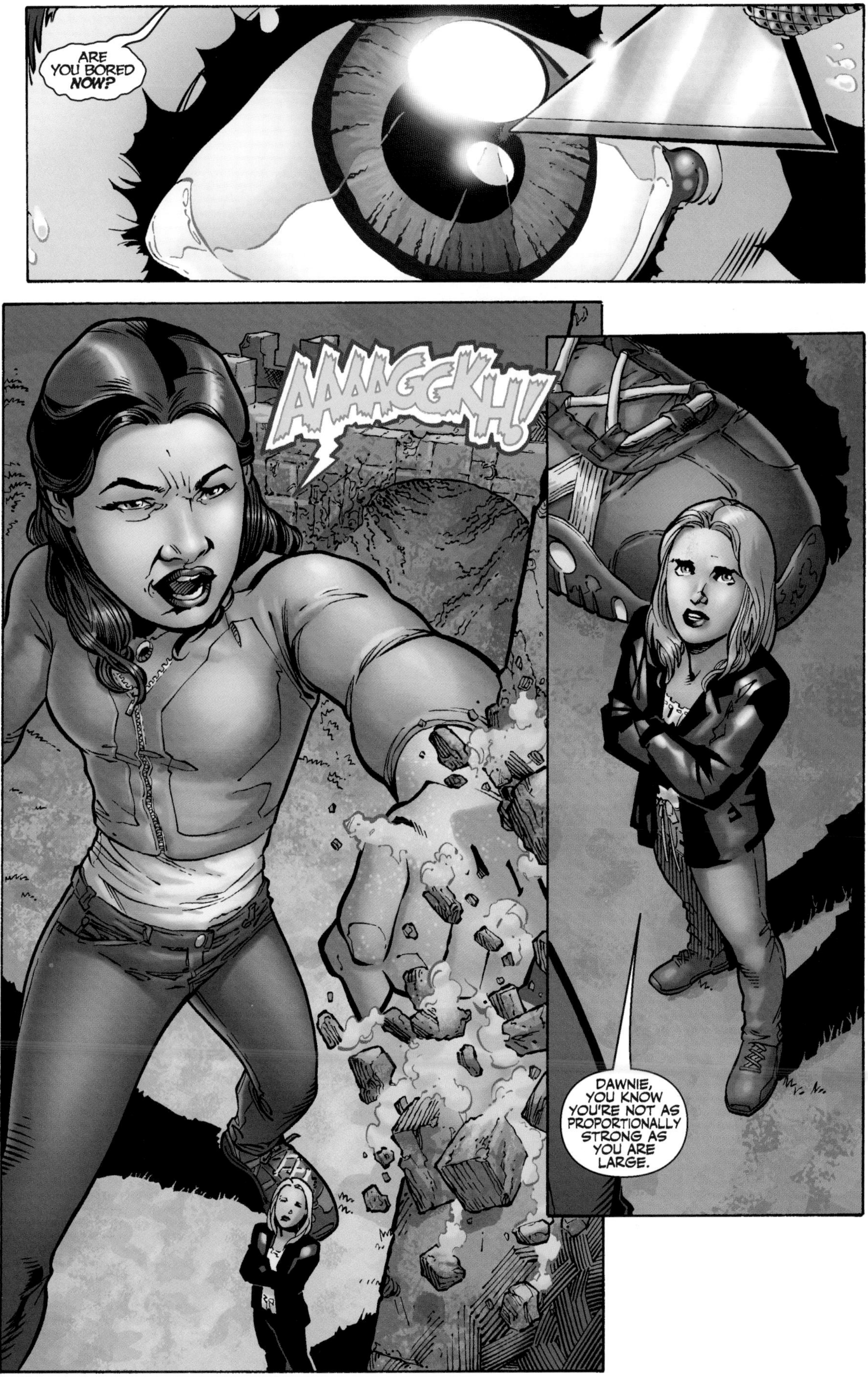
ARE YOU BORED *NOW?*
AAAAGGKH!!
DAWNIE, YOU KNOW YOU'RE NOT AS PROPORTIONALLY STRONG AS YOU ARE LARGE.

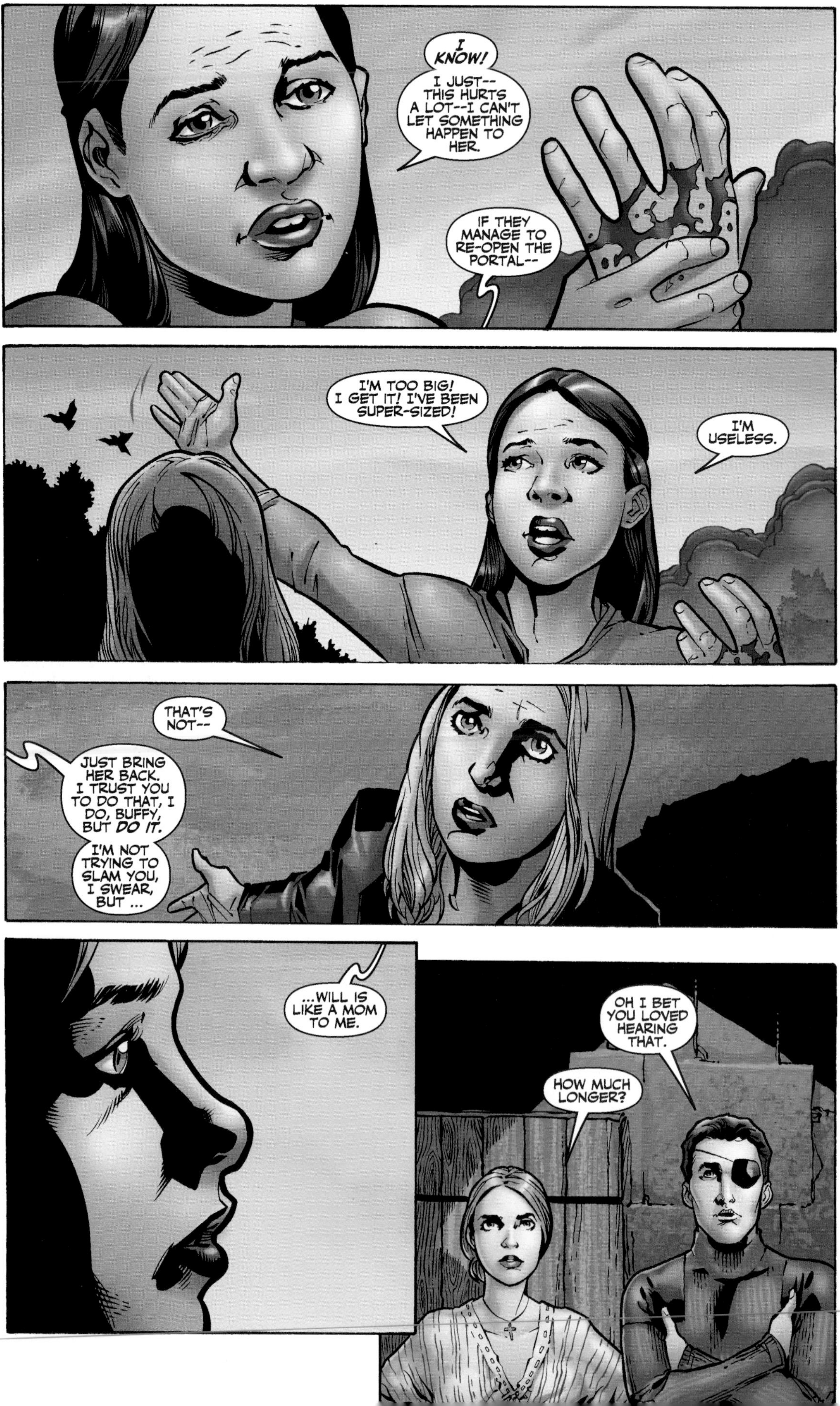
I KNOW!
I JUST--THIS HURTS A LOT--I CAN'T LET SOMETHING HAPPEN TO HER.
IF THEY MANAGE TO RE-OPEN THE PORTAL--
I'M TOO BIG! I GET IT! I'VE BEEN SUPER-SIZED!
I'M USELESS.
THAT'S NOT--
JUST BRING HER BACK. I TRUST YOU TO DO THAT, I DO, BUFFY, BUT DO IT.
I'M NOT TRYING TO SLAM YOU, I SWEAR, BUT ...
...WILL IS LIKE A MOM TO ME.
OH I BET YOU LOVED HEARING THAT.
HOW MUCH LONGER?

TELEPORTATION'S NOT AN EXACT MAGIC, BUFFY. AND GOOD AS THESE GIRLS ARE, WE'RE NOT SPORTIN' A GILES, SO...

THEY SAY A COUPLE HOURS. PORTAL ECHO BIG ENOUGH FOR ... MAYBE ONE OR TWO GUYS, TOPS.

WHAT CAN I DO?

FIGURE OUT WHO YOUR MOVING BUDDY IS.

XANDER...

I'M NOT A FIGHTER, I GOT NO MAGIC. IF THERE'S ANY KIND OF SATELLITE BOUNCE I'M YOUR EYES AND EARS, THAT'S IT.

IT'S WILL. WE PLAY IT SMART.

AND WE REMEMBER SHE'S STRONGER THAN ALL OF US.

AND THEREIN LIES, IT'S VERY OPERATIC, YOUR DOWNFALL.

YOU'RE JUST SO **STRONG.**

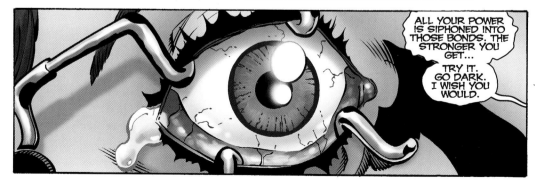

ALL YOUR POWER IS SIPHONED INTO THOSE BONDS. THE STRONGER YOU GET...

TRY IT. GO DARK. I WISH YOU WOULD.

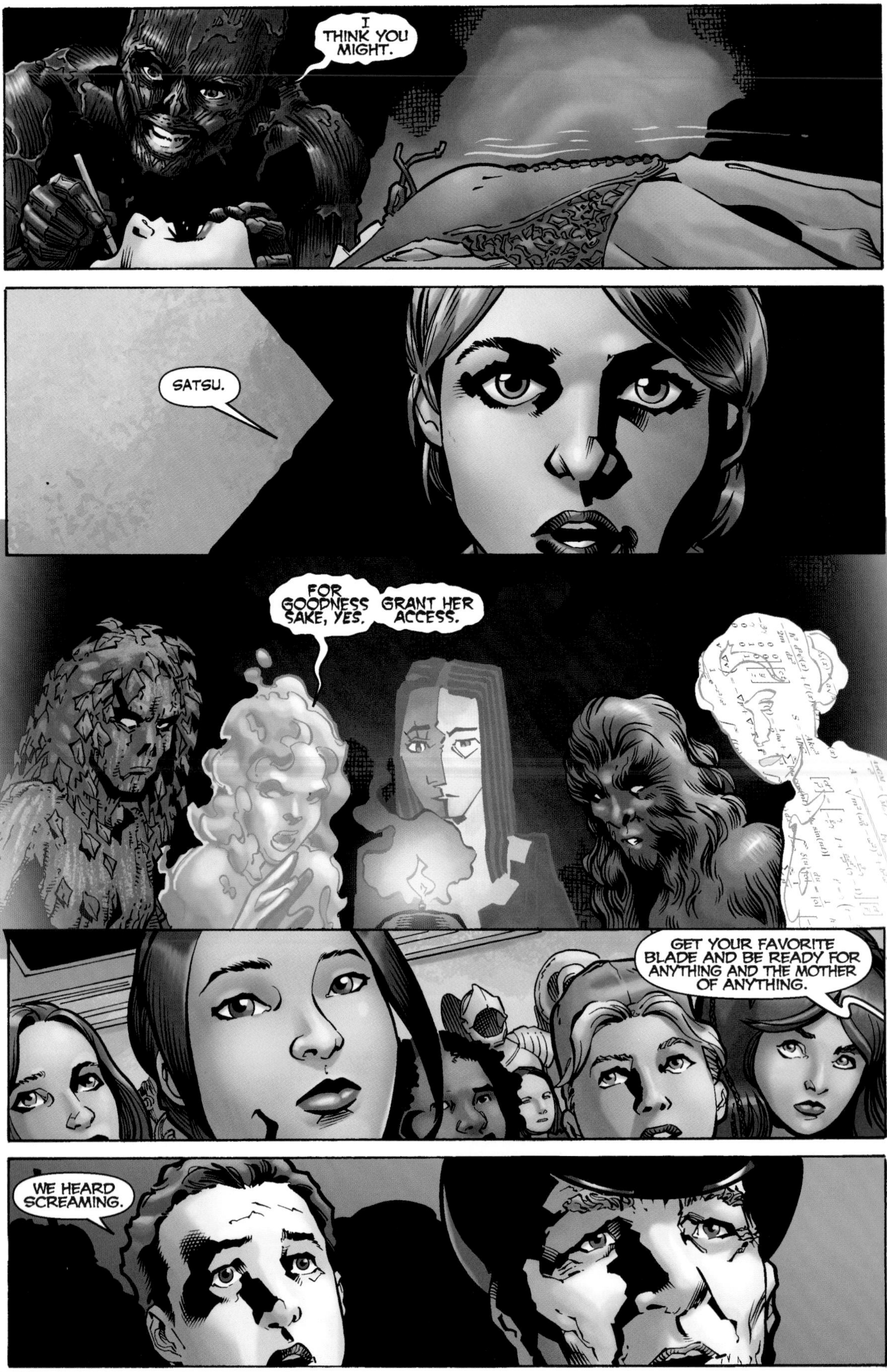
I THINK YOU MIGHT.
SATSU.
FOR GOODNESS SAKE, YES.
GRANT HER ACCESS.
GET YOUR FAVORITE BLADE AND BE READY FOR ANYTHING AND THE MOTHER OF ANYTHING.
WE HEARD SCREAMING.

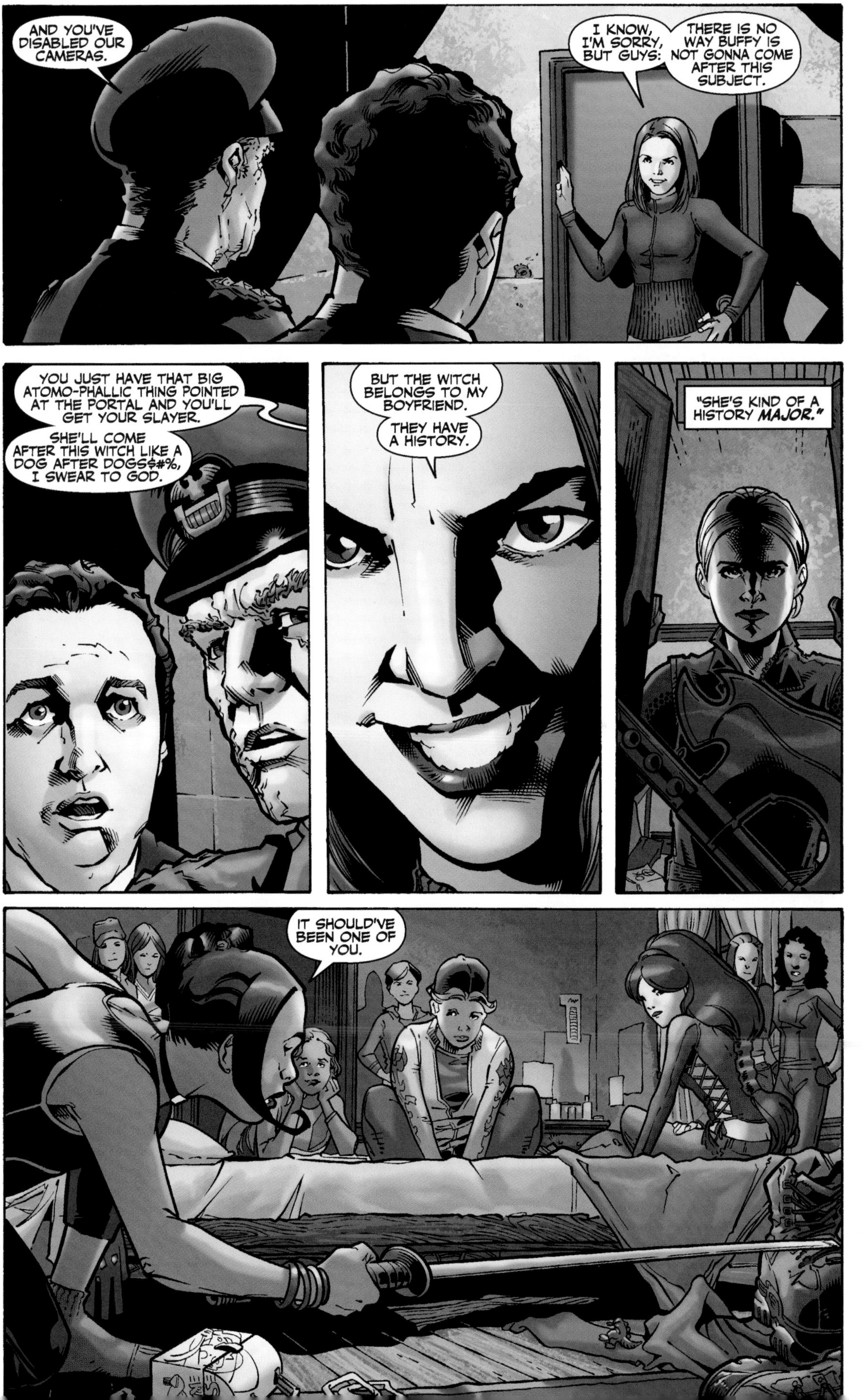
AND YOU'VE DISABLED OUR CAMERAS.
I KNOW, I'M SORRY, BUT GUYS:
THERE IS NO WAY BUFFY IS NOT GONNA COME AFTER THIS SUBJECT.
YOU JUST HAVE THAT BIG ATOMO-PHALLIC THING POINTED AT THE PORTAL AND YOU'LL GET YOUR SLAYER.
SHE'LL COME AFTER THIS WITCH LIKE A DOG AFTER DOGS$#%, I SWEAR TO GOD.
BUT THE WITCH BELONGS TO MY BOYFRIEND.
THEY HAVE A HISTORY.
"SHE'S KIND OF A HISTORY *MAJOR.*"
IT SHOULD'VE BEEN ONE OF YOU.

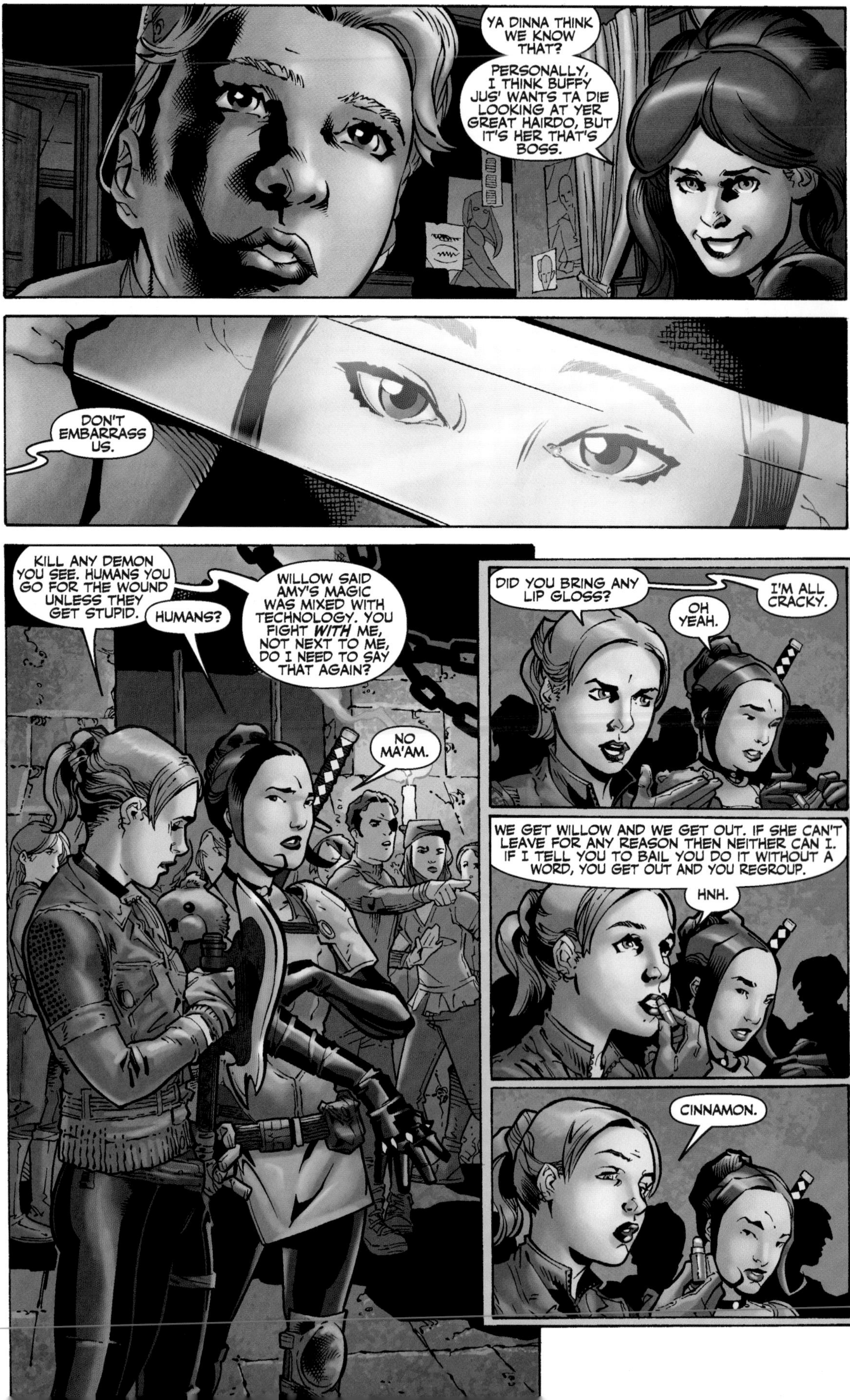
YA DINNA THINK WE KNOW THAT?
PERSONALLY, I THINK BUFFY JUS' WANTS TA DIE LOOKING AT YER GREAT HAIRDO, BUT IT'S HER THAT'S BOSS.
DON'T EMBARRASS US.
KILL ANY DEMON YOU SEE. HUMANS YOU GO FOR THE WOUND UNLESS THEY GET STUPID.
HUMANS?
WILLOW SAID AMY'S MAGIC WAS MIXED WITH TECHNOLOGY. YOU FIGHT *WITH* ME, NOT NEXT TO ME, DO I NEED TO SAY THAT AGAIN?
NO MA'AM.
DID YOU BRING ANY LIP GLOSS?
I'M ALL CRACKY.
OH YEAH.
WE GET WILLOW AND WE GET OUT. IF SHE CAN'T LEAVE FOR ANY REASON THEN NEITHER CAN I. IF I TELL YOU TO BAIL YOU DO IT WITHOUT A WORD, YOU GET OUT AND YOU REGROUP.
HNH.
CINNAMON.

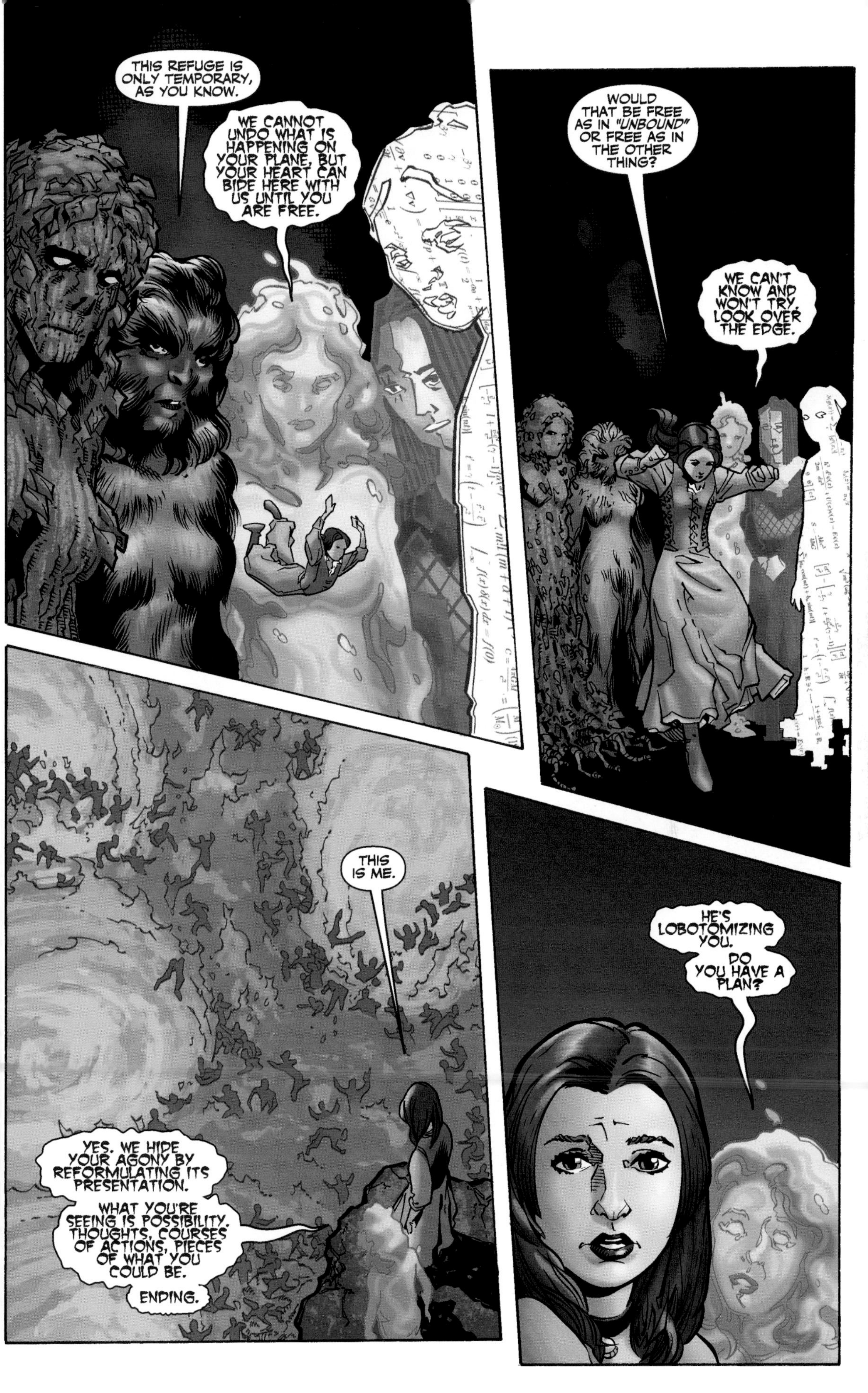
THIS REFUGE IS ONLY TEMPORARY, AS YOU KNOW.
WE CANNOT UNDO WHAT IS HAPPENING ON YOUR PLANE, BUT YOUR HEART CAN BIDE HERE WITH US UNTIL YOU ARE FREE.
WOULD THAT BE FREE AS IN *"UNBOUND"* OR FREE AS IN THE OTHER THING?
WE CAN'T KNOW AND WON'T TRY. LOOK OVER THE EDGE.
THIS IS ME.
YES. WE HIDE YOUR AGONY BY REFORMULATING ITS PRESENTATION.
WHAT YOU'RE SEEING IS POSSIBILITY. THOUGHTS, COURSES OF ACTIONS, PIECES OF WHAT YOU COULD BE.
ENDING.
HE'S LOBOTOMIZING YOU.
DO YOU HAVE A PLAN?

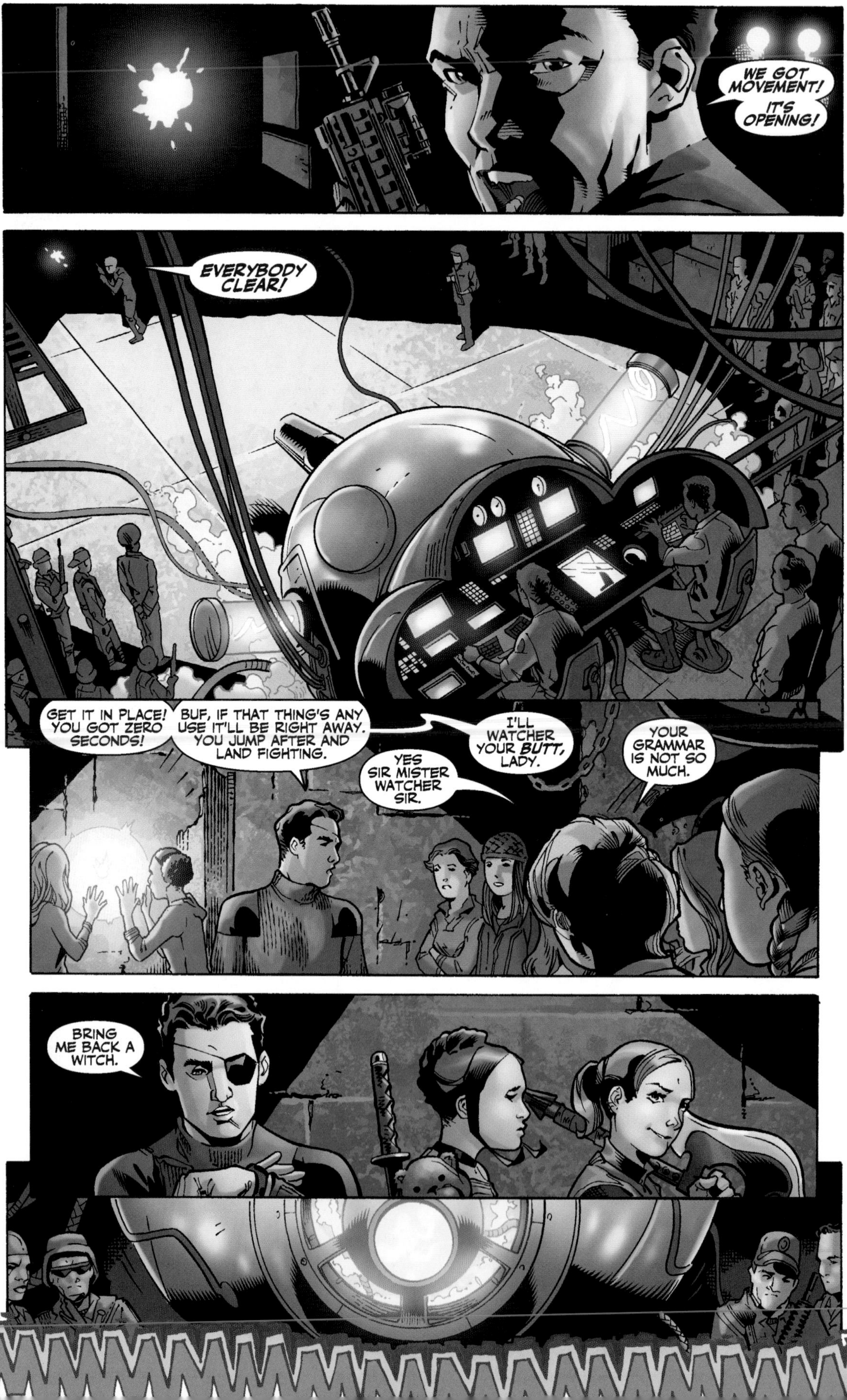
WE GOT MOVEMENT!
IT'S OPENING!
EVERYBODY CLEAR!
GET IT IN PLACE! YOU GOT ZERO SECONDS!
BUF, IF THAT THING'S ANY USE IT'LL BE RIGHT AWAY. YOU JUMP AFTER AND LAND FIGHTING.
YES SIR MISTER WATCHER SIR.
I'LL WATCHER YOUR *BUTT*, LADY.
YOUR GRAMMAR IS NOT SO MUCH.
BRING ME BACK A WITCH.

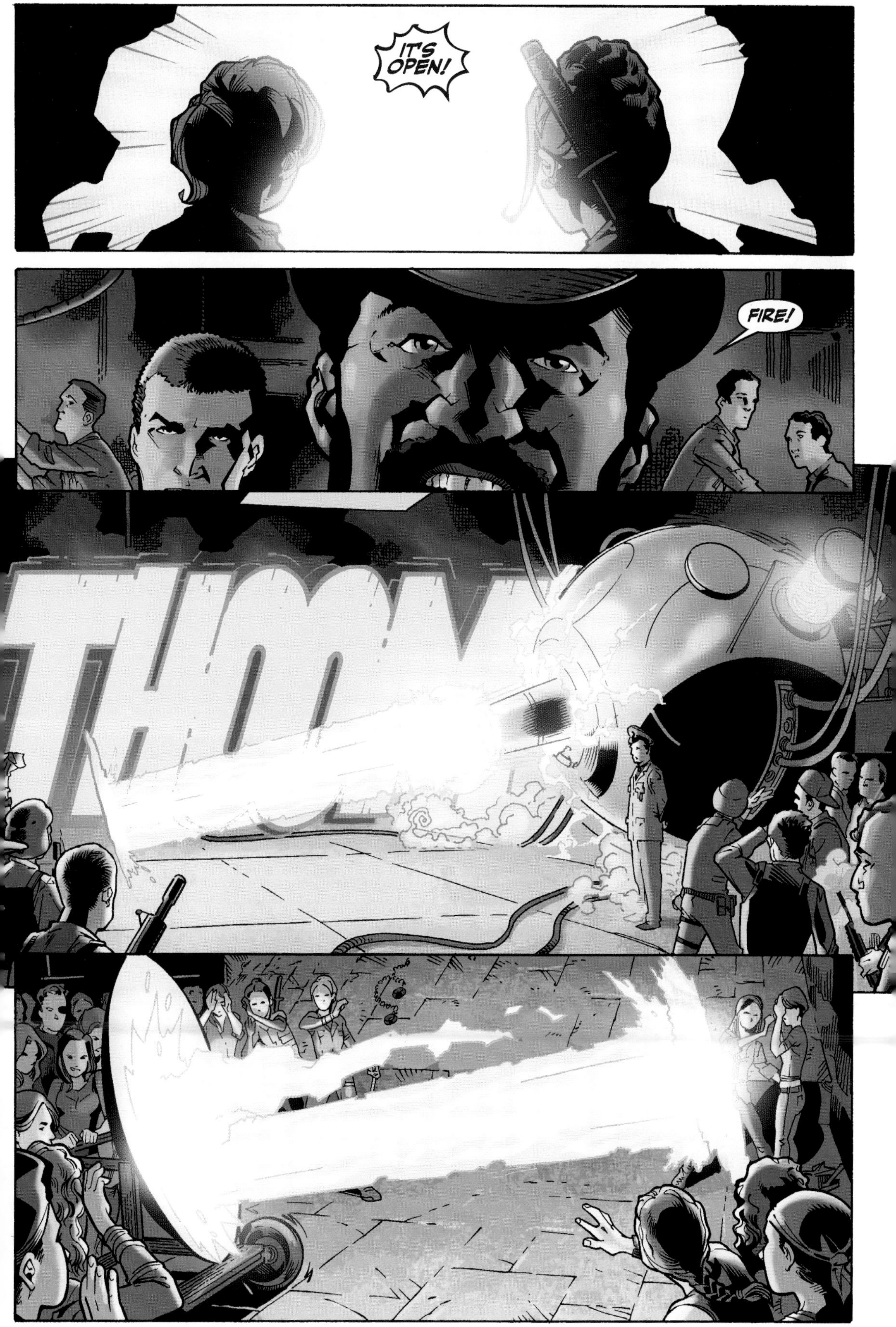
IT'S OPEN!
FIRE!
THOOM

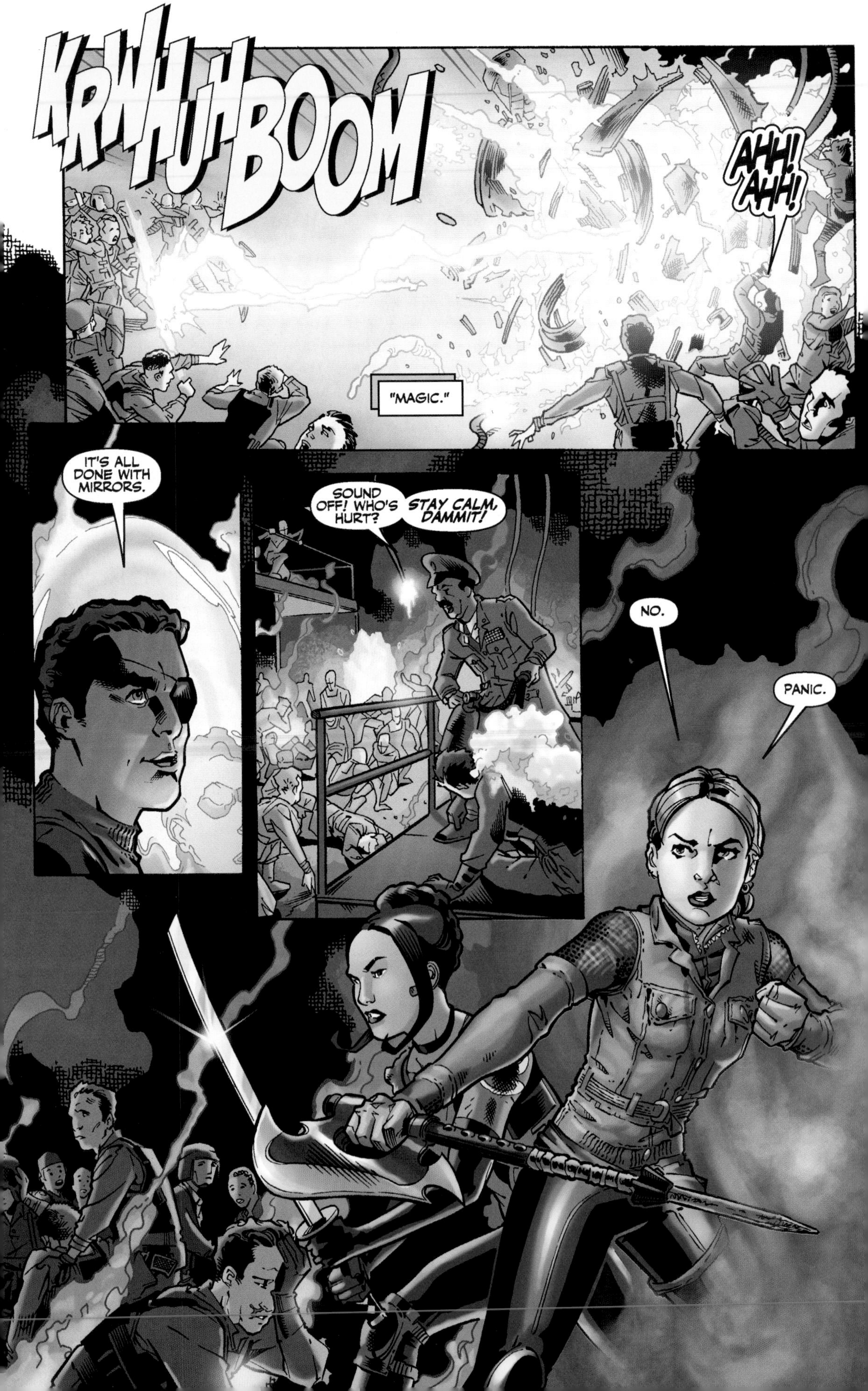

KRWHUHBOOM
AHH! AHH!
"MAGIC."
IT'S ALL DONE WITH MIRRORS.
SOUND OFF! WHO'S HURT?
STAY CALM, DAMMIT!
NO.
PANIC.

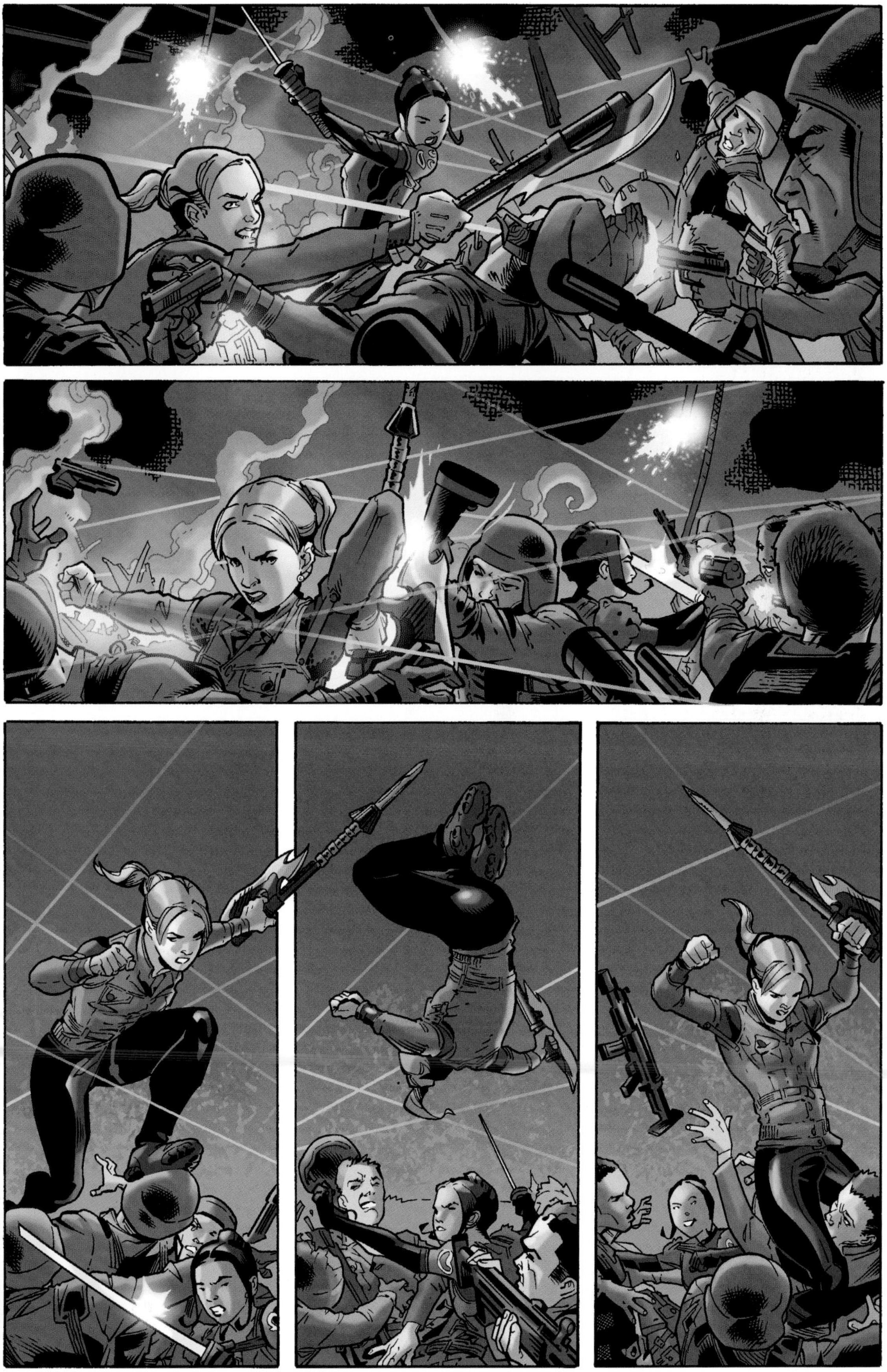

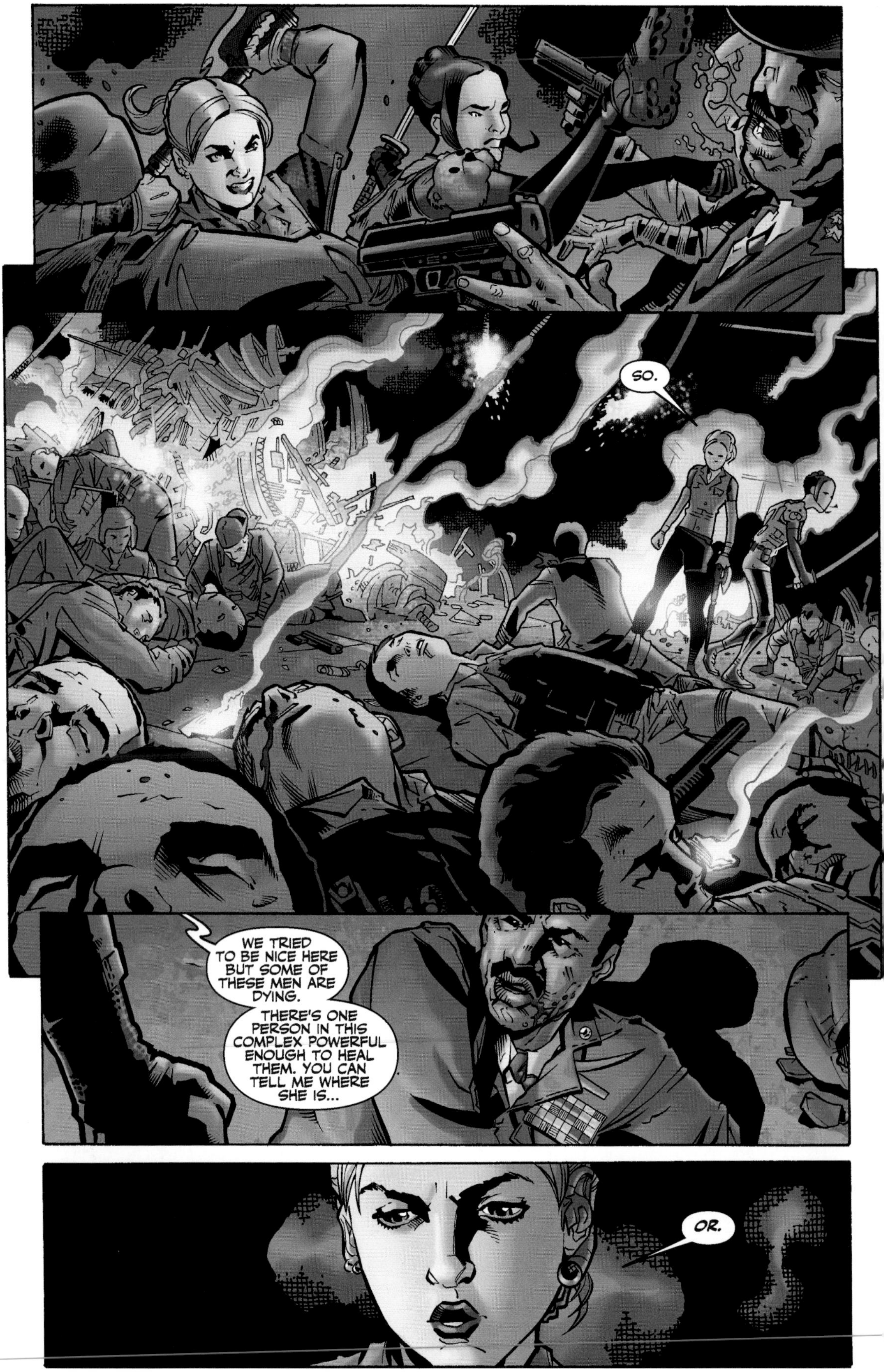
SO.
WE TRIED TO BE NICE HERE BUT SOME OF THESE MEN ARE DYING.
THERE'S ONE PERSON IN THIS COMPLEX POWERFUL ENOUGH TO HEAL THEM. YOU CAN TELL ME WHERE SHE IS...
OR.

HEY, WE'RE UP! WHAT'S THE WHAT?

WILLOW?

MILITARY INSTALLATION. INITIATIVE-Y, BUT WAY MORE OF YOUR TAX DOLLARS AT WORK.

WE'RE EN ROUTE.

AMY'LL BE WAITING FOR YOU.

WHUMP

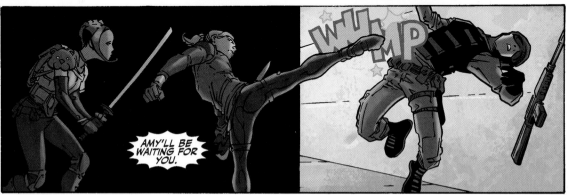

YOU GOT ANY IDEA WHERE ALL THIS IS?

YEAH, G.P.S. IS COMING UP... WOW.

WHERE ARE WE?

ABOUT TWO MILES SOUTH OF SUNNYDALE.

SUNNYDALE.

WELL.

I'M THE ONE WHO WANTED TO GO HOME.

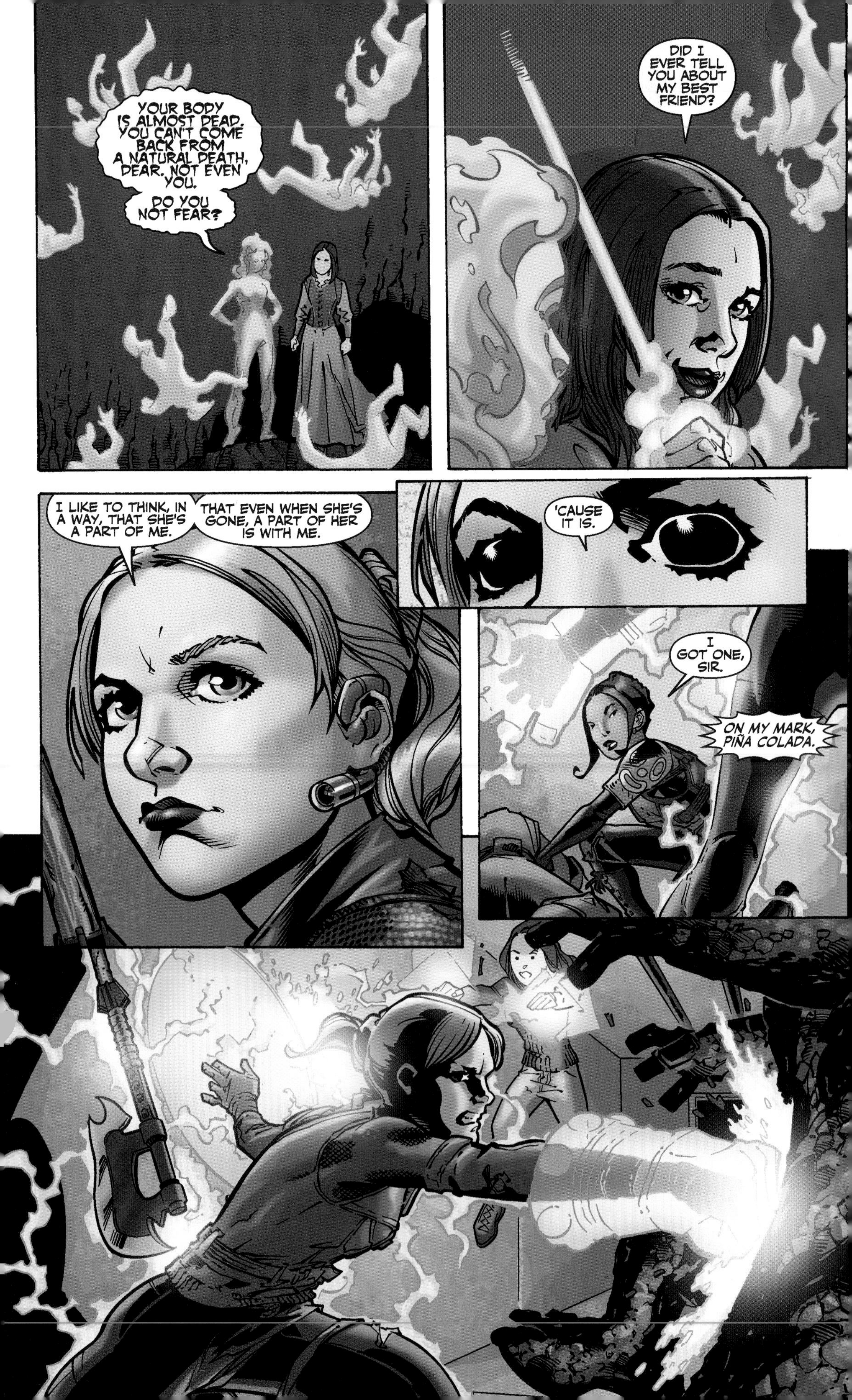
YOUR BODY IS ALMOST DEAD. YOU CAN'T COME BACK FROM A NATURAL DEATH, DEAR. NOT EVEN YOU.
DO YOU NOT FEAR?
DID I EVER TELL YOU ABOUT MY BEST FRIEND?
I LIKE TO THINK, IN A WAY, THAT SHE'S A PART OF ME.
THAT EVEN WHEN SHE'S GONE, A PART OF HER IS WITH ME.
'CAUSE IT IS.
I GOT ONE, SIR.
ON MY MARK, PIÑA COLADA.

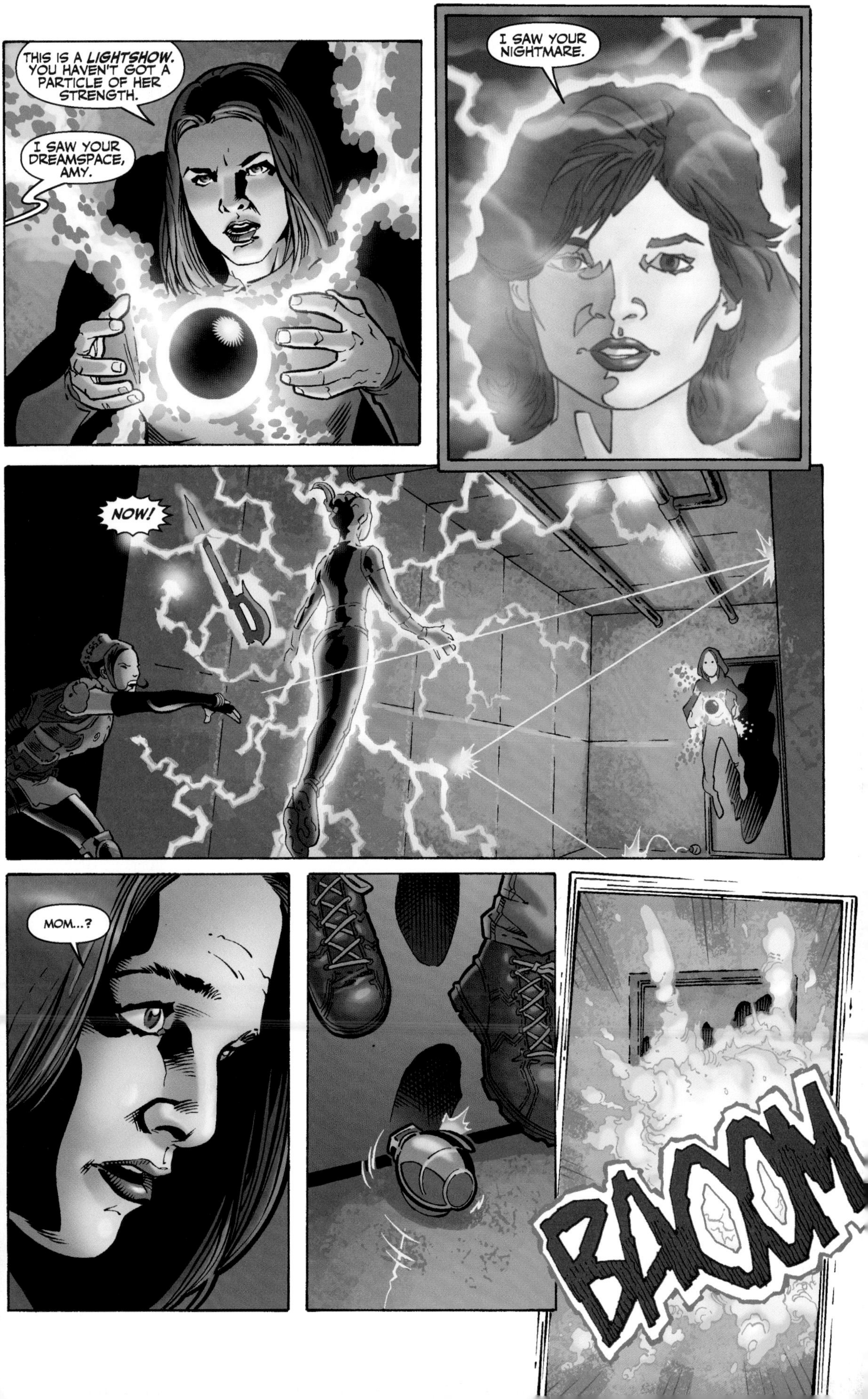
THIS IS A *LIGHTSHOW*. YOU HAVEN'T GOT A PARTICLE OF HER STRENGTH.
I SAW YOUR DREAMSPACE, AMY.
I SAW YOUR NIGHTMARE.
NOW!
MOM...?
BAOOM

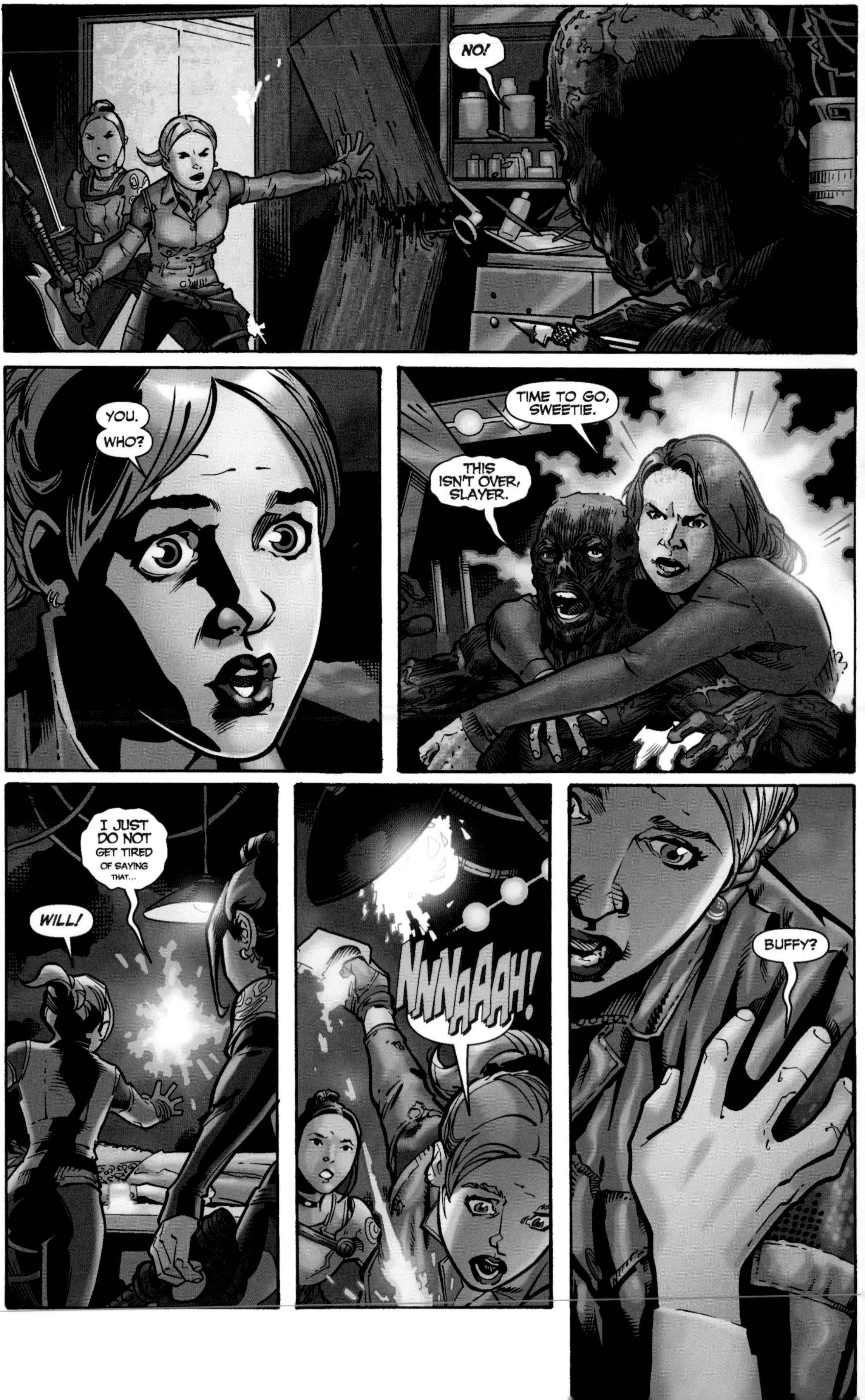
NO!
YOU.
WHO?
TIME TO GO, SWEETIE.
THIS ISN'T OVER, SLAYER.
I JUST DO NOT GET TIRED OF SAYING THAT...
WILL!
NNNAAAH!
BUFFY?

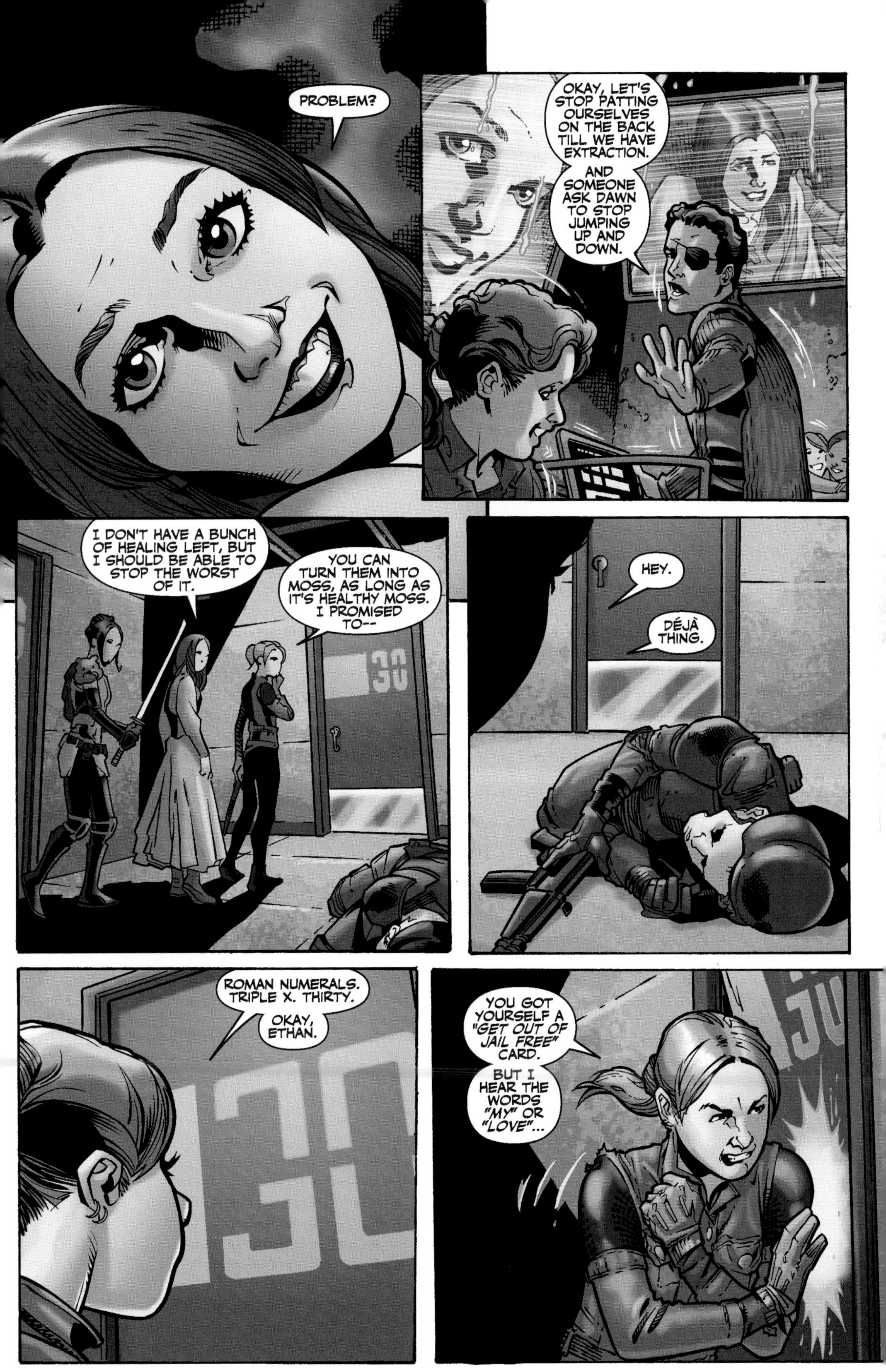
PROBLEM?
OKAY, LET'S STOP PATTING OURSELVES ON THE BACK TILL WE HAVE EXTRACTION.
AND SOMEONE ASK DAWN TO STOP JUMPING UP AND DOWN.
I DON'T HAVE A BUNCH OF HEALING LEFT, BUT I SHOULD BE ABLE TO STOP THE WORST OF IT.
YOU CAN TURN THEM INTO MOSS, AS LONG AS IT'S HEALTHY MOSS. I PROMISED TO--
HEY.
DÉJÀ THING.
ROMAN NUMERALS. TRIPLE X. THIRTY.
OKAY, ETHAN.
YOU GOT YOURSELF A "GET OUT OF JAIL FREE" CARD.
BUT I HEAR THE WORDS "MY" OR "LOVE"...

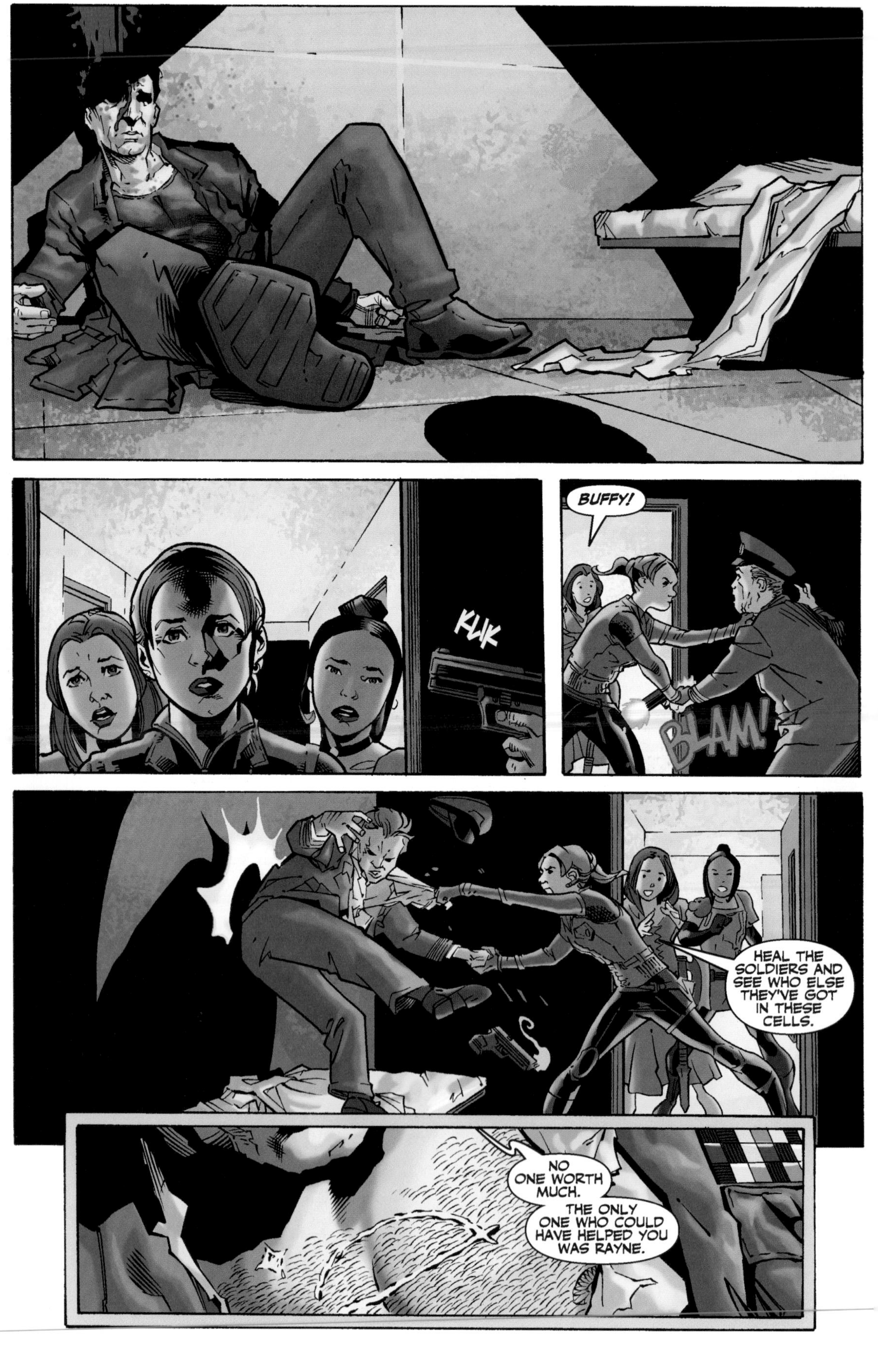

KLIK
BUFFY!
BLAM!
HEAL THE SOLDIERS AND SEE WHO ELSE THEY'VE GOT IN THESE CELLS.
NO ONE WORTH MUCH.
THE ONLY ONE WHO COULD HAVE HELPED YOU WAS RAYNE.

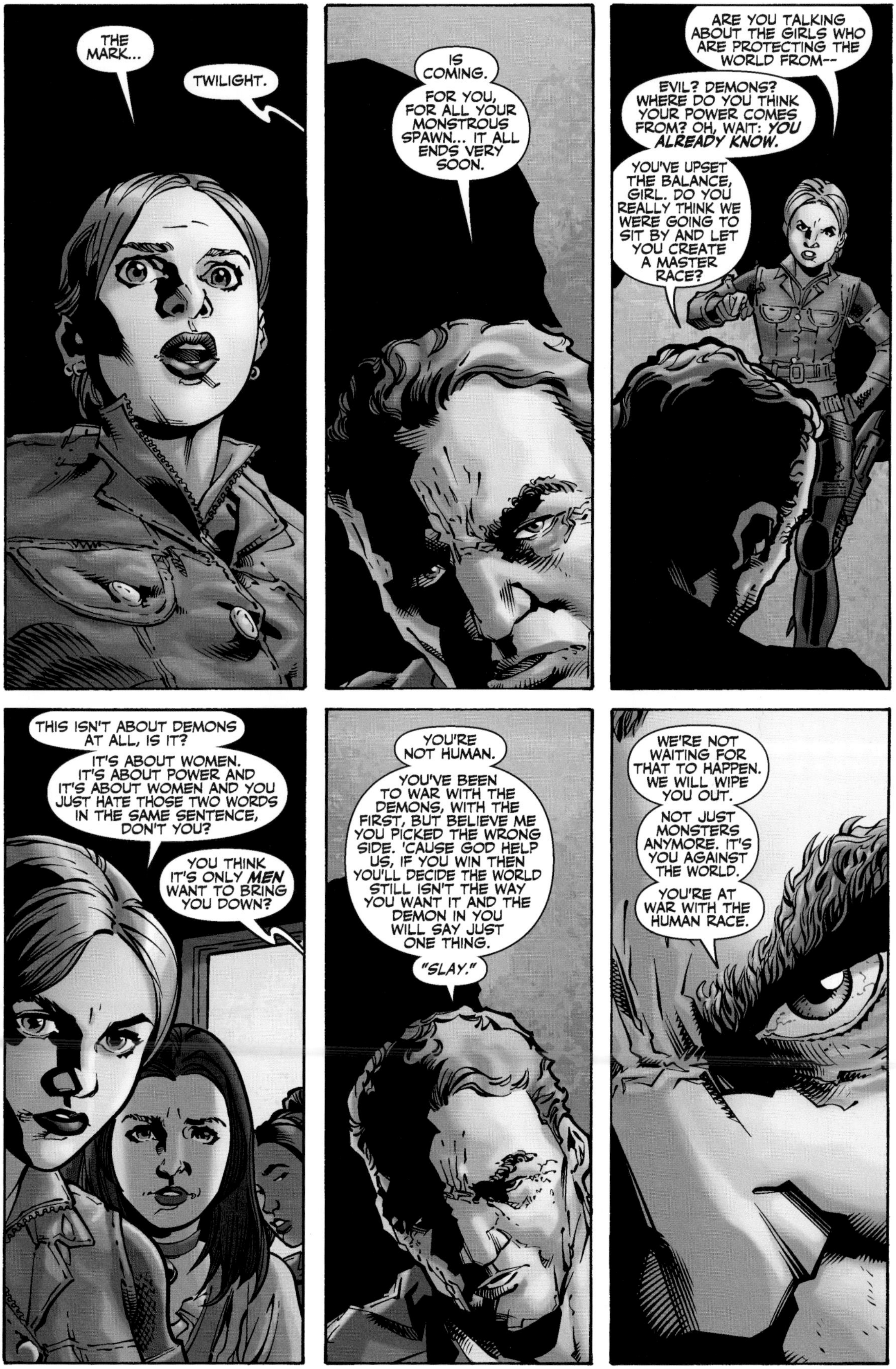
THE MARK...
TWILIGHT.
IS COMING.
FOR YOU, FOR ALL YOUR MONSTROUS SPAWN... IT ALL ENDS VERY SOON.
ARE YOU TALKING ABOUT THE GIRLS WHO ARE PROTECTING THE WORLD FROM--
EVIL? DEMONS? WHERE DO YOU THINK YOUR POWER COMES FROM? OH, WAIT: *YOU ALREADY KNOW.*
YOU'VE UPSET THE BALANCE, GIRL. DO YOU REALLY THINK WE WERE GOING TO SIT BY AND LET YOU CREATE A MASTER RACE?
THIS ISN'T ABOUT DEMONS AT ALL, IS IT?
IT'S ABOUT WOMEN. IT'S ABOUT POWER AND IT'S ABOUT WOMEN AND YOU JUST HATE THOSE TWO WORDS IN THE SAME SENTENCE, DON'T YOU?
YOU THINK IT'S ONLY *MEN* WANT TO BRING YOU DOWN?
YOU'RE NOT HUMAN.
YOU'VE BEEN TO WAR WITH THE DEMONS, WITH THE FIRST, BUT BELIEVE ME YOU PICKED THE WRONG SIDE. 'CAUSE GOD HELP US, IF YOU WIN THEN YOU'LL DECIDE THE WORLD STILL ISN'T THE WAY YOU WANT IT AND THE DEMON IN YOU WILL SAY JUST ONE THING.
"SLAY."
WE'RE NOT WAITING FOR THAT TO HAPPEN. WE WILL WIPE YOU OUT.
NOT JUST MONSTERS ANYMORE. IT'S YOU AGAINST THE WORLD.
YOU'RE AT WAR WITH THE HUMAN RACE.

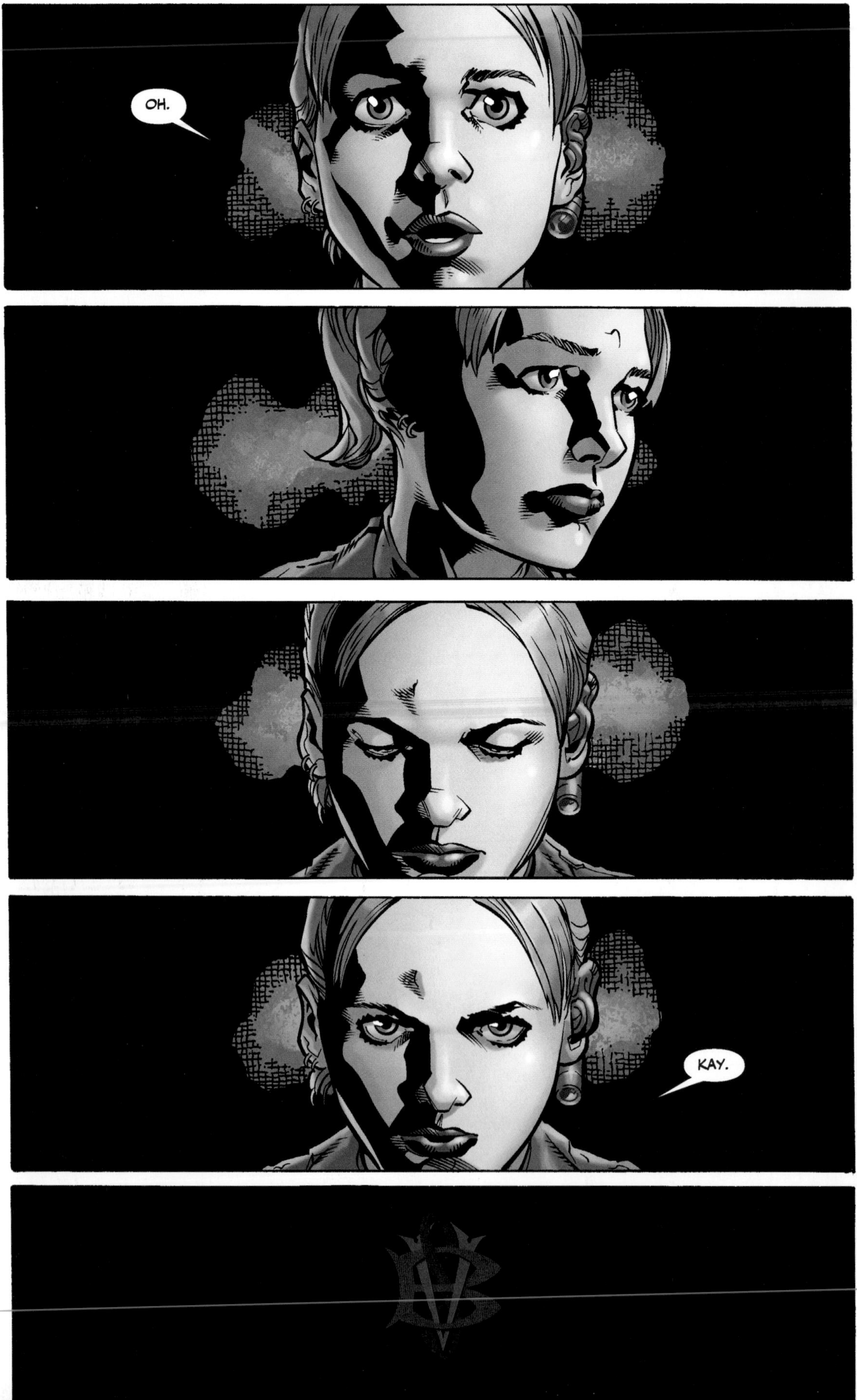
OH.
KAY.

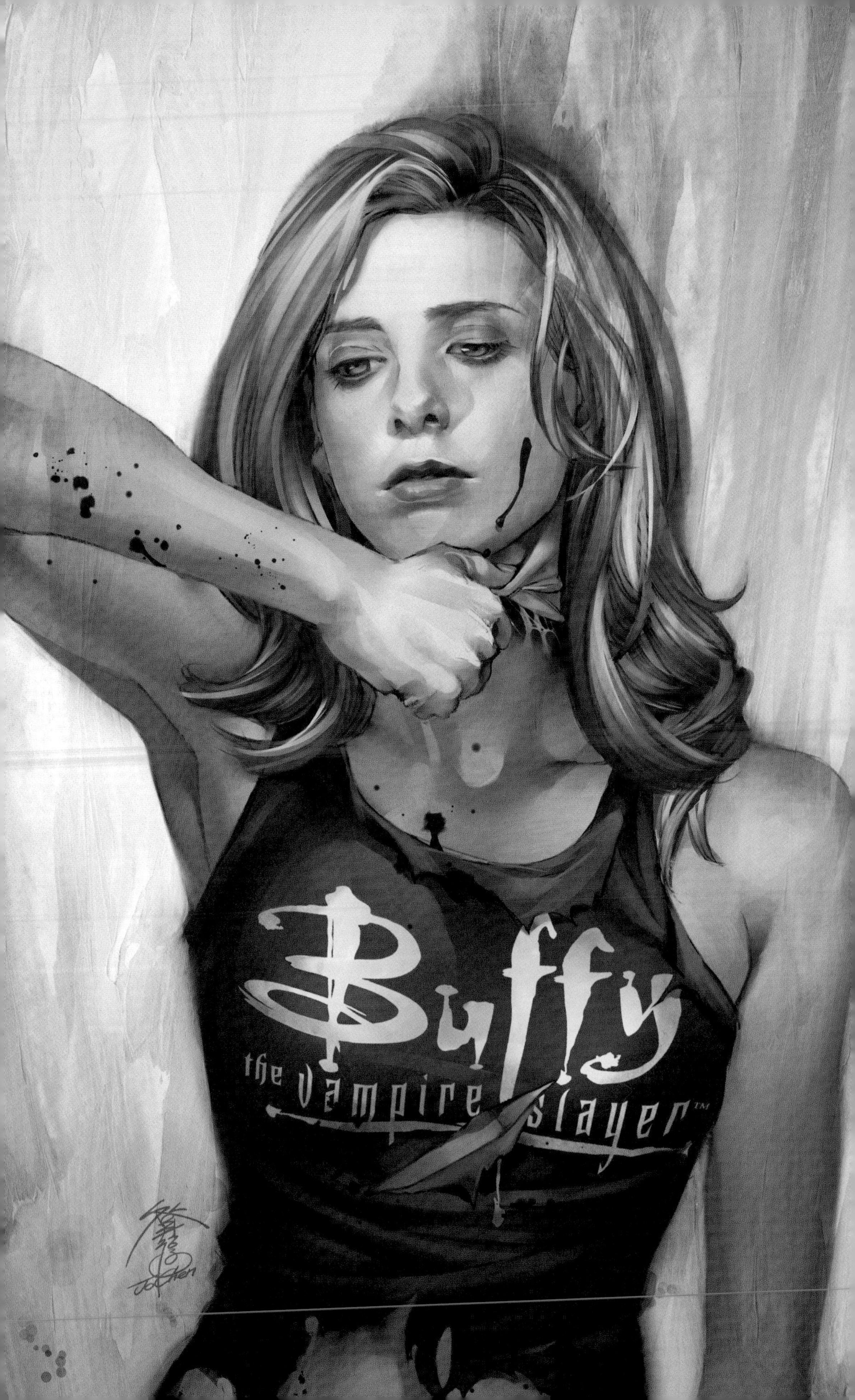
Buffy
the Vampire Slayer™

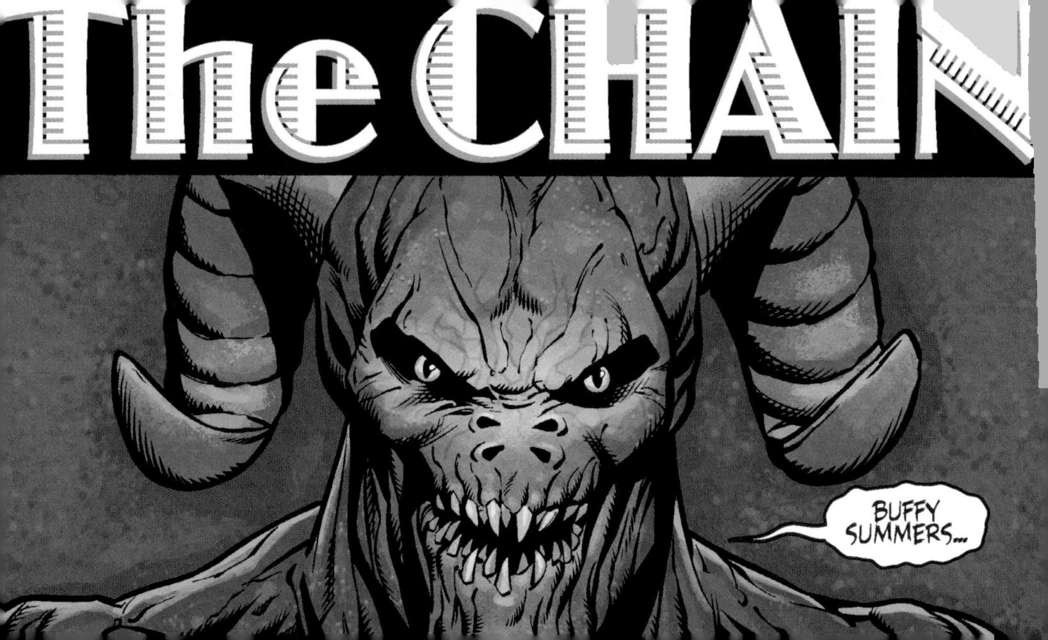
The CHAIN
BUFFY SUMMERS...

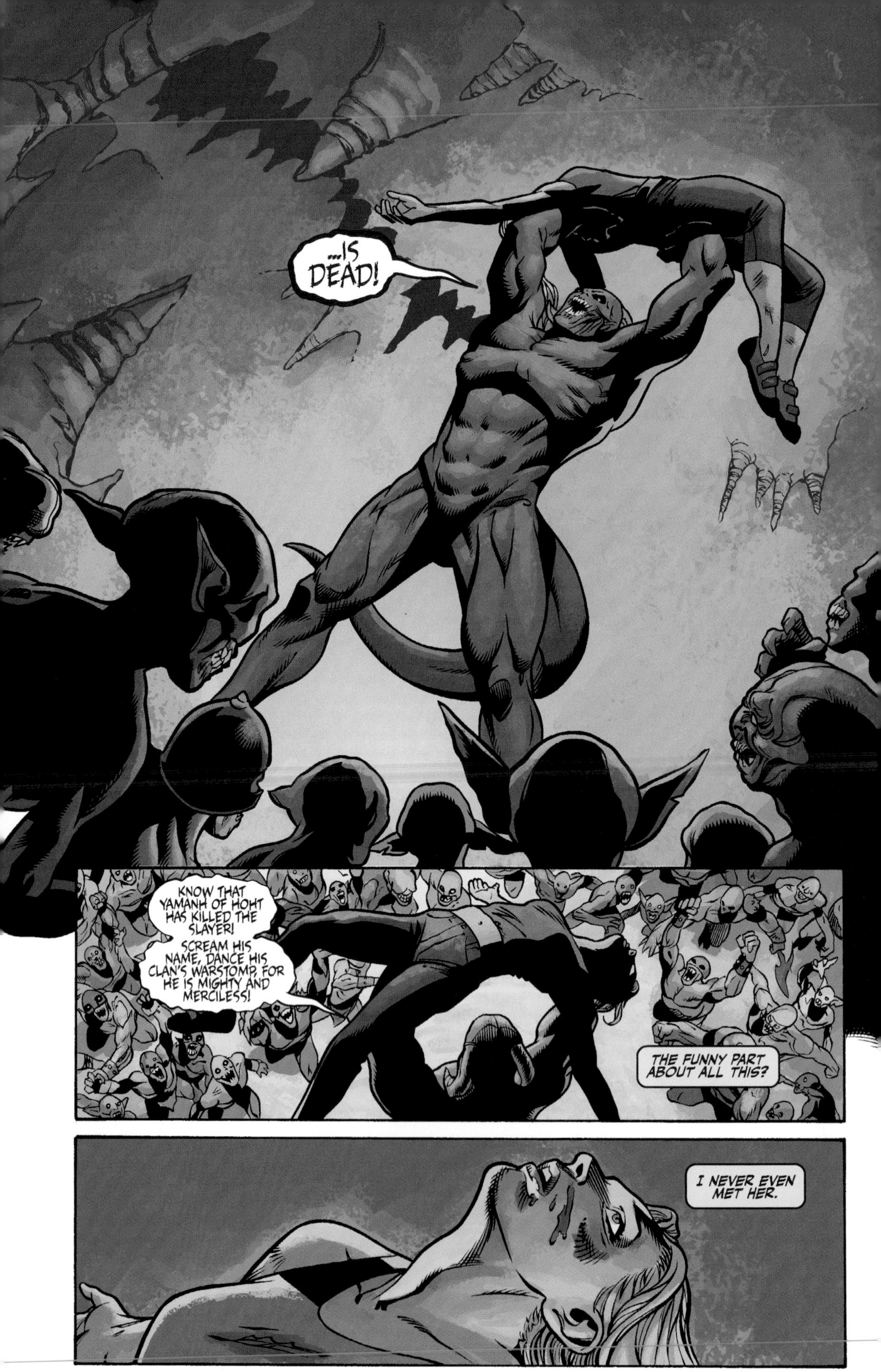
...IS DEAD!
KNOW THAT YAMANH OF HOHT HAS KILLED THE SLAYER!
SCREAM HIS NAME, DANCE HIS CLAN'S WARSTOMP, FOR HE IS MIGHTY AND MERCILESS!
THE FUNNY PART ABOUT ALL THIS?
I NEVER EVEN MET HER.

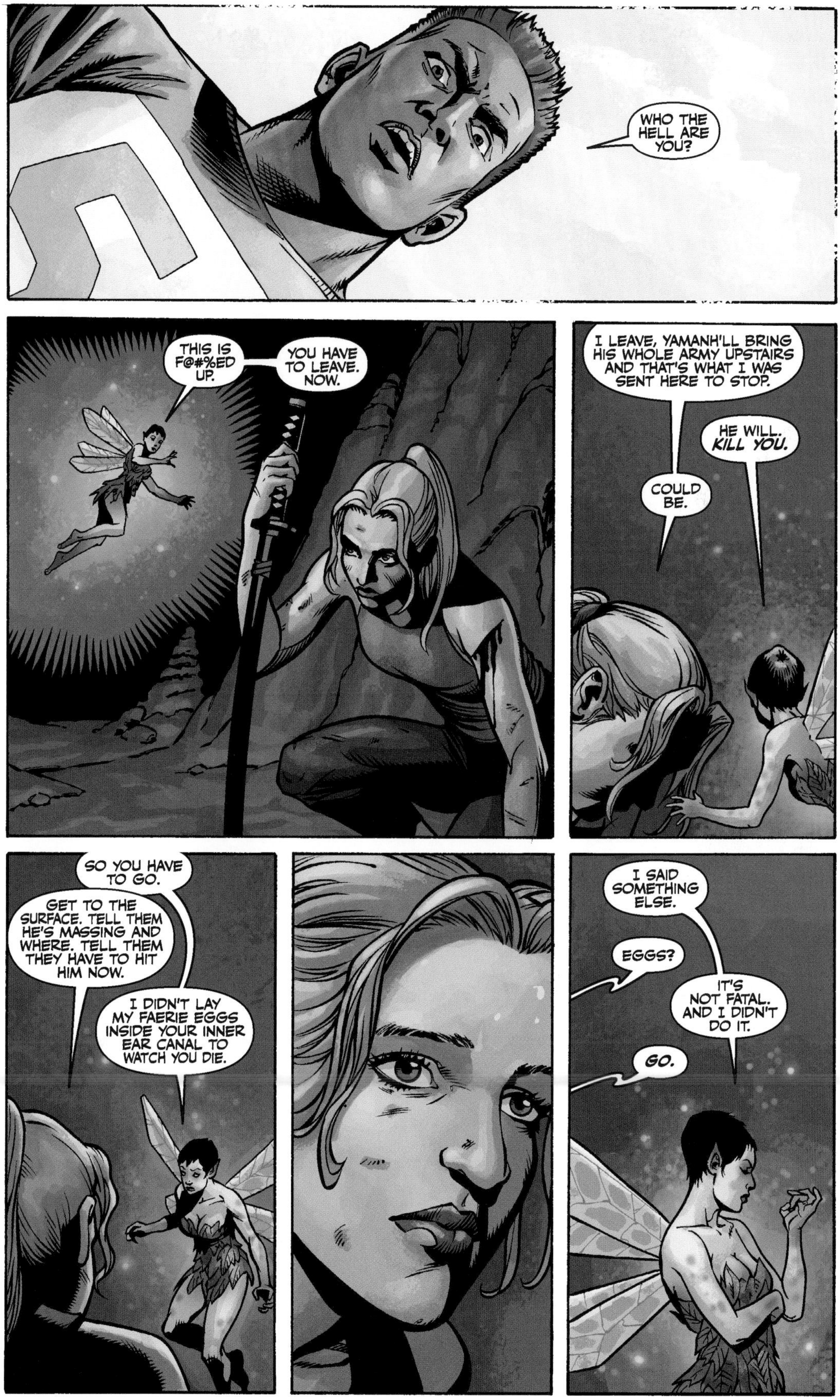
WHO THE HELL ARE YOU?
THIS IS F@#%ED UP.
YOU HAVE TO LEAVE. NOW.
I LEAVE, YAMANH'LL BRING HIS WHOLE ARMY UPSTAIRS AND THAT'S WHAT I WAS SENT HERE TO STOP.
HE WILL. KILL YOU.
COULD BE.
SO YOU HAVE TO GO.
GET TO THE SURFACE. TELL THEM HE'S MASSING AND WHERE. TELL THEM THEY HAVE TO HIT HIM NOW.
I DIDN'T LAY MY FAERIE EGGS INSIDE YOUR INNER EAR CANAL TO WATCH YOU DIE.
I SAID SOMETHING ELSE.
EGGS?
IT'S NOT FATAL. AND I DIDN'T DO IT.
GO.

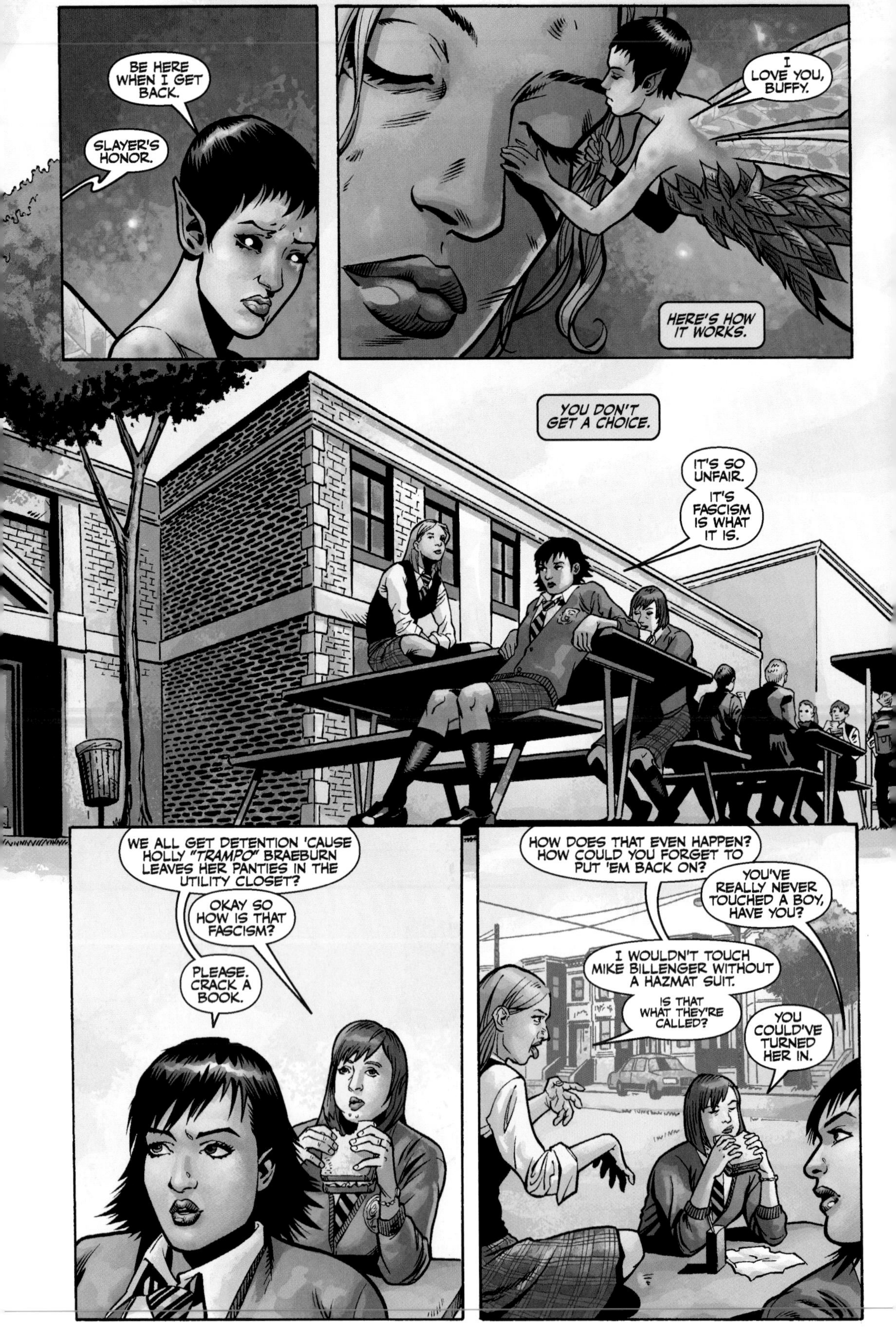
BE HERE WHEN I GET BACK.
SLAYER'S HONOR.
I LOVE YOU, BUFFY.
HERE'S HOW IT WORKS.
YOU DON'T GET A CHOICE.
IT'S SO UNFAIR.
IT'S FASCISM IS WHAT IT IS.
WE ALL GET DETENTION 'CAUSE HOLLY *"TRAMPO"* BRAEBURN LEAVES HER PANTIES IN THE UTILITY CLOSET?
OKAY SO HOW IS THAT FASCISM?
PLEASE. CRACK A BOOK.
HOW DOES THAT EVEN HAPPEN? HOW COULD YOU FORGET TO PUT 'EM BACK ON?
YOU'VE REALLY NEVER TOUCHED A BOY, HAVE YOU?
I WOULDN'T TOUCH MIKE BILLENGER WITHOUT A HAZMAT SUIT.
IS THAT WHAT THEY'RE CALLED?
YOU COULD'VE TURNED HER IN.

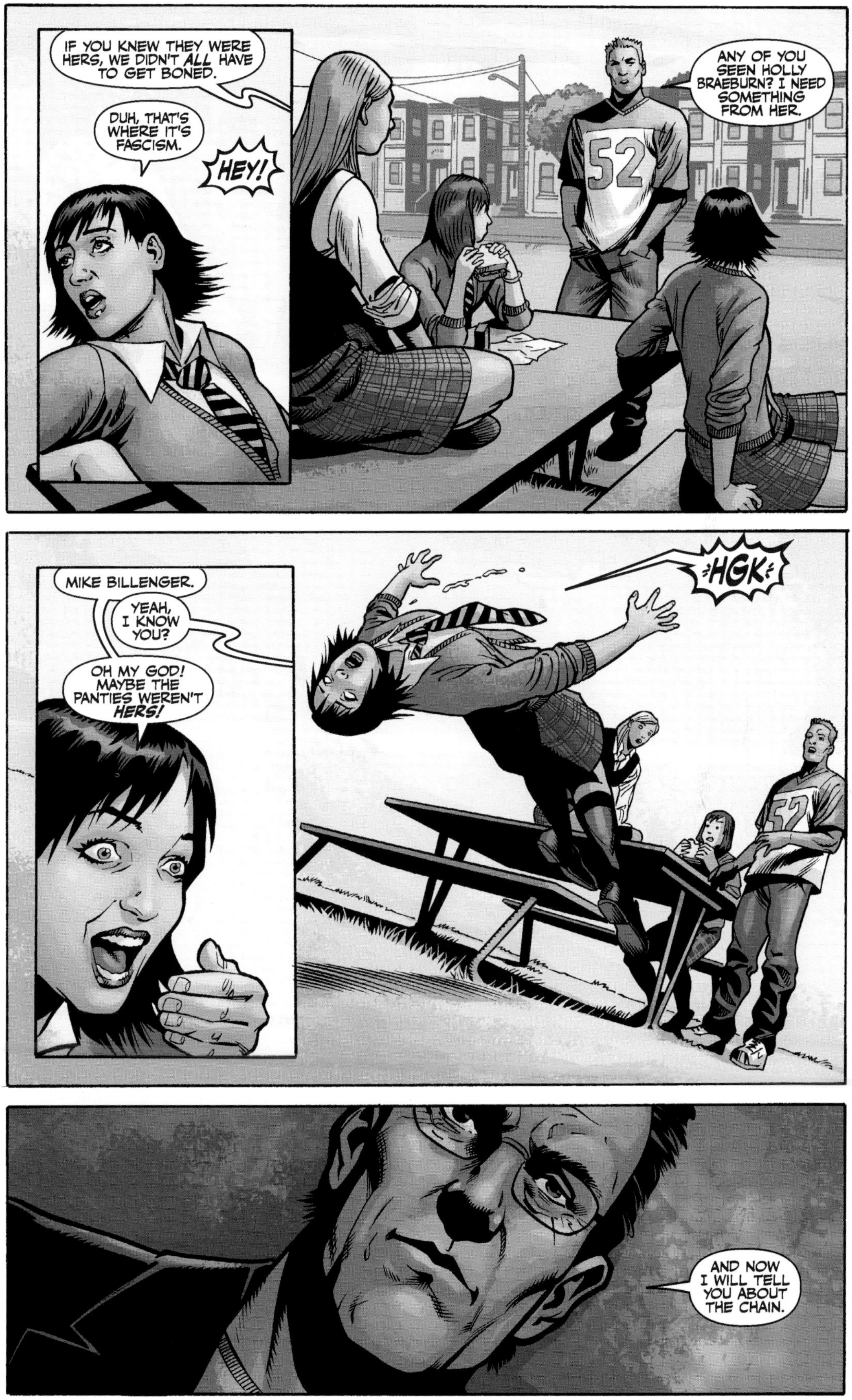
IF YOU KNEW THEY WERE HERS, WE DIDN'T *ALL* HAVE TO GET BONED.
DUH, THAT'S WHERE IT'S FASCISM.
HEY!
ANY OF YOU SEEN HOLLY BRAEBURN? I NEED SOMETHING FROM HER.
52
MIKE BILLENGER.
YEAH, I KNOW YOU?
OH MY GOD! MAYBE THE PANTIES WEREN'T *HERS!*
HGK
AND NOW I WILL TELL YOU ABOUT THE CHAIN.

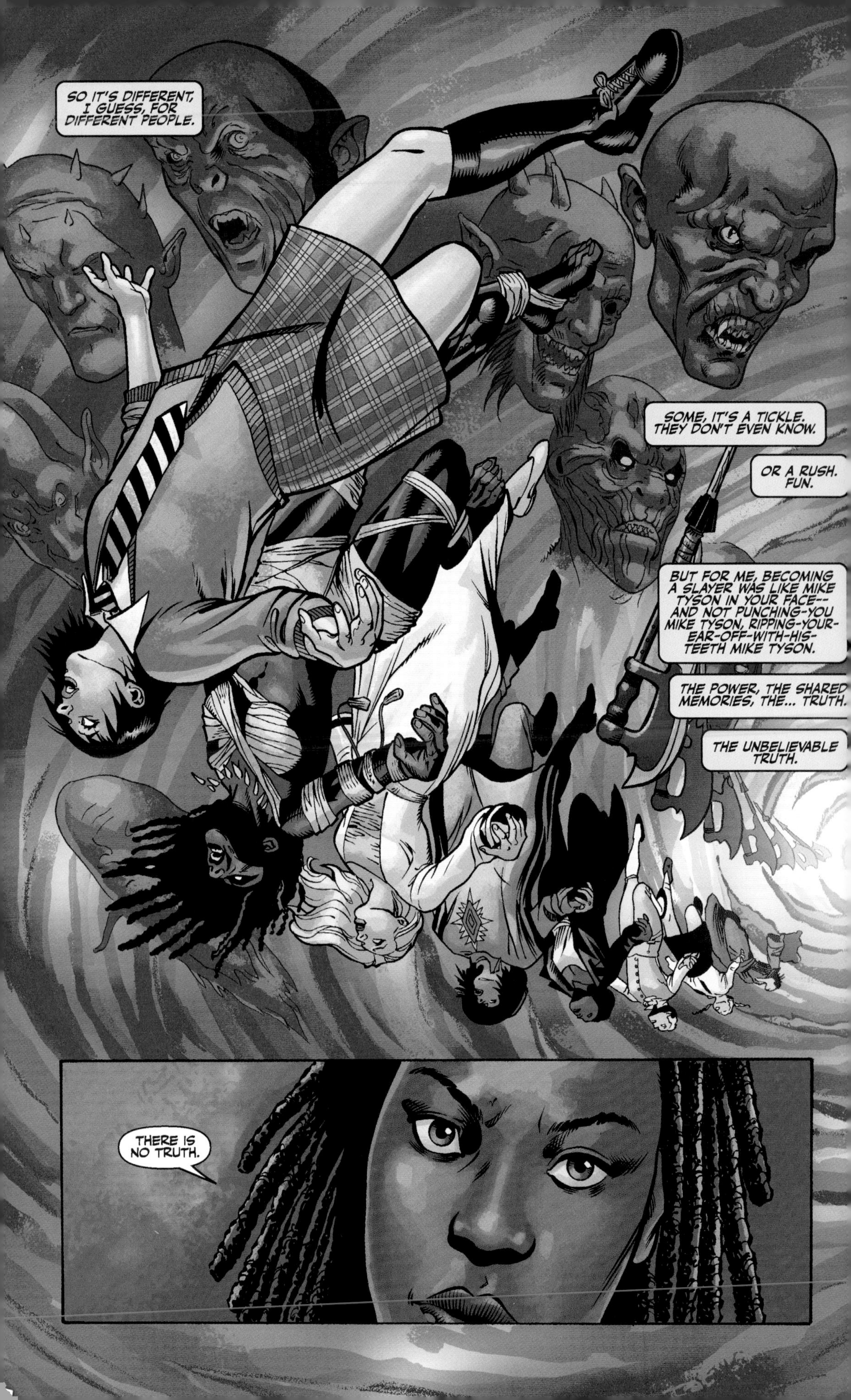
SO IT'S DIFFERENT, I GUESS, FOR DIFFERENT PEOPLE.
SOME, IT'S A TICKLE. THEY DON'T EVEN KNOW.
OR A RUSH. FUN.
BUT FOR ME, BECOMING A SLAYER WAS LIKE MIKE TYSON IN YOUR FACE-- AND NOT PUNCHING-YOU MIKE TYSON, RIPPING-YOUR-EAR-OFF-WITH-HIS-TEETH MIKE TYSON.
THE POWER, THE SHARED MEMORIES, THE... TRUTH.
THE UNBELIEVABLE TRUTH.
THERE IS NO TRUTH.

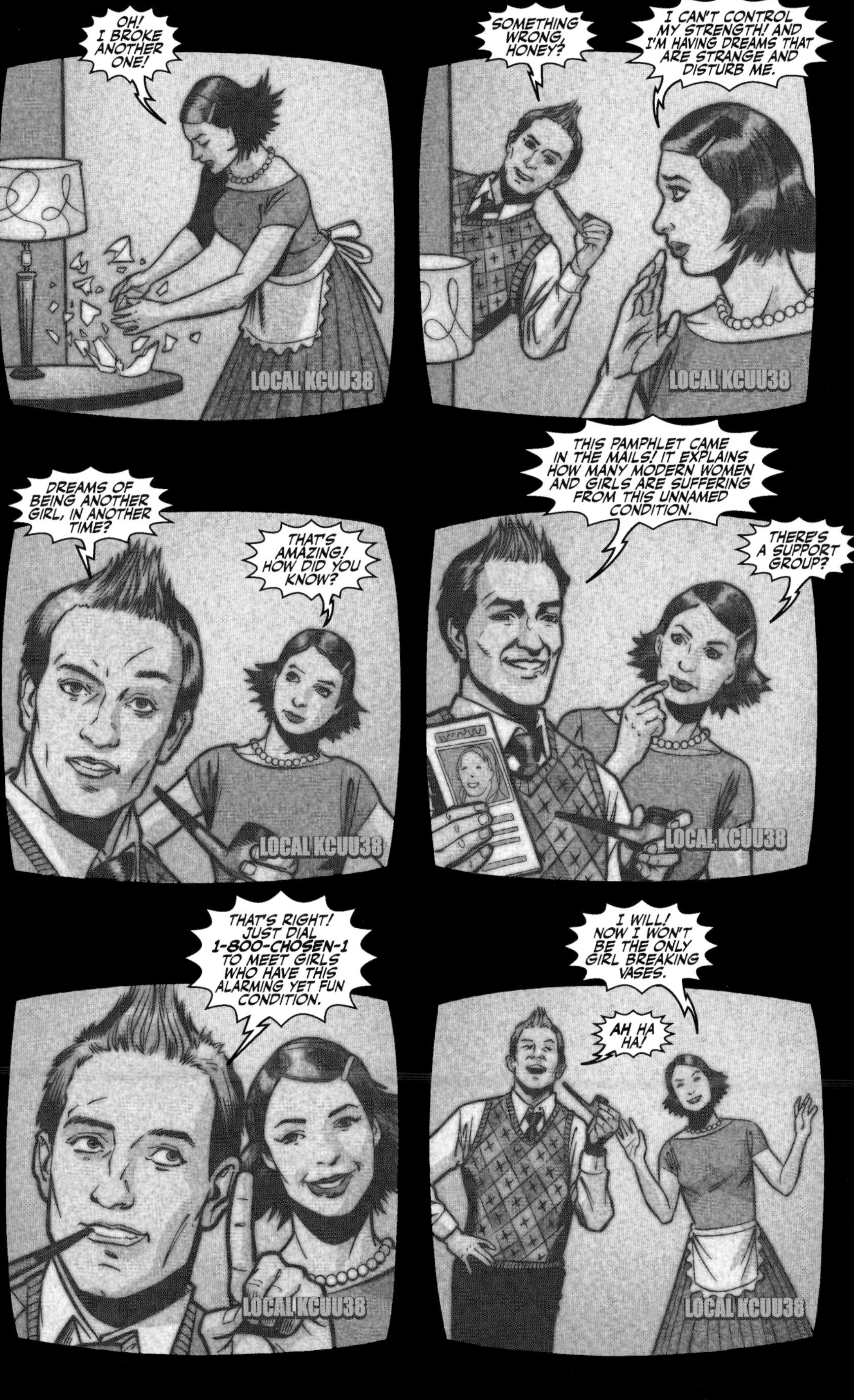
OH! I BROKE ANOTHER ONE!
LOCAL KCUU38
SOMETHING WRONG, HONEY?
I CAN'T CONTROL MY STRENGTH! AND I'M HAVING DREAMS THAT ARE STRANGE AND DISTURB ME.
LOCAL KCUU38
DREAMS OF BEING ANOTHER GIRL, IN ANOTHER TIME?
THAT'S AMAZING! HOW DID YOU KNOW?
LOCAL KCUU38
THIS PAMPHLET CAME IN THE MAILS! IT EXPLAINS HOW MANY MODERN WOMEN AND GIRLS ARE SUFFERING FROM THIS UNNAMED CONDITION.
THERE'S A SUPPORT GROUP?
LOCAL KCUU38
THAT'S RIGHT! JUST DIAL 1-800-CHOSEN-1 TO MEET GIRLS WHO HAVE THIS ALARMING YET FUN CONDITION.
LOCAL KCUU38
I WILL! NOW I WON'T BE THE ONLY GIRL BREAKING VASES.
AH HA HA!
LOCAL KCUU38

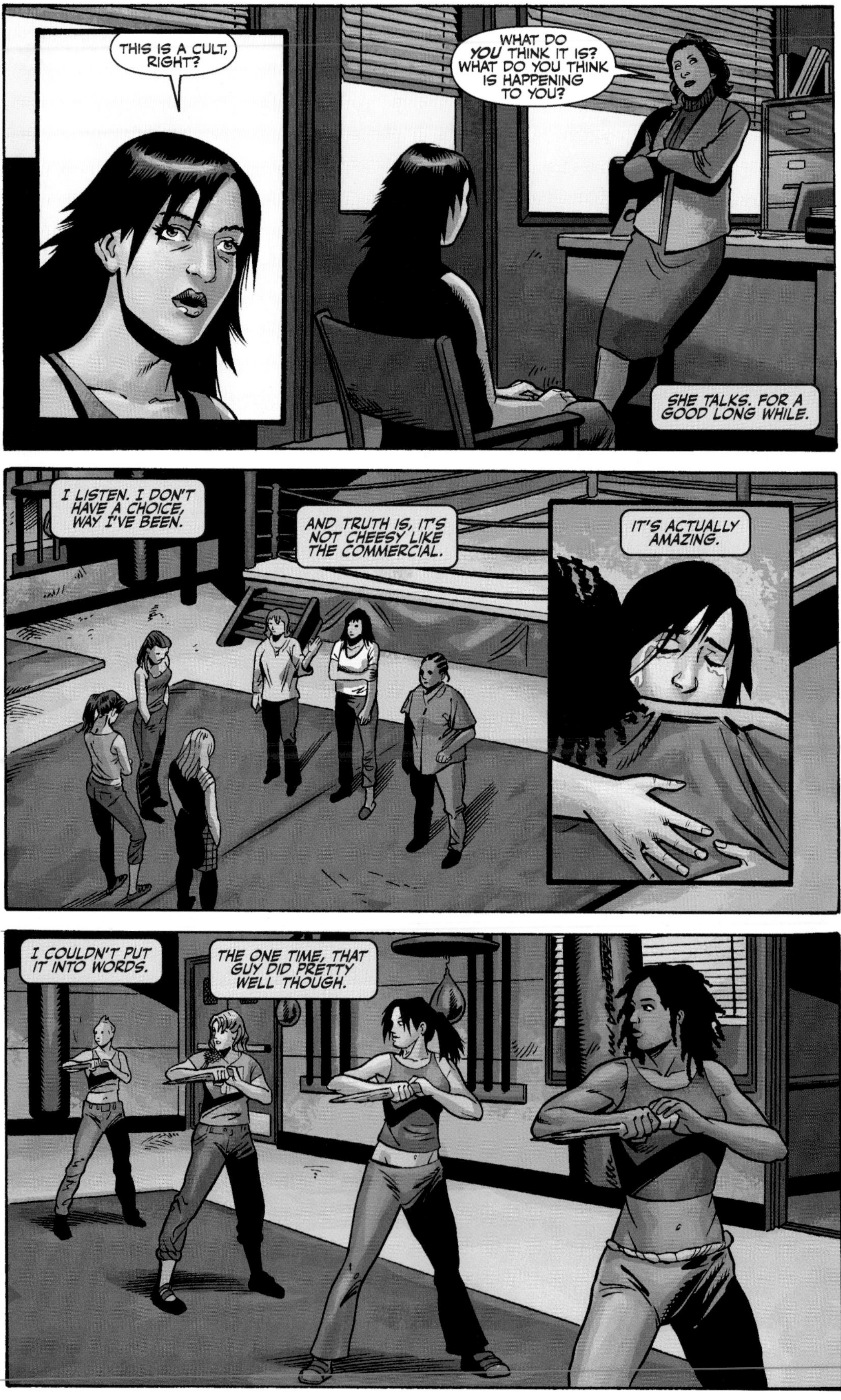

THIS IS A CULT, RIGHT?
WHAT DO *YOU* THINK IT IS? WHAT DO YOU THINK IS HAPPENING TO YOU?
SHE TALKS. FOR A GOOD LONG WHILE.
I LISTEN. I DON'T HAVE A CHOICE, WAY I'VE BEEN.
AND TRUTH IS, IT'S NOT CHEESY LIKE THE COMMERCIAL.
IT'S ACTUALLY AMAZING.
I COULDN'T PUT IT INTO WORDS.
THE ONE TIME, THAT GUY DID PRETTY WELL THOUGH.

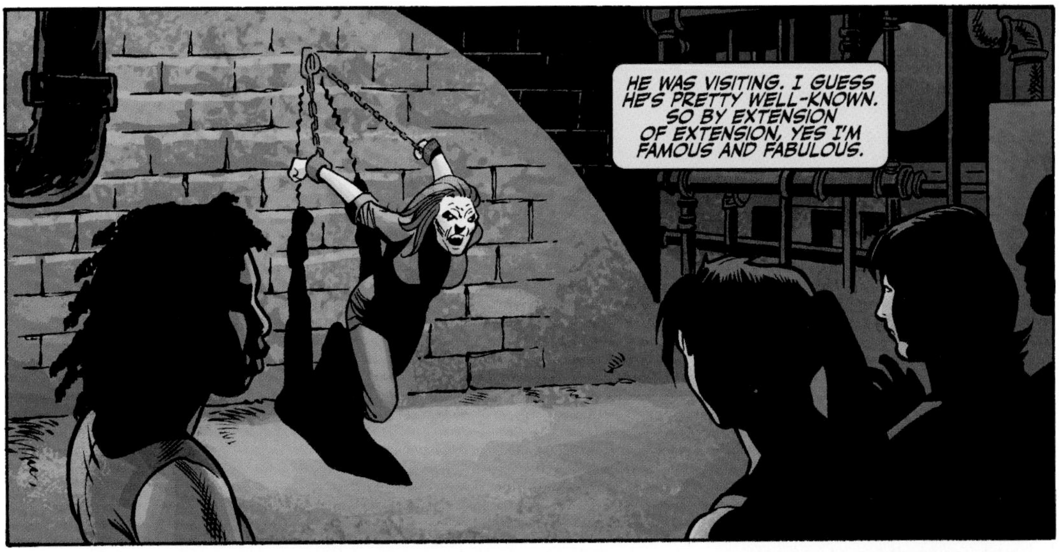
HE WAS VISITING. I GUESS HE'S PRETTY WELL-KNOWN. SO BY EXTENSION OF EXTENSION, YES I'M FAMOUS AND FABULOUS.

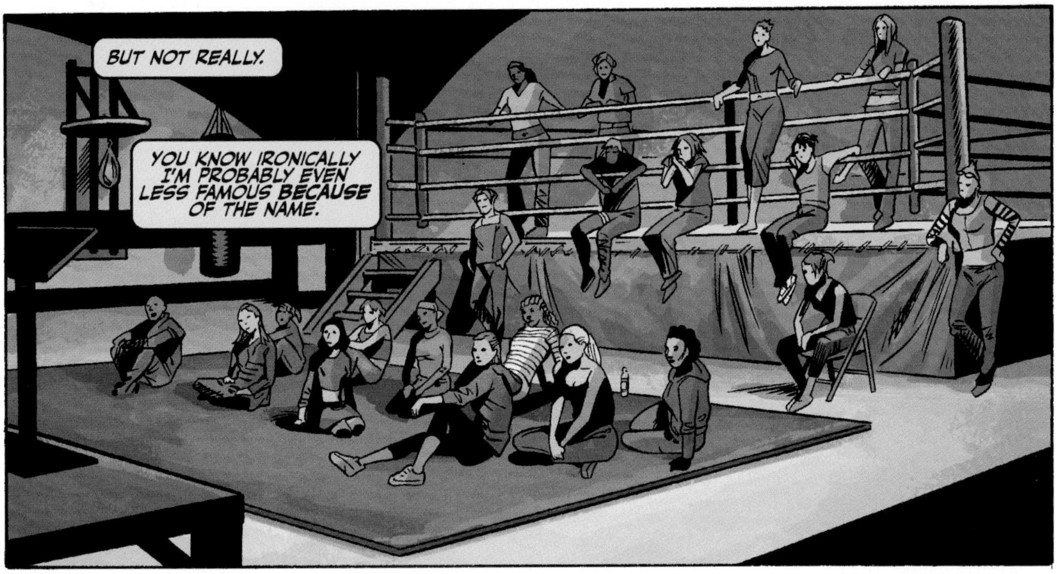
BUT NOT REALLY.
YOU KNOW IRONICALLY I'M PROBABLY EVEN LESS FAMOUS BECAUSE OF THE NAME.

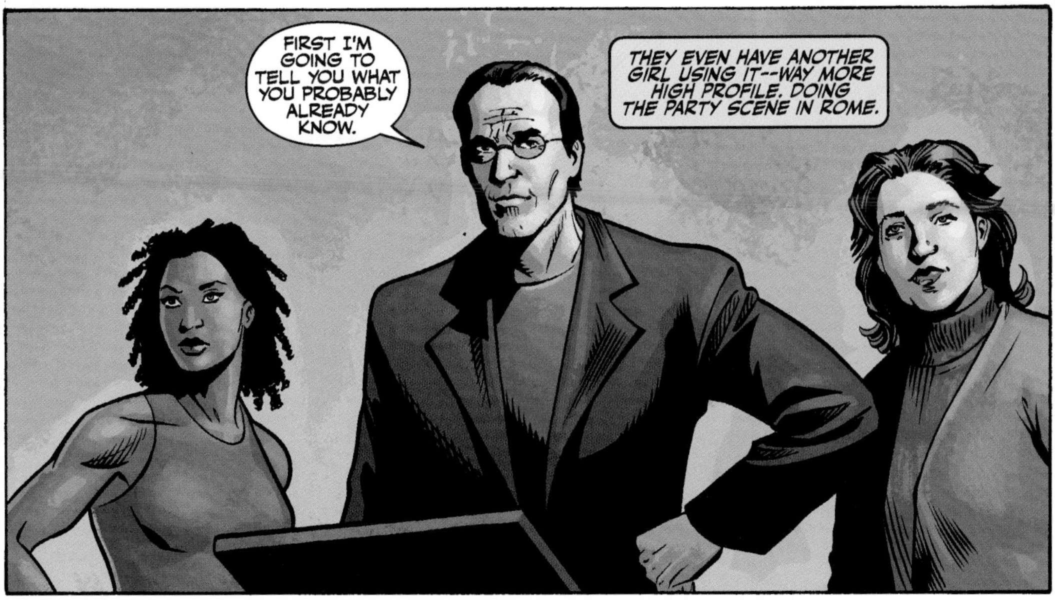
FIRST I'M GOING TO TELL YOU WHAT YOU PROBABLY ALREADY KNOW.
THEY EVEN HAVE ANOTHER GIRL USING IT--WAY MORE HIGH PROFILE. DOING THE PARTY SCENE IN ROME.

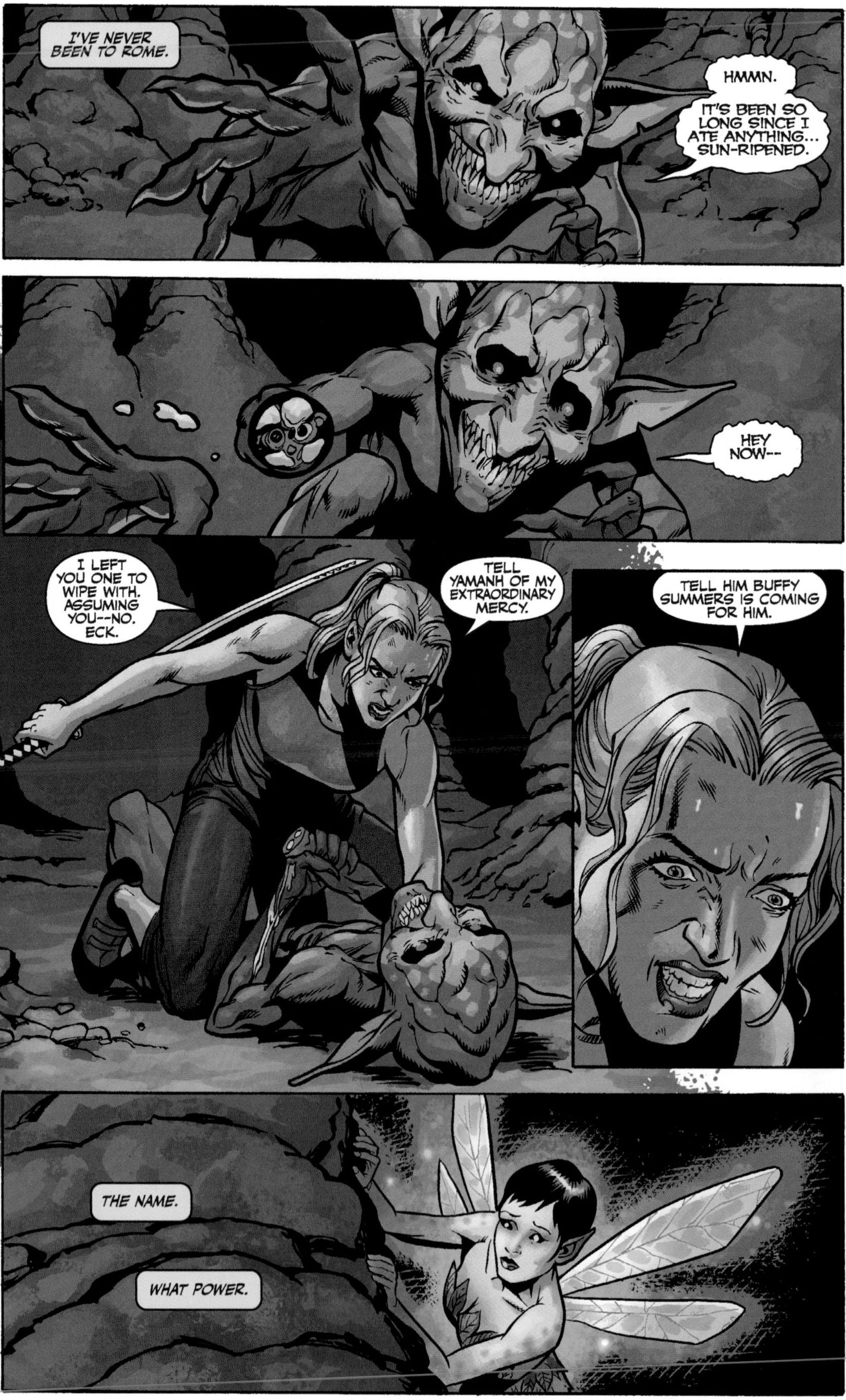
I'VE NEVER BEEN TO ROME.
HMMN.
IT'S BEEN SO LONG SINCE I ATE ANYTHING... SUN-RIPENED.
HEY NOW--
I LEFT YOU ONE TO WIPE WITH. ASSUMING YOU--NO. ECK.
TELL YAMANH OF MY EXTRAORDINARY MERCY.
TELL HIM BUFFY SUMMERS IS COMING FOR HIM.
THE NAME.
WHAT POWER.

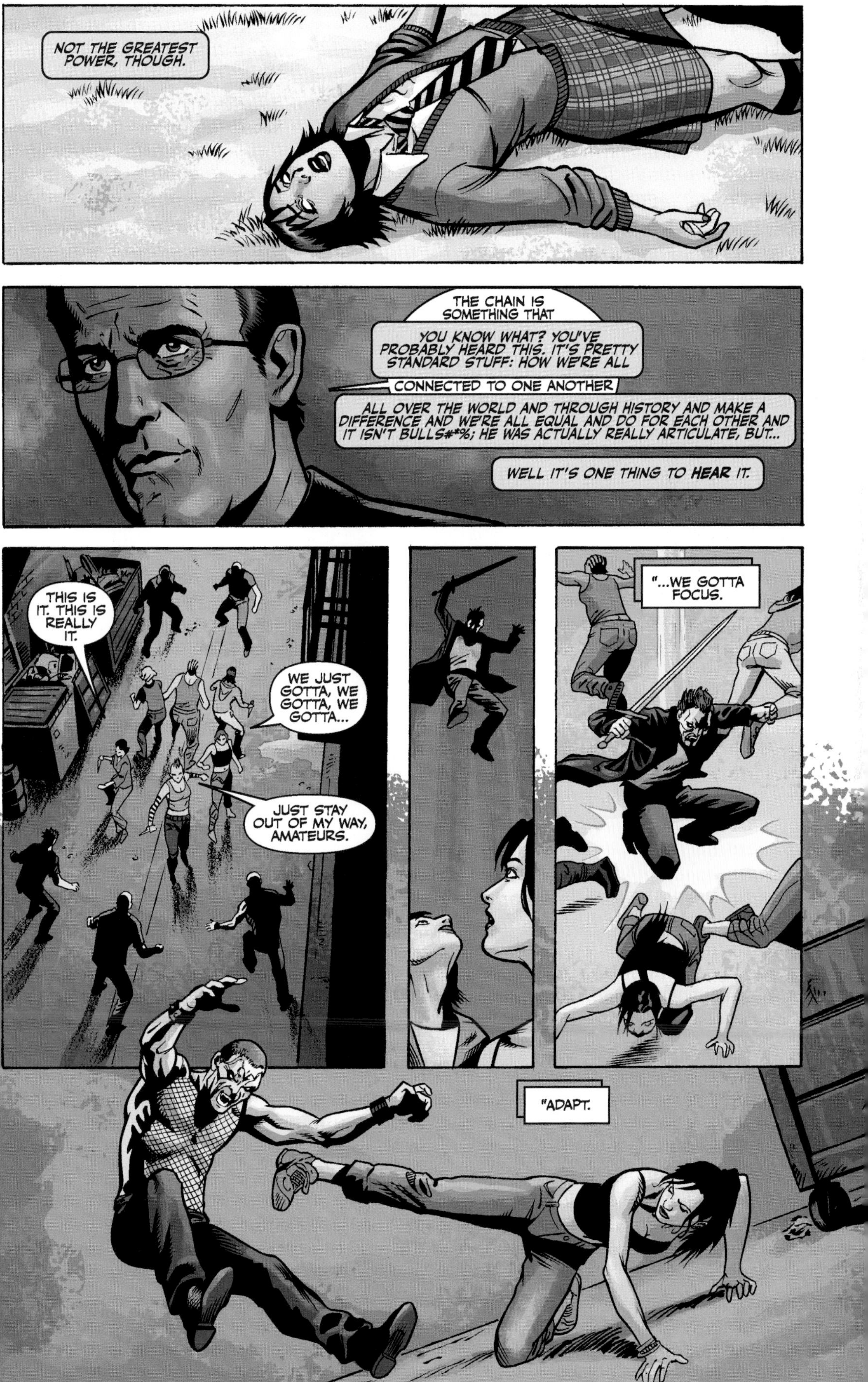
NOT THE GREATEST POWER, THOUGH.
THE CHAIN IS SOMETHING THAT
YOU KNOW WHAT? YOU'VE PROBABLY HEARD THIS. IT'S PRETTY STANDARD STUFF: HOW WE'RE ALL
CONNECTED TO ONE ANOTHER
ALL OVER THE WORLD AND THROUGH HISTORY AND MAKE A DIFFERENCE AND WE'RE ALL EQUAL AND DO FOR EACH OTHER AND IT ISN'T BULLS#*%; HE WAS ACTUALLY REALLY ARTICULATE, BUT...
WELL IT'S ONE THING TO HEAR IT.
THIS IS IT. THIS IS REALLY IT.
WE JUST GOTTA, WE GOTTA, WE GOTTA...
JUST STAY OUT OF MY WAY, AMATEURS.
"...WE GOTTA FOCUS.
"ADAPT.

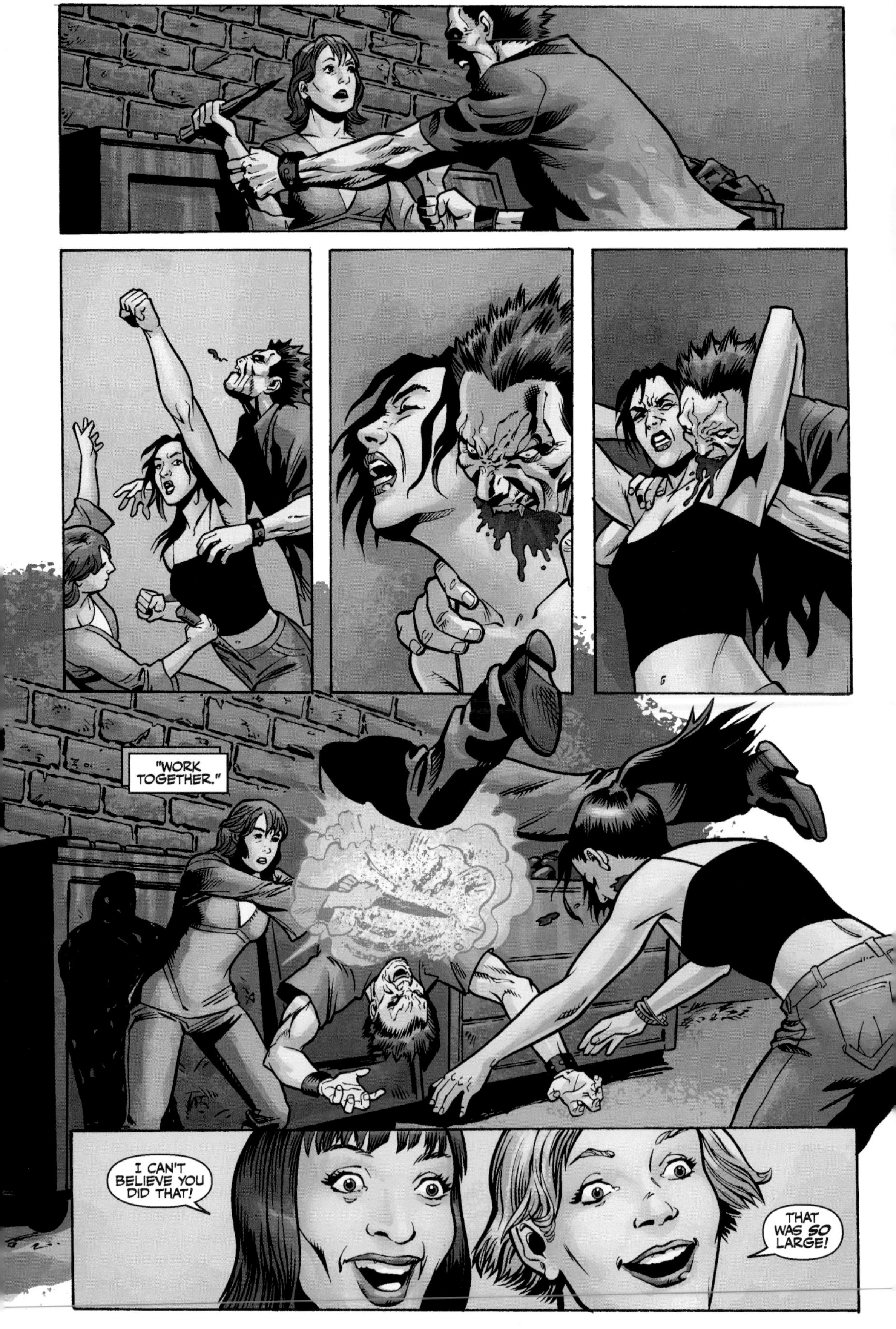
"WORK TOGETHER."
I CAN'T BELIEVE YOU DID THAT!
THAT WAS SO LARGE!

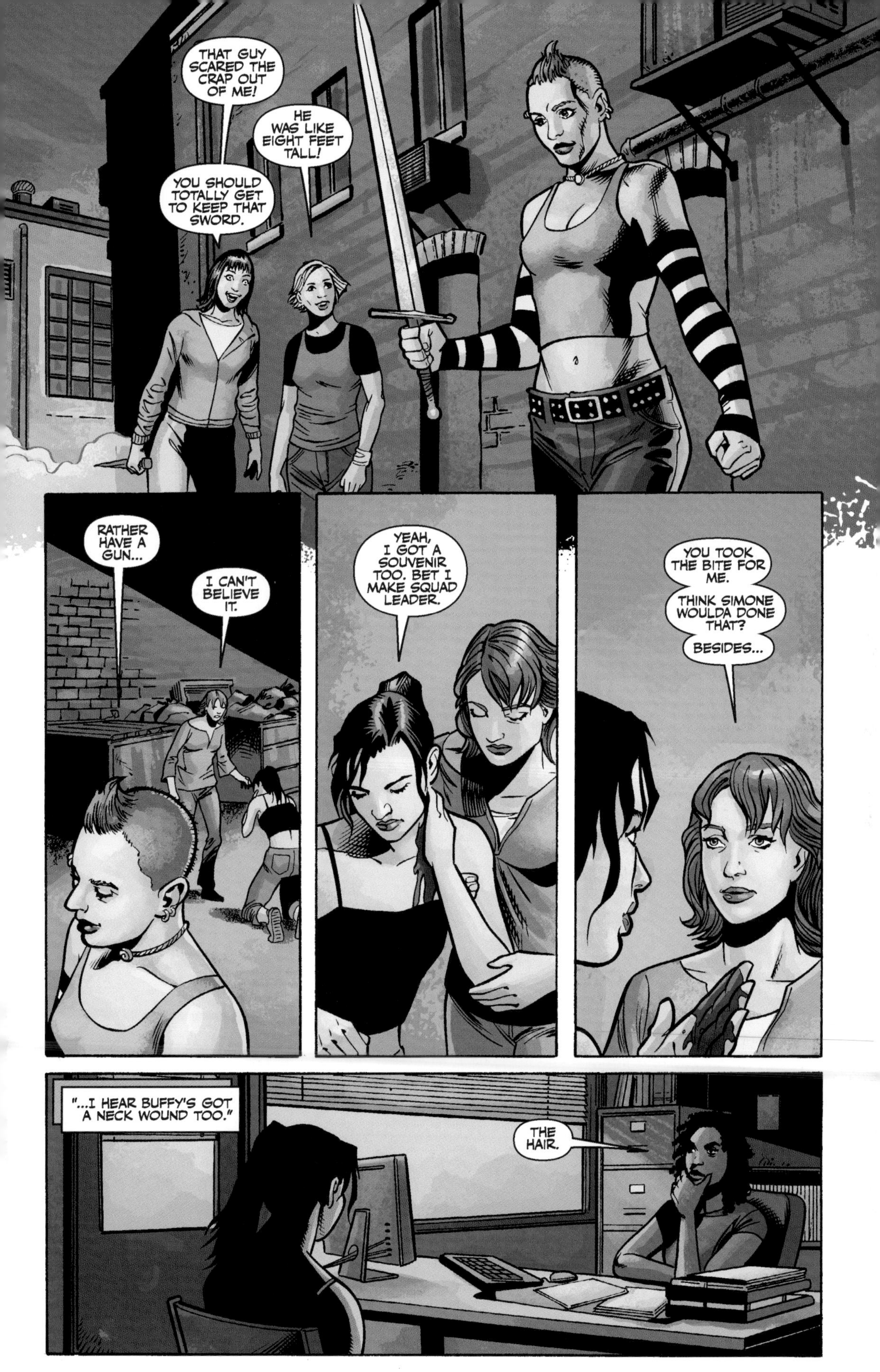
THAT GUY SCARED THE CRAP OUT OF ME!
HE WAS LIKE EIGHT FEET TALL!
YOU SHOULD TOTALLY GET TO KEEP THAT SWORD.
RATHER HAVE A GUN...
I CAN'T BELIEVE IT.
YEAH, I GOT A SOUVENIR TOO. BET I MAKE SQUAD LEADER.
YOU TOOK THE BITE FOR ME.
THINK SIMONE WOULDA DONE THAT?
BESIDES...
"...I HEAR BUFFY'S GOT A NECK WOUND TOO."
THE HAIR.

NEED A SERIOUS DYE JOB, AND YOU'D HAVE TO MAINTAIN IT YOURSELF.

BODY TYPE, HEIGHT ARE GOOD... HAVE TO PAD THE BRA A LITTLE, BUT... WE'RE COUNTING ON THESE GUYS NEVER TO HAVE ACTUALLY SEEN HER.

YOU GET WHAT ALL THIS IS?

YOU WANT ME TO BE BUFFY.

SOUNDS A LOT MORE GLAM THAN IT IS. WE'D BE SENDING YOU UNDERGROUND. UNDER ACTUAL GROUND.

NO ONE UP HERE CAN KNOW YOU'RE HER, NO ONE DOWN THERE CAN KNOW YOU'RE NOT.

IT'S DEEP COVER AND IT'S UNBELIEVABLY DANGEROUS. WE KNOW NEXT TO NOTHING ABOUT THE UNDER-COMMUNITY, EXCEPT THEY'RE STRONG AND THEY MIGHT BE HEADED UP. YAMANH'S THE NAME DOWN THERE.

IF YOU KNOW HIS NAME...

... THEN HE PROBABLY KNOWS HERS, SO YEAH, A DECOY MIGHT KEEP HIM OCCUPIED, MIGHT DO SOME INTERNAL DAMAGE.

I'M LOOKIN' AT YOU FOR THIS SO I GOTTA FIGURE YOU WANT THE TRUTH.

AS IN...

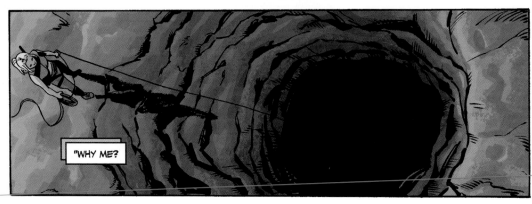

"WHY ME?

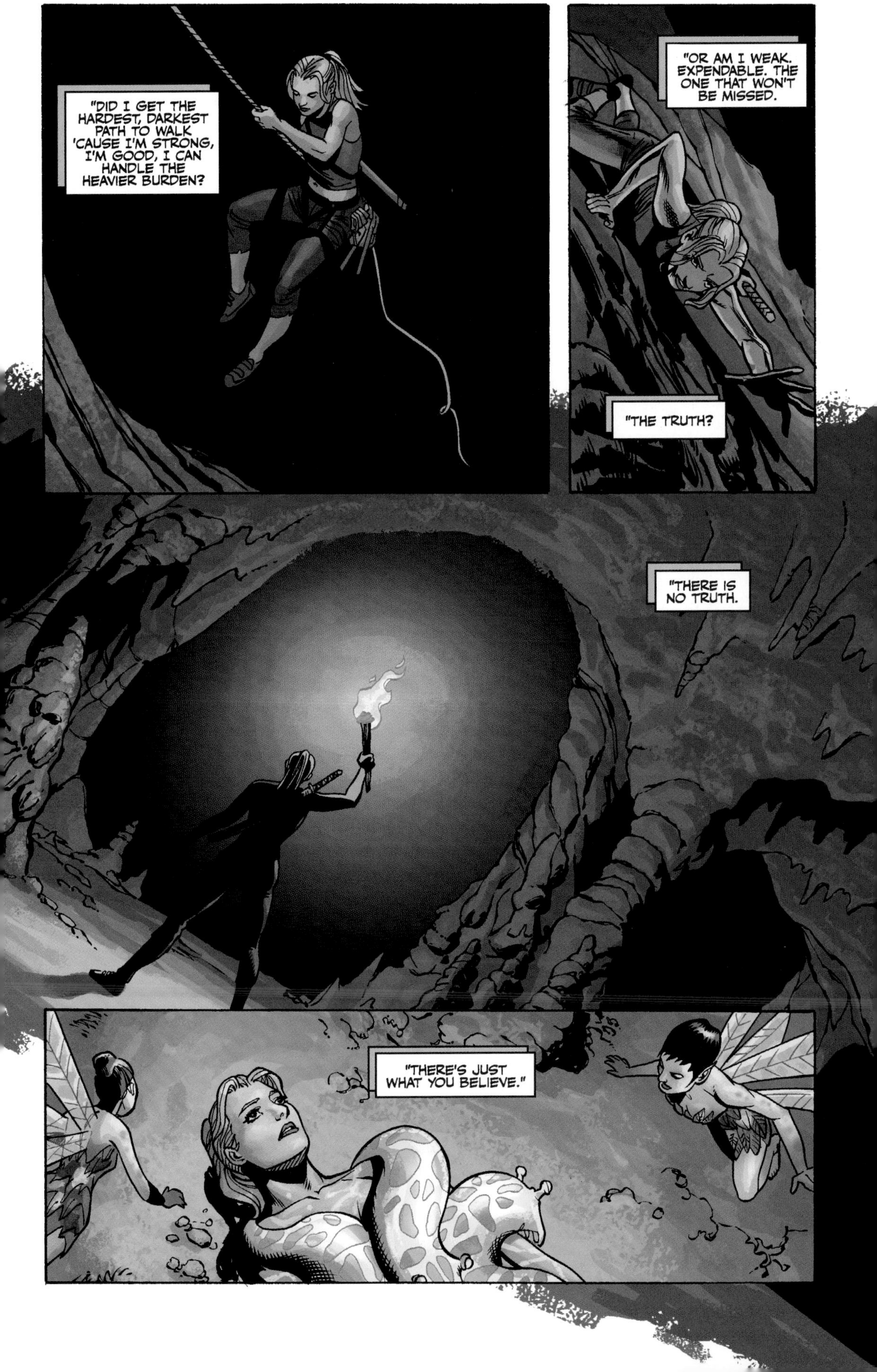
"DID I GET THE HARDEST, DARKEST PATH TO WALK 'CAUSE I'M STRONG, I'M GOOD, I CAN HANDLE THE HEAVIER BURDEN?
"OR AM I WEAK. EXPENDABLE. THE ONE THAT WON'T BE MISSED.
"THE TRUTH?
"THERE IS NO TRUTH.
"THERE'S JUST WHAT YOU BELIEVE."

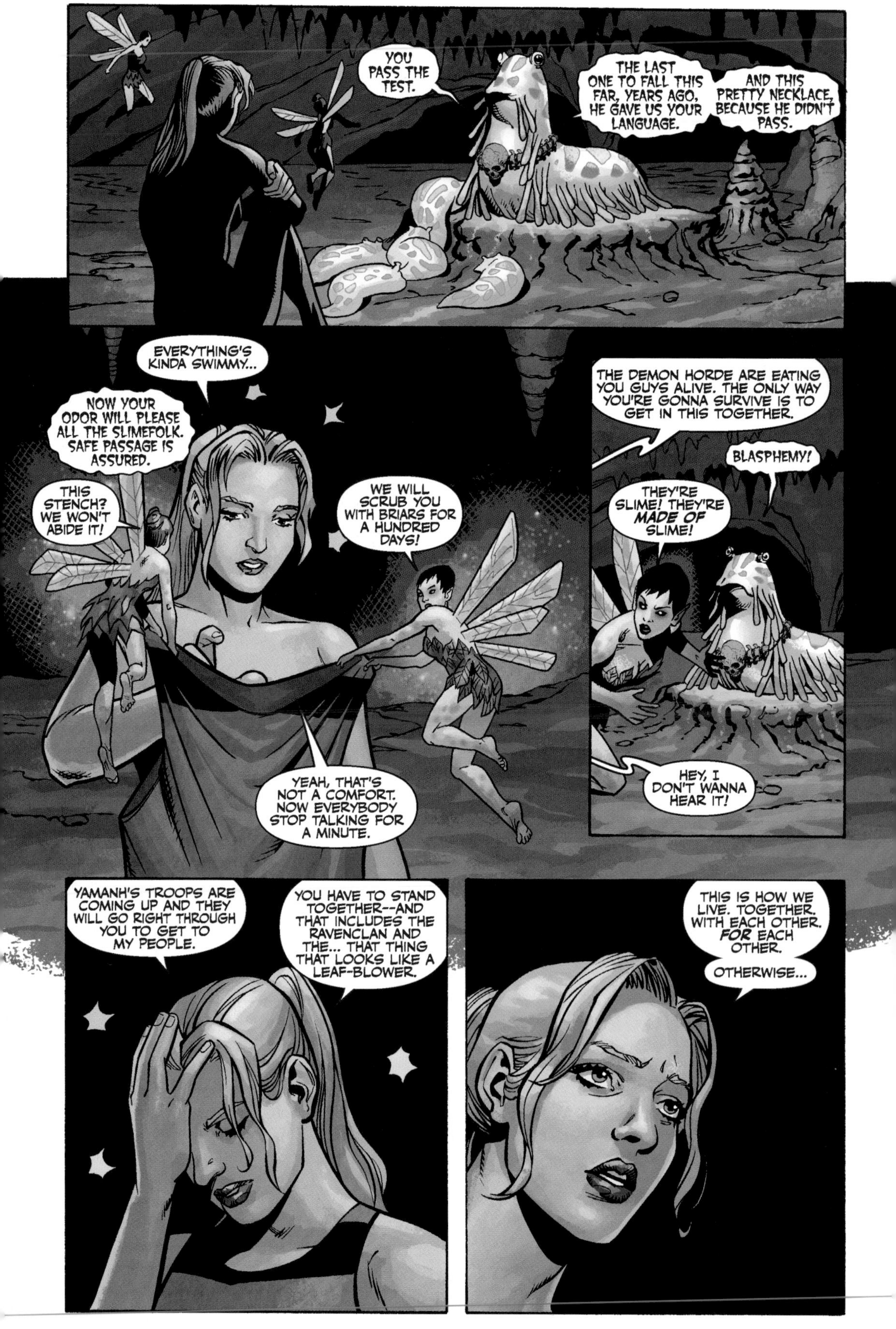
YOU PASS THE TEST.
THE LAST ONE TO FALL THIS FAR, YEARS AGO, HE GAVE US YOUR LANGUAGE.
AND THIS PRETTY NECKLACE, BECAUSE HE DIDN'T PASS.
EVERYTHING'S KINDA SWIMMY...
NOW YOUR ODOR WILL PLEASE ALL THE SLIMEFOLK. SAFE PASSAGE IS ASSURED.
THIS STENCH? WE WON'T ABIDE IT!
WE WILL SCRUB YOU WITH BRIARS FOR A HUNDRED DAYS!
YEAH, THAT'S NOT A COMFORT. NOW EVERYBODY STOP TALKING FOR A MINUTE.
THE DEMON HORDE ARE EATING YOU GUYS ALIVE. THE ONLY WAY YOU'RE GONNA SURVIVE IS TO GET IN THIS TOGETHER.
BLASPHEMY!
THEY'RE SLIME! THEY'RE MADE OF SLIME!
HEY, I DON'T WANNA HEAR IT!
YAMANH'S TROOPS ARE COMING UP AND THEY WILL GO RIGHT THROUGH YOU TO GET TO MY PEOPLE.
YOU HAVE TO STAND TOGETHER--AND THAT INCLUDES THE RAVENCLAN AND THE... THAT THING THAT LOOKS LIKE A LEAF-BLOWER.
THIS IS HOW WE LIVE. TOGETHER. WITH EACH OTHER. FOR EACH OTHER.
OTHERWISE...

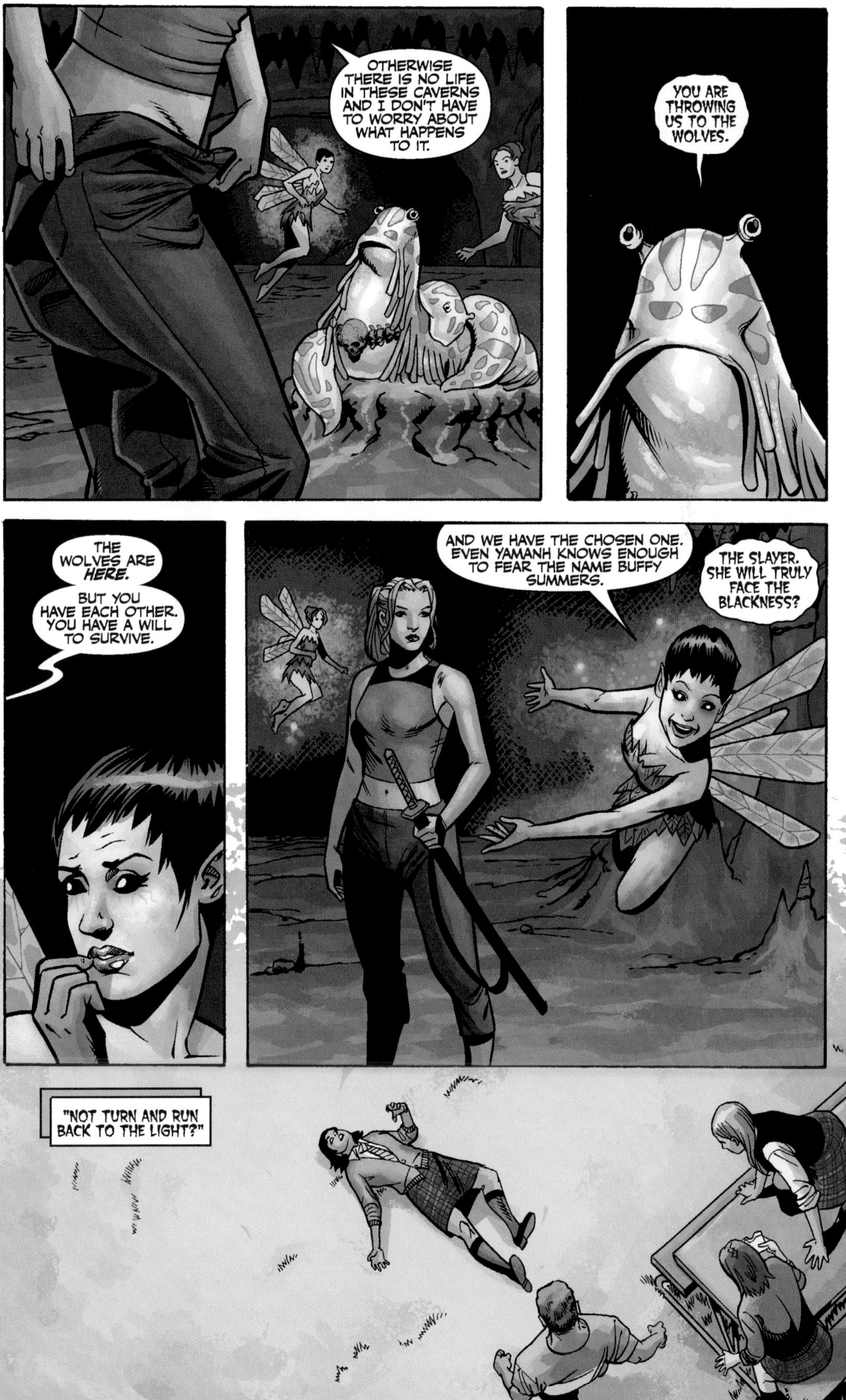
OTHERWISE THERE IS NO LIFE IN THESE CAVERNS AND I DON'T HAVE TO WORRY ABOUT WHAT HAPPENS TO IT.
YOU ARE THROWING US TO THE WOLVES.
THE WOLVES ARE HERE.
BUT YOU HAVE EACH OTHER. YOU HAVE A WILL TO SURVIVE.
AND WE HAVE THE CHOSEN ONE. EVEN YAMANH KNOWS ENOUGH TO FEAR THE NAME BUFFY SUMMERS.
THE SLAYER. SHE WILL TRULY FACE THE BLACKNESS?
"NOT TURN AND RUN BACK TO THE LIGHT?"

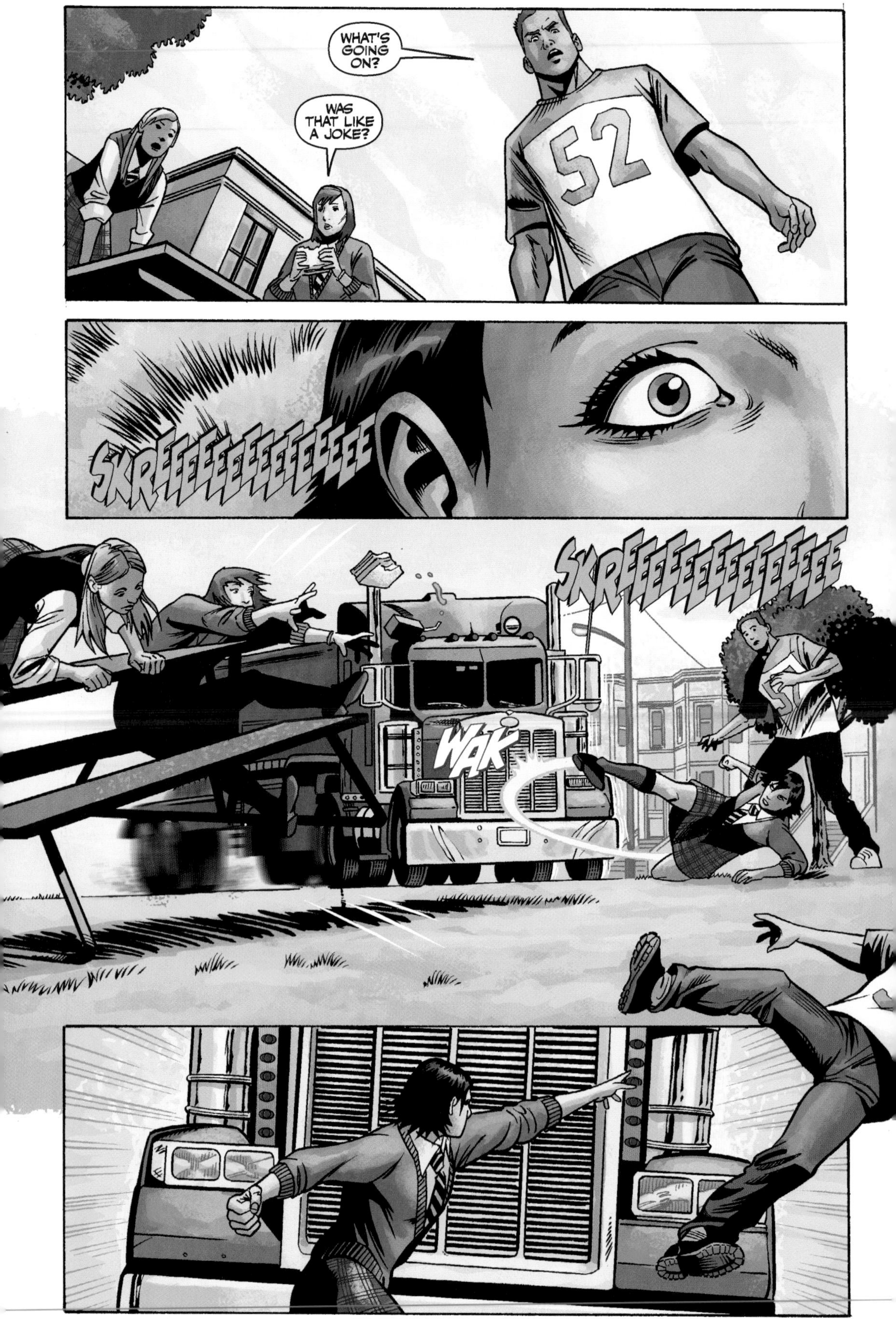
WHAT'S GOING ON?
WAS THAT LIKE A JOKE?
SKREEEEEEEEEEEEEE
SKREEEEEEEEEEEEEE
WAK

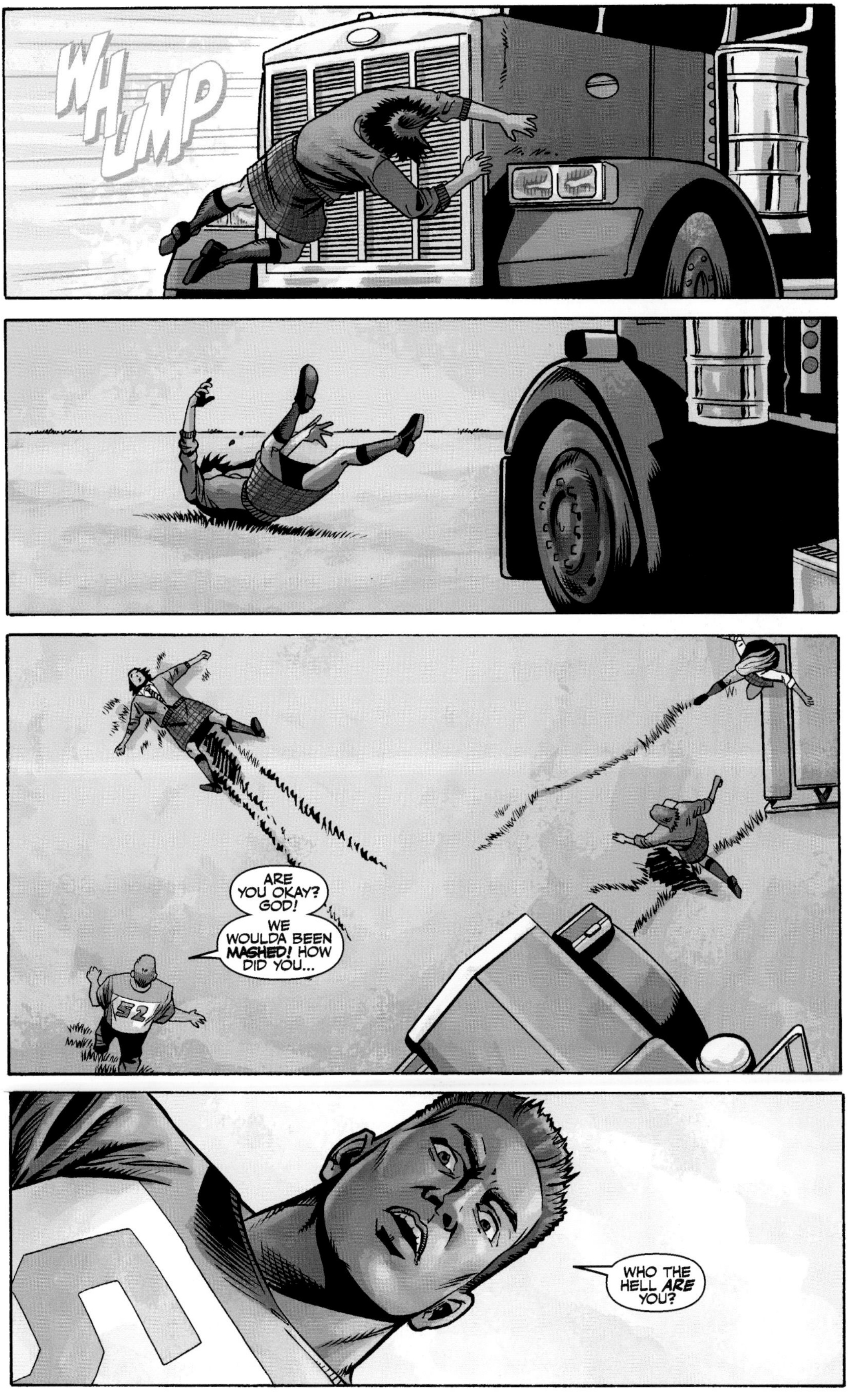
WHUMP
ARE YOU OKAY? GOD!
WE WOULDA BEEN MASHED! HOW DID YOU...
52
WHO THE HELL ARE YOU?

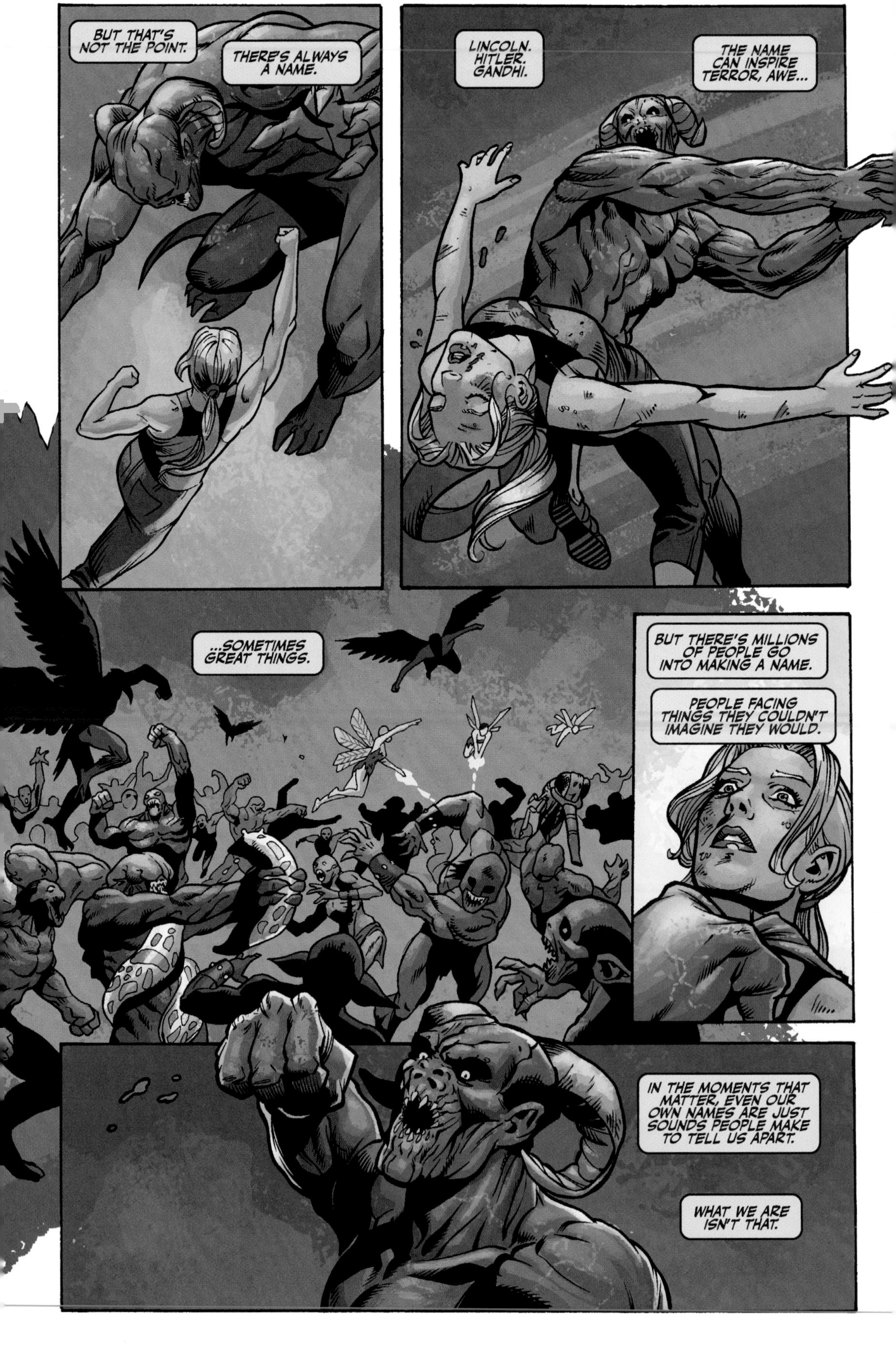
BUT THAT'S NOT THE POINT.
THERE'S ALWAYS A NAME.
LINCOLN. HITLER. GANDHI.
THE NAME CAN INSPIRE TERROR, AWE...
...SOMETIMES GREAT THINGS.
BUT THERE'S MILLIONS OF PEOPLE GO INTO MAKING A NAME.
PEOPLE FACING THINGS THEY COULDN'T IMAGINE THEY WOULD.
IN THE MOMENTS THAT MATTER, EVEN OUR OWN NAMES ARE JUST SOUNDS PEOPLE MAKE TO TELL US APART.
WHAT WE ARE ISN'T THAT.

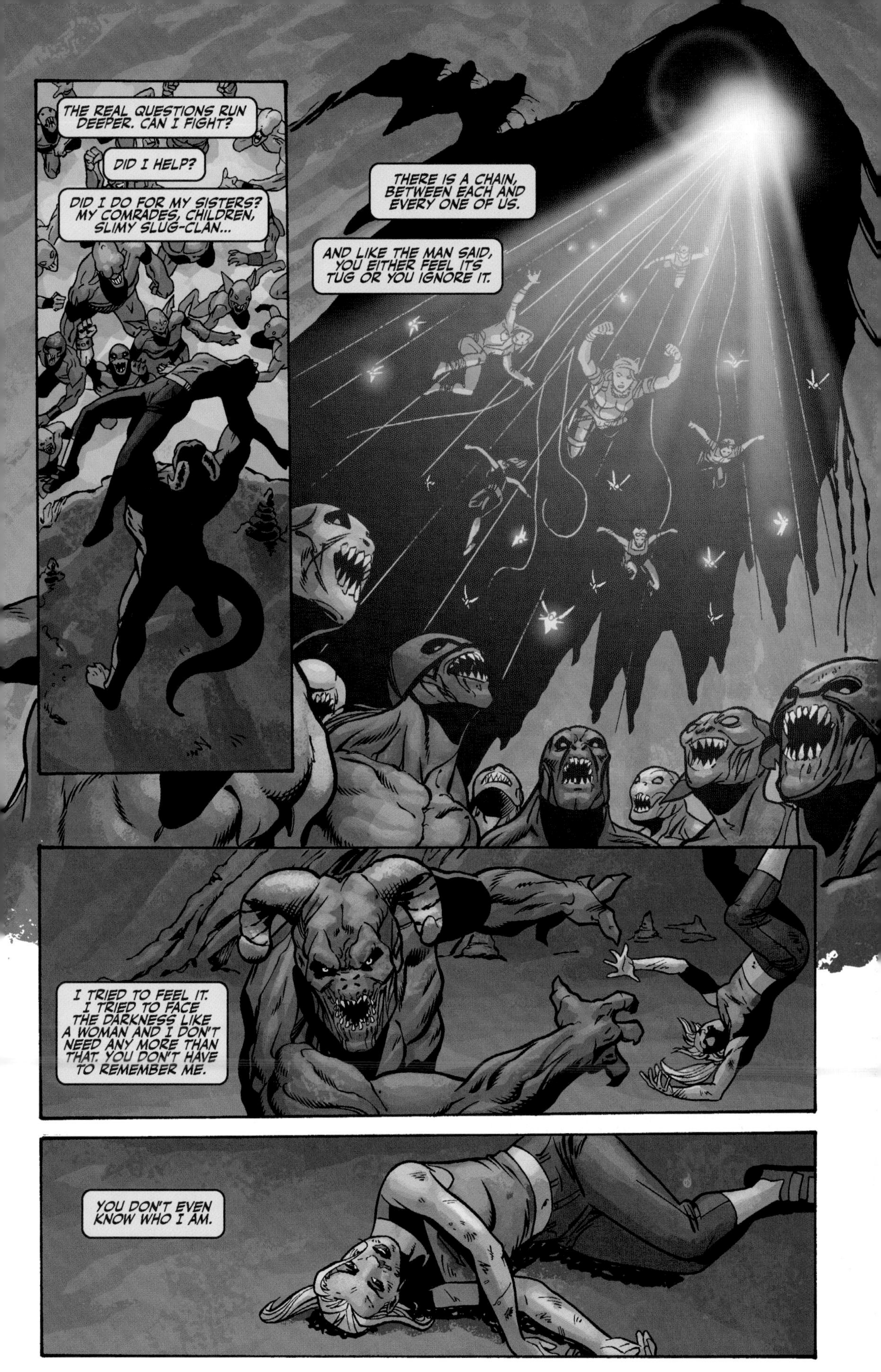
THE REAL QUESTIONS RUN DEEPER. CAN I FIGHT?
DID I HELP?
DID I DO FOR MY SISTERS? MY COMRADES, CHILDREN, SLIMY SLUG-CLAN...
THERE IS A CHAIN, BETWEEN EACH AND EVERY ONE OF US.
AND LIKE THE MAN SAID, YOU EITHER FEEL ITS TUG OR YOU IGNORE IT.
I TRIED TO FEEL IT. I TRIED TO FACE THE DARKNESS LIKE A WOMAN AND I DON'T NEED ANY MORE THAN THAT. YOU DON'T HAVE TO REMEMBER ME.
YOU DON'T EVEN KNOW WHO I AM.

BUT I DO.

FOR
JANIE
KLEINMAN

COVERS FROM
BUFFY THE VAMPIRE SLAYER
ISSUES #2–5

By

GEORGES JEANTY

&

PAUL LEE

with

ANDY OWENS

DEXTER " MUGEN" VINES

& DAVE STEWART

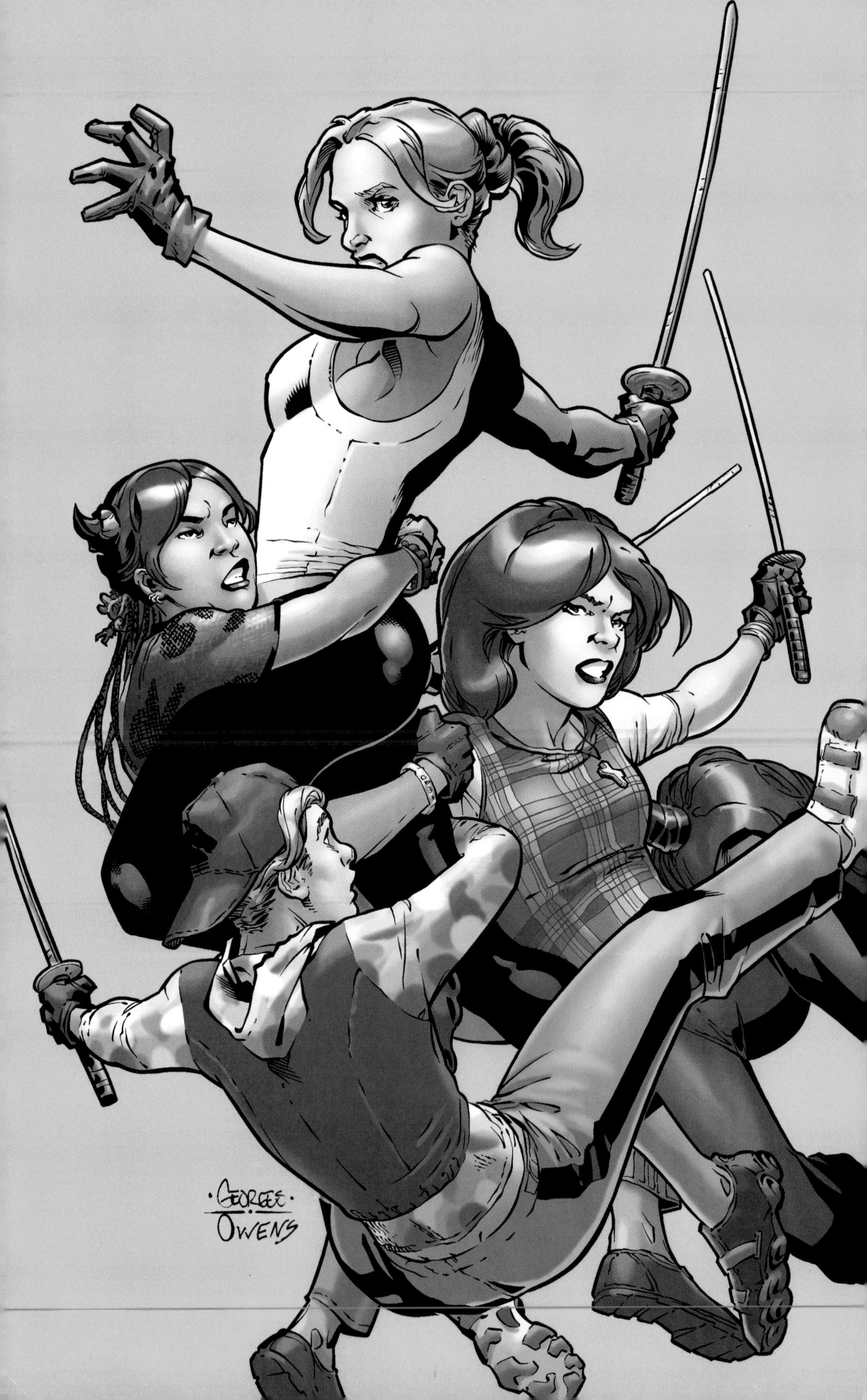
GEORGES
OWENS

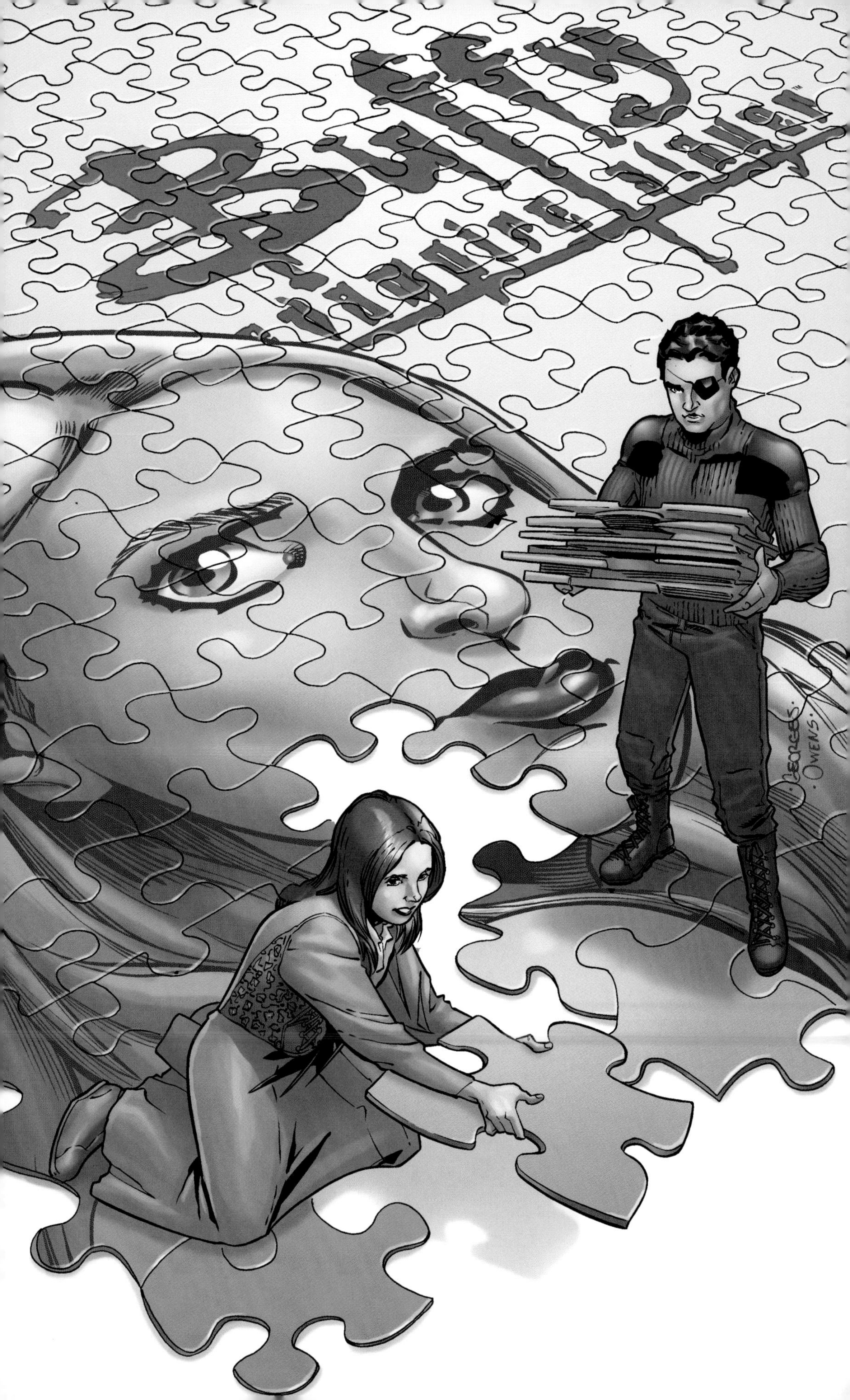

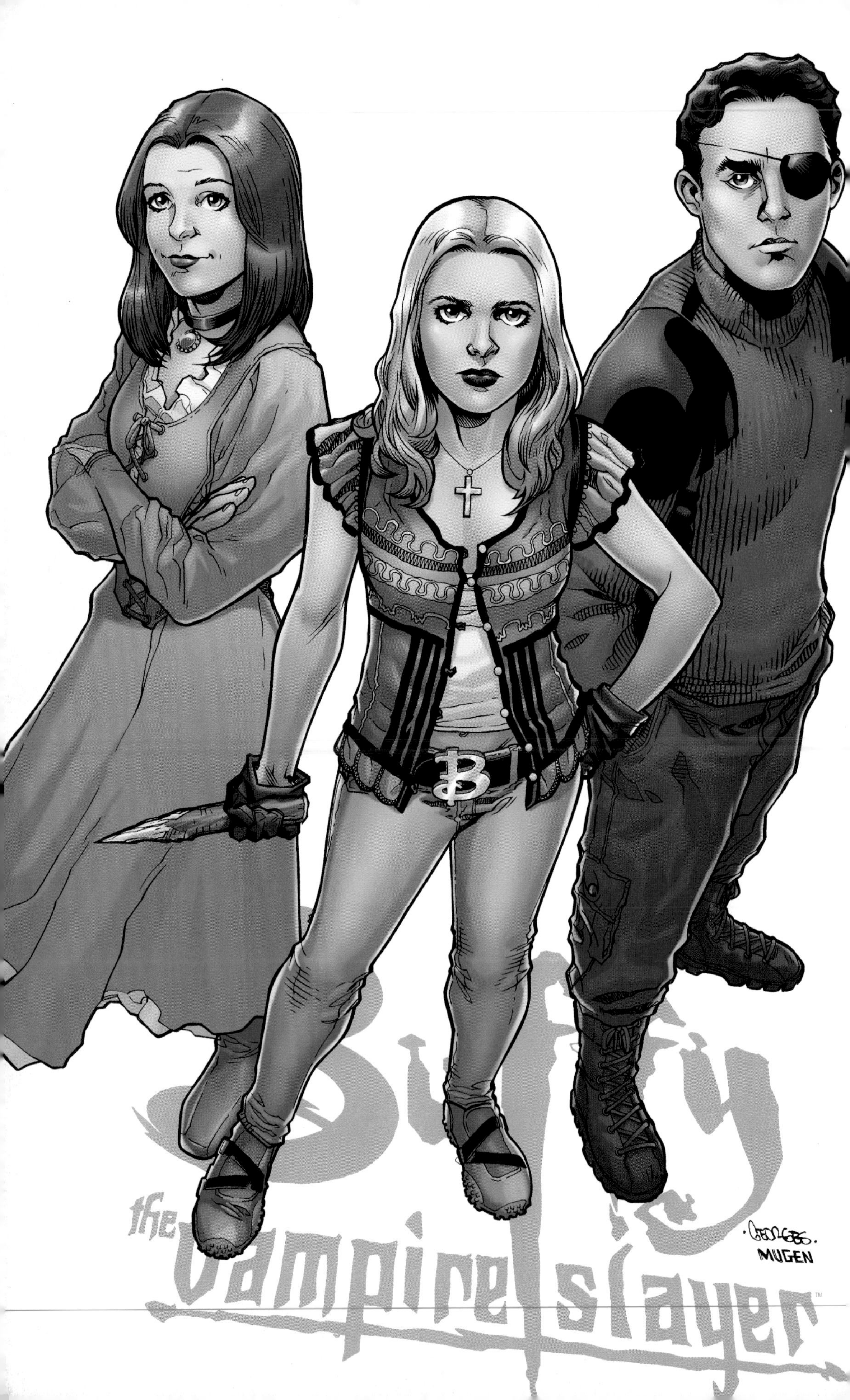
Buffy
the vampire slayer
MUGEN

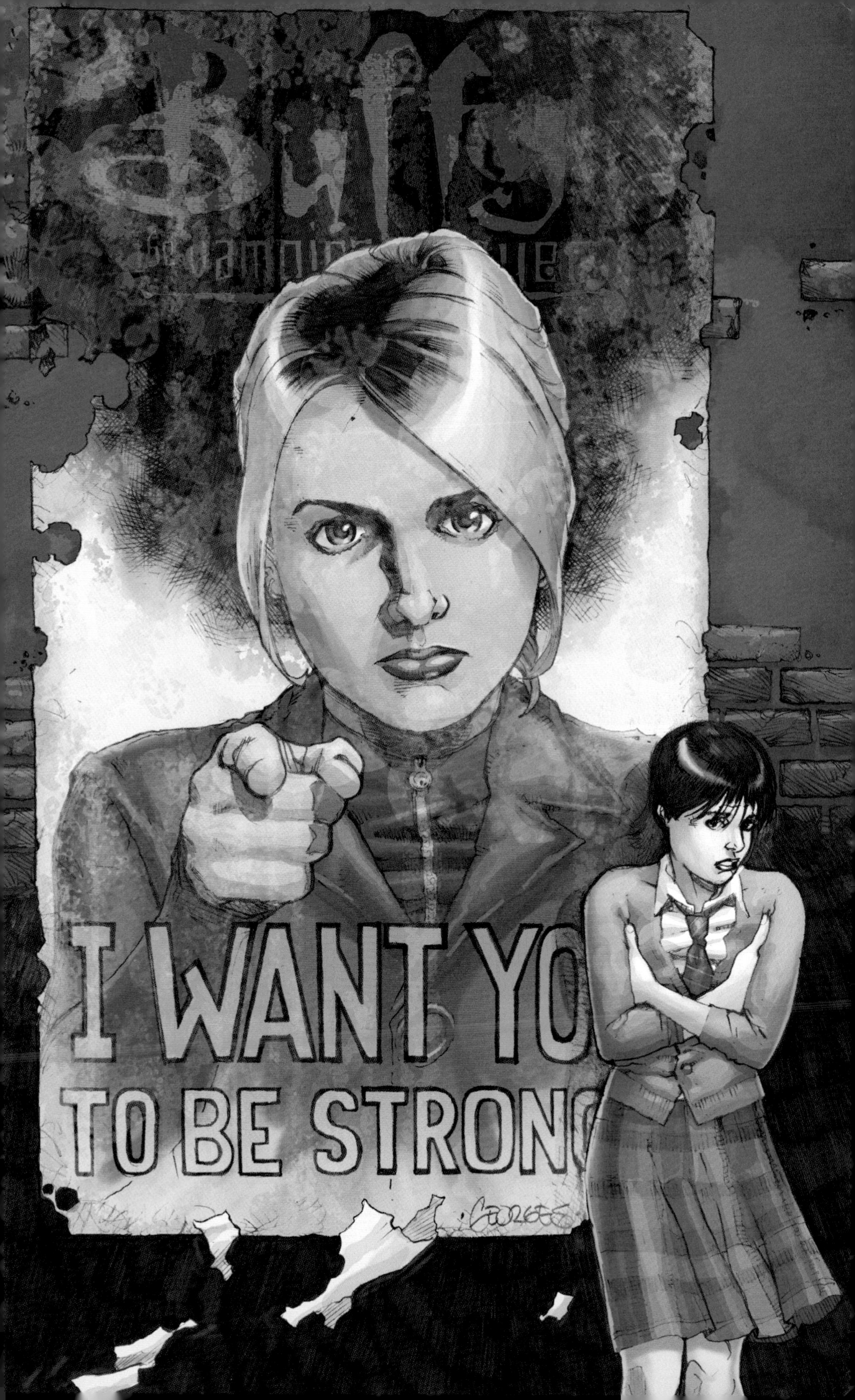

Buffy
I WANT YO
TO BE STRON

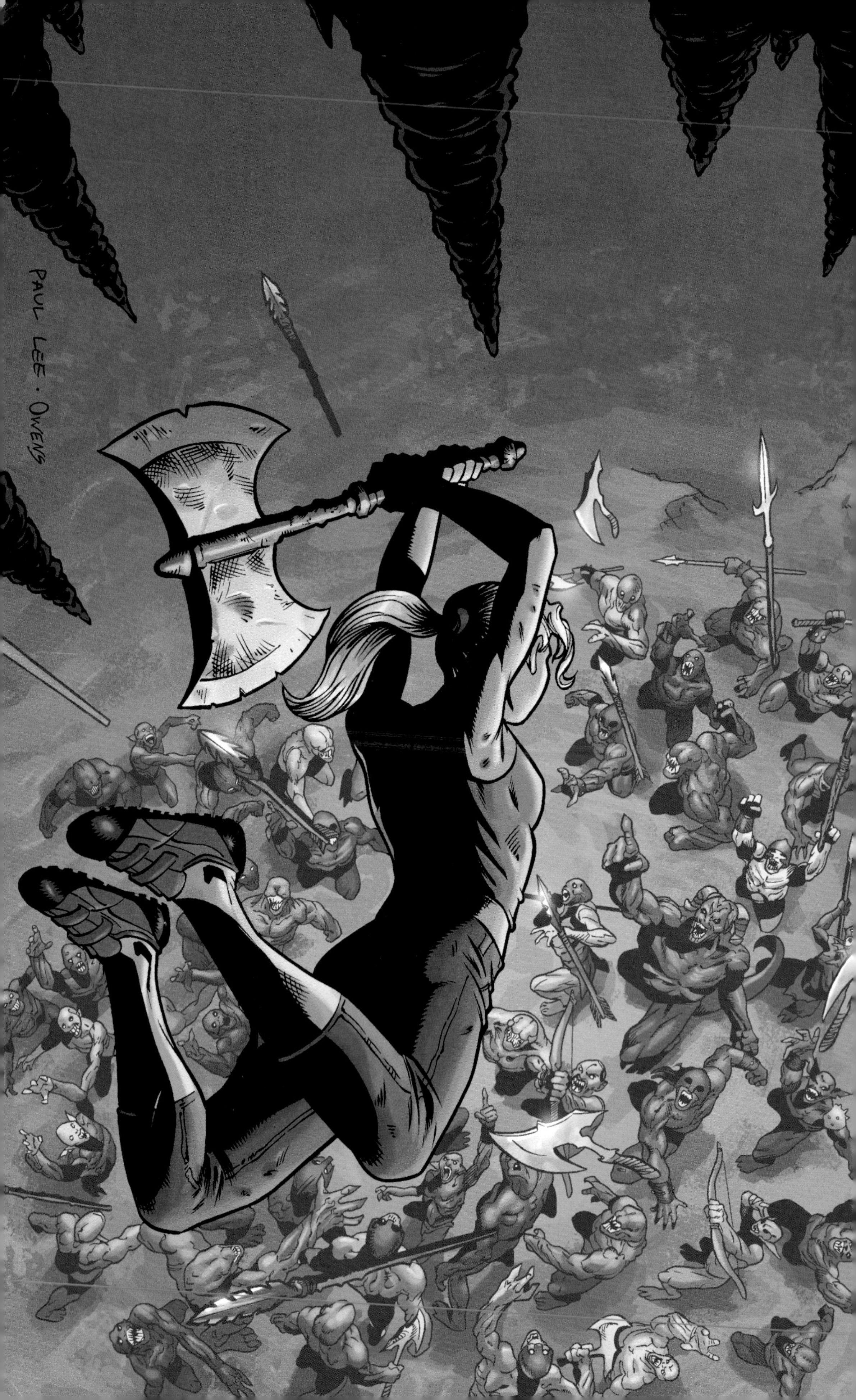
PAUL LEE · OWENS

ALSO FROM JOSS WHEDON AND THE BUFFYVERSE!

FROM THE CREATOR OF Buffy THE VAMPIRE SLAYER
TALES OF THE
slayers

BUFFY THE VAMPIRE SLAYER: TALES OF THE SLAYERS
Joss Whedon, Leinil Francis Yu, Tim Sale, Brett Matthews, and others

Buffy Summers is only the latest in a long line of women who have battled vampires, demons, and other forces of evil as the Slayer. Now, hear the stories behind other Slayers, past and future, told by the writers of the hit television show and illustrated by some of the most acclaimed artists in comics.

ISBN-10: 1-56971-605-6 / ISBN-13: 978-1-56971-605-2
$14.95

FROM THE CREATOR OF Buffy THE VAMPIRE SLAYER
tales of the
VAMPIRES

BUFFY THE VAMPIRE SLAYER: TALES OF THE VAMPIRES
Joss Whedon, Brett Matthews, Cameron Stewart, Tim Sale, and others

The creator of Buffy the Vampire Slayer reunites with the writers from his hit TV show for a frightening look into the history of vampires. Illustrated by some of comics' greatest artists, the stories span medieval times to today, including Buffy's rematch with Dracula, and Angel's ongoing battle with his own demons.

ISBN-10: 1-56971-749-4 / ISBN-13: 978-1-56971-749-3
$15.95

joss whedon
karl moline
andy owens
FRAY

FRAY
Joss Whedon, Karl Moline, and Andy Owens

In a future Manhattan so poisoned it doesn't notice the monsters on its streets, it's up to a gutter punk named Fray to unite a fallen city against a demonic plot to consume mankind. But will this girl who thought she had no future embrace her destiny—as the first Vampire Slayer in centuries—in time?

ISBN-10: 1-56971-751-6 / ISBN-13: 978-1-56971-751-6
$19.95

SERENITY
THOSE LEFT BEHIND
JOSS WHEDON BRETT MATTHEWS WILL CONRAD

SERENITY: THOSE LEFT BEHIND
Joss Whedon, Brett Matthews, Will Conrad, and Adam Hughes

Joss Whedon, creator of Buffy the Vampire Slayer and scribe of Marvel's *Astonishing X-Men*, unveils a previously unknown chapter in the lives of his favorite band of space brigands in this comics prequel of the *Serenity* feature film, bridging the gap from Whedon's cult-hit TV show *Firefly*.

ISBN-10: 1-59307-449-2 / ISBN-13: 978-1-59307-449-4
$9.95

AVAILABLE AT YOUR LOCAL COMICS SHOP OR BOOKSTORE! • To find a comics shop in your area, call 1-888-266-4226. For more information or to order direct visit darkhorse.com or call 1-800-862-0052 Mon.–Fri. 9 A.M. to 5 P.M. Pacific Time *Prices and availability subject to change without notice

DARK HORSE COMICS *drawing on your nightmares*
darkhorse.com

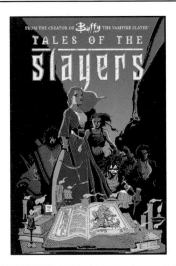

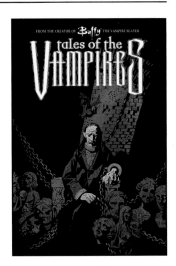

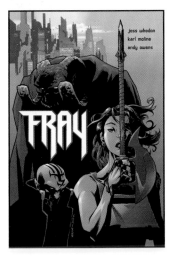

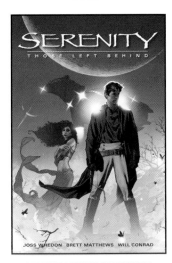

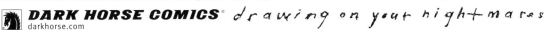

ALSO FROM DARK HORSE BOOKS!

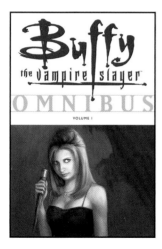

Buffy
the vampire slayer
OMNIBUS
VOLUME I

BUFFY THE VAMPIRE SLAYER OMNIBUS, VOLUME 1

The definitive comics collection of all things *Buffy* starts here. This first massive volume begins at the beginning—*The Origin*, a faithful adaptation of creator Joss Whedon's original screenplay for the film that started it all—and leads into the first season of *Buffy the Vampire Slayer.*

ISBN-10: 1-59307-784-X / ISBN-13: 978-1-59307-784-6

$24.95

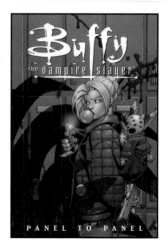

Buffy
the vampire slayer
PANEL TO PANEL

BUFFY THE VAMPIRE SLAYER: PANEL TO PANEL

Buffy the Vampire Slayer has been captivating audiences for nearly a decade, during which she's been drawn by some of the greatest luminaries in comics: Chris Bachalo, J. Scott Campbell, Jeff Matsuda, Mike Mignola, Terry Moore, and others. *Buffy the Vampire Slayer: Panel to Panel* takes a look back at the most dynamic and memorable line art and paintings of almost ten years of *Buffy* comics!

ISBN-10: 1-59307-836-6 / ISBN-13: 978-1-59307-836-2

$19.95

THE ESCAPISTS

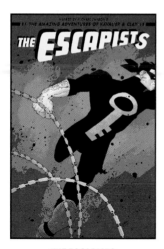

THE ESCAPISTS

Brian K. Vaughan, Jason Shawn Alexander, Steve Rolston, Philip Bond, Eduardo Barreto

Inspired by Michael Chabon's Pulitzer Prize–winning novel *The Amazing Adventures of Kavalier and Clay*, this is Vaughan's love letter to his chosen medium, a story about what it takes to start out with nothing and end up with a comic so hot a major corporation wants to steal it from you! This hardcover edition of *The Escapists* also includes an introduction by Michael Chabon!

ISBN-10: 1-59307-831-5 / ISBN-13: 978-1-59307-831-7

$19.95

THE GOON
ROUGH STUFF
by Eric Powell

THE GOON VOLUME 0: ROUGH STUFF

Eric Powell

Dark Horse Comics brings you the origin of Eric Powell's Eisner Award–winning series *The Goon*, the earliest stories published for the very first time in color! The Zombie Priest has just set up shop on Lonely Street and intends to build an undead army, and the Goon's the only man who can stop him! In this volume, we also meet his circus-freak clan and learn how he came to be the head of a notorious crime family. Also included in this volume is a special "Evolution of The Goon" sketchbook section.

ISBN-10: 1-59307-086-1 / ISBN-13: 978-1-59307-086-1

$12.95

AVAILABLE AT YOUR LOCAL COMICS SHOP OR BOOKSTORE!

To find a comics shop in your area, call 1-888-266-4226.

For more information or to order direct visit darkhorse.com or call 1-800-862-0052 Mon.–Fri. 9 A.M. to 5 P.M. Pacific Time

*Prices and availability subject to change without notice